LYDDIE

"The courage of boys in the working world has been dealt with often . . . but novels of this kind about girls are rare. *Lyddie* is outstanding because of the nature of its setting. . . . This is a rich story packed with a great variety of characters. . . . *Lyddie* is full of life, full of *lives*, full of reality."
—*The New York Times Book Review*

"Readers will sympathize with Lyddie's hardships and admire her determination to create a better life for herself. . . . Impeccably researched and expertly crafted, this book is sure to satisfy those interested in America's industrialization period."
—*Publishers Weekly*

"[A] superb novel. . . . Paterson has brought a troubling time and place vividly to life, but she has also given readers great hope in the spirited person of Lyddie Worthen."
—*School Library Journal*, starred review

"The story and characterizations are Paterson at her best. Readers will carry the image of Lyddie with them for many years."
—*Voice of Youth Advocates*

"A memorable portrait of an untutored but intelligent young woman making her way against fierce odds."
—*Kirkus Reviews*, pointer review

KATHERINE PATERSON

Lyddie

PUFFIN BOOKS

PUFFIN BOOKS
Published by the Penguin Group
Penguin Books USA Inc., 375 Hudson Street, New York, New York 10014, U.S.A.
Penguin Books Ltd, 27 Wrights Lane, London W8 5TZ, England
Penguin Books Australia Ltd, Ringwood, Victoria, Australia
Penguin Books Canada Ltd, 10 Alcorn Avenue, Toronto, Ontario, Canada M4V 3B2
Penguin Books (N.Z.) Ltd, 182–190 Wairau Road, Auckland 10, New Zealand

Penguin Books Ltd, Registered Offices: Harmondsworth, Middlesex, England

First published in the United States of America by Lodestar Books,
an affiliate of Dutton Children's Books, a division of Penguin Books USA Inc., 1991
First paperback edition published in Puffin Books, 1992
First trade paperback edition published in Puffin Books, 1995

20

THE LIBRARY OF CONGRESS HAS CATALOGED THE PREVIOUS PUFFIN EDITION AS FOLLOWS:
Paterson, Katherine.
Lyddie / by Katherine Paterson.   p.   cm.
Summary: Impoverished Vermont farm girl Lyddie Worthen is determined to gain her
independence by becoming a factory worker in Lowell, Massachusetts, in the 1840s.
ISBN 0-14-034981-2
[1. Self-reliance—Fiction. 2. Work—Fiction. 3. Factories—Fiction.
4. Textile workers—Fiction. 5. Lowell (Mass.)—Fiction.] I. Title.
[PZ7.P273Ly 1992]   [Fic]—dc20   92-20304   CIP   AC

Puffin Books trade paperback ISBN 0-14-037389-6

Printed in the United States of America
Set in Janson

for *Stephen Pierce*
our third son
and Friend in deed

Contents

1

The Bear

The bear had been their undoing, though at the time they had
all laughed. No, Mama had never laughed, but Lyddie and
Charles and the babies had laughed until their bellies ached.
Lyddie still thought of them as the babies. She probably always
would. Agnes had been four and Rachel six that November of
1843—the year of the bear.

It had been Charles's fault, if fault there was. He had fetched
in wood from the shed and left the door ajar. But the door
had not shut tight for some time, so perhaps he'd shut it as
best he could. Who knows?

At any rate, Lyddie looked up from the pot of oatmeal she
was stirring over the fire, and there in the doorway was a
massive black head, the nose up and smelling, the tiny eyes
bright with hungry anticipation.

"Don't nobody yell," she said softly. "Just back up slow and
quiet to the ladder and climb up to the loft. Charlie, you get
Agnes, and Mama, you take Rachel." She heard her mother
whimper. "Shhh," she continued, her voice absolutely even.
"It's all right long as nobody gets upset. Just take it nice and
gentle, ey? I'm watching him all the way, and I'll yank the
ladder up after me."

They obeyed her, even Mama, though Lyddie could hear
her sucking in her breath. Behind Lyddie's back, the ladder

creaked, as two by two, first Charles and Agnes, then Mama and Rachel, climbed up into the loft. Lyddie glared straight into the bear's eyes, daring him to step forward into the cabin. Then when the ladder was silent and she could hear the slight rustling above her as the family settled themselves on the straw mattresses, she backed up to the ladder and, never taking her eyes off the bear, inched her way up to the loft. At the top she almost fell backward onto the platform. Charles dragged her onto the mattress beside her mother.

The racket released the bear from the charm Lyddie seemed to have placed on him. He banged the door aside and rushed in toward the ladder, but Charles snatched it. The bottom rungs swung out, hitting the beast in the nose. The blow startled him momentarily, giving Lyddie a chance to help Charles haul the ladder up onto the platform and out of reach. The old bear roared in frustration and waved at the empty air with his huge paws, then reared up on his hind legs. He was so tall that his nose nearly touched the edge of the loft. The little girls cried out. Their mother screamed, "Oh Lord, deliver us!"

"Hush," Lyddie commanded. "You'll just make him madder." The cries were swallowed up in anxious gasps of breath. Charles's arms went around the little ones, and Lyddie put a firm grip on her mother's shoulder. It was trembling, so Lyddie relaxed her fingers and began to stroke. "It's all right," she murmured. "He can't reach us."

But could he climb the supports? It didn't seem likely. Could he, in his frustration, take a mighty leap and . . . No, she tried to breathe deeply and evenly and keep her eyes fixed on those of the beast. He fell to all fours and, tossing his head, broke off from her gaze as though embarrassed. He began to explore the cabin. He was hungry, obviously, and looking for the source of the smell that had drawn him in. He knocked over the churning jug and licked tentatively at the blade, but Lyddie had cleaned it too well after churning that morning and the critter soon gave up trying to find nourishment in the wood.

Before he found the great pot of oatmeal in the kettle over the fire, he had turned over the table and the benches and upended the spinning wheel. Lyddie held her breath, praying that he wouldn't break anything. Charles and she would try to mend, but he was only ten and she thirteen. They hadn't their father's skill or experience. *Don't break nothing*, she begged silently. They couldn't afford to replace any of the household goods.

Next the beast knocked over a jar of apple butter, but the skin lid was tied on tightly, and, flail away at it as he might with his awkward paw, he could not dislodge it. He smacked it across the floor where it hit the overturned bench, but, thank the Lord, the heavy pottery did not shatter.

At last he came to the oatmeal, bubbling—by the smell of it, scorching—over the fire. He thrust his head deep into the kettle and howled with pain as his nose met the boiling porridge. He threw back his head, but in doing so jerked the kettle off the hook, and when he turned, he was wearing it over his head like a black pumpkin. The bear was too stunned, it seemed, simply to lower his neck and let the kettle fall off. He danced about the room in pain on four, then two legs, the kettle covering his head, the boiling oatmeal raining down his thick neck and coat.

He knocked about, searching for the way out, but when he found the open door, managed to push it shut. Battering the door with his kettle-covered head, he tore it off its leather hinges and loped out into the dark. For a long time they could hear him crashing through the bush until, at last, the November night gathered about them once more with its accustomed quiet.

Then they began to laugh. Rachel first, throwing back her dark curls and showing the spaces where her pretty little teeth had been only last summer. Then Agnes joined in with her shrill four-year-old shout, and next Charles's not yet manly giggle.

"Whew," Lyddie said. "Lucky I'm so ugly. A pretty girl couldn't a scared that old rascal!"

"You ain't ugly!" Rachel cried. But they laughed louder than ever, Lyddie the loudest of all, until the tears of laughter and relief ran down her thin cheeks, and her belly cramped and doubled over. When had she laughed so much? She could not remember.

Her mother's shoulders were shaking, but Lyddie couldn't see her face. Mama must be laughing too. Lyddie dared to hope that her mother might laugh. Oh, there was the door to mend and the mess to be cleaned up, and the wasted porridge. But tomorrow she and Charles would find the kettle. The bear couldn't have taken it far and he was sure to have left more than an adequate trail with all that crashing through the underbrush. Let her be laughing, she prayed.

"Mama," she whispered, leaning her mouth close to her mother's ear. "You all right, ey?"

Her mother whirled toward her. "It's the sign," she said.

"What sign, Mama?" Lyddie asked, though she did not want an answer.

"Clarissa said when the end drew near, the devil would walk the earth."

"That weren't no devil, Mama," Charles said. "It were only a black bear."

" 'Your adversary the devil prowls around like a roaring lion, seeking whom he may devour.' "

"Aunt Clarissa don't know, Mama," Lyddie said as firmly as she could, though a shudder went through her body.

"It were only a black bear." Rachel's anxious little voice echoed her brother's, and then, "Weren't it, Lyddie? Weren't it a bear?"

4

Lyddie nodded, so as not to seem to be contradicting their mother out loud.

"Tomorrow we're going to Poultney," their mother said. "I aim to be with the faithful when the end comes."

"I don't want to be with the fate full," Rachel said. "I want to be with Lyddie."

"Lyddie will come too," their mother said.

"But how will Papa find us if we've left home?" Charles asked.

"Your father went out searching for vain riches. He ain't never coming back."

"He will! He will!" Rachel cried. "He promised." Though how could she remember? She'd been barely three when he'd left.

It was hard for the babies to go to sleep. Their stomachs were empty since the porridge had been ruined, and Mama would not hear of fixing more. Charles helped Lyddie clean the cabin. They propped up the door and put the chest against it to keep it in place until they could fix it in the morning. Then he climbed up the ladder to bed.

Lyddie stayed below. The fire must be banked for the night. She knelt down on the hearth. Behind her left shoulder sat Mama in the one chair, a rocker she had brought from Poultney when she came as a bride. Lyddie stole a glance at her. She was rocking like one dazed, staring unblinking into the fire.

The truth be told, Mama had gone somewhat queer in the head after their father had left. Lyddie had to acknowledge it. Not so strange as her sister, Clarissa, and her end-of-the-world-shouting husband, Judah—surely not. But now the bear seemed to have pushed her too far. "Don't let's go, Mama," Lyddie pleaded softly. "Please, Mama." But her mama only stared at the fireplace, rocking slowly back and forth, her eyes blank and still as though her spirit had gone away and left the body there rocking on and on.

It was useless to argue, and Lyddie gave up, hoping that the mood would pass, like her mother's times of craziness always had. But the next morning her mother had not forgotten her determination. "If it ain't Clarissa's, it will soon be the poor farm," she said.

The only charity Lyddie dreaded more than Aunt Clarissa's was that of the township's poor farm. It was to escape that specter that their father had headed West.

"I can't stop you to go," Lyddie said, "but I can't go with you. I can't leave the farm." When her mother opened her mouth to argue, Lyddie went on. "The sow won't fetch enough to provide coach fare for the lot of us."

She sent Charles along to make sure her mother and the babies arrived safely at Uncle Judah's farm. Charlie was a funny sight, hardly higher than a currant bush, but drawn up like a man in his worn boots and his father's old woolen shirt with the sleeves rolled. He loaded up the barrow; they'd sold the horse cart for seeds last year. "It's only ten miles to Cutler's, where the coach stops. The little ones can ride when they get too tired," he said. He put in their mother's old skin trunk, which had carried her meager trousseau to this mountain and most of the food she'd managed to preserve before she gave up trying. Between them, he and Lyddie wrestled the old sow to the ground and tied her, squealing, to a shaft of the barrow.

"You want I should go with you as far as the village?" she asked him. But they agreed it would be better for her to tend the cow and horse and protect the house from the wild critters.

"You watch out for yourself," he said anxiously.

"I'll do fine," she said. "Now remember, you got to get enough for the pig to pay coach fare for everyone."

"And for me to come back again," he said, as a promise that she would not be left alone on the mountain farm. He glanced about to make sure his mother wasn't in hearing distance. "You mustn't be afraid to go down and ask the Quaker Stevens for help, Lyddie. They mean to be good neighbors to us, no matter what Mama says."

"Well, I'll see how it goes, ey?" she said, tossing her thin plaits behind her shoulders. He should know she was not going to be beholden to the neighbors for anything so trivial as her own comfort. Their mother didn't approve of heathens or abolitionists, and since she considered their Quaker neighbors a bit of both, she forbade the children to have anything to do with the Stevenses. "Ain't no Worthen gonna have truck with the devil," she said. Early last summer, when Mama was having one of her spells and not paying much attention, Charlie had again sneaked the cow down the mountain to the Stevenses' place. As long as Lyddie could remember, long before their father had left, they had made use of the Stevenses' bull. If their mother ever wondered about those calves that were born like miracles every spring, she never mentioned it. She knew as well as Lyddie and Charles that they could never have managed without the cash money those calves brought in.

Lyddie didn't care one way or the other about the neighbors' radical ideas and peculiar ways, she minded mightily being beholden. It couldn't be helped. The use of a bull was a necessity she couldn't manage on her own, but she would starve to death rather than go begging before this year's calf was safely born and it was time to mate the cow once more.

She needn't have worried. Charlie came back in about two weeks, and together they made it through the winter. They shot rabbits and peeled bark for soup to eke out their scarce provisions. They ran out of flour for bread, so the churn stood idle, but "I never craved churning," said Lyddie.

When the time for the calving drew near, they reluctantly let the cow go dry. They had no need for butter without any bread, but they'd miss the milk and cheese sorely. Nonetheless, they were farmers enough to do what was best for their only cow.

The calf was born to great rejoicing and a new abundance of milk and cream. Lyddie and Charles felt rich as townsfolk. A sweet little heifer she was, arriving on the first warm day of March, the same day that they bored holes in the sugar maples and inserted the spills that they had made to catch the sap flow. They were able to make enough syrup and sugar for themselves. Hardly enough for a cash crop, but they were learning, and in another year, after another harvest, they would be experienced old farmers and sugarers, they told each other.

Years later she would remember that morning. The late May sky was brilliant dare-you-to-wink blue, and the cheek of the hillside wore a three-day growth of green. High in one of the apple trees a bluebird warbled his full spring song, *chera, weera, wee-it, cheerily-cheerily.* Lyddie's own spirit rose in reply. Her rough hands were stretched to grasp the satin-smooth wooden shafts of the old plow. With Charles at the horse's head, they urged and pushed the heavy metal blade through the rocky earth. The plow cast up the clean, damp smell of new turned soil. *Cheerily-cheerily.*

Then into that perfect spring morning a horse and rider had come round the narrow curve of the road, slowly, the horse gingerly picking its way across the deep, dried ruts of mud left from the thaws of April and early May.

"Charlie," she said quietly, hardly daring to move, because for a moment she hoped it might be Papa, but only for a moment. It was plainly a woman riding sidesaddle, and not their mother, either. She never rode since she fell years ago and miscarried the baby that would have come between Lyddie and Charles.

"Charlie," Lyddie repeated. "Someone's coming."

Mrs. Peck, for she was the rider, had brought a letter from

the general store in the village. "I thought you might be wanting this," she said. Lyddie fetched the coins for the postage from their almost empty cash box. The shopkeeper's wife waited a bit, hoping, perhaps, that Lyddie would read the letter aloud, but she didn't. Lyddie was not much of a reader, so it was later, the short wisps of hair around her face plastered with sweat, that she held the letter close to the fire and managed to make out the words in her mother's cramped and painfully childish hand.

Dear Lyddie,
    The world hav not come to the end yit. But we can stil hop. Meentime I hav hire you out to M. Cutler at the tavern and fer yr. brother to Bakers mill. The paschur, feelds and sugar bush is lent to M. Wescott to repay dets. Also cow and horse. Lv. at wuns you git this.
Yr. loving mother,
Mattie M. Worthen

Lyddie burst into tears. "I'm sorry, Charlie," she said to her brother's amazed and anxious face. "I never expected this. We were doing so good, ey? You and me."

He took a deep breath, reached into his pocket, and handed her a ragged kerchief.

"It's all right, Lyddie," he said. "It's all right." When she kept her tear-streaked face buried in his kerchief, he gave one of her braids a tweak. "The world have not come to the end yit, ey?" He took the letter from her lap, and when she wiped her face and tried to smile, he grinned anxiously and pointed to their mother's primitive spelling. "See, we can stil hop."

Lyddie laughed uncertainly. Her spelling was no better than their mother's, so she did not really see the joke at first. But Charlie laughed, and so she began to laugh, though it was the kind of laughter that caught like briars in her chest and felt very much like pain.

2
Kindly Friends

"She didn't say nothing about the calf," Lyddie said suddenly in the midst of their sorrowful packing up.

"She got no cause to," Charles said. "We never tell her about it."

"You know, Charlie, that calf is rightfully ours."

He looked at her, his honest head cocked, his eyes dubious.

"No, truly. We was the ones asked Quaker Stevens to lend us use of his bull. Mama didn't have nothing to do with it."

"But if they's debts . . ."

"She's letting out the fields and the horse and cow. She's sending you to be a miller's boy and me to housemaid. She's got us body and soul. We got no call to give her the calf." She set one hand on her waist and straightened her aching back.

"What do you aim to do with it?"

"Hush. I'm studying on it." Obediently, he quieted and stared in the same direction at the spindly maples that made up their stand of sugar bush.

"It's a nice fat heifer," she said. "We kept it so long on its mother's milk. We'll get a good price for it."

"We'd be bound to give the money to her."

"No." Her voice was sharper than she meant, ground as it was on three years of unspoken anger. "We always done that and look where it's got us. No," she said again, this time softly. "The money don't go there. She'll give it away to Uncle Judah, who'll give it to that preacher who says you don't need nothing 'cause the world is going to end." She turned to her brother. "Charlie, you and me can't think about that. We got to think about keeping this farm for when Papa comes back. We should take that money and bury it someplace, so when we get free we can come back here and have a little seed cash to start over with."

"Maybe she'll sell the farm."

"She can't. Not so long as Papa's alive."

"But maybe . . ."

"We don't know that, now do we? We got to believe he's coming back—or he's sending for us."

"I hope he don't send for us."

"We'll persuade him to stay," she said. She wanted for a minute to put her arm around his thin shoulders, but she held back. She didn't want him to think that she considered him less than the man he had so bravely sought to be. "We're a good team, ey, Charlie?"

"Ox or mule?" he asked, grinning.

"A little of both, I reckon."

They cleaned the cabin and swept out the splintery plank floor. They knew it was a rough and homely place compared to the farmhouses along the road and the ample mansions around the village green. But their father, the seventh son of a poor Connecticut Valley farmer, had bought the land and built the cabin with his own hands before their birth, promising every year to sell enough maple sugar, or oats, or potash to build a larger, proper house with a real barn attached instead of a shed which must be found through rain or blizzard. His sugar bush was scraggly and his oat crop barely enough to feed his growing family. There were stumps to burn aplenty as he cleared the land, but suddenly there was no need for potash in England and hardly any demand in Vermont. He borrowed heavily to buy himself three sheep, and the bottom dropped out of the wool market the very year he had had enough wool to think of it as a cash crop. He was an unlucky man. Even his children sensed that, but he loved them and worked hard for them, and they loved him fiercely in return.

Pulling shut the door, which, despite all Charles's efforts, still did not close quite flush, they remembered the bear and wondered how they could keep the wild creatures from destroying the cabin in their absence. Finally, Charles suggested that they take all the wood left in the woodpile and stack it in front of the door. It took them close to an hour to accomplish the move, but, sweating and breathing hard, they admired their fortress effect.

That made it a little easier for them to go. Charlie rode bareback astride the plow horse, his brown heels dug into the horse's wide flanks. Lyddie, leading the cow, followed close by. She carried a gunnysack, which held her other dress and night shift. Her outgrown boots were joined by the laces and slung over her shoulder. The long walk would be more easily done with her feet free and bare. There was no need to tie the calf. It danced around its mother's backside, bleating constantly for her to stand still long enough for a meal.

It was the end of May. The mud was drying in the deeply rutted roadway, but Lyddie did not watch her feet. Birds were playing in and out of the tall trees on either side of the road, calling and singing in the pale lacy greens and rusts of the new growth and the deep green of the pines and firs. Here and there wildflowers dared to dance in full summer dress, forgetting that any night might bring a killing frost.

Lyddie breathed in the sweet air. "It's spring," she said. Charles nodded.

"Do you mind too much going to the mill?" she asked.

He shrugged. "I don't rightly know. Don't seem too bad. Dusty, I reckon. And not much time to be lazy, ey?"

She laughed. "You wouldn't know how to be lazy, Charlie."

He smiled at the compliment. "I'd rather be home."

She sighed. "We'll be back, Charlie, I promise." They were both quiet a moment remembering their father saying almost the same words. "Truly," she added. "I'm sure of it."

He smiled. "Sure," he said.

They were in sight now of Quaker Stevens's farm. They could see him, his broad-brimmed straight black hat surrounded by the black hats of his three grown sons. They had the oxen yoked to a sled, which was already half loaded with stones, and were digging away at more stones buried in a newly cleared field.

Their farmhouse, close to the road, had been added onto over the years. The outlines of the first saltbox could be made out on the northern end, which melted on the backside into a larger frame Cape Cod, then an ell that served as shed, storage, privy, and corridor to two barns, the larger one growing out of the smaller. They were rich for all their Quaker adherence to the simple life.

Envy crept up like a noxious vine. Lyddie snapped it off, but the roots were deep and beyond her reach.

Before they called out, the farmer had seen them. He waved, took off his hat to wipe his head and face on the sleeve of his homespun shirt, replaced his hat, and made his way across the field to the road.

"I see my bull served thee well," he said, smiling. His face was broad and red, his hair curly and gray about his ears. Great caterpillar eyebrows crowned his kindly eyes.

"We come to thank you," Lyddie began, thinking fast, wanting to be fair and honest but at the same time wanting a large price for the calf that she knew in her heart was partly his.

"Thee brought these beasts five miles down the road for that?" he asked, his woolly eyebrows high up on his forehead.

Lyddie blushed. "The truth is, we're taking the horse and cow to Mr. Westcott—in payment of debt, and we're obliged to sell off this pretty calf straight away. Our mother's put us out to work."

"Thee's leaving thy land?"

"It's let as well," she said, allowing just a tiny hint of sadness to creep into her voice. "Charles here and I was waiting for our father to come back from the West, but . . ."

"Thee's been alone all winter, just thee two children?"

She could feel Charles stiffen beside her. "We managed fine," she said.

He took off his hat again and wiped his face and neck. "I should have come to call on my neighbors," he said quietly.

She sensed a weakness. "You wouldn't be interested . . . no, surely not. You got a mighty herd already."

"I'll give thee twenty dollars for the calf," he said quickly. "No, twenty-five. I know the sire and he's of a good line." He smiled.

Lyddie pretended to think. "Seems mighty high," she said.

"She's half yours by rights," Charles blurted out before Lyddie could elbow him quiet. His honesty would be her death yet.

But the kind man persisted. "It's a fair price for a nice fat little heifer. Thee's kept her well."

He invited them in to complete their business transaction and, before they were done, they found themselves eating a hearty noon dinner with the family. The room they sat down in was larger than the whole cabin with the shed thrown in. It was kitchen and parlor with a corner for spinning and weaving. The Quakers were rich enough to own their own loom. The meal spread out on the long oak table looked like a king's feast to children who, until the cow freshened, had lived mostly

old cow and horse away. Next to Westcott's sleek stock, they'd look like hungry sparrows pecking in a hen yard.

At a livelier clip they took the river road toward Baker's Mill. "I can walk from here easy," Charles protested, but Luke shook him off. "Faster I get home, sooner I'm hauling rocks," he said, laughing.

She didn't want Luke Stevens watching while she bid Charles good-bye, but again maybe it was better. She might weaken if they were alone, and that would never do.

"I'll only be in the village," she said. "Maybe you can drop up."

Charles put his little hand on her arm. "You mustn't worry, ey Lyddie," he said. "You'll be all right."

She nearly laughed. He was trying to comfort her. Or maybe she nearly cried. She watched the gaping mouth of the mill swallow up his small form. He turned in the immense doorway—it was large enough to drive a high wagon through—and waved. "Let's be going," she said. "It's late."

Luke nodded his head with a dip of his funny black hat. "This here is Cutler's Tavern," he said. They hadn't spoken since they left the mill. "Shall I come to the door with thee?" The wagon had stopped before a low stone wall, hung with a rail gate.

She was horrified. "No, no need," she said. "They might not understand me riding up with a . . ." She scrambled to the ground.

He grinned. "I hope to see thee before too much time is up," he said. "Meantime, I'll see to thy house." He leaned over the seat. "I'll give a look in on thy Charlie, too," he said. "He's a good boy."

She didn't know whether to be pleased or annoyed, but he clicked his tongue and the wagon pulled away, leaving her alone in her new life.

3

Cutler's Tavern

Lyddie stood outside the gate, waiting until Luke and his wagon disappeared around the curve of the road. Then she watched a pair of swallows dive and soar around the huge chimney in the center of the main house. The tavern was larger than the Stevenses' farmhouse. Addition after addition, porch, shed, and a couple of barns, the end one at least four stories high. The whole complex, recently painted with a mix of red ochre and buttermilk, stood against the sky like a row of giant beets popped clear of the earth.

The pastures, a lush new green, were dotted with merino sheep and fat milk cows. There was a huge sugar maple in front of what must be the parlor door, and another at the porch, which, from the presence of churns and cooling pans, must lead into the kitchen.

Once I walk in that gate, I ain't free anymore, she thought. No matter how handsome the house, once I enter I'm a servant girl—no more than a black slave. She had been queen of the cabin and the straggly fields and sugar bush up there on the hill. But now someone else would call the tune. How could her mother have done such a thing? She was sure her father would be horrified—she and Charlie drudges on someone else's place. It didn't matter that plenty of poor people put out their children for hire to save having to feed them. She and Charlie could have fed themselves—just one good harvest—one good sugaring—that was all they needed. And they could have stayed together.

She was startled out of her dreaming by a hideous roar, and before she could figure out what animal could have made such a noise, a stagecoach appeared, drawn by two spans of sweating Morgan horses, shaking their great heads, showing their fierce teeth, saliva foaming on their iron bits. The coach had rounded the curve, its horn bellowing.

The driver was yelling as well, and then, just in time, she realized that he was yelling at her. She jumped hard against the wall. He was still yelling back at her as he pulled up the reins, the coach itself now on the very spot where she had been standing seconds before.

Should she apologize? No, he wasn't paying her any attention now. He was turning the team over to a boy who had run out of the shed. A woman was hurrying out of the kitchen door to welcome the passengers, who were climbing stiffly from the coach. Lyddie stared. They were very grand looking. One of the gentlemen, a man in a beaver hat and frilled shirt, turned to hand a woman down the coach step. The lady's face was hidden by a fancy straw bonnet, the brim decorated with roses that matched her gown. Was it silk? Lyddie couldn't be sure, never having seen a real silk dress before, but it was smooth and pink like a baby's cheek. Around her shoulders the lady wore a shawl woven in a deeper shade of pink. Lyddie marveled that the woman would wear something so delicate for a ride to the northland in a dusty coach.

Safely on the ground, the woman lifted her head and looked about her. Her face was thin and white, her features elegant. She caught Lyddie's eyes and smiled. It was a very nice smile, not at all haughty. Lyddie realized that she had been staring. She closed her mouth and quickly looked away.

Then the encounter was over, for the stout woman who had come out of the kitchen door was hustling the lady, her escort, and two other passengers through the low gate and around to the main door at the north end of the tavern.

Suddenly she saw Lyddie. She came over to the wall and whispered hoarsely across it to her. "What are you doing here?" She was looking Lyddie up and down as she asked, as though Lyddie were a stray dog who had wandered too close to her house.

Lyddie was aware, as she might not have been minutes before, that she had no bonnet and that her hair and braids were dusty from the road. She crossed her arms, trying to cover her worn brown homespun with the gunnysack. The dress was tight across her newly budding chest, and it hung unevenly to just above her ankles in a ragged hem. Her brown feet were bare, her outgrown boots still slung over her shoulder. She should have remembered to put them on before she got off Luke's wagon.

Self-consciously, she raised her sleeve and wiped her nose and mouth under the woman's unforgiving stare. "Go along," the woman was saying. "This is a respectable tavern, not the township poor farm."

Lyddie could feel the rage oozing up like sap on a March morning. She cleared her throat and stood up straight. "I'm Lydia Worthen," she said. "I got a letter from my mother . . ."

The woman looked horrified. "You're the new girl?"

"I reckon I am," Lyddie said, clutching her gunnysack more tightly.

"Well, I've no time to bother with you now," the woman said. "Go into the kitchen and ask Triphena to tell you where you can wash. We keep a clean place here."

Lyddie bit her lip to keep from answering back. She looked straight into the woman's face until the woman blinked and turned, running a little to catch up with the guests who were waiting for her at the main door.

The cook was as busy as the mistress and not eager to involve herself with a dirty new servant just when she was putting the meal on the table. "Sit over there." Triphena shook her head at a low stool near the huge fireplace. Lyddie would rather have stood after the long, bumpy ride in the Stevenses' wagon, but she chose not to cause a problem with the cook as well as with the mistress in the first ten minutes of her employment.

The kitchen was three times the size of the whole Worthen cabin. Its center was the huge fireplace. Lyddie could have stretched out full length in front of it and her head and toes would have remained on the hearth with room to spare.

Built into the right side of the brick chimney was a huge beehive-shaped oven, and the smell of fresh-baked loaves made Lyddie forget the generous dinner she'd shared noontime. The trouble with eating good, she thought later, is you get too used to it. You think you ought to have it regular, not just for a treat.

Over the fire hung a kettle so large that both the babies could have bathed in it together. It was bubbling with a meat stew chock-full of carrots and onions and beans and potatoes in a thick brown broth. There were chickens turning on a spit, which seemed to be magically going round and round on its own. But as Lyddie's eyes followed a leather strap upward, she saw, above the fireplace, the mechanism from which hung a huge metal pendulum. She wished her father could see it. He could make one perhaps from wood and then no one would have to tediously turn the spit by hand. But perhaps it was something you'd have to order from the blacksmith—in which case it was likely to be so dear that only the rich could afford one. She couldn't remember seeing one at the Stevenses', and they were rich enough to own their own loom.

"Move," the cook said. The large woman was beginning to take the food from the fire. She gave Lyddie a quick glance. "Lucky you're so plain. Guests couldn't leave the last girl be." She was ladling stew into a large serving basin. "Won't have no trouble with you, will we?"

Lyddie picked up the stool and moved to a corner of the room. She knew she was no beauty, never had been, but she was a fierce worker. She'd prove that to the woman. Should she offer to help now? But the cook was too busy moving the food from the fire to the long wooden table in the center of the room to pay her any mind. Lyddie scrunched her body into itself and tucked her bare feet under the low stool, fearful of seeming in the way. Would all the guests come in here to eat? And if so, where should she hide?

As if to answer her question, the mistress pushed through the door with a boy behind her. "Hurry," she said. She supervised while the last of the food was transferred from the iron kettles into great china basins, which the cook and the boy carried from the kitchen to some other part of the house. The mistress mumbled and grumped orders, and in between complained of the guest who made herself out to be a lady when she was nothing but a factory girl putting on fancy airs.

If the mistress saw Lyddie sitting in the corner, she never let on. Lyddie was glad to be ignored. She needed time and a chance to wash and change her dusty clothes. If only she hadn't worn her better homespun to travel in. The one in the gunnysack was even tighter and more ragged. She hadn't had a new dress since they sold the sheep four years ago. Since then, her body had begun to make those strange changes to womanhood that exasperated her. Why couldn't she be as thin and straight as a boy? Why couldn't she have been a boy? Perhaps, then, her father would not have had to leave. With an older son to help, maybe he could have made a living for them on the hill farm.

But, hard as she wished, hard as she tried, she was only a girl. She was, as girls go, scrawny and muscular, yet her boyish frame had in the last year betrayed her. Her breasts were small and her hips only slightly curved, but she couldn't help resenting these visible signs that she was doomed to be female.

Even the last year before Papa left, he had begun sending her in to help her mother. "She never really got over the baby's birth," he'd say. But once there was no more wool to spin, she felt as though her presence in the house just made her mother try less. One by one, the household tasks had been turned over to Lyddie—cooking and churning and cleaning and caring for the babies. For a while her mother spun the flax. They had no loom and paid the village weaver in spun flax for cloth. Her father had left them in a new shirt her mother had made. But that was the last garment her mother sewed. Lyddie tried to keep up the spinning, but when she had to take her father's place outdoors, she was too exhausted to try to spin and sew in the dim candlelight.

Last winter she sewed one shirt. She had made it for Charlie because he, too, was outgrowing his clothes, and the old wool shirt their father had left behind hung on him like a nightdress.

As it turned out, Mistress Cutler provided her with a store-bought calico gown. It was softer than her rough brown homespun and fit her much better, but somehow it suited her less. How could she enjoy the garment of her servitude? She was fit with new boots as well. They pinched her feet and made her long to go barefoot, but she wore them, if not meekly, at least with determined obedience. After a few weeks and many blisters, they softened a little, and she was able to forget them for an hour or so at a time.

The people at Cutler's were not so easy to forget. The mistress was large in body and seemed to be everywhere on watch. How could a woman so obviously rich in this world's goods be so mean in the use of them? Her eyes were narrow and close and always on the sharp for the least bit of spilt flour or the odd crumb on the lip.

Not that Lyddie would stoop to steal a bite of bread. But the boy, Willie Hyde, was given to snatching the last of the loaf as he carried the breadbasket from the table to the kitchen. He was a year or so older than Charles and growing like red birch, and to hear the mistress carry on, about as useless. He was sent to shed or barn or field whenever he was not needed in the tavern itself. Lyddie would not have said so, but she envied him the chance to be outdoors and out of boots so often.

Mistress Cutler watched Lyddie like a barn cat on a sparrow, but Lyddie was determined not to give her cause for complaint. She had worked hard since she could remember. But now she worked even harder, for who was there to share a moment's leisure with? Who would listen with her to a bird call, stare at the sunset, or watch a calf stumble on its long, funny legs toward its mother? Missing Charlie was like wearing a stone around her neck.

She slept under the eaves in a windowless passage, which was hot and airless even in late spring. She was ordered to bed late and obliged to rise early, for the mistress was determined that no paying guest in the windowed rooms across the narrow passageway should know that they shared the floor with the kitchen girl.

She spoke rarely, but she listened intently, storing up stories for Charlie. She didn't consider writing him. She was ashamed to have Charlie see her poor penmanship and crude spelling and, besides, there was no money for paper or postage—nothing except the calf money, and she would not spent a half penny of that. Indeed, at night when she was too tired or too hot to sleep, she would take the gunnysack out from under her straw mattress and count the money in the darkness. It's like little Agnes sucking her thumb, she scolded herself, but she didn't stop. It was the only comfort she had that summer.

* * *

It was nearly September when she saw the pink silk lady again. She had come this time on the coach from Burlington, and was headed, Lyddie overheard her say at supper, for Lowell, Massachusetts. When another traveler asked her business in Lowell, she smiled and said, "Why I work in the Hamilton Mill there. Yes," she added, answering her questioner's stare, "I'm one of those *factory girls.*"

The man murmured something and turned his face toward his bowl of stew.

The lady watched him, still smiling, and then, catching Lyddie's eye, smiled even more broadly, as though to imply that Lyddie was a comrade in some peculiar way.

Indeed, when the men had left the dining room to go into the taproom, she stayed behind, reading a book she had taken from a small silk purse that matched her lovely dress.

"I've seen you before, haven't I?"

Lyddie looked around to see to whom the lady was speaking, then realized the room was empty except for the two of them.

"In late May, when I was headed home to the farm for the summer."

Lyddie cleared her throat. She had lost the habit of conversation. She nodded.

"You're not one of the family here."

Lyddie shook her head.

"You're a good worker. I can see that."

Lyddie nodded again to acknowledge the compliment and turned again to loading the dirty dishes on her tray.

"You'd do well in the mill, you know. You'd clear at least two dollars a week. And"—she paused—"you'd be independent."

She was lying, Lyddie was sure of it. No girl could make that much money in a week's time.

25

"It's hard work, but maybe easier than what you do here, and you'd have some time to yourself, to study or just rest."

"My mother's promised me here," Lyddie said quickly because the door from the kitchen was moving and suddenly Mistress Cutler was in the dining room. The woman looked from the lady to Lyddie, opening her mouth to speak, but Lyddie didn't wait. She hurried past her into the kitchen.

That night, again she counted the calf money. The lady had been lying, of course. But still, how had a farmer's daughter bought a silk dress?

4

Frog in a
Butter Churn

When Lyddie first came to the tavern, Willie built up the
morning fire. But he overslept often and several times the fire
went out and someone had to be sent to the neighbor's for live
coals. The mistress was too mean to invest in a tinderbox, but
she was mortified to be thought a careless housewife who let
her kitchen fire die, so she put Lyddie in charge of it.

The first few nights Lyddie was fearful that she would not
wake up early enough in her windowless room and slept on
the hearth all night, so as to be sure to be the first up in the
morning.

Triphena came in one morning and found her there, but
instead of scolding, took pity. A sort of friendship began that
morning. The cook was past her middle years and homely. She
had never married, preferring, as she said, "not to be a slave
to any man." She was large and vigorous, impatient with Willie, who had to be told things more than once, but, as the days
wore on, won over by Lyddie's hard work and quiet ways.

One morning while Lyddie was churning, just as the cream
was breaking into curdles, the cook told Lyddie about the two
frogs who fell into the pail of milk. "One drowned right off,"
she said, nodding her head in the direction of the door, which
had just slammed shut behind Willie's back. "But the other

kicked and kicked, and in the morning they found him there, floating on a big pat of butter."

Lyddie smiled despite herself.

"Ehyeh," Triphena continued. "Some folks are natural born kickers. They can always find a way to turn disaster into butter."

We can stil hop. Lyddie nearly laughed out loud.

Triphena cocked her head in question, but Lyddie only smiled and shook her head. She couldn't share Charlie's joke with someone else.

Autumn came all too quickly. The days grew suddenly short. And never, though she dreamed and plotted as she scrubbed the iron kettles and churned the butter and bellowed up the fire, never a chance to take the calf money home.

There was no word from Charlie. Not that she truly expected a letter—they had neither money for stationery and postage nor the time or energy for composition. She tried to keep him in her mind—to picture, as she lay upon her own cot, how he was growing and what he was doing. She rarely thought of Rachel and Agnes or their mother. The three of them seemed to belong to another, sadder life. The possibility of their father's return slipped into a back corner of her mind. She wondered once if he were dead, and that was why she seldom thought of him now. There was no pain in the thought, only a kind of numb curiosity.

She and Charlie had left their mother's note and notes of their own to Papa on the table in the cabin, weighted down by the heavy iron candlestick, so, in case he returned, he would know where they were. But the old vision of him coming up the narrow track had faded like a worn-out garment. When she realized that the dream she'd clutched for three years had slipped from her grasp, she wondered if she should feel bad that she had lost it. Her own voice said crossly within her head: "He shouldn't have gone. He should never have left us."

The flaming hills of early October died abruptly. At last, the dreary rains of late fall turned into the first sputterings of snow until the world was beautiful once more with the silver branches of the bare trees and the lush tones of the evergreens against the gleaming banks of snow, so white you had to squint your eyes against it on a sunny day.

The master put the wagons and carriages in the shed and set Willie to cleaning the mud off wheels and undercarriages, and the sleds were brought out. The stagecoach came less often now. Though there was plenty of work to be done in the short winter days, there were not many guests to feed or look after. The few who came seemed as closed and secretive as the freezing grayness of the weather, bent on some narrow business of their own. "Slave catcher," Triphena was heard to mutter after one dark, sleekly well-dressed gentleman departed. "I don't like the smell of them."

If she had been home, she might have spent the dark afternoons spinning or sewing, but the mistress bought her woolens and calicoes at the village stores. She did not even card or spin the wool from their own sheep. It was sent to Nashua or Lowell, where it could be done in a gigantic water-powered mill. All the wealth that had once been Vermont's seemed to be trickling south or west. In fact, the master was heard to say that come spring, the sheep would be sold, because the western railroads were bringing such cheap wool to the Lowell factories that a New England sheep farmer could no longer compete.

It was what her own father had said, but his flock had been much smaller than Cutler's, so their family had felt the pinch years sooner.

One late morning, as she was peeling and cutting potatoes for the boiled noon meal, she felt a presence behind her shoulder. Then someone tweaked her right braid. She looked about, annoyed, expecting to say a sharp word to the bothersome Willie, when she saw it was Charlie.

She stood up, the knife and potato still in her hand. "Oh," she said. "Oh, you surprised me."

He was grinning. "I meant to," he said. "You look well."

"You're taller," she said, but it was a lie. He looked smaller than she remembered, but he would have been pained to hear that. "How are you, Charlie?" It wasn't a pleasantry, she really needed to know.

"Stil hopping," he said with a grin. "Work is slow in winter, so they let me come to see how you were."

Now that she was seeing him at last, she hardly knew what to say. "Have you heard anything from Mama and the babies?" she asked.

He shook his head. His hair was longer, but neater somehow. A better barber than she had trimmed it, she realized with a pang.

"You're busy," he said. "I don't mean to hinder you."

It was a stupid conversation. But both the cook and Willie were in the kitchen, and the mistress would be in and out. How could they say anything that mattered?

"Have you been to home at all?" she asked, turning back to her work and motioning him to sit on a low stool beside her.

"No," he said. "Nor you, ey?"

She shook her head. She wanted to tell him about the money. How she wanted to get it safely home. Ask him what she should do, but she couldn't, of course, with others about.

"I saw Luke a few times," he said. "He's been up once or twice to look at the farm. The house is fine." He lowered his voice. "He had a bit of a laugh about the way we blocked the door. He had to climb in the window."

She didn't like the idea of Luke or anyone else climbing in

the window. It made the cabin seem less secure. A coon or a bear might climb through the window as well, or a tramp. But she didn't comment.

"Do they work you hard?" she asked softly. He looked so small and thin.

"They're fair. The miller works as hard as any of us hands. The food is plenty and good."

Then why aren't you bigger? she wanted to ask him, but she held her tongue.

After he had gone, she thought of a hundred things she wished she had said. She could have told him about the frogs, if she'd remembered to. He would have laughed, and she longed to hear his laugh. She was much lonelier after he went. His presence for an hour had rubbed off some of her protection, leaving her feeling raw and exposed. He had left about noon, carrying some bread and cheese Triphena had pressed on him for his journey. He was wearing snowshoes that looked nearly as long as he was tall. Suppose it began to snow before he got back safely? Suppose he got lost? She tried to shake off her anxieties. Would someone let her know if something were to happen to him? It would be days, for they would let her mother know first, and then she might or might not write to Lyddie. It was too hard being separated like this. It was not right.

"The weather will hold, ey?" Triphena said, reading her mind. Lyddie sighed deeply. "You're worse than a little mother," the woman chided, but her eyes were softer than usual.

The weather did hold for another three days, and then the blizzard of the winter came. The stock was watered and fed, the cows were milked, but there was little that Otis and Enoch, the two hired men, could do outdoors, so the kitchen was crowded with men, seeking the warmth of the great fire as they made spills for the March sugaring, whittling four-inch segments of sumac, which they hollowed out with red-hot pokers. She thought of how she and Charlie had made spills last winter for tapping their own maples. Their own efforts were so childish compared to the practiced skill of these hired men.

She could hardly move in the kitchen, large as it was, without tripping over the gangly legs of a man or having one of them bar her path to the fireplace with a poker. Triphena grumbled continuously under her breath and rejoiced audibly when they left to tend to the livestock.

But Lyddie didn't mind so much. Their bodies were in the way of everything she had to do, but as they worked they talked, and the talk was a welcome window into the world beyond the tavern.

"They caught another slave up near Ferrisburg."

"The legislature can say all they want to about not giving up runaways, but as long as them rewards are high, somebody's going to report them."

"Well, you gotta decide." Enoch spat at the fire. His spit sizzled like fat on a hot griddle. "Who's in charge? Down in Washington slavery is the law of the land. Man buys a horse fair and legal, he sure as hell going after it if it bolts. You pay for something, it's yours. If the law says a man can own slaves, he's got a right to go after them if they bolt. Ain't no difference I can see."

"And if I happen to return somebody's property, seems to me I deserve a reward." Otis paused to pull his poker from the flames and thrust it smoking through the center of the sumac spill he held. "None of them high and mighty folks in Montpelier offered to pay me a hundred dollars *not* to report a runaway, now have they?"

"Well, this weather they likely to be froze 'fore you find 'em. You reckon the reward holds froze or thawed?"

"Why you suppose anyone'd try to run in winter? Don't they know how easy it is to track a critter in the snow?"

"Way I figure, it's not snowing down there where they come from, ey? They don't know what it's like up this way. They just see a chance to run, they run. They don't give it good thought."

I'd give it good thought, Lyddie said to herself. I'd get it all figured out close and choose my time right. If I was running, I'd pick me a early summer night with a lot of moon. I'd just travel by night, sleep in the day . . .

"Can you believe these fools?" Triphena was saying in her ear. "They don't know what it's like to be trapped."

Lyddie had never seen a black person. She tried to imagine how one might look and act. In a way, she'd like to see one, but what would she do? What would she say? And supposing it *was* a fugitive, what then? One hundred dollars! Would they really give you a hundred dollars for turning in a runaway slave? Surely, with that much money, she could pay off her father's debts and go back home.

March came. The sap began to rise in the sugar bush, and Cutler's was in a frenzy of activity. Willie went with the hired men to help in the gathering and boiling of the sap. Mr. Cutler had built a large sugaring shed two summers ago, and the only time any of the men were around the big house was when the livestock needed tending to. Even then, Lyddie was called on to help with the milking and the feeding and watering of the stock.

Added to all her other chores was the task of clarifying the syrup brought up to the house. They had never bothered much with clarifying at the farm as there had hardly been enough syrup or sugar for the family, but the mistress was very particular and stood over Lyddie directing her.

It was hot and exhausting work—beating milk and ash lye with the syrup and boiling the mixture until the impurities rose to the top in a scum and could be skimmed off—but the mistress, who only watched and commanded, declared the light, clear syrup worth the effort.

Some of the clarified syrup was boiled until it turned to sugar and was molded into fancy shapes. Lyddie's favorite among the lead molds was the head of George Washington, though sometimes the nose stuck and it was ruined.

It was because of the molded sugar that Lyddie's dream of taking the calf money home came true, though she couldn't have known how that dream was going to come out.

5

Going Home

By the second week of April, the sap had ceased to run, but it had been a good sugaring season. The mistress decided to take a large selection of the molded maple sugar to Boston. She could pay for her trip by selling the sugar, and it would give her a chance to see the big city and her perpetually ailing sister.

Work did not disappear with the departure of the mistress, but it became as pleasant as a holiday. "If I could make life so happy for others just by going away, I'd go more often," Triphena said. In two weeks Lyddie and Triphena and Willie, when they could catch him, turned the huge house inside out with scrubbing and cleaning. It smelled as good as the air of coming spring. And though there was a bit of fresh snow toward the end of the month, Lyddie knew it for the sham winter it was. Spring could not be denied forever.

"Well," said the cook one night. "The mistress earned herself a trip. I think the rest of us have, too."

"Where will you go, ey?" asked Lyddie wistfully.

"Me?" Triphena said. She was knitting and her worn red hands fairly flew over the yarn. "I got no place I want to visit. I been to Montpelier twice. That's enough. Boston's too big and too dirty. I wouldn't like it. Where would you go?"

"Home," said Lyddie, her voice no more than a whisper.

"Home? But that's hardly ten miles."

Lyddie nodded. It might as well be ten thousand.

"You can go and be back in no more than a couple of days at most."

What was the woman saying?

"Go on. Tomorrow, if you like."

Lyddie couldn't believe her ears. "But . . ."

"Who's going to care with the mistress gone?" She turned the row and began to purl without ever looking down.

"Would it be all right?"

"If I say so," Triphena said. "With her gone, I'm in charge, ey?" Lyddie wasn't going to argue. "If you was to wait, the ground would thaw to mud. Better go tomorrow if it's fair. Take a little sugar to your brother on the way."

Lyddie opened her mouth to ask again if it would be all right, but decided not to. If Triphena said she could go, who was Lyddie to question?

She was up before the sun, but she could tell the day would be a good one. She took a lunch bucket of bread and cheese and a little packet of molded sugar. The snow in the roadway was already turning to mud, and she slung a pair of snowshoes on her back in case the tracks up the mountain were still deep in snow.

She reached the mill in less than an hour, but to her disappointment Charlie was not there.

"I think he's off somewheres," one of the men said. "But you can ask up at the house."

A pretty, rather plump woman answered Lyddie's knock. "Yes?" she said, but she was smiling.

"I come to see Charles Worthen." Lyddie seemed to stumble over the words, which made her flush with embarrassment. "I'm his sister."

"Of course," the woman said. "Come in."

Lyddie stopped to leave her snowshoes and lunch bucket on the porch, then followed the woman into a large, fragrant kitchen. "I was just starting dinner," the woman said as if in apology as she hurried to stir the stew bubbling over the fire in the stone fireplace. "Charles is at school today." She replaced the lid on the kettle. "He's a very bright boy."

"Yes," said Lyddie. She would not be envious of Charlie. They were nearly the same person, weren't they?

"My husband is growing very fond of him."

What did she mean? Who was growing fond of Charlie? Charlie was not their child, not even their apprentice. She felt a need to explain to the woman that Charlie belonged to her, but she couldn't figure out how.

"Just tell him I was here, ey?" she said awkwardly. At the door she remembered the sugar and shoved it at the woman. "Some sugar," she mumbled.

"We'd be happy for you to stay awhile," the woman said, but Lyddie was already picking up her things. "I have to go," she said. "Not much time."

She realized later that she had forgotten to say thank you. But there was no going back. Besides she was in a hurry to get to the farm. She'd have time to clean the house well and check the roofs, as well as find a good place to hide the money. She'd just spend the night there, as it would be almost dark by the time she got everything done.

If she got an early start the next day, perhaps she could stop by once more at the mill . . . but, no . . . She couldn't stop by again and ask for Charlie and have him at school again. What would they think of her? And it might embarrass Charlie to have his sister clucking over him like an old biddy hen. She couldn't stand the thought of Charlie being mortified by her in front of these people who thought so highly of him.

Well, she was glad. Hadn't she felt bad that he didn't have a father and mother like Luke Stevens had to watch over him? But these weren't his real family. She was his real family. More than their mother, really, who had shucked them off like corn husks to follow her craziness.

37

Her anger, or whatever emotion it was that kept her head reeling, kept her feet moving as well. She was walking past the Stevenses' farm by noon. She never stopped to eat, but on the last leg of the trip she suddenly realized her hunger and chewed on the now hard roll and dry cheese as she climbed the narrow track toward the farm.

There was still plenty of snow on the track, but it was better packed than she had imagined. Mr. Westcott must be going back and forth to see to his cows. And then she realized there was snow on the pastures. There'd be no animals up in the fields. But of course—the sugaring. He had gone back and forth gathering sap from the sugar bush.

When she rounded the bend, she half expected the cabin to have disappeared. But there it sat, sagging a bit, squat and honest as her father had built it. The firewood was stacked against the door as she and Charlie had left it. The roofs seemed undamaged from the snow—thanks, perhaps, to Luke Stevens. Those must be his tracks around the cabin. She felt kindly toward the tall, awkward young Quaker for taking care.

She fetched the short ladder from the shed and propped it against one of the two south windows. Then she fetched a piece of split wood from the pile at the front door. The window should be easy to pry open unless it had swollen, but it hadn't. Indeed, it seemed to open quite smoothly, as though welcoming her home. Lyddie propped it up with the wood. She put her right leg over the sill and scrunched her head down onto her chest to squeeze into the opening.

Then she saw it at the fireplace—a shadowy form. She stifled a scream. "Luke?" she whispered. "That you?"

The form turned and stood up. She could barely make it out in the gloom of the cabin. It was a tall man. But not Luke. There was a strange man in her home—the whites of his eyes seemed enormous. And then she realized what was so strange about him. In the dim light his face and hands were very dark. Only his eyes shone. She was looking at a black man.

6

Ezekial

With one leg over the windowsill and her body pressed up under the window frame, there seemed no way to run. But why should she run? It was her house, after all, and what was one measly man, black or white, compared to a bear? Besides—she broke into a cold sweat—this man was likely to be worth one hundred dollars. Keeping her eyes on the intruder as though he *were* a bear, she managed to get her left foot across the sill and straighten herself to a sitting position on the window ledge. Pretending courage seemed to manufacture it, so she was just about to open her mouth to ask the man who he was and what he was doing in her house when he spoke to her.

"Verily, verily I say unto you, he that entereth not by the door but climbeth up some other way, the same is a thief and a robber." His voice was deep and smooth, almost like thick, brushed fur. She knew his words were from the Bible, but she was so astonished by the music of them that she sat there open-mouthed, unable to protest that whatever *he* might be, she was no thief.

"Never fear, little miss. My heart assures me that you're neither a thief nor a robber."

"No," she said, and then louder to show her authority, "I'm mistress here."

"Ah," he said, "we meet at last. You must be Miss Lydia Worthen, my hostess. Forgive my intrusion."

"How do you know my name, ey?" She had meant to ask his, or at least what he was doing in her house, but, as before, he'd gotten the better of her with his fancy talk and quick mind.

"Brother Stevens," he said. "He felt you would be understanding." He glanced at her, and for the first time since he had spied her at the window his expression seemed uncertain. "I hope he was not mistaken." He smiled apologetically. "Here, do come down from there and share a cup of tea with me. You've had a long journey, I'd imagine, and a rude shock, finding your home occupied by a stranger."

What else was she to do? She took the hand he held out to her, surprised by its roughness, as his skin looked like satin in the dim light.

He helped her to the floor. She followed as he led her to the rocker, and then she sat perched on the edge of the chair as he handed her a cup of birch tea. Why hadn't she spied smoke, coming up the road? But the man's fire was tiny, so perhaps there was none to see. The cabin was cold, though warmer than the outdoors. The man poured himself a cup and pulled up a stool on the other side of the fireplace to sit down facing her.

"You've come from the village," he said.

She nodded. The man could hardly be a runaway slave. He talked like a congregational preacher. But he was in hiding, that was plain.

"I should introduce myself," he said, reading her mind. "I'm Ezekial Abernathy, or was so called formerly. I was on the way northward when the snow delayed me last November."

Then he *was* a fugitive.

"I was conveyed to Brother Stevens's farm, where I stayed until it became clear that someone was watching their farm.

40

That was when young Luke spirited me here. He thought your log pile at the door would discourage curiosity."

"We done it to keep out wild critters."

"Yes," he said. "And you succeeded. I've been quite safe from wild ones here." He took a sip of his tea, keeping his eyes on the rim of the cup. "So far." He glanced up at her. "I would have left at once, but I was inconveniently ill. In the cold my lungs have been slow to clear."

"You talk like a preacher."

He relaxed a little. "Well, I am, or rather, I was."

"Then you ain't a slave?"

"Some have considered me a slave."

"But you talk nice." She hadn't meant to put it that way, but it came out unthought.

He smiled. "So do you."

"No," she said, "I mean you've had schooling—"

"I was my own schoolmaster," he said. 'At first I only wanted to read the Bible so I could preach to my people. But" —he smiled again, showing his lovely, even teeth—"a little reading is an exceedingly dangerous thing."

"Reading the Bible?"

"Especially the Bible," he said. "It gave me notions."

"So you just left, ey? Just set out walking?"

He leaned his head back, remembering. "Something like that," he said, but she could tell from his eyes that it was nothing like that at all.

"I couldn't leave my home," she said.

"No? And yet you did."

"I had no choice," she said hotly. "I was made to."

"So many slaves," he said softly.

"I ain't a slave," she said. "I just—I just—" Just what? "There was the debt my father left, so . . ." Whatever she said only made it seem worse. "But we own the land. We're free-men of the State of Vermont." He looked at her. "Well, my

41

father is, or was, till he left, and my brother will be . . ." But Charlie was at school and living with strangers. She hated the man for making her think this way.

"I left the only home I knew," he said quietly. "I left a wife and child behind, vowing I would send for them or come for them within a few months. And here I sit, sick and penniless, hiding for my life, totally dependent on the kindnesses of others for everything." He shook his head and she was sorry she had had a moment's hate of him. Somewhere, perhaps, her father was saying those very same words.

After a while he stood up. "I can offer you a little rabbit stew," he said. "I'm afraid that's about all I have at the moment. Brother Luke will be coming up tonight with more food, I think, but if you're hungry—"

"I have some bread and cheese," she said.

"A veritable feast," he said, his good humor returned.

"When I first saw you"—they were eating and somehow she needed to let him know—"I . . . thought . . ." But she was ashamed to finish the sentence.

"It's a lot of money," he said gently. "I'd be tempted myself if I were you."

She could feel herself go hot and red. "But I won't," she said fiercely. "Now I know you, I couldn't ever."

"Thank you," he said. "A compliment as beautiful as the giver."

"It's dark in here," Lyddie said. "Or you could see I'm plain as sod."

"Or lovely as the earth." He used such fancy words, but she knew he wasn't using words to make fun of her.

Luke did come in the night, but she had slept so soundly that she didn't hear him. The proof was the odor of porridge bubbling over the fire when she awoke. She had slept in her clothes, and scrambled down the loft ladder at once.

42

"Ah, the sleeper awaketh!"

"It's late," she said. "I have to go." But he made her wait long enough to eat.

It was a strange good-bye. She did not hope to see Ezekial again. She hoped that he could cross the border fast as a fox—far away from the snares of those who would trap him. How could she have imagined for one minute that she could betray him? "I hope you get to Canada safe," she said. "And I hope your family can join you real soon." And then, without even thinking, she thrust her hand into her pocket and held out to him the calf-money bag. "You might need something along the way," she said.

The coins jangled as she passed them over.

"But this is yours. You'll need it. You earned it."

"No," she said. "I didn't earn it. It come from selling the calf. I was only going to bury it—till it was needed."

"Will you think of it as a loan, then?" he asked. "When I get established, I'll send it to you care of the Stevenses. With interest, if I can."

"There's no hurry. Wait till your family comes. I don't know when my brother and I can ever get back." She felt leaden with sadness. She pushed the stool to the window and climbed up. He held the window open as she climbed out. Someone—Luke perhaps—had left the short ladder in place.

"I can never thank you, my friend," Ezekial said.

"It was half Stevenses' calf by rights," she said, trying to diminish for both of them the enormity of what she had done. "It was their bull."

"I hope you find your freedom as well, Miss Lydia," he said. It wasn't until she was well down the road that she began to try to figure out what he had meant. And he was right. At Cutler's, despite Triphena's friendship, she was no more than a slave. She worked from before dawn until well after dark, and what did she have to show for it? She was no closer to paying off the debt and coming home than she'd been a year ago. She needed cash money for that. She needed work that would pay and pay well. And there was only one place in New England where a girl could get a good cash wage for her work—and that was in Lowell, in the mills.

The weather held and the trip back was mostly downhill, so she was back by early afternoon. She hung the unused snowshoes in the shed and the lunch bucket in the pantry before she entered the warm kitchen.

"So! You've decided to honor us with a visit!" The mistress's face was red with heat or rage. Behind her, Triphena grimaced an apology.

She stood in the doorway, trying to frame an excuse or apology, but as usual the words did not come quickly enough to mind.

"You're dismissed!" the woman said.

"The best one you ever had," Triphena muttered.

"Unless—"

"No," Lyddie said quickly. "I know I done wrong to go off when you wasn't here. I'll just collect my things and be gone, ey?"

"You're wearing my dress!"

"Yes, ma'am. Shall I wash it before I go or—?"

"Don't be impertinent!"

Lyddie went past the angry woman without a word and up the back staircase to her tiny, windowless room. She pulled off the calico dress and put on the tight homespun, but it was like laying off a great burden. She felt more lighthearted than she had since the day Mrs. Peck brought the letter.

Triphena had followed her up. "Just stay out of sight today. By tomorrow she'll have come to her senses. She knows you're the best worker she's ever likely to get—and at no price at all.

Why she sends your mother fifty cents a week, and then, only if I remind her."

"I'm going to be a factory girl, Triphena."

"You what?"

"I'm free. She's set me free. I can do anything I want. I can go to Lowell and make real money to pay off the debt so I can go home."

"But your brother—"

"He'll be all right. He's in a good place where he's cared for. They're even letting him go to school."

"How can you get to Massachusetts? You've no money for coach fare."

"I'll walk," she said proudly. "A person should walk to freedom."

"A person's feet will get mighty sore," muttered Triphena.

7

South to Freedom

Lyddie set out at once. Or nearly at once. First Triphena made the girl put on her own second-best pair of boots. They were, of course, too large for Lyddie, so she had to wait while the cook fetched two extra pairs of stockings and paper with which to stuff the toes. When Lyddie objected, Triphena kept muttering, "A person can't walk to Massachusetts barefoot, not in April, she can't."

Next, Triphena made her wait while she packed her a parcel of food large enough to feed a table of harvesters. And, finally, she gave her a tiny cloth purse with five silver dollars in it.

"It's too much," Lyddie protested.

"I'm not having your dead body on my conscience," the cook said. "It will be enough for coach fare and the stops along the way. The only tavern food I trust is my own."

"But the mistress . . ."

"You leave the mistress to me."

"I'll pay you back the money—with interest when I can," Lyddie promised. Triphena only shook her head, and gave her a pat on the buttocks as though she were five years old.

"Just don't forget me, ey? Give your old friend a thought now and again. That's all the interest I'll be wanting."

It was three in the afternoon before she could even start her journey, but she would not let Triphena persuade her to wait.

She might let the mistress talk her into staying or lose her nerve if she didn't set out at once.

Her heart was light even if her feet felt clumsy in their makeshift boots and oversized stockings. She remembered Ezekial and thought: He walked north for freedom and I am walking south.

She had forgotten in the excitement that she had already walked above ten miles that day, but her feet remembered. Long before dark they were chafing in the unaccustomed bindings of stockings and ill-fitting boots, reminding her that they had done too much. She sat down on a rock and took the boots off. But before long she felt chilled, so she put them on again and started out, but more slowly than before.

Then, just at dusk, the sky opened, and it began to rain—not light spring showers, but cold, soaking torrents of rain, streaming down her face, icicling rivulets down her chest and legs.

She was obliged, reluctantly, to stop in the next village and seek shelter for the night. The mistress of the local inn was at first shocked to see a young girl traveling alone and then solicitous. "You look near drowned!" she cried, and asked her where she thought she was headed.

"Lowell, is it? Well, the stagecoach will be coming through the end of the week. Work for me till then and I'll give you your board."

Lyddie hesitated, but her sodden clothes and blistered feet reminded her how unsuited she was to continue the journey. She gratefully accepted the mistress's offer and worked so hard that before the week was out the woman was begging her to forget Lowell and stay on. But Lyddie was not to be persuaded.

She boarded the coach on Thursday in the same dismal rain she'd arrived in. Handing over three of her precious dollars to the driver, she settled herself in the corner of the carriage. There were only two other passengers—a man and a woman who seemed to be married, though they hardly spoke to each

47

other. The woman gave Lyddie's dress and shawl and strange boots a critical going over with her eyes, then settled again to her knitting, which the bumping of the coach made difficult.

With the muddy roads, it took two days to get to Windsor. They had not even left Vermont. Lyddie often wished she had saved her dollars and walked—rain or no rain. Surely she could have made it just as fast. But at least the disagreeable people left the coach at Windsor. The bed in the inn was infested with bugs, so she felt both filthy and itchy the next morning, and was not happily surprised that the coach, which had seemed overcrowded with three, was now to carry six as far as Lowell.

One of the passengers was a girl about her own age. Lyddie wanted to ask her if she, too, was going for a factory girl, but she had a young man with her who appeared to be her brother, so Lyddie was hesitant to speak. Then, too, she remembered the look the previous female passenger had given her.

The six of them were jammed into the carriage. There was hardly room for any of them to move, yet the rolling and pitching of the coach seemed worse rather than better for the load. Lyddie tried to sit delicately on one hip and then the other—to spread the bruising out if possible. One of the gentlemen lit a large pipe and the odor of it nearly made her retch. Fortunately, another gentleman reminded him sternly that there were ladies present, and the first man reluctantly tapped his pipe against the metal fixings of the door. But the stench had already been added to the air of foul breath and strong body odors. Lyddie longed for a healthy smell of a farmyard. People were so much fouler than critters.

And still, when the others weren't concentrating on keeping their seats in the swaying coach, they were looking at her—at her clothes especially. At first she was mortified, but the longer they rode, the angrier she became. How rude they were, these so-called gentry.

Everyone's clothes were a disgrace before they'd reached Lowell. The thaw and spring rains had turned parts of the roadway into muddy sloughs, and despite the coachman's skill, early on the last morning they were stuck fast. The passengers were all obliged to alight, and the four men ordered by the coachman to push the wheels out of the rut.

Lyddie watched the hapless gentlemen heave and shove and sweat, all to no avail. The coachman yelled encouragement from above. The men grunted and cursed below as their fancy breeches and overcoats turned brown with the mud and their lovely beaver hats went rolling off down the road.

After at least a quarter of an hour of watching, she could stand their stupidity no longer. Lyddie took off her worn shawl, tied it about her waist, and tucked up her skirts under it. She found a flat stone and put it under the mired wheel. Then she waded in, her narrow shoulders shoving two of the gaping men aside as she set her own strong right shoulder against the rear wheel, ordered the men to the rear boot, and called out; "One, two, three, heave!"

Above, she heard the laughter of the coachman. The men beside her were not smiling, but they did push together. The wheel rolled over the stone, and the coach was free to continue the journey.

She was filthy, but she hardly cared. She could only think of how ignorant, how useless her fellow passengers had been. None of them thanked her, but she hardly noticed. She was eager to be going, but not to ride inside. She looked up at the still smiling coachman. "Can I come up?" she called.

He nodded. Lyddie scrambled up beside him. None of the gentlemen offered her a hand, but she needed none, having spent her life climbing trees and ladders and roofs.

The coachman was still chuckling as he gave the horses a crack of the whip. Cries of protest rose up from the passengers below. He jerked the reins, his eyes twinkling, as more cries came up from the irate inmates as they tried to disentangle their bodies in the carriage and settle themselves on the seats once more.

He shook his head at Lyddie and held the pawing team for a few moments until the jostling in the carriage finally ceased. "You're a hardy one, you are," he said, reaching into the box behind him to pull out a heavy robe. "Here, this will keep the chill off."

She wrapped the robe around her head and body. "Silly fools," she said. "Not the common sense of a quill pig 'mongst the lot of them. Why didn't you tell them what to do, ey?"

"What?" he said. "And lose the entertainment?"

Lyddie couldn't help but laugh, remembering the sight of those sweating, swearing, filthy gentlemen, and now they were further poisoning the already stale air of the carriage with their odor and road mud. Indeed, someone was already raising the shade to let in a bit of cold, fresh air.

"So, you're for the factory life?"

Lyddie nodded. "I need the money."

He glanced sideways at her. "Those young women dress like Boston ladies," he said.

"I don't care for the fancy dress. There's debts on my farm . . ."

"And it's your farm, now is it?"

"My father's," she said. "But he headed West four years ago, and we haven't heard . . ."

"You're a stout one," he said. "Ain't you brothers to help?"

"One," she said. "And he'd be a great help, only my mother put him out to a miller, so until—"

"Have you someone to look out for you in Lowell? A relative, or a friend?"

She shook her head. "I'll do all right on my own."

"I've no doubt of that," he said. "But a friend to put in a word can't hurt. Let me take you to my sister's. She runs a boardinghouse, Number Five, it is, of the Concord Manufacturing Corporation."

"I'm obliged for your kindness, but—"

"Think of it as payment for your help."

"You could have had it out in no time, had you—"

"But never such fun. Coaching can be a wearisome, lonesome job, my girl. I take my pleasure where I can. Did you see those gentlemen's faces, having to be rescued by a slip of a farm girl?"

They crossed the bridge into the city late that afternoon. And city it surely was. It seemed to Lyddie that there were as many buildings crowded before her as sheep in a shearing shed. But they were not soft and murmuring as sheep. They were huge and foreboding in the gray light of afternoon. She would not have believed that the world contained as much brick as there was in a single building here. They were giants—five and six stories high and as long as the length of a large pasture. Chimneys, belching smoke, reached to the low hanging sky.

And the noise of it! Her impulse was to cover her ears, but she held her hands tightly in her lap. She would not begin to be afraid now, she who had stared down a bear and conversed easily with a runaway slave.

The other passengers in their muddy clothing and with their various trunks alighted at the Merrimack Hotel. Lyddie could tell at a glance it was too grand for her purse and person.

In the end, she waited until the coachman had seen the horses and carriage taken care of and then let him walk her to his sister's boardinghouse. "I've brought you a little chip of Vermont granite," he explained to the plump, smiling woman who met them at the door. Then he added, "We'd best come in by the back. Run into a little muddy stretch on the way down."

8
Number Five, Concord Corporation

At first she thought it was the bear, clanging the oatmeal pot against the furniture, but then the tiny attic came alive with girls. One struck a stick against a box, making the flash and odor of a tiny hell. And all this was just to light a candle that barely softened the predawn gloom of the attic. In the clatter of five girls dressing and squabbling over a single basin, Lyddie was forced fully awake and began to remember where she was.

Filthy as she had been, Mrs. Bedlow, the coachman's sister, had kindly taken her in. The boardinghouse keeper hurriedly gave her brother a cup of tea and sent him on his way. Then she had her son, a boy about Charlie's age, fill a tub of hot water in her own bedroom and ordered Lyddie to bathe. The mud-caked dress and shawl she carried away as soon as Lyddie shed them and plopped them directly in a pot of boiling water on the black iron cook stove.

And what a stove it was! Lyddie had only heard rumors of such modern wonders. When she came in from the boarding-house keeper's bedroom, her face scrubbed barn red, her warm, lazy body straining every seam of her one remaining dress, the first thing her eyes lit upon was the stove. She stared at it as though it were an exotic monster from the depths of the sea. If she could have chosen, Lyddie would have pulled a chair close to it and felt its wonderful warmth and studied its marvels, but Mrs. Bedlow urged her into the dining room, which was soon filled with a noisy army of almost thirty young women, still full of energy after their long day in the factory. Lyddie's own head nearly settled into the plate of pork and beans, so that long before the others had finished, Mrs. Bedlow helped her up the four flights of stairs to the attic room, where she fell into bed hardly awake enough to mumble thanks for the woman's kindness.

And now, on this first morning of her new life, she lay in bed a few minutes to relish the quiet of the empty attic. Three days rattling in a coach, then to share a room with five others—indeed, a bed with a stranger who woke Lyddie in the middle of the night with her tossing and snoring—to be clanged awake by a bell, and to have her head punctured by shrieks and squeals and the rattle of voices—it made the windowless alcove she had left behind at Cutler's seem a haven of peace. But she would not look back. She threw off the quilt. She had nothing to wear but her much too small homespun. It couldn't be helped. She dressed herself and padded down the four flights of stairs in her darned and redarned stockings.

The front room was crowded with the two large dining tables that Tim, Mrs. Bedlow's son, was scurrying to set. Wonderful smells of coffee and apple pie and hash and—would it be fish?—wafted through the house from the magical stove as though to prove how many separate wonders it could perform at once.

"I've left my boots . . ." Lyddie started.

Mrs. Bedlow looked up, her round face radiant from the heat. "They're by the stove drying, but they won't do, you know."

"Ey?"

"Your clothes. Your boots. They simply won't do. That dress

is only fit now to be burned. Or what's left of it. I'm afraid it turned to mud stew in my kettle. What could my crazy brother have been thinking of letting a mere girl . . . ?"

"Oh, it wasn't his fault, ma'am," said Lyddie, slipping her feet into Triphena's boots, now stiff from a night beside the stove. "It was the men. They were so stupid . . ."

"You needn't tell me. I know that brother of mine. He was sitting up on top laughing, not giving a word of direction."

"But he had the coach and team . . ."

"Nonsense. He does it to amuse himself and humiliate his betters. He'd wreck a coach if he thought it would give him a rollicking story to tell in the tavern that night. And all at the cost of your clothes and dignity."

"Well, I ain't lost much either way."

"Have you any money at all?"

Lyddie hesitated. She really didn't. It was Triphena's money, not her own.

"If I'm to recommend you to the Concord Corporation, you need to look decent. They like to hire a good class of girls here."

Lyddie reddened.

"Of course, you're as good as anyone, a better worker than most, I suspect, but at the factory they'll look at your clothes and shoes to decide. The Almighty may look at the heart, but 'man looketh on the outward appearance' as the Good Book says, and that goes for women too, I fear. So you'll have to do better than . . ." She looked sadly at Lyddie's tight home-spun and stiff, worn boots.

Lyddie hung her head. "I have a bit left over from the trip. But it's on loan."

"You can pay it back after you're working. Now, would you like to give me a hand? I think the girls will be home for breakfast early. The river's too high and the mill wheels are likely slowing. It means a holiday for them, but not for me."

Lyddie hastened to grab a cloth and take a pie Mrs. Bedlow

was removing from the bowels of the stove. "Yes," Mrs. Bedlow continued, "there'll be a few days off now till the water goes down." She smiled. "Time enough to get you proper clothes and a place in the factory as well."

If the girls had seemed noisy before, it was nothing compared to their entrance to breakfast. They burst through the door, each high-pitched voice shrieking to be heard over the others. There was an air of holiday that hardly paused for a blessing over the food and that erupted full blast before the echo of the "amen" died.

Lyddie, her feet alternately sloshing about and being pinched by Triphena's shoes, determinedly helped Tim serve both large tables. They brought in great platters of fried cod, hash, potato balls, pumpkin mush with huge pitchers of cream, toast and butter, apple pie, and pitchers of coffee and milk. Lyddie had never seen harvesters eat so much or so noisily. And these were supposed to be ladies.

"Hello, there," a voice cut through the din. "We didn't really meet you."

The room was suddenly quiet. "Don't be rude, Betsy," another said. "She was tired last night." Lyddie turned to see who had said this last because it was her idea of a lady's voice. The young woman who had spoken was smiling. "You only came in last night, didn't you, my dear?"

Lyddie nodded.

"There, don't be shy. We were all new once, even our Betsy." There was a titter from the rest. "I'm Amelia Cate." Her name was aristocratic—Amelia. It suited her. She was almost as pretty as the lady in pink that had come through the inn last year. Her skin was white and her face and hands long and delicate. And she was respected, or the others wouldn't have stopped chattering when she spoke.

"And you?"

"Lyddie Worthen. *Lydia* Worthen." With a rough finger she

scratched at the tight homespun across her chest. It seemed to Lyddie that the room was full of young women, all well-dressed, all delicate, all beautiful. And she a crow among peacocks.

"Vermont, isn't it?" said the one called Betsy, and a few of the others laughed.

"What's the matter with Vermont?" The voice had a bare trace of a Green Mountain twang. "I'm from near Rutland myself. Where do you hail from, Lyddie?"

Lyddie turned to see a girl not much older than herself, but, like all the others, whiter of complexion. She had light hair braided in a crown about her head and a serious face that a few freckles failed to relieve. Lyddie pulled at her own straggly brown plaits, grateful when attention shifted and the room was once again filled with chattering.

After breakfast, Amelia and the Rutland girl, whose name was Prudence Allen, offered to take her shopping for a proper dress, work apron, shoes, and bonnet. As they were leaving, Mrs. Bedlow pressed something into Amelia's hand, which turned out to be a dollar that Mrs. Bedlow claimed was a payment from her roguish brother for damages to Lyddie's clothing on the way.

Much to Lyddie's distress, it took all the money she had left, including the coachman's dollar, to dress her in a manner that satisfied Amelia and Prudence. She was so pained at the waste of money that she couldn't enjoy any of the new things, though she was pressed to wear the shoes home. In her heart she knew that she had never had a better-fitting pair—even the stiffness that she felt around the toes and heels and ankles was simply a reminder that she had on grand new city boots. When they were broken in, she would be able to walk anywhere in such shoes—even home.

Lyddie never quite knew how it was decided, but Mrs. Bedlow told her that evening that she would move her things from the attic to Amelia and Prudence's room on the third floor.

The other girls might grumble, which indeed they did, being passed over for a choice room by a newcomer, but Amelia had persuaded Mrs. Bedlow that since Lyddie had no relatives or friends in the house, indeed in the city, she needed their particular caring. Mrs. Bedlow, still feeling guilty about her brother, gave in. So Lyddie was moved to a smaller bedroom on the third floor to be with Amelia, Prudence, and the obviously disgruntled Betsy, who, since their previous roommate had gone home to New Hampshire the week before, had had the luxury of a bed to herself.

Four to a room was in itself a luxury, as most of the rooms held six. But even so, there was hardly any space to walk around the two double beds, the two tiny nightstands, and the various trunks and bandboxes of the inhabitants. There was no place to sit except on the beds, but then, on a regular workday there was no leisure time except the less than three hours between supper and curfew. Most of the girls spent their short measure of free time down in the parlor/dining room or out in town where there were shops and lectures and even dances, all run by honest citizens bent on parting the working girls from their wages.

"Now," said Amelia, who was far more conscientious about her duties as caretaker than Lyddie would have wished, "where will you be going to church on the Sabbath?"

Lyddie looked up in alarm. Living as far as they had from the village, the Worthens had never even bothered to pay pew rent in the village congregational church. "I—I hadn't thought to go."

Amelia sighed, reminding Lyddie that she was proving a harder case than the older girl had bargained for. "Oh, but you must," she said.

"What Amelia means," Betsy said, looking up from her novel, "is that regardless of the state of your immortal soul, the corporation requires regular attendance of all its girls. It makes us look respectable, even those of us who waste our precious minds on novels."

"Oh, do behave yourself, Betsy."

"Sorry, Amelia, but if I let you carry on about her moral duties when the girl plainly has no notion of them herself, this conversation will last all night." She put down her book and looked Lyddie straight in the face. "They'll probably make you put in an appearance from time to time somewhere. The Methodists don't press girls for pew rent, so if you're short on money, best go there. You have to pay for it in longer sermons, but nonetheless I always recommend the Methodists to new girls with no particular desire to go anywhere."

"Betsy!"

"Betsy likes to sound shocking," Prudence explained patiently. "Don't take it to heart." She was brushing out her long blonde hair and looked like a princess in a fairy tale, though her voice was far too matter-of-fact for a story book.

"But—" How should Lyddie explain it? "But, ain't Massachusetts a free country?"

"Of course, my dear," Amelia said. "But there are rules and regulations here as in any civilized establishment. They are meant for our own good, my dear. You'll see."

Betsy rolled her eyes and went back to her novel.

The next morning Mrs. Bedlow led Lyddie down the street past all the corporation boardinghouses to the bridge that led to the factory complex. Between two low brick buildings was a tall wooden fence. The gate of the fence was locked like a jail yard, but Mrs. Bedlow wasn't deterred. She simply went to the door of one of the low buildings and walked in. Lyddie followed, dragging her feet, for the room they entered was larger than the main floor of Cutler's Tavern, and it was crowded with tables and scriveners' desks. There were a few men working about the huge room, who looked up over their pens and account books as the two women passed, but it was clear that nothing much was being accomplished even in the counting room now that the water was too high to drive the mill wheel.

Mrs. Bedlow walked straight through the room and out the door on the opposite side into a courtyard large enough, it seemed to Lyddie, for the whole of their mountain farm to fit inside. The front gate and low south buildings—the counting house, offices, and storerooms, as Mrs. Bedlow explained—formed part of the enclosure. The two slightly shorter sides were taller frame structures—the machine shops and repair shops—and across the whole north end of the compound was the cotton mill itself—a gigantic six-story brick building. At one end ran the frame structure of the outdoor staircase. From the brick face, six even rows of windows seemed to glower down at her through the gray April drizzle like so many unfriendly eyes. A bell tower rose from the long roof, making the building seem even taller and more forbidding.

"It must seem imposing to a farm girl," Mrs. Bedlow said.

Lyddie nodded and tightened her grip on her shawl to keep from trembling.

Mrs. Bedlow turned back toward the low south building and knocked on a door marked "Agent."

"I've brought you a new girl," she said cheerily to the young man who opened the door. "Fresh from the farm and very healthy, as you can see."

The young man hardly gave Lyddie a glance, but stepped back and held the door for them to come in. "I'll see if Mr. Graves can spare a minute," he said haughtily.

"These clerks do put on airs," Mrs. Bedlow whispered, but if she was trying to make Lyddie feel more at ease, she failed. Nor was the sight of the agent himself any comfort.

"Mrs. Bedlow, isn't it?" He was a fat, prosperous-looking man, but without the manners to stand when a middle-aged lady came into his office.

Mrs. Bedlow talked very fast, her face flushed. Lyddie was sure the man would turn them both away—he looked barely patient as Mrs. Bedlow rattled on. But in the end, he said he would give Lyddie a contract for one year. There was a shortage in the weaving room at the moment. Mr. Thurston, the clerk, would give the girl the broadside with the regulations for the Concord and arrange for her to have her smallpox vaccination the following morning.

They were dismissed with a nod. Mrs. Bedlow punched Lyddie and prompted her to thank the agent for his kindness. Lyddie's voice could hardly manage a whisper, but it didn't matter. The gentleman wasn't paying her any attention.

She signed the paper where the clerk pointed, tried to listen carefully to all his warnings about what the contract demanded, and stuffed the broadside that he handed her into her apron pocket. She would study it tonight, she decided, her heart sinking. She could tell at a glance that it would be almost impossible for her to make out the meaning of such a paper. Oh, if only Charlie were here to read it aloud to her and explain the long words. Factory girls were not supposed to be ignorant, it would seem.

It would be several months before she could read with ease the "Regulations for the Boarding Houses of the Concord Corporation." But she found out the next day that it concealed unpleasant truths. The first of these was the vaccination. Mrs. Bedlow marched her over to the hospital after dinner where a doctor cruelly gouged her leg and poured a mysterious liquid directly into the wound.

Lyddie was even more distressed when the wound turned into a nasty sore in a few days' time, but she was only laughed at for her distress and told it was all for her own good. She'd never get the pox now, so she should be grateful. Amelia, indeed, was always instructing her to be grateful about things that Lyddie, try as she might, could not summon the least whiff of gratitude over. But finally, when she had been alternately shocked and bored for the better part of two weeks, the announcement was made at supper that work was to begin again the next day, and Lyddie felt a surge of gratitude that her days of idleness were over. She would be a true factory girl in a few hours' time.

Lyddie was mostly disappointed, but perhaps a tiny bit relieved, when Mrs. Bedlow announced that she would take her over to the weaving room after dinner. The large noonday meal must be out of the way and the dishes washed before the housekeeper could spare a moment, she said. Besides, it wouldn't do to be totally worn out the first day. Four hours would be plenty to start with.

The gate was locked. "They don't want tardy girls slipping past," Mrs. Bedlow explained. "You must always take care to be here when the bell rings." They entered the factory complex through the counting room as they had two weeks before, but this time it was teeming with men, all dressed like gentlemen. Every head seemed to rise, and every eye looked their way. Despite her new clothes, Lyddie could feel the shame burning through her rough brown cheeks. She ducked her bonneted head and hurried through as fast as she could, almost shoving Mrs. Bedlow in her haste.

Once in the yard, she was acutely aware of the thudding. The pulse of the factory boomed through the massive brick wall, and she could feel the vibrations of the machinery as they made their way up the shadowy wooden staircase, which clung for dear life to the side of the building.

Mrs. Bedlow huffed ahead, stopping more than once to catch her breath on the climb to the fourth floor. Once there, she jerked open the door, and the thudding beat exploded into a roar. She gave Lyddie a little push toward the racket. "Mr. Marsden is expecting you!" she yelled. "He'll see you settled in." And she was gone.

9

The Weaving Room

Creation! What a noise! Clatter and clack, great shuddering moans, groans, creaks, and rattles. The shrieks and whistles of huge leather belts on wheels. And when her brain cleared enough, Lyddie saw through the murky air row upon row of machines, eerily like the old hand loom in Quaker Stevens's house, but as unlike as a nightmare, for these creatures had come to life. They seemed moved by eyes alone—the eyes of neat, vigilant young women—needing only the occasional, swift intervention of a human hand to keep them clattering.

From the overarching metal frame crowning each machine, wooden harnesses, carrying hundreds of warp threads drawn from a massive beam at the back of each loom, clanked up and down. Shuttles holding the weft thread hurtled themselves like beasts of prey through the tall forests of warp threads, and beaters slammed the threads tightly into place. With alarming speed, inches of finished cloth rolled up on the beams at the front of the looms.

The girls didn't seem afraid or even amazed. As she walked by with the overseer, girls glanced up. A few smiled, some stared. No one seemed to mind the deafening din. How could they stand it? She had thought a single stagecoach struggling to hold back the horses on a downhill run was unbearably noisy. A single stagecoach! A factory was a hundred stagecoaches all inside one's skull, banging their wheels against the bone. Her impulse was to turn and run to the door, down the rickety stairs, through the yard and counting room, across the narrow bridge, past the row of boardinghouses, down the street—out of this hellish city and back, back, back to the green hills and quiet pastures.

But of course she didn't move a step. She didn't even cover her ears against the assault. She just stood quietly in front of the machine that the overseer had led her to and pretended she could hear what he was saying to her. His mouth was moving, a strange little red mouth peeping out from under his bushy black mustache. The luxuriant growth of the mustache was all the more peculiar because the overseer had hardly any hair on his head. His pate gleamed like polished wood.

Suddenly, to Lyddie's astonishment, the man put his red mouth quite close to her ear. She jerked her head away before she realized he was shouting the words: "Is that quite clear?"

Lyddie stared at him in terror. Nothing was clear at all. What did the man mean? Did he seriously think she could possibly have heard any of his mysterious mouthings? But how could she say she had heard nothing but the beastly racket of the looms? How could she say she could see hardly anything in the morning gloom of the huge, barnlike room, the very air a soup of dust and lint?

She was simply standing there, her mouth open with no words coming out, when an arm went around her shoulders. She shrank again from the touch before she saw it was one of the young women who tended the looms. Her head was close enough to Lyddie's left ear so that Lyddie could hear her say to the overseer, "Don't worry, Mr. Marsden, I'll see she settles in."

The overseer nodded, obviously relieved not to have to deal with Lyddie or the loom he'd assigned her.

"We'll work together," the girl shouted in her ear. "My

two machines are just next to you here. I'm Diana." She motioned for Lyddie to stand close behind her right shoulder, so although Lyddie wasn't in her way as she worked, the older girl could speak into Lyddie's left ear by turning her head slightly to the right.

Suddenly, Diana banged a metal lever at the right of the machine and the loom shivered to a halt. At either end of the shed, made by the crisscrossing of warp threads, was a narrow wooden trough. From the trough on the left she retrieved the shuttle. The shuttle was wood, pointed and tipped at either end with copper. It was about the shape of a corncob, only a little larger and hollowed out so that it could carry a bobbin or quill of weft thread. With her hands moving so quickly that Lyddie could hardly follow them, Diana popped out a nearly empty quill of thread and thrust in a full one from a wooden box of bobbins near her feet. Then she put her mouth to a small hole near one end of the shuttle and sucked out the end of the weft thread.

"We call it the kiss of death," she shouted, smiling wryly to soften the words. She pulled out a foot or more of the thread, wound it quickly around one of two iron hooks, and rehung the hooks into the last row of woven cloth. The hooks were attached by a yard or so of leather cord to a bell-shaped iron weight. "You have to keep moving your temple hooks," Diana said. "Pulls the web down snug as you go." She pointed to the new inches of woven fabric.

"Now," said Diana, speaking into Lyddie's ear, "make sure the shuttle is all the way at the end of the race—always on your right here." She placed the shuttle snug against the right-hand end of the trough. "We don't want any flying shuttles. All right, then, we're ready to go again." Diana grasped the metal lever, pulled it toward the loom, and jammed it into a slot. The loom shuddered once more to life.

For the first hour or so Lyddie watched, trying mostly to

stay out of Diana's way as she moved among the three machines, two opposite and one adjoining. The older girl refilled the shuttles when they ran low and rehung the temple hooks to keep the web tight. Then, without warning, for no reason that Lyddie could see, Diana slammed off one of the looms.

"See," she said, pointing at the shed, "a warp thread's snapped. If we don't catch that, we're in trouble." An empty shuttle might damage a few inches of goods, she explained, but a broken warp could leave a flaw through yards of cloth. "We don't get paid when we ruin a piece." She pinched a tiny bag hung from the metal frame of the loom. It spit out a puff of talc, which she rubbed into her fingertips. Then fishing out the broken ends of warp, she showed Lyddie how to fasten them together with a weaver's knot. When Diana tied the ends, they seemed to melt together, leaving the knot invisible. She stepped aside. "Now you start it," she said.

Lyddie was a farm girl. She took pride in her strength, but it took all of her might to yank the metal lever into place. She broke into a sweat like some untried plow horse. The temples were not much larger than apples, but when Diana asked her to move one, she felt as though someone had tied a gigantic field stone to the end of the leather cord. Still, the physical strength the work required paled beside the dexterity needed to rethread a shuttle quickly, or, heaven help her, tie one of those infernal weaver's knots.

Everything happened too fast—a bobbin of weft thread lasted hardly five minutes before it had to be replaced—and it was painfully deafening. But tall, quiet Diana moved from loom to loom like the silent angel in the lion's den, keeping Daniel from harm.

There were moments when all three looms were running as they ought—all the shuttles bearing full quills, all three temples hung high on the cloth, no warp threads snapping. During one of these respites, Diana drew Lyddie to the nearest window.

The sill was alive with flowers blooming in pots, and around the frame someone had pasted single pages of books and magazines. Diana pressed down a curling corner of a poem. Most of the sheets were yellowing. "Not so much time to read these days," Diana said. "We used to have more time. Do you like to read, Lyddie?"

Lyddie thought of the regulations that she was still trying laboriously to decipher when no one was looking. "I've not much schooling."

"Well, you can remedy that," the older girl said. "I'll help, if you like, some evening."

Lyddie looked up gratefully. She felt no need with Diana to apologize or to be ashamed of her ignorance. "I'm needing a bit of help with the regulations . . ."

"I shouldn't wonder. They're a trial for us all," Diana said. "Why don't you bring the broadside over to Number Three tonight and we'll slog through that wretched thing together."

Amelia was not pleased that evening after supper when she realized that Lyddie was getting ready to go out. "Your first day. You ought to rest."

"I'm all right," said Lyddie. And, indeed, once the noise of the weaving room was out of her ears, she did feel quite all right. A bit tired, but certainly not overweary. "I aim to do a bit of studying," she said. It made her feel proud to say such a thing.

"Studying? With whom?"

"The girl I'm working with in the weaving room. Diana—" She realized that she didn't know Diana's surname.

Amelia, Prudence, and Betsy worked in the spinning room on the third floor, so she supposed they did not know Diana. Betsy looked up from her ever-present novel. "Diana Goss?" she asked.

"I don't know. Just Diana. She was very kind to me today."

66

"Diana Goss?" echoed Amelia. "Oh Lyddie, don't be taken in."

Lyddie couldn't believe her ears. "Ey?"

"If it's Diana Goss," Prudence said, "she's a known radical, and Amelia is concerned—"

"Ey?"

Betsy laughed. "I don't think our little country cousin is acquainted with any radicals, known or unknown."

"I know Quakers," Lyddie said. "Creation! They're abolitionists, every one, ey?"

"Hoorah for you." Betsy put down her novel and made a little show of clapping her hands.

Amelia was sewing new ribbons on her Sunday bonnet and, watching Betsy's performance, managed to jab the needle into her finger instead of the hat brim. She stuck her finger in her mouth and looked up annoyed. "I wish you wouldn't keep saying things like 'creation' and 'ey,' Lyddie. It's so—so—"

"Only the *new* girls from Vermont speak like that," said Prudence, whose own mountain speech was well tamed.

Lyddie didn't quite know what to do. She had no desire to anger her roommates, but she was quite set on going to see Diana. It wasn't just the foolish regulations. She wanted to learn everything—to become as quietly competent as the tall girl. She knew enough about factory life already to realize that good workers in the weaving room made good money. It wasn't like being a maid where hard work only earned you a bonus in exhaustion.

"Well," she said, tying her bonnet, "I'll be back soon."

"I'd rather you wouldn't go at all," Amelia said coolly.

Lyddie smiled. She didn't mean to seem unfriendly or even ungrateful, though it was tiresome to be always beholden to Amelia. "I don't want you to worry after me. I'm able to do for myself, ey?"

"Hah!" Betsy's short laugh came out like a snort.

"It's just—" Prudence said "—it's just that you haven't been here long enough to know about certain things. Amelia doesn't—well, none of us—want you to find yourself in an awkward situation."

For a moment Lyddie was afraid that Amelia or even Prudence would start in to lecture her, so she grabbed her shawl and said as she was moving out of the bedroom door, "I'll watch out." Though what she was promising to look out for, she had no idea.

Diana's boardinghouse was only two houses away from her own. The architecture was identical—a four-story brick building—lined with rows of windows that blinked like sleepy eyes as lamps and candles were lit against the dusk of an April evening.

The front door was unlocked, so she walked into the large front room, like Mrs. Bedlow's, nearly filled with two large dining tables but with the semblance of a living area on one side. And just as in Mrs. Bedlow's parlor, chairs had been pulled away from the tables and girls were chatting and sewing and reading in the living area. It was as noisy and busy as a chicken yard. Peddlers had come off the street to tempt the girls with ribbons and cheap jewelry. A local phrenologist was in one corner measuring a girl's skull and preparing to read her character from his findings. Several girls were watching this consultation transfixed.

Lyddie pushed the door shut but stood just inside, uncertain how to proceed. How could she ask for Diana when she wasn't even sure of her proper name?

But she needn't have worried. Out of the chattering mass of bodies, Diana rose from her chair in the corner and came to where Lyddie stood. She smiled and her long, serious face creased into dimples. "I'm so glad you came. Let's go upstairs where we can speak in something less than a shout."

What a relief it was to climb the stairs and leave most of

the racket two floors behind. There was no one else in Diana's room. "What a treat," Diana said, as though reading Lyddie's mind. "Sometimes I'd sell my soul for a moment of quiet, wouldn't you?"

Lyddie nodded. She suddenly felt shy around Diana, who seemed even more imposing away from the looms when her lovely, elegant voice was pitched rich and low like the call of a mourning dove.

"First, we need to get properly introduced," she said. "I'm Diana Goss." She must have noted a flicker of something in Lyddie's face, because she added, "The *infamous* Diana Goss," and dimpled into her lovely smile.

Lyddie reddened.

"So you've been warned."

"Not really—"

"Well, then, you will be. I'm a friend of Sarah Bagley's." She watched Lyddie's face for a reaction to the name, and when she got none tried another. "Amelia Sargeant? Mary Emerson? Huldah Stone? No? Well, you'll hear those names soon enough. Our crime has been to speak out for better working conditions." She looked at Lyddie again. "Yes, why, then, should the operatives themselves fear us? It is, dear Lyddie, the nature of slavery to make the slave fear freedom."

"I'm not a slave," Lyddie said, more fiercely than she intended.

"You're not here for a lecture. I'm sorry. Tell me about yourself."

It was hard for Lyddie to talk about herself. She'd had no practice. With Amelia and Prudence and Betsy, she didn't need to. They—especially Amelia—seemed always to be telling her about herself or trying to make her like themselves. Besides, what was interesting about her? What would someone like Diana want to know?

"There's Charlie," she began. And before she knew it, she

was explaining that she was here to earn the money to pay off her father's debts, so she and Charlie could go home.

Diana did not smile ironically or laugh as Betsy was sure to. She did not once lecture her as though she were a slow child the way Amelia often did—or offer a single explanation as Prudence would have felt obliged to. No, the tall girl perched on the edge of a bed and listened silently and intently until Lyddie ran out of story to tell. Lyddie was a bit breathless, never having said so many words in the space of so few minutes in her life. And then, embarrassed to have talked so long about herself, she asked, "But I reckon you know how it is with families, ey?"

"Not really. I can hardly remember mine. Only my aunt that kept me until I was ten. And she's gone now."

Lyddie made as if to sympathize, but Diana shook it off. "I think of the mill as my family. It gives me plenty of sisters to worry about. But," she said, "I don't think I need to worry about you. You don't know what it is *not* to work hard, do you?"

"I don't mind work. The noise—"

Diana laughed. "Yes, the noise is terrible at the beginning, but you get accustomed to it somehow."

Lyddie found that hard to believe, but if Diana said so . . .

"And I don't suppose you think a thirteen-hour day overly long, either."

Lyddie's days had never been run on clocks. "I just work until the work is done," she said. "But I never had leave to go paying calls in the evenings before."

"And the wages seem fair?"

"I ain't been paid yet, but from what I hear—"

"What did you get at the inn?"

"I don't know. Fifty cents the week, I think. They sent it to Mama. Triphena said the mistress was like to forget as not.

I suppose Charlie—" Lyddie stopped speaking. Neither Charlie nor her mother knew where she was!

"Is something the matter, Lyddie?"

"I haven't wrote them. Charlie nor my mother. They don't know where I am." Suppose they needed her? How would they find her? Lyddie felt the panic rising. She was cut off from them all. She might as well have gone to the other side of the world. She was out of their reach. "When will they pay me?"

"If it's paper you need—"

"It's postage, too. I'd have to prepay. They don't have the money to pay at that end."

"I could manage postage."

"I can't borrow. I borrowed too much already."

But Diana quietly insisted. Lyddie owed it to her family to let them know right away, she said. She brought out paper, pen and ink, and a sturdy board for Lyddie to write upon. Lyddie would have felt shy about forming her letters so laboriously in front of Diana, but Diana took up a book and made Lyddie feel as though she were alone.

Dear Mother,
    You will be surprize to no I am gone to Lowell to work. I am in the weving rum at the Concord Corp. I bord at number 5 if you rit me. Everwun is kind and the food is plenty and tasty. I am saving my muny to pay the dets.
    I am well. I trus you and the babbies are well to.
                                        Yr. fathfull dater,
                                        Lydia Worthen

It seemed extravagant to take another sheet to write to Charlie, but Diana had said that she ought to write to him as well.

Dear Bruther,
    Do not be surprize. I am gone to Lowell for a factry girl.

Everwun is kind. The work is alrite, but masheens is nosy, beleev me. The muny is good. I will save and pay off the dets. So we can stil hop. (Ha ha)

Yr. loving sister,
Lydia Worthen

P.S. I am at Concord Corp. Number 5 if you can rit. Excuse al mistaks. I am in grate hurry.

She folded the letters, sealed them with Diana's wax, and addressed them. Before she could ask further about posting them, Diana took the letters from her hand. "I have to go tomorrow anyhow. Let me mail them for you."

"I'll pay you back as soon as I get paid." She sighed. "As soon as I pay Triphena—"

"No," said Diana. "This time it's my welcoming gift. You mustn't try to repay a gift."

The bell rang for curfew. "We haven't looked at the silly regulations," Diana said. "Well, another time . . ."

Diana walked her to Number Five. It was a bright, cool night, though in the city, the stars seemed dim and far away. "Until tomorrow," Diana said at the door.

"I'm obliged to you for everything," Lyddie said.

Diana shook her head. "They need to know. They'll worry."

The roommates were already getting into bed. "You're late," Amelia said.

"I come as soon as the bell rung—"

"Oh, you're not really late," said Betsy. "Amelia just doesn't approve of where you've been."

"It *was* Diana Goss, wasn't it?" Amelia asked.

"Yes."

"And?" Lyddie was taking off her bonnet, then her shawl. And what? What did Amelia mean? Amelia answered her own question. "Did she try to make you join?"

Lyddie folded her shawl, still uncomprehending.

"She means," said Betsy, "did she tie you up and torture

72

you until you promised to join the Female Labor Reform Association?"

"Oh, Betsy," said Prudence.

"She never mentioned such," Lyddie said. She made her way around Amelia and Prudence's bed and trunks to the side of the bed that she shared with Betsy. She sat on the edge and began to take off her shoes and stockings.

"Then what were you doing all that time?"

Betsy slammed her book shut. "What affair is it of yours, Amelia?"

"It's all right," Lyddie said. She had no desire to get her roommates stirred up over nothing. "She just give me paper to write to my family to tell them where I was."

"Oh Lyddie," Prudence said. "How thoughtless of us. We never offered."

"No matter," Lyddie said. "I done it now."

"She's devious," Amelia muttered. "You have to watch her. Believe me, Lyddie. I'm only thinking of your own good."

Betsy snorted, reached over, and blew out the candle as the final curfew bell began to clang.

10

Oliver

The four-thirty bell clanged the house awake. From every direction, Lyddie could hear the shrill voices of girls calling to one another, even singing. Someone on another floor was imitating a rooster. From the other side of the bed Betsy groaned and turned over, but Lyddie was up, dressing quickly in the dark as she had always done in the windowless attic of the inn.

Her stomach rumbled, but she ignored it. There would be no breakfast until seven, and that was two and a half hours away. By five the girls had crowded through the main gate, jostled their way up the outside staircase on the far end of the mill, cleaned their machines, and stood waiting for the workday to begin.

"Not too tired this morning?" Diana asked by way of greeting.

Lyddie shook her head. Her feet were sore, but she'd felt tireder after a day behind the plow.

"Good. Today will be something more strenuous, I fear. We'll work all three looms together, all right? Until you feel quite sure of everything."

Lyddie felt a bit as though the older girl were whispering in church. It seemed almost that quiet in the great loom room. The only real noise was the creaking from the ceiling of the leather belts that connected the wheels in the weaving room to the gigantic waterwheel in the basement.

The overseer came in, nodded good morning, and pushed a low wooden stool under a cord dangling from the assembly of wheels and belts above his head. His little red mouth pursed, he stepped up on the stool and pulled out his pocket watch. At the same moment, the bell in the tower above the roof began to ring. He yanked the cord, the wide leather belt above him shifted from a loose to a tight pulley, and suddenly all the hundred or so silent looms, in raucous concert, shuddered and groaned into fearsome life. Lyddie's first full day as a factory girl had begun.

Within five minutes, her head felt like a log being split to splinters. She kept shaking it, as though she could rid it of the noise, or at least the pain, but both only seemed to grow more intense. If that weren't trial enough, a few hours of standing in her proud new boots and her feet had swollen so that the laces cut into her flesh. She bent down quickly to loosen them, and when she found the right lace was knotted, she nearly burst into tears. Or perhaps the tears were caused by the swirling dust and lint.

Now that she thought of it, she could hardly breathe, the air was so laden with moisture and debris. She snatched a moment to run to the window. She had to get air, but the window was nailed shut against the April morning. She leaned her forehead against it; even the glass seemed hot. Her apron brushed the pots of red geraniums crowding the wide sill. They were flourishing in this hot house. She coughed, trying to free her throat and lungs for breath.

Then she felt, rather than saw, Diana. "Mr. Marsden has his eye on you," the older girl said gently, and put her arm on Lyddie's shoulder to turn her back toward the looms. She pointed to the stalled loom and the broken warp thread that must be tied. Even though Diana had stopped the loom, Lyddie stood rubbing the powder into her fingertips, hesitating to plunge her hands into the bowels of the machine. Diana urged her with a light touch.

I stared down a black bear, Lyddie reminded herself. She

took a deep breath, fished out the broken ends, and began to
tie the weaver's knot that Diana had shown her over and over
again the afternoon before. Finally, Lyddie managed to make
a clumsy knot, and Diana pulled the lever, and the loom shuddered to life once more.

How could she ever get accustomed to this inferno? Even
when the girls were set free at 7:00, it was to push and shove
their way across the bridge and down the street to their boardinghouses, bolt down their hearty breakfast, and rush back,
stomachs still churning, for "ring in" at 7:35. Nearly half the
mealtime was spent simply going up and down the staircase,
across the mill yard and bridge, down the row of houses—just
getting to and from the meal. And the din in the dining room
was nearly as loud as the racket in the mill—thirty young
women chewing and calling at the same time, reaching for the
platters of flapjacks and pitchers of syrup, ignoring cries from
the other end of the table to pass anything.

Her quiet meals in the corner of the kitchen with Triphena,
even her meager bowls of bark soup in the cabin with the
seldom talkative Charlie, seemed like feasts compared to the
huge, rushed, noisy affairs in Mrs. Bedlow's house. The half
hour at noonday dinner with more food than she had ever had
set before her at one time was worse than breakfast.

At last the evening bell rang, and Mr. Marsden pulled the
cord to end the day. Diana walked with her to the place by
the door where the girls hung their bonnets and shawls, and
handed Lyddie hers. "Let's forget about studying those regulations tonight," she said. "It's been too long a day already."

Lyddie nodded. Yesterday seemed years in the past. She
couldn't even remember why she'd thought the regulations important enough to bother with.

She had lost all appetite. The very smell of supper made
her nauseous—beans heavy with pork fat and brown injun
bread with orange cheese, fried potatoes, of course, and flap-

jacks with apple sauce, baked Indian pudding with cream and plum cake for dessert. Lyddie nibbled at the brown bread and washed it down with a little scalding tea. How could the others eat so heartily and with such a clatter of dishes and shrieks of conversation? She longed only to get to the room, take off her boots, massage her abused feet, and lay down her aching head. While the other girls pulled their chairs from the table and scraped them about to form little circles in the parlor area, Lyddie dragged herself from the table and up the stairs.

Betsy was already there before her, her current novel in her hand. She laughed at the sight of Lyddie. "The first full day! And up to now you thought yourself a strapping country farm girl who could do anything, didn't you?"

Lyddie did not try to answer back. She simply sank to her side of the double bed and took off the offending shoes and began to rub her swollen feet.

"If you've got an older pair"—Betsy's voice was almost gentle—"more stretched and softer . . ."

Lyddie nodded. Tomorrow she'd wear Triphena's without the stuffing. They were still stiff from the trip and she'd be awkward rushing back and forth to meals, but at least there'd be room for her feet to swell.

She undressed, slipped on her shabby night shift, and slid under the quilt. Betsy glanced over at her. "To bed so soon?"

Lyddie could only nod again. It was as though she could not possibly squeeze a word through her lips. Betsy smiled again. She ain't laughing at me, Lyddie realized. She's remembering how it was.

"Shall I read to you?" Betsy asked.

Lyddie nodded gratefully and closed her eyes and turned her back against the candlelight.

Betsy did not give any explanation of the novel she was reading, simply commenced to read aloud where she had broken off reading to herself. Even though Lyddie's head was still choked with lint and battered with noise, she struggled to get the sense of the story.

The child was in some kind of poorhouse, it seemed, and he was hungry. Lyddie knew about hungry children. Rachel, Agnes, Charlie—they had all been hungry that winter of the bear. The hungry little boy in the story had held up his bowl to the poorhouse overseer and said:

"Please sir, I want some more."

And for this the overseer—she could see his little rosebud mouth rounded in horror—for this the overseer had screamed out at the child. In her mind's eye little Oliver Twist looked exactly like a younger Charlie. The cruel overseer had screamed and hauled the boy before a sort of agent. And for what crime? For the monstrous crime of wanting more to eat.

"That boy will be hung," the agent had prophesied. "I know that boy will be hung."

She fought sleep, ravenous for every word. She had not had any appetite for the bountiful meal downstairs, but now she was feeling a hunger she knew nothing about. She had to know what would happen to little Oliver. Would he indeed be hanged just because he wanted more gruel?

She opened her eyes and turned to watch Betsy, who was absorbed in her reading. Then Betsy sensed her watching, and looked up from the book. "It's a marvelous story, isn't it? I saw the author once—Mr. Charles Dickens. He visited our factory. Let me see—I was already in the spinning room—it must have been in—"

But Lyddie cared nothing for authors or dates. "Don't stop reading the story, please," she croaked out.

"Never fear, little Lyddie. No more interruptions," Betsy promised, and read on, though her voice grew raspy with fatigue, until the bell rang for curfew. She stuck a hair ribbon in the place. "Till tomorrow night," she whispered as the feet of an army of girls could be heard thundering up the staircase.

11
The Admirable Choice

The next day in the mill, the noise was just as jarring and her feet in Triphena's old boots swelled just as large, but now and again she caught herself humming. Why am I suddenly happy? What wonderful thing is about to happen to me? And then she remembered. Tonight after supper, Betsy would read to her again. She was, of course, afraid for Oliver, who was all mixed up in her mind with Charlie. But there was a delicious anticipation, like molded sugar on her tongue. She had to know what would happen to him, how his story would unfold.

Diana noticed the change. "You're settling in faster than I thought," she said. But Lyddie didn't tell her. She didn't quite know how to explain to anyone, that it wasn't so much that she had gotten used to the mill, but she had found a way to escape its grasp. The pasted sheets of poetry or Scripture in the window frames, the geraniums on the sill, those must be some other girl's way, she decided. But hers was a story.

As the days melted into weeks, she tried not to think how very kind it was of Betsy to keep reading to her. There were nights, of course, when she could not, when there was shopping or washing that had to be done. On Saturday evenings they were let out two hours early and Amelia corralled Lyddie and Prudence for long walks along the river before it grew too dark. Betsy, of course, did whatever she liked regardless of

Amelia. Sundays Amelia dragged the reluctant Lyddie to church. At first Lyddie had been afraid Betsy would go on reading without her, but Betsy waited until Sunday afternoon, when Amelia and Prudence were down in the dining room writing their weekly letters home, and she picked up the story just where she had stopped on the previous Friday evening.

It was several weeks before Lyddie caught on that the novel was from the lending library and thus cost Betsy five cents a week to borrow. On her own, Betsy could have read it much faster, Lyddie was sure of that. As much as she hated to spend the money, on her first payday, Lyddie insisted on giving Betsy a full ten cents to help with *Oliver*'s rent. Betsy laughed, but she took it. She, too, was saving her money, she confessed quietly to Lyddie and asked her not to tell, to go for an education. There was a college out West in Ohio that took female students—a real college, not a young ladies' seminary. "But don't tell Amelia," she said, her voice returning to its usual ironic tone, "she'd think it unladylike to want to go to Oberlin."

It seemed strange to Lyddie that Betsy should care at all what Amelia thought. But Lyddie, who had never had any ambition to be thought a lady, did find herself asking, What would Amelia think?—and censoring her own behavior from time to time accordingly.

Then, all too soon, the book was done. It seemed to have flown by, and there was so much, especially at the beginning—when Lyddie was too tired and, try as she might, could not listen properly—so much at the beginning that she needed to hear again. Actually, she needed to hear the whole book again, even the terrible parts, dear Nancy's killing and the death of Sikes.

She wished she dared to ask Betsy to read more, but she could not. Betsy had given her hours and hours of time and voice. And besides, with July nearly upon them, the three roommates were making plans for going home. The very word was like a blow to her chest. Home. If only she could go. But she had signed with the corporation for a full year of work. If she left, even just to see the cabin and visit for an hour or so with Charlie, she would lose her position. "And if you leave without an honorable discharge," the clerk had said, "not only will you never work at the Concord Corporation again, but no other mill in Lowell will ever engage you." Blacklisted! The word sent chills down her backbone.

So she watched her roommates pack their trunks and listened as they chattered about whom they would see and what they would do, and tried not to mind. Amelia would go to New Hampshire where her clergyman father had a country church. Her mother would welcome her help around the manse and with the tutoring of the farm children in the parish Sunday School. Prudence was bound for the family farm near Rutland, where, Amelia hinted, a suitor on a neighboring farm was primed to snatch her away from factory life forever. Betsy's parents were dead, but there was an uncle in Maine who was always glad for her to come and help with the cooking. Haying season would soon be here, and there would be many mouths to feed. There was a chance, as well, Betsy said, of seeing her brother. But again, he might be too pressed with invitations from his university mates to find time for a visit with a sister who was only an old spinster and a factory girl to boot.

After they are gone, I will be earning and saving, Lyddie said to comfort herself. I may earn even more. If the weaving room is short of workers, Mr. Marsden may assign me another loom. Then I could turn out many more pieces each week. For she was proficient now. Weeks before she had begun tending her own loom without Diana's help.

She hadn't imagined that Diana would go on holiday as well, but when Diana told her she was going, she felt a little thrill. Mr. Marsden was sure to give her charge of at least two looms, perhaps a third. She didn't want Diana to think she was rejoicing in her absence, but she was not skilled at feigning feelings she did not own. "I'll miss you," she said.

Diana laughed at her. "Oh, you'll be glad enough to see me gone," she said. "There'll be three looms for you to tend, a nice fat raise to your wages for these several weeks." Lyddie blushed. "You needn't feel bad. Enjoy the money. I think you'll find you've earned every penny. It's hot as Hades up here in July."

"But where will you be going?" Lyddie asked, trying to shift attention from herself. She quickly repented, remembering too late that Diana had no family waiting to see her.

"It's all right," Diana said in reply to Lyddie's pained look. "I was orphaned young. I'm used to it. I suppose this mill is as much home as I can claim. I started here as a doffer when I was ten. So I've fifteen years here. But only a scant handful of Julys."

Lyddie wanted to ask, then, if she had no home to go to, where she was headed, but it wasn't rightly her business, and Diana didn't offer the information except to say when the noise of the machines insured that no one could overhear, "There'll be a mass meeting at Woburn on Independence Day." When Lyddie looked puzzled, she went on, "Of the movement. The ten-hour movement. Miss Bagley will speak, as well as some of the men." When Lyddie still said nothing, she continued, "There'll be a picnic lunch, a real Fourth of July celebration. How about it? I promise no one will make you sign your name to anything."

Lyddie pressed her lips together and shook her head. "No," she said. "I expect I'll be busy."

July was hot, as Diana had so inelegantly predicted. Reluctantly, Lyddie spent a dollar on a light summer work dress as her spring calico proved unbearable. Her other expenditure was at the lending library, where she borrowed *Oliver Twist*.

This time she would read it on her own. It didn't occur to her that she was teaching herself as she laboriously chopped apart the words that had rolled like rainwater off Betsy's tongue. She was so hungry to hear the story again that, exhausted as she was after her thirteen hours in the weaving room, she lay sweating across her bed mouthing in whispers the sounds of Mr. Dickens's narrative.

She was grateful to be alone in the room. There was no one there to make fun of her efforts, or even to try to help. She didn't want help. She didn't want to share this reading with anyone. She was determined to learn the book so well that she would be able to read it aloud to Charlie someday. And wouldn't he be surprised? His Lyddie a real scholar? He'd be monstrous proud.

During the day at the looms, she went over in her head the bits of the story that she had puzzled out the night before. Then it occurred to her that she could copy out pages and paste them up and practice reading them whenever she had a pause. There were not a lot of pauses when she had three machines to tend, so she pasted the copied page on the frame of one of the looms where she could snatch a glance at it as she worked.

July was halfway gone when she made her momentous decision. One fair evening as soon as supper was done, she dressed in her calico, which was nicer than her light summer cotton, put on her bonnet and good boots, and went out on the street. She was trembling when she got to the door of the shop, but she pushed it open. A little bell rang as she did so, and a gentleman who was seated on a high stool behind a slanting desktop looked up at her over his spectacles. "How may I help you, miss?" he asked politely.

She tried to control the shaking in her voice, but in the end was unable to. "I—I come to purchase the book," she said.

The gentleman slid off his stool and waited for her to continue. But Lyddie had already made her rehearsed speech. She didn't have any more words prepared. Finally, he leaned toward her and said in the kindliest sort of voice, "What book did you have in mind, my dear?"

How stupid she must seem to him! The shop was nothing but shelves and shelves of books, hundreds, perhaps thousands of books. "Uh-uh *Oliver Twist*, if you please, sir," she managed to stammer out.

"Ah," he said. "Mr. Dickens. An admirable choice."

He showed her several editions, some rudely printed on cheap paper with only paper backing, but there was only one she wanted. It was beautifully bound in leather with gold letters stamped on its spine. It would take all her money, she knew. Maybe it would be more than she had. She looked fearfully at the kind clerk.

"That will be two dollars," he said. "Shall I wrap it for you?"

She handed him two silver dollars from her purse. "Yes," she said, sighing with relief, "Yes, thank you, sir." And clutching her treasure, she ran from the shop and would have run all the way back to the boardinghouse except that she realized that people on the street were turning to stare.

The Sundays of July were too precious to think of going to church. She didn't even go to the big Sunday School Union picnic on the Fourth, though the sound of the fireworks sent her running from her room to the kitchen. There was no one at home to explain the fearsome racket, but she satisfied herself that the iron cook stove had not blown up, and returned to her sweltering bedroom to continue reading and copying. Mrs. Bedlow gave a general reminder at breakfast on the third Sabbath that many of her boarders were neglecting divine worship, and that the corporation would be most vexed if attendance did not soon improve among the inhabitants of Number Five.

Lyddie slipped a copied page of her book into her pocket and managed to read through the long Methodist sermon. In this way, she only lost a little study time during the two-hour service. She was startled once into attention during the Scripture reading. "Why do you, a Jew, ask water of me a Samaritan?" the woman asked Jesus in the Gospel story. Jesus a Jew? Just like the wicked Fagin? No one had ever told her that Jesus was a Jew before. Just like Fagin, and yet not like Fagin at all.

Lyddie studied on it as she walked home after the service. "Will you watch where you're going, please." She had walked straight into a stout woman in her Sunday best. Lyddie murmured an apology, but the woman humphed angrily and readjusted her bonnet, mumbling something under her breath that ended in "factory girls."

The sidewalk was too crowded for daydreaming. Lyddie packed her wonderings away in her head to think about some other time and began to watch where she was going.

It was then that she saw Diana, or thought she did. At any rate she saw a couple, a handsome, bearded gentleman with a well-dressed lady on his arm, walking toward her on the opposite side of Merrimack Street. The woman was Diana, Lyddie was sure of it. Without thinking, Lyddie called out to her.

But the woman turned her head away. Perhaps she was embarrassed to have a girl yelling rudely at her across a public thoroughfare. Then several carriages and a cart rolled past them, and before Lyddie could see them again, the man and woman had disappeared into the crowd of Sunday strollers. She must have been mistaken. Diana would have recognized her and come across to speak.

12

I Will Not Be
a Slave

She was good at her work—fast, nimble-fingered, diligent, and even in the nearly unbearable heat of the weaving room, apparently indefatigable. The overseer noticed from his high corner stool. Lyddie saw him watching, and she could tell by the smile on his little round lips that he was pleased with her. One afternoon a pair of foreign dignitaries toured the mill, and Mr. Marsden brought them over to watch Lyddie work. She tried to smile politely, but she felt like a prize sow at a village auction.

They didn't pause long. One of them spent the whole time mopping his face and neck and muttering foreign phrases which Lyddie was sure had to do with the temperature rather than the marvels of the Concord Corporation. The other stood by blinking the perspiration from his eyes, looking as though he might faint at any moment. "One of our best girls," Mr. Marsden said, beaming. "One of our very best."

The pay reflected her proficiency. She was making almost $2.50 a week above her $1.75 board. While the other girls grumbled that their piece rates had dropped so that it had hardly been worth slaving through the summer heat, she kept her silence. With Diana gone, she had no friends in the weaving room. She worked too hard to waste precious time getting a drink at the water bucket or running out to the staircase to snatch a breath of air. Besides, her *Oliver* was pasted up, and any free moment her eyes went to the text. She read and reread the page for the day until she nearly had the words by heart.

In this way, she found that even the words that had seemed impossible to decipher on first reading began to make sense as she discovered their place in the story. The names, though peculiar, were the easiest because she remembered them well from Betsy's reading. She liked the names—Mr. Bumble, a villain, but, like her bear, a clumsy one. You had to laugh at his attempts to be somebody in a world that obviously despised him.

Bill Sikes—a name like a rapier—a real villain with nothing to dilute the evil of him, not even Nancy's love. She did not ask herself how a woman could stay with a man like Sikes. Even in her short life she had known of women who clung to fearsome husbands.

Fagin she understood a bit. If the world despised you so much, you were apt to seek revenge on it. The boy thieves—what choice did they have with no homes or families—only workhouses that pretended Christian charity and dealt out despair?

She knew with a shudder how close the family had come to being on the mercy of the town that winter her mother had fled with the babies. Was it to save them from the poor farm that she had gone? Lyddie had not thought of it that way before. Her mother might have realized that she and Charlie on their own were stout enough to manage, but with the extra burden of their mother and the babies . . . Had their mother really thought the bear was the devil on earth? Had she really thought the end was near? Lyddie wondered if she'd ever know the truth of that, anymore than she would ever know what had become of their father.

A letter came to Number Five in her mother's handwriting.

Lyddie felt a pang as she ran to fetch the coins to reimburse Mrs. Bedlow for the postage. She hadn't yet sent any money to her mother. She'd been meaning to. She even had a few dollars set aside for the purpose, but her head had been tied up in other things—her work, the boardinghouse, the dream world of a book—and she had neglected the poor who were her own flesh.

She wanted not to have to open the letter. She wanted the letter never to have arrived, but there it was, and it had to be faced.

Dear Datter,
    I was exceding surpriz to get your letter consern yr mov to Lowell. I do not no to say. if you can send muny it will be help to Judah and Clarissa. They fel a grate burdun. Babby Agnes is gone to God. Rachel is porely. Miny hav died, but Gods will be dun.

Yr. loving mother,
Mattie M. Worthen

She tried to remember Agnes's little face. She strained, squenching her eyes tight to get a picture of her sister, now gone forever. She was a baby. She couldn't have been more than four the winter of the bear, but that was now nearly two years past. She would have changed. Maybe she didn't even remember me, Lyddie thought. Could she have forgotten me and Charlie? Me, Lyddie, who washed and fed her and dear Charlie who made her laugh? She wanted to cry but no tears came, only a hard, dry knot in the place where her heart should have been.

She must work harder. She must earn all the money to pay what they owed, so she could gather her family together back on the farm while she still had family left to gather. The idea of living alone and orphaned and without brother or sister—a life barren of land and family like Diana's . . .

So it was that when the Concord Corporation once again speeded up the machinery, she, almost alone, did not complain. She only had two looms to tend instead of the four she'd tended during the summer. She needed the money. She had to have the money. Some of the girls had no sooner come back from their summer holidays than they went home again. They could not keep up the pace. Lyddie was given another loom and then another, and even at the increased speed of each loom, she could tend all four and felt a satisfying disdain for those who could not do the work.

Prudence was the first of the roommates to go home for good. The suitor in Rutland was urging her to give up factory life, but there was a more compelling reason for her to return. She had begun coughing, a dry, painful cough through the night that kept both Betsy and Amelia awake, though not Lyddie. She slept like a caterpillar in winter. Indeed, she was cocooned from all the rest. Betsy had not offered to read another novel to Lyddie since the summer. She and several other operatives had formed study groups, one in Latin and another in botany. On Tuesday and Thursday evenings they commandeered half the parlor of Number Five and hired their own teacher. When Betsy wasn't downstairs with her group, she was in the room preparing for her next session. "Would you like me to read the text to you?" she asked Lyddie once, taking her nose out from between the pages of her botany book.

Lyddie smiled and shook her head. She knew about plants and flowers, at least as much as she craved to know. She didn't know enough about Oliver Twist.

With Prudence gone and the parlor congested, Amelia was often in the room. She insisted on talking, though Betsy, when there, ignored her and Lyddie tried hard to.

"The two of you should be exercising your bodies instead of holing up in this stuffy room reading," Amelia said.

No answer.

"Or at the least, stretching your souls."

No reply, though both Lyddie and Betsy knew that Amelia was reminding them that it was the Sabbath and neither of them had gone to services earlier.

"What are you reading, Lyddie?"

Maybe if I pretend not to hear, she'll leave me be.

"Lyddie!" This time she spoke so sharply that Lyddie looked up, startled. "Get your nose out of that book and come take a walk with me. We won't have many more lovely Sunday afternoons like this. It will be getting cold soon."

"I'm busy," Lyddie mumbled.

Amelia came closer. "You've been reading that same book for months." She reached over and took *Oliver Twist* out of Lyddie's hands.

"That's my book, ey!"

"Come on, Lyddie. Just a short walk by the river before supper. It will do you good."

'Will you get her out of here before I gag her with my bonnet ribbons and lash her to the bedpost?" Betsy said tightly, never taking her eyes off her own book.

"She can walk by herself. I got to read my book." Lyddie stretched her hand to take the book back, but Amelia held it up just out of reach.

"Oh, come," she said. "You've already read this book. I've seen you, and besides, it's only a silly novel—not fit for reading, and a sin on the Sabbath—"

Lyddie could feel the gorge rising in her throat. Silly novel? It was life and death. "You ain't read it," she said, forgetting her grammar in her anger. "How can you know?"

Amelia flushed and her eyes blinked rapidly. She was no longer teasing. "I know about novels," she said, her voice high and a little shaky. "They are the devil's instrument to draw impressionable young minds to perdition."

Lyddie stared at Amelia with her mouth wide open.

It was Betsy who spoke. "For pity's sake, Amelia. Where did you ever hear such pompous nonsense?"

Amelia's face grew redder. "You are unbelievers and scoffers, and I don't see how I can continue to live in the same room with you."

"Oh, hush." Betsy's tones were gentler than her words. "We do you no harm. Can't we just live and let live?"

Amelia began to cry. Her chiseled marble features crumbled into the angry, helpless rage of a child. As Lyddie watched, she could feel the hardness inside herself breaking, like jagged cracks across granite.

She got a clean handkerchief from her own box and handed it to the older girl. "Here," she said.

Amelia glanced quickly at the hanky—making sure it was a clean one, Lyddie thought wryly—but she murmured a thank you and blew her nose. "I don't know what possessed me," she said, more in her old tone.

"We're all working like black slaves, is what," said Betsy. "I've half a mind to sign the blooming petition."

"Oh Betsy, you wouldn't!" Amelia lifted her nose out of the handkerchief, her eyes wide.

"Wouldn't I just? When I started in the spinning room, I could do a thirteen-hour day and to spare. But in those days I had a hundred thirty spindles to tend. Now I've twice that many at a speed that would make the devil curse. I'm worn out, Amelia. We're all worn out."

"But we'd be paid less." Couldn't Betsy understand that? "If we just work ten hours, we'd be paid much less."

"Time is more precious than money, Lyddie girl. If only I had two more free hours of an evening—what I couldn't do."

"Should you sign the petition, Betsy, they'll dismiss you. I know they will." Amelia folded the handkerchief and handed it back to Lyddie with a nod.

"And would you miss me, Amelia? I thought you'd consider

it good riddance. I thought I was the blister on your heel these last four years."

"I'm thinking of you. What will you do with no job? You'd be blacklisted. No other corporation would hire you."

"Oh," said Betsy, "maybe I'd just take off West. I've nearly the money." She smiled slyly at Lyddie. "I'm thinking of going out to Ohio."

"Ohio?"

"Hurrah!" Betsy cried out. "That's it! I wait till I've got all the money I need, sign the petition, and exit this city of spindles in a veritable fireworks of defiance."

"No!" Lyddie was startled herself that she had spoken so sharply. Both girls looked at her. "I mean, please, don't sign. I can't. I got to have the money. I got to pay the debts before—"

"Oh Lyddie, hasn't your friend Diana explained it all to you? We're working longer hours, tending more machines, all of which have been speeded to demon pace, so the corporation can make a packet of money. Our real wages have gone down more often than they've gone up. Merciful heaven! Why waste our time on a paper petition? Why not a good old-fashioned turnout?" Betsy put her botany book on the counterpane face down to save the place, hugged her knees, and began to sing in a high childlike soprano:

> "Oh! Isn't it a pity such a pretty girl as I
> Should be sent to the factory to pine away and
>   die?
> Oh! I cannot be a slave,
> I will not be a slave,
> For I'm so fond of liberty
> That I cannot be a slave."

"I ain't a slave!" said Lyddie fiercely. "I ain't a slave."

"Of course you aren't." Amelia's confidence had returned and with it her schoolmarm manner.

"At the inn I worked sometimes fifteen, sixteen hours a day and they paid my mother fifty cents a week, if they remembered. Here—"

"Oh shush, girl. Nobody's calling you a slave. I was just singing the old song."

"How do you know that radical song?" Amelia asked.

"I was a doffer back in '36. At ten you learn all the songs."

"And did you join the turnout?" Now Amelia looked like a schoolmarm who had caught a child in mischief.

Betsy's eyes blazed. "At ten? I led out my whole floor— running all the way. It was the most exciting day of my life!"

"It does no good to rebel against authority."

"Well, it does me good. I'm sick of being a sniveling wage slave." Betsy picked up her botany book again as though closing the discussion.

"I mean it's . . . it's unladylike and . . . and against the Scriptures." Amelia's voice was shaking as she spoke.

"Against the Bible to fight injustice? Oh, come now, Amelia. I think you've got the wrong book at that church of yours."

Lyddie looked from one angry face to the other. She cared nothing for being a lady or being religious. She was making far more money than she ever had at home in Vermont or was ever likely to. Why couldn't people just live and let live?

The clang of the curfew bell quieted the argument but not Lyddie's anxiety.

13

Speed Up

Lyddie could not keep the silly song out of her head. It clacked
and whistled along with the machinery.

> Oh! I cannot be a slave,
> I will not be a slave . . .

She *wasn't* a slave. She was a free woman of the state of
Vermont, earning her own way in the world. Whatever Diana,
or even Betsy, might think, she, Lyddie, was far less a slave
than most any girl she knew of. They mustn't spoil it for her
with their petitions and turnouts. They mustn't meddle with
the system and bring it all clanging down to ruin.

She liked Diana, really she did, yet she found herself avoiding her friend as though radicalism were something catching,
like diptheria. She knew Mr. Marsden was beginning to keep
track of the girls who stopped by Diana's looms. She could see
him watching and taking mental note.

When Diana came her way, Lyddie could feel herself stiff-
ening up. And when Diana invited her to one of the Tuesday
night meetings, Lyddie said *"No!"* so fiercely that she scared
herself. Diana didn't ask again. It ain't about you, Lyddie
wanted to say. It's me. I just want to go home. Please understand, Diana, it ain't about you.

The ten-hour people were putting out a weekly newspaper,

The Voice of Industry. Lyddie tried to keep her eyes from straying toward the copies of the weekly, which were thrown with seeming carelessness on the parlor table. Then one night after supper she and Amelia came upstairs to find Betsy chortling over the paper in their bedroom.

"Here!" she said, holding it out to Lyddie. "Read this! Those plucky women are going after the legislature now!"

Lyddie recoiled as though someone had offered her the hot end of a poker.

"Oh Lyddie," Betsy said. "Don't be afraid to read something you might not agree with."

"Leave Lyddie alone, Betsy. You'll only get her into trouble."

"Never fret, Amelia. Our Lyddie loves money too much to risk trouble."

Lyddie flushed furiously. She *was* worried about the money, but she wished Betsy wouldn't put it like that. She wanted to explain to them—to justify herself. Maybe if she told them about the bear—about how close her family'd come to moving to the poor farm. Maybe if she told them about Charlie—how bright he was and how she knew he could do as good at college as Betsy's stuckup brother. Only Charlie wasn't at Harvard. He was sweeping chaff off a mill floor. And little Agnes had gone to God. She shuddered and held her peace. It might sound like cowardly excuses when the words were formed. But it didn't matter if they understood or not. As much as she admired Diana, she wouldn't be tricked by her, or even by Betsy, to joining any protest. Just another year or two and she could go home—home free. I got to write Mama, she thought. I got to tell her how hard I'm working to pay off the debt.

Dear Mother,
   I was made quite sad by your letter telling of my sister Agnes's death. I am consern that you are not taking proper

care of your health. I have enclose one dollar. Please get
yourself and little Rachel good food and if possible a warm
shawl for the winter. I will send more next payday. I try to
save for the debt, but you must tell me how much it is
exakly. And do I send it direct to Mr. Wescott or to some
bank? I am well. I work hard.

> Your loving daughter,
> Lydia Worthen

She checked her spelling in *Oliver*. The grammar as well.
She felt a little thrill of pride. She knew she was improving in
her writing. Not that her mother would be able to tell, but
Charlie would. She took a second sheet to begin a letter to
him, then hesitated, suddenly shy. It had been so long. She
hardly knew what to say. I must go to see him soon as my
year is up, she thought. I'll lose touch. Or—he'll forget me.
She jerked her head to loosen the thought. Charlie would no
more forget her than the snow would forget to fall on Camel's
Hump Mountain. But she should write. He might think she
had forgotten him.

Dear Charlie,

No, "Dear Charles." (He was nearly a man now and might
not like a pet name.)

Dear Charles,

She held the pen so tight her fingers cramped.

I have heard from Mother that little Agnes has died. Did
she write you as well this sad news? We must get Mother
and Rachel home soon. I am saving most of my wages for
the debt. I am working hard and making good pay. We can
go home soon I stil hop. (ha ha). I trust you are well.

> I am as ever your loving sister,
> Lydia Worthen

A great blob of ink fell from the pen right at her name. She blotted it, but the black spread up into the body of the letter. She tried to tell herself that it didn't matter—that Charlie would not be bothered, but she was too bothered by it herself. She'd meant the letter to show him how well she was doing—how she was learning and studying as well as working, but the black stain ruined it. She destroyed the page and could not seem to start another.

No matter how fast the machines speeded up, Lyddie was somehow able to keep pace. She never wasted energy worrying or complaining. It was almost as if they had exchanged natures, as though she had become the machine, perfectly tuned to the roaring, clattering beasts in her care. Think of them as bears she'd tell herself. Great, clumsy bears. You can face down bears.

From his high stool at the back corner of the great room, she could almost feel the eyes of the overseer upon her. Indeed, when Mr. Marsden got up to stroll the room he always stopped at her looms. She was often startled by the touch of his puffy white hand upon her sleeve, and when she turned, his little mouth would be forming something she took to be complimentary, for his eyes were crinkled as though the skin about them had cracked in the attempt to smile.

She would nod acknowledgment and turn back to her machines, which at least did not reach out and pat you when you weren't watching.

He was a strange little man. Lyddie tried once to imagine him dressing in the morning. His impeccable wife tying that impeccable tie, brushing down that black coat, which by six A.M. would be white with the lint blowing about the gigantic room. Did she polish his head as well? And with what? You couldn't use shoeblack of course. Was there a head grease that could be applied and then rubbed to a high shine? She saw the overseer's impeccable wife with the end of a towel in either hand briskly polishing her husband's head, just above the ears, then carefully combing back the few strands of grayish hair from one ear to the other. It was hard to put a face on the overseer's wife. Was she a meek, obedient little woman, or someone like Mrs. Cutler, who would rule him as he ruled the girls under his watchful eye? Not a happy woman, though, for Mr. Marsden did not seem to be the stuff from which contentment could be woven.

Soon there was little time to wonder and daydream. She had done so well on her two, then three, machines that Mr. Marsden gave her a fourth loom to tend. Now she hardly noticed people anymore. At mealtimes the noise and complaints and banter of the other girls were like the commotion of a distant parade. She paid no attention that the food was not as bountiful as it had once been. There was still more than she could eat. Nor did she notice that the taste of the meat was a bit off or the potatoes moldy. She ate the food set before her steadily, with no attempt to bolt as much as possible in the short time allotted. When the bell rang, it didn't matter what was left untasted, she simply pushed back from the table and went back to her bears.

She was too tired now at night to copy out a page of *Oliver* to paste to her loom. It hardly mattered. When would she have had time to study it? After supper she stumbled upstairs, hardly taking time to wash, changed to her shift, and fell into bed.

Though Amelia cajoled and Mrs. Bedlow made announcements at mealtime, Lyddie did not attempt to go to church. Her body wouldn't have cooperated even if she'd had the desire to go. She slept out Sunday mornings and forced herself up for dinner, which she ate, as she ate all her meals now, automatically and without conversation. She was as likely to nap again in the afternoon as not.

"It's like being a racehorse," Betsy was saying. "The harder we work, the bigger prize they get."

Amelia murmured something in reply, which Lyddie was too near sleep to make out.

"I've made up my mind to sign the next petition."

"You wouldn't!"

"Wouldn't I just?" Betsy laughed. "The golden lad finishes Harvard this spring. His fees are paid up, and I've got nearly the money I need now. My Latin is done. So as soon as I complete my botany course, I'll be ready to leave this insane asylum."

Even Lyddie's sleep-drugged mind could feel a twinge. She did not want Betsy to go.

"It would be grand—going out with the bang of a dishonorable dismissal."

"But where would you go? You've always said you could never settle in Maine."

"Not to Maine, Amelia. To Ohio. I'm aiming to go to college."

"To college?"

"Do I surprise you, Amelia? Betsy, in public the devourer of novels, in secret a woman of great ambition?"

"College. I wouldn't have imagined—"

"If they dismiss me, I'd have to stop stalling and blathering and get myself to Oberlin College and a new life." By now, Lyddie was propped up on her elbow listening, torn between pride for Betsy and horror at what she was proposing. "So, you're awake after all, our sleeping beauty."

"Lyddie, tell her not to be foolish."

"I'd hate you to leave," Lyddie said quietly.

Betsy snorted. "I'd be gone a month and a half before you'd ever notice," she said.

The overseers were being offered premiums—prizes to the men whose girls produced the most goods in a pay period—

99

which was why the machines were speeded and why the girls hardly dared take time off even when they were feverish.

"If you can't do the work," Lyddie heard Mr. Marsden say to a girl at the breakfast break, "there's many a girl who can and will. We've no place for sickly girls in this room."

Many girls—those with families who could support them or sweethearts ready to marry them—went home, and new girls came in to replace them. Their speech was strange and their clothing even stranger. They didn't live in the corporation boardinghouses but in that part of the city known as "the Acre."

The Acre wasn't part of the tour for foreign dignitaries who came to view the splendor of Lowell—the model factory city of the New World. Near the Northern Canal, sprouting up like toadstools, rose the squat shacks of rough boards and turf with only a tiny window and a few holes to let in light. And each jammed with Irish Catholics who, it was said, bred like wharf rats. Rumor also had it that these papists were willing to work for lower wages, and, since the corporations did not subsidize their board and keep, the Irish girls were cheaper still to hire.

Diana was helping the new girls settle in, teaching them just as she had taught Lyddie in the spring. Lyddie herself was far too busy to help anyone else. She could not fall behind in her production, else her pay would drop and before she knew it one of these cussed papists would have her job.

Often, now, the tune came unbidden to her head:

> Oh! I cannot be a slave,
> I will not be a slave . . .

It was a dreary December without the abundance of snow that Lyddie yearned for. What snow fell soon turned to a filthy sludge under the feet of too many people and the soot and ashes from too many chimneys. Her body itched even more than it usually did in winter. The tub of hot water, that first night in Mrs. Bedlow's bedroom, proved to be her only full bath in the city, for, like most of the companies, the Concord Corporation had not seen fit to provide bathhouses for their workers. The girls were obliged to wash themselves using only the wash basins in their rooms, to which Tim hauled a pitcher of cold water once a day.

Despite the winter temperatures, the factory stayed hot with the heat of the machinery, the hundreds of whale oil lamps lit against the winter's short, dark days, and the steam piped into the rooms to keep the air humid lest warp threads break needlessly and precious time and materials be wasted.

Lyddie went to work in the icy darkness and returned again at night. She never saw the sun. The brief noon break did not help. The sky was always oppressive and gray, and the smoke of thousands of chimneys hung low and menacing.

At the Lawrence Corporation, just down the riverbank from the Concord, a girl had slipped on the icy staircase in the rush to dinner. She had broken her neck in the fall. And the very same day, a man loading finished bolts of cloth onto the railroad cars in the Lawrence mill yard had been run over and crushed. There were no deaths at the Concord Corporation, but one of the little Irish girls in the spinning room had caught her hair in the machinery and was badly hurt.

Diana took up a collection for the hospital fees, but Lyddie had no money on her person. Besides, how could she give a contribution to some foreigner when she had her own poor baby sister to think of? She vowed to send her mother something next payday. She had opened a bank account and it was growing. She watched it the way one watched a heifer, hardly patient for the time to come when you could milk it. She tried not to resent withdrawing money to send to her mother, but she could see the balance grow each payday. She hadn't seen her mother for two years. She had no way of knowing what her true needs were. And surely, as mean as Judah was and as crazy as Clarissa might be, they would not let their own sister or her child go hungry.

Christmas was not a holiday. It came and went hardly noticed. Amelia had a New Year's gift from her mother—a pair of woolen gloves, which she wrapped again in the paper they had come in and hid in her trunk. Only someone fresh from the farm or one of the Irish would wear a pair of homemade gloves in Lowell. Betsy's brother sent her a volume of essays "to improve my mind." She laughed about his gift, knowing that it had been bought out of the money she sent him each month for his school allowance. "Oh, well," she said. "Only a few more months and our golden lad will be on his own. Ah, if only our sexes had been reversed! Imagine him putting *me* through college."

Lyddie received no gifts, indeed expected none, but she did get a note from Triphena, who thanked her for returning the loan. There was little news to report from Cutler's. She asked after Lyddie's health and complained that the mistress was as harsh as ever. Willie had run off at last, and the new boy and girl weren't worth two blasts on a penny whistle. Lyddie had to smile. Poor Triphena.

Was she thinking of Triphena when it happened? Or was she overtired? It was late on Friday—the hardest time of the week. Was she careless when she replaced the shuttle in the right-hand box or had there been a knot in the weft thread? She would never know. She remembered rethreading the shuttle and putting it back in the race, yanking the lever into its slot . . . Before she could think she was on the floor, blood pouring through the hair near her right temple . . . the shuttle, the blasted shuttle. She tried to rise, she needed to stop the loom, but Diana got there almost at once, racing along the row, tripping with both hands the levers of her own machines and Lyddie's four as she ran. She knelt down beside Lyddie.

"Dear God," she said, cradling Lyddie's head in her lap. She pulled her handkerchief from her pocket and held it tight against Lyddie's temple. It filled immediately with blood. She eased her apron out from under Lyddie's head, snatched it off her shoulders, and pressed it against the soaked handkerchief.

Girls had begun to gather. "Get me some cold water, Delia—clean!" she cried after the girl. "And handkerchiefs, please. All of you!" she cried to the girls crowding about them.

Mr. Marsden's head appeared in the circle of heads above them. The girls shifted to make room for the overseer. "What's this here?" His voice was stern, but his face went ashen as he looked down at the two girls.

"She was hit by the shuttle," Diana said.

"What?" he yelled above the noise.

"Shuttle—shuttle—shuttle." The word whished back and forth across the circle like a shuttle in a race.

"Well . . . well . . . get her out of here." He clamped a large blue pocket handkerchief over his nose and mouth and hurried back to his high stool.

"Not partial to the sight of blood, are we?" The speaker was kneeling on the floor beside Diana, offering her the dainty white handkerchiefs she had collected from the operatives.

The cool water came at last. Diana lifted her apron from Lyddie's temple. The first gush of blood had eased now to a trickle. She dipped a handkerchief into the water and, gently as a cow licking its newborn, cleaned the wound. "Can you see all right?" she asked.

"I think so." Lyddie's head pounded, but when she opened her eyes she could see nearly as well as she ever could in the dusty, lamp-lit room. She closed her eyes almost at once against the pain.

"How about your stomach? Do you feel sick?" Lyddie shook her head, then stopped. Any movement seemed to make the pain worse.

There was a sound of ripping cloth at Lyddie's ear. She opened her eyes. "Your apron," Lyddie said. "Don't—" Aprons cost money.

Diana seemed not to hear, continuing to tear until her apron was in shreds. She bound the least bloodied pieces around Lyddie's head and tied them in place with a narrower strip. "Do you think you could stand up?" she asked.

In answer, Lyddie started to get up. Diana and Delia helped her to her feet. "Just stand here for a minute," Diana said. "Don't try to move yet."

The room spun. She reached out toward the beam of the loom to steady herself. Diana put her arm around Lyddie's shoulders. "Lean on me," she said. "I'll take you home."

"The bell ain't rung," Lyddie protested weakly.

"Oh Lyddie, Lyddie," Diana said, "whatever shall we do with you?" She sighed and pulled Lyddie close. "Delia, help us down the stairs, please. I think I can get her the rest of the way by myself."

Slowly, slowly they went, stopping every few feet to rest. "We don't want to open that cut again," Diana said. "Easy, easy." Mrs. Bedlow helped Diana take Lyddie up the stairs to the second-floor infirmary, not her own room as she wished. But Lyddie's head pounded too much for her to insist that they take her up still another flight of stairs.

"I'll send Tim for Dr. Morris," she heard Mrs. Bedlow saying. No, no, Lyddie wanted to say. Doctors cost money.

"No," Diana was saying. "Not Dr. Morris. Dr. Craven. On Fletcher Street."

She was asleep when the doctor arrived, but she opened her eyes when she heard the murmur of voices above her. "Lyddie," Diana was saying softly, "Dr. Craven needs to look at the wound."

They were there, the two of them standing above her, Diana's familiar face flushed, smiling anxiously down at her, and the doctor's . . . He was a handsome, bearded gentleman— young, his dark brown eyes studying her own, his long, thin hands already reaching to loosen Diana's makeshift bandage. "Now let's look at that cut of yours," he said in a tone compounded of concern and assurance—the perfect doctor.

Lyddie gasped.

He drew his hands back. "Are you in pain?" he asked.

Lyddie shook her head. It was not pain that had startled her. It was the doctor himself. She had seen him before—with Diana—last summer on Merrimack Street.

14

Ills and Petitions

By Saturday afternoon she was back in her own room, and by Sunday the pain had dulled. Dr. Craven had cut her hair away from the wound and bound her head in a proper bandage, but she took it off. She was going back to work the next day, bald spot and all. She'd never been vain—never had anything to be vain about, to tell the truth. No need to start in fussing over her looks now.

At first Amelia and Mrs. Bedlow objected to her returning to work so soon, but they quickly gave up. Lyddie would go to work no matter what. "If you can't do the work . . . ," Mr. Marsden had said. Besides, Diana came by Sunday evening and said she was looking quite fit again. Diana should know, shouldn't she?

She went to bed early, but she couldn't sleep. Her head seemed to throb more when she was lying down. She thought about her family—suppose that cussed shuttle had killed her, or put out her eye? What would they do? And Diana. What was Lyddie to think? She hadn't dared ask about Dr. Craven. Diana hadn't explained why she sent for him instead of Dr. Morris, who usually cared for the girls at Number Five. Dr. Craven seemed as good a doctor as any—better. He didn't leave a bill.

The curfew bell rang. Amelia came to bed. Betsy did too,

106

though she kept her candle burning, studying into the night as she often did. At last she blew out the light, and slid down under the quilts. Then it began, that awful tearing sound that Lyddie would come to dread with every knotted inch of nerves through her whole silently screeching body. Finally it stopped.

"Betsy, I *do* wish you'd see Dr. Morris about that cough." Amelia's voice came from the next bed.

"I'm a big girl, Amelia. Don't nag."

"I'm not nagging. If you weren't so stubborn . . ."

"What would he tell me, Amelia? To rest? How can I do that? I've only got a few more months to go. If I stop now—"

"*I'm* going to stop."

"What?"

There was a sigh in the darkness. "I'm leaving—going home."

"Home?"

"I—I've come to hate factory life. Oh Betsy, I hate what it's doing to me. I don't even know myself anymore. This corporation is turning me into a sour old spinster."

"It's just the winter." Betsy's voice was kinder than usual. "It's hard to stay cheerful in the dark. Come spring you'll be our resident saint once more."

Amelia ignored the tease. "I've been through winter before," she said. "It's not the season." She sighed again, more deeply than before. "I'm tired, Betsy. I can't keep up the pace."

"Who can? Except our Amazonian Lyddie?" Betsy's laugh turned abruptly into a cough that shook the whole bed.

Lyddie scrunched up tightly into herself and tried to block out the sound and the rusty saw hacking through her own chest. Had Betsy been coughing like this for long? Why hadn't she heard it before? Surely there must be some syrup or tonic, even opium . . .

"You *must* see the doctor about that cough," Amelia said. "Promise me you will."

"I'll make a pact with you, Amelia. I'll see the doctor if you'll promise to stay until summer. I can't think of Number Five without you." She stopped to cough, then cleared her throat and said in a still husky voice, "How could I manage? You're the plague of my life—my—my guardian angel."

There was a funny kind of closeness between her roommates after that night, but even so, Amelia went home the last week of January to visit and didn't come back. She wrote that her father had found her a teaching post in the next village. "Forgive me, Betsy," she wrote. "And do, please, I beg you, go to see the doctor."

With a bed to herself, Lyddie was less distressed by Betsy's coughing. And though Betsy never quite got around to seeing Dr. Morris, she was better, Lyddie told herself. Surely the cough was less wracking than it had been. Lyddie missed Amelia. She would have imagined that she'd feel relief to have her gone, but Betsy was right. They both needed her in an odd sort of way—their nettlesome guardian angel.

Her cut was quite healed. Her hair grew out and covered the scar. She was working as well and as hard as ever. Her January pay came to eleven dollars and twenty cents, exclusive of board. Everything was going well for her when Mr. Marsden stopped her one evening as she was about to leave. The machines were quiet, so she could not pretend deafness.

"You're feeling fine again? No problems with the—the head?" She nodded and made as if to go. "You have to take care of yourself. You're my best girl, you know." He put his hand on her sleeve. She looked down at it, and he slipped it off. His face reddened slightly, and his little round mouth worked a bit on the next sentence.

"We're getting new operators in tomorrow—not nearly so

clever as you, but promising. If I could put one in your care—let her work as a spare hand on one of your machines."

Oh, hang it all. How could she say no? How could she explain that she must not be slowed down? She couldn't have some dummy monkeying with her looms. "I got to make my pieces," she muttered.

"Yes," he said, "of course you do. It would only be for a day or so. I wouldn't let anyone hinder you." He smiled with his mouth and not his eyes. "You're my prize girl here."

I'm not your girl. I'm not anybody's girl but my own.

"So—it's settled," he said, reaching out as though to pat her again, but Lyddie quickly shifted her arm to escape the touch.

The new girl, Brigid, was from the Acre—an Irish papist through and through, wearing layers of strange capes and smelling even worse than Lyddie herself. Lyddie scented more than poverty and winter sweat. She whiffed disaster. The girl's only asset was a better command of proper New England speech than most of her lot. Not that she spoke often. She seemed deafened by the machinery and too cowed to ask questions even when she needed to.

As for tying knots, a basic weaver's knot, the girl simply couldn't do them. Lyddie demonstrated—her powdered fingers pinching, looping, slipping, pulling—all in one fluid motion that magically produced a healed warp thread with no hint of a lump to betray the break.

"You don't even watch!" the girl cried out in alarm. And, of course, Lyddie didn't. She had no need to. Her fingers could have tied that knot in a privy at midnight, and it would have held. It would have been invisible as well.

"Here," she said, barely clinging to patience. "I'll do it more slowly." She slapped off all four machines. With her scissors, she cut two threads from a bobbin and, taking the girl to the window where the light was best, she wasted at least five precious minutes tying and retying the useless knot until, finally, the girl was able, however clumsily, to tie a lumpy knot herself.

Lyddie jerked a nod. "It will get better with practice," she said gruffly, anxious to get the stilled looms roaring once more.

Threading the shuttle was, if anything, worse. Lyddie popped the full bobbin into the shuttle and then, as always, put her mouth to the hole and sucked the thread through, pulled it to length, wrapped it quickly on a hook of the temple, dropped the shuttle into the race, and restarted the loom. The next time the quill had to be replaced, she had Brigid thread it, and, as she watched the girl put her mouth over the hole and suck out the thread, the words *kiss of death* came to mind. She had always thought the words a joke among the weavers, but here was this strange-smelling foreigner sucking Lyddie's shuttles, leaving her spittle all over the thread hole. Lyddie wiped the point quickly on her apron before she banged the shuttle against the far end of the race. "We don't want any flying shuttles," she yelled, her face nearly as crimson as the Irish girl's.

By the end of the first day, the girl was far from ready to operate her own machine, but Lyddie had run out of patience. She told Mr. Marsden to assign the girl a loom next to her own. "I'll watch out for her and tend my own machines as well."

Before the noon break of the next day, a flying shuttle had grazed the girl's shoulder, and she had let the shuttle run out of weft, ruining several inches of cloth. When a warp thread snapped, instead of instantly hitting the lever to stall the loom, she threw her apron over her head and burst into tears.

"Shut off your loom," Lyddie yelled over to her. "You can tie the knot this time. You should know how by now, ey?" The girl burst into tears again, and before Lyddie could decide what to do with her, Diana was there, slapping off the loom. Burning with shame, Lyddie glanced over as Diana, without a quiver of impatience, helped the girl retrieve the broken ends and tie a weaver's knot. When, finally, Diana stood back and told the girl to pull the lever into place, Lyddie touched Diana's shoulder. "Sorry," she mouthed.

Diana nodded and went back to work. At the last bell Lyddie found herself going down the stairs beside Diana.

"She's going to do fine, your Brigid," Diana said.

"Oh, I don't know," Lyddie said, wondering how Diana knew the girl's name and then annoyed that the foreigner should be "hers." Surely Lyddie had never wanted her. "She seems all thumbs and tears. They be such fools, those Irish."

Diana gave a wry smile. "We're all allowed to be fools the first week or two, aren't we?"

Lyddie blushed furiously. "I never thanked you proper for taking care of me before," she said. "And your doctor—he never sent a bill. Mind you, I'm not complaining, but—"

Diana didn't comment on the doctor. "Your head seems to have quite recovered. How do you feel? No pain, I hope."

"Oh, I'm all right," Lyddie said. "Just ornery as a old sow."

"Ornery enough to add your name to the petition?" Diana whispered.

She was teasing her, Lyddie was sure of it. "I don't reckon I aim to ever get that ornery," Lyddie said.

Betsy signed the petition. One of the Female Labor Reform girls caught her in an apothecary shop one evening and got her to write in her name.

Lyddie was furious. "They got you when you was feeling low," she said. "They go creeping around the city taking advantage when girls are feeling sick or worn out. Now you'll be blacklisted, and what will I do without you?"

"Better to go out with a flourish than a whine, don't you think?" But Betsy was never allowed her imagined exit. She was to be neither blacklisted nor dismissed.

Her cough got no better. She asked for a transfer to the drawing room. The work of drawing the warp threads from the beam through the harness and reeds had to be done painstakingly by hand. The air was cleaner in the drawing room, and there was much less noise. Though the threading took skill, it did not take the physical strength demanded in the machine rooms, and the girls sat on high stools as they worked. The drawing room was a welcome change for Betsy, but the move came too late to help. The coughing persisted. She began to spend days in their bedroom, then the house infirmary, until, finally, when blood showed up in her phlegm, Mrs. Bedlow demanded that she be removed to the hospital.

On Sunday Lyddie went to see her, taking her botany text and a couple of novels that cost Lyddie twenty cents at the lending library.

"You've got to get me out of here," Betsy said between fits of coughing. "They'll bleed me of every penny I've saved." But where could Betsy go? Mrs. Bedlow would not have her in the house, unwilling to bear the responsibility, and Dr. Morris had declared her too weak to travel to Maine to her uncle's.

Lyddie wrote the brother. He was only in Cambridge—less than a day away by coach or train—but there was a three-week delay before he wrote to say that he was studying for his final examinations and would, perhaps, be able to come for a visit at the end of the term.

Betsy only laughed. "Well," she said, "he's our darling baby boy." Then she fell to coughing. There was a red stain on her handkerchief.

"But you sent him all the way through that college of his."

"Wouldn't you do as much for your Charlie?"

"But Charlie is—" Lyddie was going to say "nice" and stopped herself just in time.

"Our parents are dead, and he's the son and heir," Betsy said as though that explained everything.

Betsy grew a little stronger as the weather warmed, and in April her uncle came to take her to Maine. By then her savings were gone, along with her good looks. "Keep my bed for me, Lyddie. I'll be back next year to start all over again. Someday I'll have enough money to go to college no matter how much the piece rate drops. I may be the oldest girl in the corporation before I have the money again, but if they let women into Oberlin at all, surely they won't fuss about gray hair and a few wrinkles."

She'll never come back, Lyddie thought sadly as she watched the buggy disappear around the corner, headed for the depot and the train north. She'll never be strong enough again to work in a mill thirteen, fourteen hours a day. When I'm ready to go myself, she thought, maybe I could sign that cussed petition. Not for me. I don't need it, but for Betsy and the others. It ain't right for this place to suck the strength of their youth, then cast them off like dry husks to the wind.

He was standing by the front door of Number Five when she came with the rush of girls for the noon meal. "Lyddie Worthen . . ." He said her name so quietly that she almost went past him without hearing. "Miss Lyddie . . ."

She turned toward the voice, which didn't seem familiar, to see a tall man she didn't know. Later she realized that he had not been wearing his broad black Quaker hat. She would have known him at once in his hat. His hair in the sunlight was the rusty red of a robin's breast. Several girls nudged her and giggled as they pushed past her up the steps to the boarding-house.

"I was hoping thee would come," he said. He was so tall he had to stoop over to speak to her. "I'm Luke Stevens." His grave brown eyes searched her face. "Has thee forgotten?"

"No," she said. "I'd not forgot. I just never expected—"

"I wondered if thee would know me in this strange garb." He was wearing shirt and trousers of coarse cotton jean—the kind of cloth the Lowell mills spit out by the mile. She would have known him at once in his Quaker hat and his mother's brown homespun. "I'm fetching some freight from down Boston way," he said almost in a whisper, glancing over his shoulder as he spoke. "They tend to look out for Friends on the road."

"Oh," she said, not really understanding.

"My pa sent thee this," he said, handing her a thick brown parcel about the size of a small book. "He didn't want to risk the post with it, and since I was coming down Boston way—"

She took the parcel from his big, rough farmer fist. "I thank you for your trouble," she said.

"It was no trouble." Was he blushing behind that sun- and wind-weathered face? How odd he seemed.

She felt a need to be polite. "Maybe Mrs. Bedlow could find you some dinner," she said. "We was just coming to eat."

"I can't stay longer. I'm due in Boston. But—but, I'm obliged," he said.

"Well . . ."

"I'd best be on my way . . ."

"Well . . ." She could hear the calls and clatter of the dinner hour even through the closed front door. She'd hardly have a minute to eat her meal if he didn't go.

"It's mighty good to see thee, Lyddie Worthen," he said. "We miss having thee up the hill."

She tried to smile at him. "Thank you for the . . ."—whatever the strange parcel was. "It was good of you to bring it all this way." When on earth would he leave?

"Thy Charlie is well," he said. "I was by the mill just last week."

Charlie. "He's doing well? Fit and—and content?"

"Cheerful as ever. He's a fine boy, Lyddie."

"Yes. I know. Give him my—my best when you see him again, ey?"

He nodded. "Thy house came through the winter in good shape." He saw her glimpse the door. "I mustn't hold thee longer from thy dinner," he said. "God keep you."

"And you," she said.

He grinned good-bye and was gone.

She didn't have time to open the parcel until after supper. Enclosed in several layers of brown paper was a strange, official-looking document, which at first she could make no sense of, and a letter in a strange hand.

My dear Miss Lydia,
  By now you have despaired of me and decided that I am a man who does not honor his word. Please forgive my tardiness. Thanks to the good offices of our friends the Stevenses (true Friends, indeed) as well as your gracious loan, I was able to make my way safely to Montreal. I have now the great joy of my family's presence. Enclosed, therefore, herein is a draft which can never repay my great debt to you.
                     With everlasting gratitude, your friend,
                     Ezekial Freeman

She could not believe it. Fifty dollars. The next day she used her dinner break to race to the bank. Yes, it was a genuine draft from a solvent Montreal bank. Fifty dollars. With one piece of paper her account had bulged like a cow about to freshen. She must find out at once what the debt was. She might already have enough to cover it. Why hadn't her mother replied to her inquiry? Did her mother even know what the debt was? Did she care? Oh mercy, had the woman always hated the farm? Was she glad to have it off her hands?

Lyddie wrote again that very night.

Dear Mother,
    You have not answered my letter of some months prevyus. I need to know the total sum of the det. Writ soon.
                                    Yr. loving daughter,
                                    Lydia Worthen

She didn't take the time to check her spelling. She sealed the letter at once. Then, reluctantly, reopened it to slip in a dollar.

She awoke once in the night and pondered on what she had once been and what she seemed to have become. She marveled that there had been a time when she had almost gladly given a perfect stranger everything she had, but now found it hard to send her own mother a dollar.

15

Rachel

She told no one about the money. She wanted to tell Diana. Diana, she knew, would rejoice with her, but she decided to wait. She was so close now to having the money she needed, and when she did, she would surprise Diana by signing the petition. Then, not more than a week after Luke had brought the money, she had a second visitor who turned her life upside down.

She had left the bedroom door open, trying to encourage a faint breeze through the stuffy room while she washed out her stockings and underwear in the basin. Suddenly she was aware of Tim, standing in the doorway. She looked up from her washing.

"There's a visitor for you in the parlor, Ma says to tell you. A gentleman."

Charlie! She was sure it must be he, all grown up to a gentleman, for who else would come to see her? She could hardly count Luke Stevens. She squeezed the water from her laundry and hastily wiped her hands upon her apron as she ran down the stairs.

But it wasn't Charlie waiting in the corner of the dining room that Mrs. Bedlow called a parlor. Nor was it Luke. She wondered why Tim had called him a "gentleman" at all. At first she was sure he was a stranger. He seemed so out of place in the room of neatly dressed, chattering factory girls, this short man, very thin, with a weathered face and the homespun clothes of a hill farmer.

"Don't you know your uncle, ey?" the man asked at the same moment she recognized him for Judah, Aunt Clarissa's husband, whom she hadn't seen since she was a small thing.

"Made it in two days," he boasted. "Slept right in the wagon."

She tried to smile, but her heart was beating like a churning blade against her breast. What could have brought him here? Anything to do with Clarissa had always spelled trouble. "What's the matter?" She spoke as quietly as she could, feeling every eye in the crowded parlor turned their way. "Why've you come?"

He sobered at once, as though remembering a solemn duty. "Your Aunt Clarissa thought you need be told—"

"Told what?" A chill went through her.

"Your ma's never been stout, you know—"

"The fever? Did she catch the fever?"

He glanced around at the girls seated in the room, who were pretending not to listen, but whose ears stood up, alert as wild creatures in a meadow. He lowered his voice, tapping his head. "Stout up here, ey?"

Lyddie stared at him. What had they done to her mother?

Judah dropped his eyes, uncomfortable under her stare. "So we been obliged—"

"What have you done to my mother?" she whispered fiercely.

"We been obliged to remand her to Brattleboro—to the asylum down there."

"But that's for crazy folk!"

Judah put on a face of hound-dog sorrow and sighed deeply. "It were just too much care for poor Clarissa, delicate as she be."

"Why didn't you ask me? I been responsible for her before. I can do it."

He cocked his head. "You waren't there, ey?"

"Where's Rachel? What have you done with the baby?"

"Why," he said, relieved to have gotten off the subject of her mother, "why she's just fine. Right out front in the wagon. I brung her to you."

Lyddie brushed past him out the door. The farm wagon stood outside; the patient oxen, oblivious to how comically out of place they looked on a city street, chewed their cuds contentedly. For all the stuffiness upstairs, it was damp and chilly down on the street, and Rachel sat shivering on the bench of the wagon, wrapped in a worn shawl that Lyddie recognized as her mother's.

She climbed up on the wagon step and lifted the child down. Rachel was too light. Boneless as a rag doll. As Lyddie went up the steps of the boardinghouse, she could feel her tiny burden trembling through the shawl. "It's all right, Rachie. It's me, Lyddie," she said, hoping the child could remember her.

She carried Rachel inside to where Judah still stood, nervously pinching the rim of his sweat-stained hat. "It's your sister, Rachie," Judah boomed out, his voice fake with hearty cheer. A gasp went up from the girls in the parlor. "Like Aunt Clarissie told you, ey? We brung you to Lyddie."

"Have you got her things?"

In answer he went out to the wagon and brought back a sack with a small lump at the bottom.

"What about my mother's things?" she asked coldly, no longer caring about the audience and what they heard.

"There waren't hardly nothing," he said. She let it go. He was nearly right. "Well," he said, looking from one sister to the other, "I'll be off, then, ey?"

"I'm coming to fetch our mother, soon as I can. As soon

as I pay off the debt. I'll take her back home and care for her myself."

He turned at the door, the hat brim rolled tight and squeezed in his big hands. "Back where?"

"Home," she repeated. "To the farm."

"We be selling it," he said, "We got to have the money— for—for Brattleboro."

"No!" Her voice was so sharp that the roomful of girls stopped everything they were doing to stare. Even little Rachel twisted in her arms to look at her with alarm. She went close to Judah and lowered her voice again to a fierce whisper. "No one can sell that land except my father."

"He give permission."

"How?" She was seized with a wild hope. Her father! They had heard from him. "When?"

"Before he left. He had it wrote out and put his mark to it. In case—ey?"

She wanted to scream at him, but how could she? She had already frightened Rachel. "You got no right," she said between her teeth.

"We got no choice," the man said stubbornly. "We be responsible." And he was gone.

Once more Lyddie was aware of the other girls in the room, who were watching her openmouthed and gaping at the dirty little bundle in her arms. She buried her face in the shawl. "Come on, Rachie," she said as much to them as to the child, "we got to go meet Mrs. Bedlow." She straightened up tall and made her way through the chairs and knees to the kitchen.

"Mrs. Bedlow?" The housekeeper was sitting in the kitchen rocker, peeling potatoes for tomorrow's hash.

"What in heaven's name?"

At the housekeeper's sharp question, Rachel's little head came up from the depths of the shawl like a turtle from a shell.

"It's Rachel, Mrs. Bedlow." Lyddie made her voice as gentle as she could. "My sister, Rachel."

She could read the warning in Mrs. Bedlow's eyes. No men, no children (except for the keeper's own) in a corporation house. But surely the woman would not have the heart . . .

"I'm begging a bath for her. She's had a long, rough journey in an ox cart, and she's chilled right through, ey Rachie?"

Rachel stiffened in her arms, but Mrs. Bedlow dropped her paring knife into the bowl of peeled potatoes, wiped her hands on her apron, and put a kettle on to boil.

It was only after they had both seen Rachel safely asleep in Lyddie's bed that Mrs. Bedlow said the words that Lyddie knew were on her mind. "It won't do, you know. She can't stay here."

"I'll get her a job. She can doff."

"You know she's not old enough or strong enough to be a doffer."

"Just till I can straighten things out," Lyddie pleaded. "Please let her stay. I'll get it all set in just a few days, ey?"

Mrs. Bedlow sighed and made to shake her head.

"I'll pay, of course. Full board. And you see how small she is. You know she won't eat a full share."

Mrs. Bedlow sat down and picked up her paring knife. Lyddie held her breath. "A week. Even then—"

"It wouldn't be more'n a fortnight. I give you my vow. I just got to write my brother."

Mrs. Bedlow looked doubtful, but she didn't say no. She just sighed and started to peel again, the long coil so thin it was almost transparent.

"I'm obliged to you, Mrs. Bedlow. I got nowhere to turn, else."

"She mustn't go outdoors. We can't have her seen about the premises."

"No, no, I swear. I'll keep her in my room. The other girls won't even know."

Mrs. Bedlow looked at Lyddie wryly. "They already know, and there's no guarantee they'll keep their peace."

"I'll beg 'em—"

"No need to coop her up more than necessary. She can come down with me during the day. I'll have Tim help her with her letters and numbers in the afternoon. She ought to be in school herself."

"She will be, Mrs. Bedlow. She will be. Soon as I can get things worked out. I swear upon my life—"

"You need to watch your language, my girl. Set an example for the little one."

"I thank you, Mrs. Bedlow. You'll not be sorry, I promise."

She wrote Charlie that night after curfew in the flickering light of a forbidden stub of candle.

Dear Brother Charles,

I hope you are well. I am sorry to trouble you with sad news, but Uncle Judah come tonight to Lowell and brung Rachel to me. They have put our mother to the asylum at Brattleboro. Now they are thinking to sell the farm. You must go and stop them. You are the man of the family. Judah won't pay me no mind. They got to listen to you. I got more than one hundred dollars to the det. Do not let them sell, Charlie. I beg you. I don't know what to do with Rachel. Children are not allowed in corporation house. If I can I will take her home, but I got to have a home to go to. It is up to you, Charlie. Please I beg you stop Uncle Judah.

Yr. loving sister,
Lydia Worthen

She could hardly keep her mind on her work. What was the use of it all anyway if the farm was gone? But it couldn't be! Not after all her sweating and saving. And what was she to do with Rachel? The child hadn't spoken a word since her arrival. She hadn't even cried. She seemed more dead than alive. And precious time must be spent finding her a place to stay and precious money put out for her keep—more if she was to go to school. Why couldn't the child work in the spinning room? There were Irish children down there who looked no older than seven or eight. They were earning their own way. Hadn't Lyddie herself been working hard since she was no more than a tadpole? And doffing wasn't as hard as farm work. Why those children hardly worked fifteen minutes out of the hour, just taking off the full spools and replacing them with empty ones. Then they just sat in the corner and played or chatted. Sometimes from the window on a clear day Lyddie had seen them running about the mill yard playing tag or marbles. It was an easy life compared to the farm, and still Rachel would be out of mischief and earning her own way.

As if she hadn't trouble enough, Brigid was crying again. Lyddie glanced over at the loom. Everything seemed in order, but the Irish girl was standing there, staring at the shuddering machine with tears running down her cheeks. Lyddie quickly checked her own looms before walking over and saying in the girl's ear, "What's the matter with you, ey?"

Brigid looked around startled. She bit her lip and shook her head.

Lyddie shrugged. It was just as well if the girl learned to bear her own troubles.

Mr. Marsden stopped Lyddie at the stairs on the way to breakfast. Her heart knotted. How could he have heard about Rachel already? Had one of the other girls tattled so soon? They were jealous of her, Lyddie knew. She was the best operator on the floor. But it was not about Rachel that Mr. Marsden wished to speak, it was about the wretched Irish girl. "You must tell her," he said, "that she must get her speed up. I can't keep her on, even as a spare hand, unless she can maintain a proper pace."

Why didn't he tell her himself? He was the overseer. Brigid did not belong to her. She hadn't asked for a spare hand—hadn't wanted one—and now he was trying to shove the responsibility off on her.

She spoke to Brigid after the break. "He says you'll have to speed up or he can't keep you on."

The girl's eyes widened in fear, reminding Lyddie, oh cuss it, of Rachel's silent face as the child sat crouched within herself in the corner of Mrs. Bedlow's kitchen. "Oh, tarnation," she hollered in Brigid's ear, "I'll help you. We'll do the five looms together for a few days—just till you get on better, ey?"

The girl smiled faintly, still frightened.

"And keep your mind on your blooming work, you hear? We can't have you catching your hair or being hit in the head by a flying shuttle because you're being stup—because your mind is someplace else."

Fresh tears started in the girl's eyes, but she bit her lip again and nodded. Lyddie could see Diana smiling approval. Good thing she couldn't hear me, Lyddie thought wryly. She wouldn't be thinking I was so kindly then.

By the seven o'clock bell, Brigid was looking a little less distraught, and Mr. Marsden came past to pat both girls proudly. Lyddie sighed and hardly bothered to dodge him. She had gotten off the fewest pieces in one day since she'd had four looms, and she still had to go home to the burden of silent little Rachel.

"Well, it won't do," said Mrs. Bedlow. "She won't talk to either Tim or me. Not a word. Just sits trembling in the corner like a frozen mouse."

"Did she manage to eat anything?"

"Did she manage to eat? She eats like she hasn't had food in a month of Sundays. I fed her with Tim. She out ate him! And he a growing boy. But never a word through it all—just shovels it in like there'll never be another plateful this side of the grave."

Lyddie looked at the housekeeper's face, pinched with anger, and then down at the top of Rachel's head. The child was trembling—like Oliver, she thought. Like Oliver.

For more? That boy will be hung. I know that boy will be hung.

Oh Rachie, Rachie. I don't want to think of you hungry. "I'll pay you more," she promised Mrs. Bedlow.

"It isn't the money . . ." But it was quite clear to Lyddie that it was indeed the money in addition to the risk, so Lyddie vowed to fetch payment from the bank the very next day. She had to buy time—at least until she heard from Charlie.

When she had finished her own supper, she fetched Rachel from the kitchen, took her out to the privy, and then led her by hand up the staircase to the bedroom. All of this was accomplished with neither of them saying a word aloud, although inside Lyddie's head lengthy conversations were bouncing about. As she tucked the quilt about the child, she tried some of her practiced lines aloud. "What did you do today, Rachie?" "Did Tim make you do some schoolwork?" "Ain't Mrs. Bedlow funny?" "She's all right, ey, just scared to break a rule . . . We got to do what the corporation says, you know, 'cause if we don't we're out of a job, and then what would we do, ey?" There was no answer. She hadn't expected any, still . . . "You musn't be worried, Rachie, Judah can't sell the farm. Charlie and me, we won't let him. We're keeping it for Papa"— was there a flicker of life in the eyes?—"and Mama—and Charlie and Rachie and Lyddie too." Did she just imagine the child had relaxed a little against the pillow, or was it a trick of the candlelight?

Maybe if she read aloud, as Betsy had to her. She opened *Oliver Twist* and commenced. When Rachel fell asleep she didn't know. Lyddie was lost in the comfort of the familiar words. When the bell rang, she blew out the candle and lay in the darkness, feeling the presence of the small body nearby. What could she do? Where could she turn for help? She couldn't keep Rachel here, and yet she, Lyddie, must live in a corporation house to keep her job. And without her job, what good could she do for any of them? But how could she put this little lost child out with strangers? She cursed her aunt and uncle—what could they have been thinking of to bring the child here? And yet, wasn't she better off here with Lyddie, who loved her, than with those two, who must not have given her enough to eat? Poor little Rachel. Poor old Lyddie. She heaved herself over in bed. She had to sleep. There was nothing she could do until she heard from Charlie. Surely Charlie could stop Judah from selling the farm, and then, debt or no debt, she'd take Rachel home. Let them try to get her off that land again. Just let them try.

In her uneasy sleep she saw the bear again, but, suddenly, in the midst of his clumsy thrashing about, he threw off the pot and was transformed, leaping like a spring buck up into the loft where they were huddled. And she could not stare him down.

16
Fever

Taking the money from the bank was like having a rooted tooth yanked from her jaw. Then, the most painful part past, she pressed two whole dollars into Mrs. Bedlow's hand before going out on the town to buy Rachel shoes and shawl and to order a dress made for her. Having spent that much, Lyddie squandered fifty pence more to get the child a beginning reader and a small paper volume of verses that the bookseller recommended. All told, Lyddie had spent more than two weeks' wages. There was less than a dollar in her pocket now left from the princely sum she had withdrawn. She tried not to think on it. It was for Rachel, wasn't it? How could she begrudge the child?

The very next day Brigid was slower than ever, and it was all that Lyddie could do to keep from screaming. Time after time she took the shuttle from the girl's clumsy hands, sucked the thread through from the bobbin, and threw it into the race, raging that a machine should stand idle for even a few seconds. Brigid was on the brink of tears all day.

At last Lyddie exploded when once again the girl's inattention caused a snarl and a ruined piece. "You must mind, girl!" she shouted. "Forget everything else but the loom."

"But I canna forget," Brigid cried out. "Me mother sick unto death and no money for a doctor."

"Here!" She snatched all the change from her apron pocket and stuffed it into Brigid's. "Here. That's for the doctor. Now—mind the machine, ey?"

The next few days went better than those before. She coaxed a few words from Rachel, and the suggestion of a smile, when she read aloud from the book of verses.

"Doctor Foster went to Gloucester
In a shower of rain;
He stepped in a puddle
Right up to his middle,
And never went there again."

"Well," said Lyddie, "that's mud season in Vermont, ey?" And Rachel smiled. Encouraged, Lyddie tried to make a rhyme for Rachel herself.

"Uncle Judah went to Bermuda
In the April rain
He sunk in the ooze
Right up to his snooze
And never was heard of again."

This time there was no mistaking the smile.

Work was going better as well. Brigid was pathetically grateful for her gift. She beat Lyddie to work in the mornings and had two of the machines oiled and gleaming before Lyddie even entered the room.

Mr. Marsden was very pleased. By Thursday, he smiled across the room continually. Lyddie resolved not to glance his way, but she could see without looking the little rosebud mouth fixed in its prissy bow.

How hot the room seemed. Of course it was always hot and steamy, but somehow . . . Perhaps if she hadn't been burning up she could have kept her head, but she was so hot, so exhausted that Thursday in May, she wasn't prepared, she had no defenses. He stopped her and made her wait until everyone had gone—just when she felt she must lie down or faint, he stopped her and put both his fat white hands heavily on either sleeve, dragging his weight on her arms. He was saying something as well, but her head was pounding and she couldn't make it out. What did he want with her? She had to go. She had to see Rachel. Her whole body was on fire. She needed a cool cloth for her head. And yet he kept holding on to her. She tried to stare him down, but her eyes were burning in their sockets. Let me go! She wanted to cry. She tried to pull back from him, but he clutched tighter. He was bringing his strange little mouth closer and closer to her fiery face.

She murmured something about not feeling well, but it made his eyes grow soft and his arm go all around her shoulder.

What made her do it? Illness? Desperation? She'd never know. But she raised her booted foot and stomped her heel down with all her might. He gave a cry, and, dropping his arms, doubled over. It was all the time she needed. She stumbled down the stairs and across the yard, nearly falling at last into the door of Number Five. He had not tried to follow.

She did not go to work the next day or for many days thereafter. Her fever raged, and she was out of her mind with it. Once, she realized that someone was putting a cold cloth on her forehead, and she raised her arm to bring it down over her burning eyelids. A tiny cool hand rested on her hot one and stroked it timidly. Somewhere, at a great distance, she heard a small voice croon: "There, there." And then her heavy arm was lifted and put back gently under the quilt.

Dr. Morris was summoned. She tried to protest. She couldn't waste money on doctors, but if the words came out at all, they came out too thickly for anyone to understand.

The bell rang, but it was far away now. It no longer rang for her. People came in and out of the darkened room. Sometimes Mrs. Bedlow was spooning broth into her, sometimes another of the boarders. Diana was there, and Brigid, though who would have sent for them?

Brigid had brought some Irish concoction that Mrs. Bedlow seemed to be trying to refuse, but the girl would not leave until she had been allowed to spoon some of it into the patient's mouth. And always, whenever Lyddie swam up the fiery pool out into consciousness, she knew that Rachel was there beside her.

She'll get sick, Lyddie tried to protest. Make her go away. Or move me to the infirmary. She's too frail. But either she never got the words out, or no one could or would understand, for whenever she was in her right mind, Rachel was there.

She woke one morning with a start. The bell was clanging, banging away at her dully aching head. She sat up abruptly. The room swooped and dipped about her. More slowly, she swung her legs over the side of the bed, but when she tried to stand, she fell over like a newborn calf. "Rachel," she called. "Help me. I got to go to work."

Rachel raised up from the other bed. "You're awake!" she cried. "Lyddie, you didn't die!"

She fell back onto her pillow. "No," she said weakly. "Not yet. We can stil hop."

17
Doffer

It had been two weeks since she fell ill, and Dr. Morris still refused to let her return to work. Her mind roared protest, but her legs could hardly carry her to the privy. Her body had never betrayed her before. She despised its weakness, and every day she heard the first bell and ordered herself up and dressed, but she would only be up a few minutes, not even through washing herself at the basin, before the sweat broke out on her forehead from the effort, and she was obliged to let Rachel help her back to bed.

There was too much time in bed. She slept and slept and still there were hours awake to worry when her mind skimpleskombled back on itself like threads in a snarled loom. Why hadn't Charlie written? She should have heard from him long ago. Perhaps her letter had been lost. That was it. She sat straight up.

"Better rest, Lyddie." Rachel was there as always. "The doctor said."

"Get me some paper and my pen and ink from the box there—the little one on top of the bandbox. I must write Charlie again."

Rachel obeyed, but even as she handed Lyddie the writing materials, she protested. "You ain't s'posed to worry, Lyddie. Doctor said."

Lyddie put her hand on Rachel's head. Her hair was soft as goose down. "It's all right, Rachie. I'm much better, ey? Nearly all well now."

Rachel's brow furrowed, but her eyes were clear, not the dead, blank eyes of her arrival. Lyddie stroked her hair. "I had me such a good nurse. I couldn't have believed it."

Rachel smiled and nodded at the writing box. "Tell Charlie," she said.

"I'll be sure to," Lyddie said. "He'll be monstrous proud."

By the next week she was feeling truly ready to go back to work and remembering with every breath her last act at the factory. Merciful heavens. There was probably no work to go back to. Had she really? Had she truly stomped on Mr. Marsden's foot with her boot heel? She hardly knew whether to laugh or cry. She sent a note to Brigid—most of the girls were wary of speaking to Diana under Mr. Marsden's nose—asking her and Diana to stop over after supper.

That evening both Diana and Brigid came as she hoped. Brigid brought more soup from her now fully recovered mother and a half bottle of Dr. Rush's Infallible Health Pills. "Me mother swears by them," she said, blushing.

Diana handed Lyddie a paperbound book—*American Notes for General Circulation*—by Mr. Charles Dickens. "Since you're such an admirer of the gentleman, I thought you might like to see what he wrote about factory life in Lowell," she said. "I suppose he was comparing us to the satanic mills of England—anyhow, it's a bit romantical, as they say."

A book. By Mr. Dickens. "How did you know—"

"My dear, anyone who copies a book out page by page and pastes it to her frame . . ."

Lyddie sent Rachel and Brigid down to beg a cup of tea from Mrs. Bedlow. "Diana, I got to ask you. Has Mr. Marsden said anything of me?"

"Well, of course. He missed you at once. You're his best girl."

Lyddie felt her face go crimson.

"I told him I'd ask after you. That's when I learned how ill you were. A lot of the girls have been out with this fever—especially the Irish. There've been many deaths in the Acre."

Lyddie looked away, out the tiny dirty window of the bedroom. Thank you, God. How could I leave my baby girl?

Diana reached over from where she was sitting on the edge of the other bed and put her hand lightly on Lyddie's arm. "I'm grateful you were spared, Lyddie," she said softly.

Lyddie pressed her lips together and gave a little nod. "I reckon I'm too ornery to die."

"I wouldn't be surprised."

"Can you recollect—can you remember just what Mr. Marsden said when he asked about me?"

"He didn't speak directly to me. He doesn't like to think that you and I are friends, you know, but I know he was worried. He wouldn't want to lose you."

"So I still got a place?"

Diana looked at her as though she were crazy. "Why on earth not?"

"I stomped his foot."

"You what?"

"I was all a fever, only I didn't know, ey, and he tried to hold me after the rest had gone. He wouldn't let me go, so I—I stomped down on his foot."

Diana threw her head back and laughed out loud.

"It ain't a joke. He'll have my place for it."

"No, no," she said, trying to recover. "No," she said, taking out her handkerchief and wiping her eyes. "No, I don't think so. He's probably more frightened than you are. Have you ever seen Mrs. Overseer Marsden, Lyddie? If word ever got to that august lady . . . ." She stopped laughing and lowered her voice, her ear cocked toward the open door. "Nonetheless, I wouldn't make attacking the overseer a regular practice, my dear. Do be more discreet in the future—that is, if you want to stay on at the corporation. The day may come when Mr. Marsden would welcome any excuse to let you go." She smiled wryly. "It sounds as though I'm advising you not to sign any petitions or consort with any known radicals."

"But maybe he meant nothing. I was burnt up with the fever. Maybe I mistook kindness for—for—" She grimaced. "You know I'm not the kind of girl men look at that way. I'm plain as plowed sod."

Diana raised an eyebrow, but Rachel and Brigid were at the door with the tea, so she said nothing more.

I'll pretend, thought Lyddie, as she tried to unsnarl her brain over the steaming cup, I'll pretend I was crazy from the fever and didn't know what I was doing—can't even remember what I did.

"I want to be a doffer, Lyddie," Rachel said. Lyddie had brushed her sister's curls and was weaving them into plaits. Rachel wanted to pin her hair up like the big girls in the house, but Lyddie insisted that the braids hang down. She couldn't bear for Rachel to look like a funny little make-believe woman. "Brigid says her little sister is a doffer and she's no bigger than me."

"Oh Rachel. You need to go to school." She loved to braid Rachel's hair, but was suddenly ashamed that she had only string to bind it with. She should have splurged on a bit of ribbon. Rachel was so pretty, for all her being too thin. She ought to have bright bows to set off the two silky curls at the end of each plait. They would brighten her drab little dress. But ribbons cost money, and string bound the hair just as well. She twisted each curl around her index finger and gave it a final brush. "We got to get you into school. You don't want to grow ignorant as your Lyddie."

"You ain't ignorant a-tall. I seed you read."

"You want I should read to you, Rachie?"

"No. I want you should let me be a doffer."

"We'll have to wait and see, ey? When we hear from Charlie . . ."

But they didn't hear from Charlie. They heard from Quaker Stevens.

> Dear Sister Worthen,
>   Thy brother asked me to look into the sale of thy farm. All inquiry has come to naught, but as I have business in thy uncle's neighborhood on Wednesday next, I will inquire directly at that time. I trust thee and the little one are in good health. Son Luke asks to be remembered to thee.
>
> > Thy friend and neighbor,
> > Jeremiah Stevens

She tried not to feel angry at Charlie for not writing to her himself. He had, after all, done the sensible thing. To the law and their uncle, they were only children. Judah would have to listen to Quaker Stevens. He was a man of substance. She was glad to know that Luke had gotten safely home. She had finally realized that the freight he had come to fetch was human.

The letter meant, though, that she could wait no longer. Something would have to be done about Rachel. The promised fortnight had passed, and she must go back to work herself on the morrow. She sent Rachel to the bedroom, stuffed the letter in her apron pocket, and went into the kitchen.

She didn't start with the request, but with an offer of help to fix dinner. Mrs. Bedlow was always grateful for an extra hand in the kitchen, even though the house was now down to only twenty girls.

"You give me more than the fortnight, Mrs. Bedlow, and I

am obliged," she said, once the cabbage had been chopped and the bread sliced.

"You were near to death, Lyddie. I'm not without heart."

"Indeed not." Lyddie smiled as warmly as she knew how. "You been more'n good to me and mine. Which is why I dare—"

"It won't do, you know. I can't keep her on indefinitely."

"But if she was a doffer—"

"She's hardly more than a baby."

"She's small, but she's a worker. Didn't she nurse me, ey?"

"She pulled you through. I wouldn't have warranted it—"

"Could you ask the agent for me? Just until I got things set with my brother? All I want to do is take her home. It wouldn't be for long, I swear. Meantime, I've not the heart to set her out with strangers."

Mrs. Bedlow was weakening. Lyddie could read it in the sag of her face. She pressed on, eagerly. "It won't be more than a few weeks, and I'd pay extra, I would. I know it's hard for you with only twenty girls here regular—"

"I'll speak to the agent, but I can't promise you—"

"I know, I know. But if you'll just ask for me. She's a fine little worker, and so eager to make good."

"I can't promise anything—"

"Would you go now and ask?"

"Now? I'm in the middle of fixing dinner—"

"I'll finish for you. Please. So I can take her over when I go back to work tomorrow . . ."

It was arranged. Lyddie suspected that Mrs. Bedlow had added a few years and several pounds in her description of Rachel to the agent, but a skeptical look was all she got from the overseer on the spinning floor when she presented Rachel for work the next morning. And Rachel looked so bright and eager and smiled so sweetly that even the skeptical look melted, and she was sent, skipping down the aisle, to meet the other doffers under the care of a kindly middle-aged spinner.

Slowly, Lyddie climbed the flight of stairs to the weaving room. Her worry for Rachel had pushed aside, for a time, her own fears of seeing Mr. Marsden again. She didn't dare look in his direction, but went straight to her looms where Brigid was already at work, cleaning and oiling.

"You're looking much the rosier," Brigid said. How pretty the girl was with her light brown hair and eyes clear blue as a bright February sky after snow. It was the smile, though, that transformed her into a real beauty. Lyddie smiled back. She did not envy other women their good looks. And even if she had been so inclined, she would never begrudge this bounty of nature to one so poor in everything else.

"We covered the machines as best we could while you were gone, me and Diana. Though"—she smiled apologetically— "you'll see from your wage, the work was not near what it would be, had you been here."

It was all they had time to say before Mr. Marsden stepped on his stool and pulled the cord that set the room to roaring and shaking. Lyddie jumped, then laughed. How quickly she'd forgotten the noise! Within minutes she had settled in and forgotten everything else—Mr. Marsden, her weakness, the farm, Charlie, even Rachel. It was good to be back with her beasts again. She belonged among them somehow.

By the breakfast bell she was almost too tired to eat. She would, if she could have chosen, sat out the break in the window alcove, but that would leave her alone on the floor. She glanced at Mr. Marsden and hurried toward the stairs. He didn't speak to her. It was as if nothing had occurred between them, except that he never came over to her loom to pat and encourage her. Not once.

She managed to eat breakfast, or some of it. Rachel was

stuffing herself like a regular factory girl, talking excitedly at the same time. She stopped only to look at Lyddie and say through her full mouth, "Eat, Lyddie. You got to eat and grow strong."

So it was she got through breakfast and dinner, but by supper she could only manage a few bites of stew before she dragged herself up to bed. Fatigue was like a toothache in her bones. She would have cursed her weakness, had she the strength.

Each day, though, she was a little stronger. At first she could not feel it, no more than a body can feel itself grow taller. But by the end of the week, she found that she had eaten a full plate at supper and was lingering in the parlor with Rachel, who was watching, fascinated, as a phrenologist sought to sell his services to the girls.

"Please, Lyddie," Rachel begged. "Let's have our heads done."

"I know about my head, Rachel. Why should I pay good money to find out it's plain as sod and stubborn as a mule?"

"And such a skinflint a penny would freeze to your fist before you'd spend it," the phrenologist snapped. "I give you that reading for free. Not that there's hope you'd pay."

The other girls in the parlor tittered. Even Lyddie tried to smile, but Rachel was indignant. "She's not mean. She's going to buy me ribbons," she declared. "Come on, Lyddie," she added, taking her hand. "Let's go read the book you bought me."

The girls laughed again, but more gently. They had never cared much for Lyddie, whom they knew to be close with her money and her friendships, but Rachel was rapidly becoming their pet.

How dry her life had been before Rachel came. It was like springs of water in the desert to have her here. She kissed her head that night before she tucked her in. "You don't think your Lyddie is a cheap old spinster, ey?"

Rachel was furious all over again. "You're the best sister in the world!"

Lyddie blew out the candle. She lay listening to Rachel's even breathing and heard in her memory the sounds of birds in the spring woods. If only she could hear from Charlie, Lyddie's happiness would be complete. The money was growing again. She had nearly caught up with the wages lost by her illness, and even though Rachel made only a pittance, it paid her room and board. She had seldom been happier.

She woke in the night, puzzled. She thought she had heard Betsy again—that wretched hacking sound that sawed through her rib cage straight into her heart. And then she was wide awake and knew it to be Rachel.

It was only a cold. Surely it was nothing. She would be over it in a week. See, the child seemed bright-eyed and lively as ever. If she were sick, really sick . . . Lyddie kept the knowledge of the night cough tight inside herself, but the fear grew like a tumor. She began to lie awake listening for the awful sound, until finally, she knew she must send the child away—anywhere, just so she was not breathing this poison air.

It will break my heart to send the child away. Lyddie could not bear the thought. It might break Rachel's heart as well. She has been sent away too often in her short life. Look, she dotes on me. Me, tough and mean as I be. She clings to me more than she ever did our mother. She needs me.

Lyddie did not know what to do, and she was too terrified to ask. No one must know. She fed Rachel the pills Brigid had brought her. She had no faith in them, but she must try. She fixed plasters for the child's chest, trying to turn it into a game, desperate to hide her own terror. And she was succeeding, wasn't she? Rachel seemed happy as ever and carefree as a kitten. Caught in a spasm of coughing, she made light of it. "Silly cough," she said. "All the girls have them."

Lyddie mustn't worry. Summer was here. The weather was warm. Rachel would be over it soon. They'd take July off. Go back to the farm, the two of them. But it was a vain dream, Lyddie knew. There would be nothing to eat there. The cow was gone and no crops planted.

Triphena. She would send Rachel to Triphena. But Triphena meant Mistress Cutler as well as that lonely, airless attic. How could she do to Rachel at eight what her mother had done to her at thirteen? It had been hard even then. And so very lonely. She hadn't realized how lonely until now—now that she was no longer alone.

Then one evening in late June—she had just read Rachel to sleep—Tim knocked on the door. "A visitor for you, Lyddie," he said. "In the parlor."

18

Charlie at Last

She hardly knew him. He was not so much taller, but bigger somehow, foreign. He wore homespun, but it was well tailored to his body. His brown hair was combed neatly against his head, and a carpetbag hung from his right hand.

"Sister," he said quietly, and the voice was one she had never heard before and would not have known for his.

"Sister," he repeated, his voice cracking on the words, "it's me, Charles."

"Yes," she said. "Charles. So—you come."

He smiled then. She looked in vain for the funny, serious little boy she knew. He wasn't thirteen yet. How could he have discarded that little child so quickly?

He glanced around the crowded room. All the staring faces quickly dived back into their sewing or knitting or conversation. "I took the railroad car," he said in quiet pride. "The stage into New Hampshire, to Concord, and then all the rest of the way by train." Then he grinned like a child, but not the child she remembered. Not quite.

She didn't know what to say. She cared nothing for railroads, those dangerous, dirty things. It was the farm she ached to know about. "Well," she said at last, "you must be tired, ey?"

She cast about the parlor for two free chairs. At her glance, three girls rose and abandoned theirs in the far corner of the room beyond the dining tables. She thanked them and led him over. It was she who felt the need to sit.

"Well," she said, arranging her apron on her lap. "Well, then?" It was as much of a question as she could manage.

"I got good news, Lyddie," he said, a little of the boy she knew creeping into his voice. Her heart rose.

"The Phinneys have taken me on as full apprentice."

"Ey?"

"More than that, truly. They treat me like their own. They don't have no child but me."

"You got a family," she said faintly.

"You'll always be my sister, Lyddie. I don't forget that. It's just . . ." He put the carpetbag on the floor and laid his cap carefully on top. His hands were big now, too large for his body. Finally he looked up at her. "It's just—I don't have to worry every morning when I get up and every night when I lie abed. I just do my work, and every day, three times, the food is there. When the work is slack, I go to school. It's a good life they give me, Lyddie—"

She wanted to scream out at him, remind him how hard she had worked for him, how hard she had tried, but she only said softly, "I wanted to do for you, Charlie. I tried—"

"Oh Lyddie, I know," he said, leaning toward her. "I know. But it weren't fair to you. You only a girl, trying to be father and mother and sister to us all. It were too much. This'll be best for you, too, ey. Don't you see?"

No! she wanted to howl. No! What will be the use of me, then? But she kept her lips pressed together against such a cry. At last she said, "There's Rachel . . ."

He smiled again, his grown-up smile that turned him into a stranger. "I have good news there, too. Mrs. Phinney asked me to bring Rachel back. She craves a daughter as well. And

142

she'll be so good to her, you'll see. She even sent a dress. She made it herself for Rachel to wear on the train. With a bonnet even." His eyes went to the carpetbag beside the chair. "She's never had a proper Ma, Rachel."

She has me. Oh Charlie, I ain't perfect, but I do my best. Can't you see? I done my best for you. She's all I got left now. How can I let her go? But even as she stormed within herself, she knew she had no choice. Like the rusty blade through her heart she felt it. *If she stays here with me, she will die. If I cling to her, I will be her death.*

She heard her own voice, calm as morning after a storm, no, quiet as death, say, "When will you be leaving?"

"The train leaves Lowell at five minutes after seven of the morning. I'll come to fetch her at half past six."

"I'll have her ready before I go to work." She stood. There was nothing more to be said.

He stood, too, cap in hand, wanting, she knew, to say more, but not knowing quite how. She waited.

"About the farm . . ." he began.

The farm. A few minutes before she had thought it was all she cared about. Now it had ceased to matter.

"Uncle Judah's bound and determined to sell."

Lyddie nodded. "Well," she said, "so be it."

He grinned wryly. "For a man who says the Lord is set to end the whole Creation at any minute, he's got a powerful concern for the vain things of this world." She realized he was trying to be funny, so she attempted a smile.

"But I near forgot . . ." He reached into an inside pocket and took out a sealed letter.

Lyddie stared at it. "He ain't sending me money?"

"Who?"

"Uncle."

"Oh, no, not him. He says anything from the sale is rightly

143

his for taking care of Ma and the babies all this time. No. This here is a letter." He handed it to her, studying her face the while. "From Luke."

"Luke who?"

"Lyddie! Our friend, Luke. Our neighbor Luke Stevens." He seemed shocked. He couldn't know she was two lifetimes away from the day Luke had driven them to the village and at least one lifetime from the day the Quaker boy had stood on the doorstep of Number Five in his peculiar disguise.

She tucked the letter in her apron pocket. "Thank you," she said, "and good-bye, I reckon. I'll not be here in the morning when you come."

"It'll be all right, Lyddie. It'll be best for us all, ey?" His voice was anxious. "It'll work out best for you, as well."

"You forgot your bag," she said.

"No, that's for Rachel." He picked it up and handed it to her. He put out his hand as if to shake hers, but hers were tightly wrapped around the handle of the bag. She nodded instead. The next she saw him he would be taller than she, Lyddie thought. If there was a next time. She led him to the door. "Good-bye," she mouthed the words. She couldn't have spoken them aloud if she'd dared.

She climbed the stairs like an old, decrepit woman, clinging to the banister and pulling herself up step by step. Rachel was fast asleep. She would not wake her. In the candlelight she studied the lovely little face. Too thin, too pale, the skin nearly transparent. Lyddie brushed back a curl that had escaped its plait and smoothed it against Rachel's cheek. Any minute she would start to cough, her little body wracked, the bed shaking. Mrs. Phinney would keep her safe. She could go to school. She would have a good life, a real mother. And she will forget me, plain, rough, miserly Lyddie who only bought her ribbons because she was shamed to it. Will she ever know how much

I loved her? How I would have gladly laid down my life and died for her? How, O Lord, I am dying this very minute for her?

She took out the dress. It was a lovely sprigged muslin. It looked too big for Rachel's tiny frame, but the child would grow into it. She would lengthen and fatten and turn once again into a stranger. Lyddie's tears were soaking the dress. She wiped her face on her own apron skirt, then laid out the new garments—the frilly little bonnet with ribbons and lace, a petticoat fit for a wedding. A length of pink ribbon was woven in and out all around the top of the hem, wasted, pure waste where no one would ever see it. Except Rachie.

She packed the bag. It took less than a minute. Rachel had so little. She remembered the primer, and then decided to keep it. Rachel would have a new one, a better one now. She took the book of verses off the nightstand and shut it in the bag, then took it out again. She got her box of writing materials, dipped her pen in the ink, and wrote in painful, careful script on the fly leaf: "For Rachel Worthen from her sister Lydia Worthen, June 24, 1846," wiping her face carefully on her apron as she wrote so as not to blot the page.

She lay awake most of the night listening to Rachel cough, the sound rasping and sawing through her own body. But the pain of it was her salvation. She knew, if she had ever doubted before, she was absolutely certain, that Rachel must leave Lowell.

When the first bell rang, instead of waking Rachel as usual, she waited until she herself was dressed and ready to go. Then she shook her gently.

Rachel awoke at once, alarmed. "I'm late! Why did you let me sleep?"

"You got a treat today, Rachie. Charlie's come to fetch you."

"Charlie? My brother Charlie?" She was as excited as if she could really remember him. Lyddie brushed away a cobweb of envy. "He's come to take you for a visit."

"He wants me to visit him?" She was plainly thrilled, but then she caught something in Lyddie's face. "You coming too, ain't you Lyddie?"

"No, not me. I got to work, ey?" The child's face darkened. "I'll come later." She stretched out her hand. "Here, up you go, you got to get ready."

Rachel took Lyddie's hand and pulled herself upright, then threw back the covers. The child always slept under a quilt, even in the terrible summer heat. "How long will I be gone, Lyddie?"

"I don't rightly know. We both, me and Charlie, we both think you should stay awhile. Make sure you get rid of that silly cough, ey? The factory is too hot in summer, anyways. Lots of the girls take off, come July."

"Will you take off, Lyddie?" She was standing in her little night shift, scratching one leg with the bare toes of the other.

"I just might. Who knows, ey?" Lyddie wrung out the cloth over the basin and handed it to Rachel to wash.

"Come with me now, Lyddie."

"Over on the other bed is a new dress for you to put on. You got to dress fancy for riding on a train."

"A railroad train?"

"Luckiest girl I know. New dress and bonnet, train ride, holiday with a handsome man . . ." She took the cloth from Rachel's hand, tipped up the child's chin, and began to wash her upturned face. "Now you learn your letters better so you can write me all about that train ride." The bell began to ring. She turned swiftly, wringing the cloth out over the basin, her face to the wall, lest she betray herself. "He'll be here to fetch you in a hour or so," she said brightly. "So get yourself dressed and go down and ask Mrs. Bedlow to give you a extra big breakfast." She turned only long enough to give Rachel a light kiss on the cheek and then hurried out the door.

"Come soon, Lyddie." Rachel's voice followed her down the stairs. "I'll miss you."

"Be a good girl for Charlie," she called back, and rushed on down the stairs with a great clatter to erase any more sounds, any more doubts.

Rachel had been gone nearly a week when she found the letter with her name written on it in small, neat handwriting. She had stuffed it into her trunk some days before and couldn't remember at first where it had come from. She unsealed it curiously.

Dear Lyddie Worthen,
  Doubtless thy Charlie has told thee about thy farm. Although our father pled on thy behalf, thy uncle could not be moved. Thus our father put down the purchase price himself, as he has four sons and not enough land for us all.
  I have spoken with thy Charlie. He has urged me to put aside my fears and speak my heart plain. Which is that I long to earn from our father the deed to thy farm. Yet thy land would be barren without thee.
  May I dare ask thee to return? Not as sister, but as wife?
  Forgive these bold words, but I know not how to fashion pretty phrases fit for such as thee.
                    In all respect, thy friend,
                    Luke Stevens

What had Charlie said to the man to make him dare write such a letter? Do they think they can buy me? Do they think I will sell myself for that land? That land I have no one to take to anymore? I have nothing left but me, Lyddie Worthen—do they think I will sell her? I will not be a slave. Nor will I be his freight—some homeless fugitive that Luke Stevens must bend down his lofty Quaker soul to rescue.

She tore the letter into tiny bits and stuffed every shred of it into Mrs. Bedlow's iron cook stove, and then, to her own amazement, burst into tears.

147

19

Diana

She had been alone before Rachel came, but she had not known what loneliness was—this sharp pain in her breastbone dragging down into a dull, persistent heaviness. My heart is heavy, she thought. It's not just a saying. It is what is—heavy, a great stone lodged in my breast, pressing down my whole being. How can I even stand straight and look out upon the world? I am doubled over into myself and, for all the weight, find only emptiness.

Workdays dragged by with nothing to look forward to at the evening bell. Rumor had it that the corporation had slowed the clocks to squeeze even more minutes out of the long summer shift. From time to time, she wondered why she was working so hard, now that the farm was sold and Rachel and Charlie lost to her. She brushed the question aside. She worked hard because work was all she knew, all she had. Everything else that had made her know herself as Lyddie Worthen was gone. Nothing but hard work—so hard that her mind became as calloused as her hands—work alone remained. She fell into bed exhausted and only felt the full burden of her grief in dreams, which, determined as she was, she could not control.

The weavers at the Massachusetts Corporation had all refused the agent's demand that they each tend four looms and take a piece rate reduction as well. They signed a pledge in defiance and none of them backed down. The word went like a whispered wave through the Concord weaving room: "Not a girl has backed down. Not a one."

Diana should have been elated. Wasn't it a victory for the Association? But when Lyddie was finally able to rouse herself from her own pain, she saw that Diana's face was drawn, the expression grim and set. Since Rachel had gone, whenever Brigid or Diana had tried to reach out to her, she had shaken them off. No one could understand her loss, she was sure. She did not have the strength to bear their vain attempts to comfort.

Then, suddenly, it was mid-July, and Lyddie realized that Diana was still at work, looking more sickly by the day. It was more than the heat of the weaving room. She's worried, Lyddie thought, she's sore troubled, and I, so bent on my own trial, never took it to mind.

Lyddie tried to speak to Diana on the stairs, but she seemed hardly to hear the greeting. Are they threatening her with dismissal? With blacklisting? A chill went through Lyddie. She thought she had nothing else to lose, but suppose Diana was to go? Diana—the one person who, from her first day on, had treated her like a proper person—the only one who had never laughed at Lyddie's queer mountain speech or demanded that she change her manners or her mind. All the girls took their burdens to Diana. She was always the one who came to help *you*. Nobody ever thought of Diana needing help.

She's ill—like Betsy and Rachel and Prudence and a host of others, Lyddie thought. She's worked here too long and too hard. How much longer could Diana last? How much longer could any of them last?

I must do something for her, Lyddie decided, give her a present. There was only one present good enough.

"Diana?" Lyddie worked her way through the jostling crowd of operatives crossing the yard. "I been thinking." She glanced around to see if anyone was listening, but all the girls were too intent on rushing home for their suppers. "About the— the—" Even now that she had made up her mind, she couldn't quite bring herself to speak the forbidden word in the very courtyard of the corporation. She took a deep breath. "I been thinking on signing."

The older girl turned to her and put her hand on Lyddie's sleeve. "Well," she said, and Lyddie couldn't quite make out the rest in the clamor of the yard, but it sounded something like: "Well, we'll see," as Diana let herself be carried away in the rushing stream of operatives.

But I mean it, thought Lyddie. I mean it.

Earlier in the spring she had known that there were girls in her own house secretly circulating the petition, but now that she had made up her mind to it, she wanted to do it for Diana. How could it be a true present otherwise? After supper she put on her bonnet and went to Diana's boardinghouse. She asked one of the girls in the front room of Number Three for Diana. "Diana Goss?" the girl asked with a sneer. "It's Tuesday. She'll be at her meeting."

"Oh."

The girl looked her up and down as though memorizing her features. Maybe the girl was a corporation spy. Stare her down, Lyddie told herself. The other was shorter than she, so when Lyddie stood tall and looked down into her eyes, the girl shifted her gaze. "It's at their reading room on Central Street." She glanced back at Lyddie. The sneer had returned. "Number Seventy-six. All are welcome. So I'm told."

In for a penny, in for a pound, thought Lyddie, and made her way into town.

The meeting had already begun. Someone was reading minutes. The forty or so girls crowded into the small room looked almost like a sewing circle, so many of the girls were doing mending or needlework.

"Hello." The young woman who seemed to be in charge interrupted the secretary's droning. "Come on in."

Lyddie stepped into the room, looking about uncertainly for a chair. To her relief she saw Diana, getting up and coming toward her. "You came," she said, her tired features relaxing into a smile. It reminded her of that first night when she had gone to see Diana, except then Diana had looked lovely and full of life. She took Lyddie to a place where there were two vacant chairs and sat beside her while the meeting carried on.

It was hard for Lyddie to follow the discussion. They were planning something for some sort of rally at the end of the month. She kept waiting for someone to mention the petition, so she could declare herself ready to sign, but no one did. At the first curfew bell, the woman in charge pronounced the meeting adjourned until the following Tuesday, and the girls broke into a buzz, gathering their sewing things together and putting on bonnets to leave.

The woman who had been in charge came over to where Lyddie was standing with Diana. She stretched out her hand. "I'm Mary Emerson," she said. "Welcome. I think this is your first time with us."

Lyddie shook the woman's hand and nodded.

"This is my friend, Lydia Worthen," Diana said. "She's thinking about joining us."

Miss Emerson turned expectantly to Lyddie. "I come to sign the—the petition," Lyddie said.

The woman cocked her head, seemingly puzzled. What was the matter with her? "The one to ask for ten-hour workdays." Why was she explaining the petition to a leader of the movement? It was crazy.

"Maybe next year," Diana was saying quietly.

"No. I made up my mind to it. I want to do it now. Tonight."

"But we've already submitted it," Miss Emerson said. "We had to. Before the legislature recessed for the year."

She had at long last made up her mind to do it, and now it was too late? "But—"

"Next year," Diana repeated, "you can put your name in the very first column, if you like."

"Yes," said Miss Emerson brightly. "That's our motto— 'We'll try again.' Since four thousand names didn't convince them, next year we'll have to get eight." She gave Lyddie the kind of encouraging smile a teacher gives to a slow pupil. "We'll need all the help we can get."

Lyddie stood there, openmouthed, looking from Diana's thin face to the other woman's robust one. Too late. She'd come too late. She was always too late. Too late to save the farm. Too late to keep her family together. Too late to do for Diana the only thing she knew to do.

"We'd better get you back to Number Five," Diana was saying. Like she was some helpless child who needed tending. "You wouldn't want to be late."

They hurried down the dimly lit streets toward the Concord boardinghouses without speaking. Lyddie wanted to explain— to say she was sorry, to somehow make it up to Diana—but she didn't know how to do it.

As they neared Number Five, Diana broke the silence. "Thank you for coming tonight."

"Oh Diana, I come too late."

"You came as soon as you could."

"I'm always too late to do any good."

"Lyddie . . ." Diana was hesitating. "I'll miss you."

What was she saying? "I ain't going nowhere. I'll be right here. Next year and the next."

"No. *I'm* the one who'll be leaving."

"But where would you be going?" Diana had always said that the mill was her family.

"Boston, I think."

"I don't understand. Are you ailing?"

"Lyddie, if I don't leave soon—right away, in fact—I'll be dismissed."

"It's because of the cussed petition. They're trying to get you—"

"No. Not that. I wish it were." They had stopped walking and stood several yards away from the steps of Number Five. They both watched the heavy door swing open and glimpsed the light inside as two girls hurried in to beat the final bell. "It's because . . . Oh Lyddie, don't despise me . . ."

"I could never do that!" How could Diana say such a thing?

"Lyddie, I've been, oh, I don't know—foolish? wicked?"

"What are you talking about? You could never be—"

"Oh, yes." She was silent for a moment as though sifting the words she needed from the chaff of her thoughts. "I'm going to have a child, Lyddie."

"A what?" Her voice had dropped to a stunned whisper. She tried to search Diana's features, but it was too dark to read her expression. "Who done this to you?" she asked finally.

"Oh Lyddie, no one 'done' it to me."

"Then he'll marry you, ey?"

"He—he's not free to marry. There's a wife . . . in Concord. She wouldn't come to live here in a factory town. Though her father is one of the owners." Diana's laugh was short and harsh.

It was that doctor. Lyddie was sure of it. He looked so kind and gentle and all the time . . . "But what will you do?" She could hear now the shrillness in her voice. She tried to tone it down. "Where can you go?"

"I've got some savings, and he's—he's determined to help as he can. I'll find work. I'll—we'll manage—the baby and I."

"It ain't right."

"I'll need to go soon. I can't bring dishonor on the Association. Any whisper of this, and our enemies will dance like dervishes with delight." She could hear the grim amusement in Diana's voice. "I won't hand them a weapon to destroy us. Not if I can possibly help it."

"How can I help you? Oh Diana, I been so blind—"

She touched Lyddie's cheek lightly. "Let's just pray everyone has been as blind. I'll write you, if I may. Tell you how things go—"

"You been so good to me—"

"I'll miss you, little Lyddie." The final bell began to clang. "Quick. Slip in before they lock you out."

"Diana—" But the older girl pushed her toward the door and hurried away down the street toward Number Three.

The word passed around the floor next morning was that Diana Goss had left, snatching an honorable dismissal while she could still get it. Much more of her radical doings and she would have been blacklisted, or so the rumors went.

20

B Is for Brigid

Brigid had two looms now and would soon be ready for a third. She stood between them proudly, the sweat pouring from her forehead in concentration. If she would wear less clothing—but no, the girls from the Acre wore the same layers of dress, summer and winter. Still, despite her craziness, Brigid was turning into a proper operative.

Mr. Marsden hardly came past Lyddie's looms these days. When their eyes met by chance, it was as though they had never been introduced. Earlier, his coldness had worried her. She feared then that he might find some reason to dismiss her, so she had been scrupulous to observe every regulation to the letter. As the days went on, she became less anxious about Mr. Marsden's state of mind, much preferring his coolness to the rosebud smiles and little pats she had endured before her illness.

She treated herself to some more books. In honor of Ezekial Freeman—what a handsome name her friend had chosen for himself—she bought *Narrative of the Life of Frederick Douglass: An American Slave Written by Himself* and a Bible. Both volumes became a quiet comfort to her Sunday loneliness, because as she read them she could hear Ezekial's rich, warm voice filling the darkness of the cabin.

She had liked Mr. Dickens's account of his travels in America—all but the Lowell part. It was, as Diana had warned her, romantical. There was no mention in its rosy descriptions of sick lungs or blacklisting or men with wives at Concord.

July wore on its weary way into August. It seemed a century since the summer just a year ago when she had read and reread *Oliver Twist* and dreamed of home. She had been such a child then—such a foolish, unknowing child. As always, many of the New England operatives had gone home. Brigid took on her third loom. More Irish girls came on as spare hands, some of the machines simply stood idle. The room was quieter. Lyddie took to copying out passages from Mr. Douglass and the Bible to paste on her looms.

She liked the Psalms best. "I will lift up mine eyes unto the hills . . ." and "By the rivers of Babylon there we sat down, yea, we wept, when we remembered Zion . . ." The Psalms were poetry, no, songs that rode the powerful rhythm of the looms.

Sometimes she composed her own. "By the rivers of Merrimack and Concord there we sat down, yea, we wept, when we remembered . . ." I must forget, she thought. I must forget them all. I cannot bear the remembering.

Lyddie was strong again. Her body no longer betrayed her into exhaustion by the end of the day, and she was past shedding tears for what might have been. It was a relief, she told herself, not to carry the burden of debt or, what was worse, the welfare of other persons. A great yoke had been lifted from her shoulders, had it not? And someday the stone would be taken from her breast as well.

Between them, she and Brigid coached several of the new spare hands, all of them wearing far too much clothing in the suffocating heat. "But me mither says me capes will cape me cool," one of the girls insisted. Lyddie let it be. She hadn't managed to persuade Brigid to take off her silly capes, how could she expect to persuade the new girls? Still, she was more patient with them than she had ever been with poor Brigid at the beginning. She had to be. Brigid herself was a paragon of gentleness, teaching the new girls all that Lyddie and Diana had taught her, never raising her voice in irritation or complaint.

Lyddie watched her snip off a length of thread from a bobbin and lead one of the clumsier girls over to the window and show her in the best light how to tie a weaver's knot. It was exactly what Lyddie remembered doing, but she knew, to her shame, that her own face had betrayed exasperation, while Brigid's was as gentle as that of a ewe nuzzling her lamb.

She smiled ruefully at Brigid as the girl returned to her own looms. Brigid smiled back broadly. "She's a bit slow, that one."

"We're all allowed to be fools the first week or two," she said, hearing Diana's voice in her head. There had been a short note from Diana telling her not to worry—that she had found a place in a seamstress's shop. But how could she not be anxious for her?

"Aye," Brigid was continuing sadly, "but I'm a fool yet." She nodded at the Psalm pasted on Lyddie's loom. "And you such a scholar."

Lyddie slid her fingers under the paper to loosen the paste and handed it to Brigid. "Here," she said, "for practice. I'll make another for myself."

Brigid shook her head. "It will do me no good. I might as well be blind, you know."

"But I sent you a note once—"

"I took it straight away to Diana to read to me."

"You've learned your letters at least?"

Shamefaced, the girl shook her head.

Lyddie sighed. She couldn't take Brigid on to teach, but how could she begrudge her a chance to start? She made papers for the girl to post.

"*A* is for agent." Beside it was a crude picture of a man in a beaver hat—the stern high priest of those invisible Boston gods who had created the corporations and to whom all in Lowell daily sacrificed their lives.

"*B* is for bobbin and Brigid, too." *B* was instantly mastered.

"*C* is for carding."

"*D* is for drawing in." She went on, using as far as possible words Brigid knew from factory life. Each day Lyddie gave her three new papers to post and learn, and, at the end of the day, to take home and practice.

So it was that day by day, without intending to be, Lyddie found herself bound letter by letter, word by word, sentence by sentence, page by page, until it was, "Come by when you've had your supper, and we'll work on the reader together." Or on a Sunday afternoon: "Meet me by the river, and I'll bring paper and pens for practice."

She did not go to Brigid's house. She was not afraid to go into the Acre. She was not frightened by rumors of robberies and assaults, but, somehow, she was reluctant to go for Brigid's sake. She did not want Brigid to have to be ashamed of the only home she had.

At last a letter came from Charlie. She had not allowed herself to look for one, but when it came she realized how she had longed to hear—just to be reminded that she had not been altogether forgotten.

Dear Sister Lyddie,

(Charlie did make his letters well!)

We are fine. We hope you are well, too. Rachel began school last month. Her cough is nearly gone, and she is growing quite fat with Mrs. Phinney's cooking.

Luke Stevens says he has had no reply. Do think kindly

on him, Lyddie. You need someone to watch out for you as well.

Your loving brother,
Charles Worthen

She almost tore this letter up, but stopped at the first tear. She had nearly ripped the page across Charlie's name.

September came. Some of the New England girls had returned to the weaving room, though the room now was mostly Irish. No Diana, of course, though there was something in Lyddie that kept waiting for her, that kept expecting to see the tall, quiet form moving toward her through the lint-filled room. She had taken something from the weaving floor with her going. There was no quiet center left in the tumult.

A letter arrived in September, on thick, expensive paper, the address decked out in curlicues. "We regret to inform you of the death of Maggie M. Worthen . . ." They hadn't even got her name right. Poor Mama. Nothing ever right for her in life or death. Lyddie squeezed her eyes closed and tried to picture her mother's face. She could see the thin, restless form rocking back and forth before the fire, the hair already streaked with gray. But the face was blurred. She had been gone so long from them. Gone long before she died.

Fall came. Not the raucous patchwork of the Green Mountains, but the sedate brocade of a Massachusetts city. The days began to shorten. Lyddie went to work in darkness and came back to supper in darkness. The whale oil lamps stayed on nearly the whole day in the factory, so water buckets were kept filled on every floor. Fire was a constant dread while the lamps burned.

As the days grew short, breakfast came before the working day began. There was, as always, barely time to swallow the meals, though the food was not as ample as it had been a year ago. At the end of the day now, she waited for Brigid, and they would go out together. Often all the other girls passed them on the stairs or in the yard, for they would be talking about what Brigid had read since the day before, and Lyddie would solve the mystery of an impossible word or the conundrum of a sentence.

Then one evening, she realized that Brigid was not beside her on the crowded stairs. She tried to wait, but the crowd of chattering operatives pushed her forward. She went down to the bottom of the stairs and stepped out of the stream. A hundred or more girls went past.

She was puzzled. Surely Brigid had been right beside her. They had been talking. Brigid had asked her what "thralldom" was. She was trying laboriously to read Mr. Douglass's book, but was yet to get through the first page of the preface.

At last the stairs were empty of clattering feet and the shrill laughter of young women at the end of a long workday. But still there was no Brigid. Lyddie hesitated. Perhaps the girl had gone ahead? Or perhaps she had forgotten something and gone back. Lyddie started across the nearly deserted yard. Her supper would be waiting and Mrs. Bedlow was insulted by tardiness. She had got nearly to the gate when something made her stop, nose up, like a doe with young in the thicket.

She hurried back and climbed the four flights to the weaving room. The lamps had been extinguished by the operatives as they left their looms, so at first her eyes could make out nothing but the hulking shapes of the machines.

Then she heard a strained, high-pitched voice. "Please, sir, please Mr. Marsden . . ."

Lyddie snatched up the fire bucket. It was full of water, but she didn't notice the weight. "Please—no—" She ran down the aisle between the looms toward the voice and saw in the shadows Brigid, eyes white with fear, and Mr. Marsden's back. His hands were clamped on Brigid's arms.

"Mr. Marsden!"

At the sound of her hoarse cry, the overseer whirled about. She crammed the fire bucket down over his shiny pate, his bulging eyes, his rosebud mouth fixed in a perfect little O. The stagnant water sloshed over his shoulders and ran down his trousers.

She let go of the bucket and grabbed Brigid's hand. They began to run, Lyddie dragging Brigid across the floor. Behind in the darkness, she thought she heard the noise of an angry bear crashing an oatmeal pot against the furniture.

She started to laugh. By the time they were at the bottom of the stairs she was weak with laughter and her side ached, but she kept running, through the empty yard, past the startled gatekeeper, across the bridge, and down the row of wide-eyed boardinghouses, dragging a bewildered Brigid behind her.

21

Turpitude

By morning the laughter was long past. She was awake and dressed, pacing the narrow corridor between the beds, before the four-thirty bell. Her breath caught high in her throat and her blood raced around her body, undecided whether to run fire through her veins, searing her despite the November chill, or freeze to the icy rivulet of a mountain brook.

She could not touch her breakfast. The smell of fried codfish turned her stomach. But she sat there amidst the chatter and clatter of the meal because it was easier to pass the time in the noise of company than in the raging silence of her room.

She was the first at the gate. It wasn't that she was eager for the day to begin, but eager for it to be over, for whatever was to happen—and she did not doubt that something dreadful must happen—for whatever must happen to be in the past.

She tried not to think of Brigid. She could not take on Brigid's fate as well as her own. If only she had not come back up the stairs. Monster! Would I have wished to leave that poor child alone? Better to feed Rachel and Agnes to the bear. And yet, Brigid was not a helpless child. She might have broken loose—stomped his foot or . . . Well, it was too late for that. Lyddie *had* gone back. She had, mercy on her, picked up that pail of filthy water and crammed it down on the overseer's neat little head. And all she had need to do was speak. When she had called his name, he had turned and let Brigid go. But, no, Lyddie could not be satisfied. She had taken that pail and rammed it till the man's shoulders were almost squeezed up under the tin. The skin on her scalp crawled . . .

Why didn't they open the gate? She was as weary of the scene in her head as if she'd actually picked up that heavy bucket and brought it down over and over again and run the length of the yard dragging Brigid behind her a thousand times over. Laughing. Of course he must have heard her. She had howled like a maniac. He must have heard.

The other operatives were crowded about, jostling her as they all waited for the bell. And still, when it rang, she jumped. It was so loud, so like an alarm clanging danger. She tried to turn against the tide, to get away while there was still time, but she was caught in the chattering, laughing trap of factory girls pushing themselves forward into the new day. She gave up and allowed the press of bodies around her to propel her to the enclosed staircase and up the four flights to the weaving room.

Brigid was not at her looms. Mr. Marsden was not on his high stool. Her execution was delayed. She felt relief, which was immediately swallowed up in anxiety. She needed it all to be over.

One of the girls from the Acre approached her. "Brigid says to tell you she's feeling a wee bit poorly this morning. You are not to worry."

The little coward. She's going to let me face it all alone, ey? When I was the one risked all to help her.

The girl glanced back over her shoulder and around the room. She bent her face close to Lyddie's neck and whispered. "The truth be told, she got word not to report this morning. But she had no wish to alarm you."

Now Lyddie was truly alarmed without even the slight armor that resentment might provide. Would they, then, be punishing Brigid instead of her? What sin had Brigid committed? What rule had she ever trespassed? And she with a sickly mother and nearly a dozen brothers and sisters to care for?

Mr. Marsden had come in. Lyddie kept her eyes carefully on her looms. The room shook and shuddered into life. Lyddie and the Irish girl beyond kept Brigid's looms going between them as best they could. She was almost busy enough to suppress her fears. And then a young man, the agent's clerk in his neat suit and cravat, appeared at her side and asked her to come with him to the agent's office. The time had come at last. She shut down her own looms and one of Brigid's, and followed the clerk down the stairs and out across the yard to the low building that housed the counting room and the offices.

The agent Graves was seated at his huge rolltop desk and did not at once turn from his papers and acknowledge her presence. The clerk had only taken her as far as the door, so she stood just inside as he closed it behind her. She tried to breathe.

She waited like that, hardly able to get a breath past her Adam's apple, until she began to feel quite faint. Would she collapse then in a heap on the rug? She studied the pattern, shades of dull browns, starting nearly black in the center and spinning out lighter and lighter to a dirty yellow at the outer edge. Dizzy, she stumbled a step forward to keep from falling. The man turned in his chair, as though annoyed. He was wearing half spectacles and he lowered his massive head and stared over them at her.

"You—you sent for me, sir?" It came out like a hen cackle. "Yes?"

"You sent for me, sir." She was glad to hear her voice grow stronger. The man kept staring as though she were a maggot on his dish. "Lydia Worthen, sir. You sent for me."

"Ah, yes, Miss Worthen." He neither stood nor asked her

to sit down. "Miss Worthen." He gathered the papers he had been working on and tamped the bottom of the pile on his desk to neaten it, and then laid the stack down on the right side of the desk. Then he scraped his chair around to face her more directly. "Miss Worthen. I've had a distressing interview with your overseer this morning."

She couldn't help but wonder how Mr. Marsden had retold last night's encounter.

"It seems," he continued, "it seems you are a troublemaker in the weaving room." He was studying her closely now, as closely as he had studied his papers before. "A troublemaker," he repeated.

"I, sir?"

"Yes. Mr. Marsden fears you are having a bad influence on the other girls there."

So there had been no report of last night. That, at least, seemed clear. "I do my work, sir," Lyddie said, gathering courage. "I have no intention of causing trouble on the floor."

"How long have you been with us, Miss Worthen?"

"A year, sir. Last April, sir."

"And how many looms are you tending at this time?"

"Four, sir."

"I see. And your wages? On the average?"

"I make a good wage, sir. Lately it's been three dollars above my board."

"Are you satisfied with these wages, then?"

"Yes, sir."

"I see. And the hours?"

"I'm used to long hours. I manage."

"I see. And none of this . . ." He waved a massive hand. "None of this ten-hour business, eh?"

"I never signed a petition." I meant to, but no need for you to know it.

There was a long pause during which the agent took off his

165

spectacles as though to see her better. "So," he said finally, "you are not one of these female reform girls?"

"No sir."

"I see," he said, replacing his spectacles and looking quite as though he saw much less than he had a few minutes before. "I see."

She took a tiny step forward. "May I ask, sir, why I'm being called a troublemaker?" She spoke very softly, but the agent heard her.

"Yes, well—"

"Maybe . . ." Her heart thumped in admiration for her own boldness. "Maybe Mr. Marsden could be called, sir? How is it, exactly, that I have displeased him?" Her voice went up to soften the request into a question.

"Yes, well . . ." He hesitated. "Open the door." And when Lyddie obeyed, he called to the clerk to summon Mr. Marsden, then turned again to Lyddie. "You may sit down, Miss Worthen," he said, and went back to the papers on his desk.

Though the chair he indicated was narrow and straight, she was grateful to sit down at last. The spurt of courage had exhausted her as much as her fear had earlier. She was glad, too, to have time to pull her rioting thoughts together. But the longer she waited, the greater the tumult inside her. So that when the clerk opened the door and Mr. Marsden appeared, she could only just keep from jumping up and crying out. She pressed her back into the spindles of the chair until she could almost feel the print of the wood through to her chest. She kept her eyes on the dizzying oval spiral of the rug.

There was a clearing of the throat and then, "You sent for me, sir?" Lyddie nearly laughed aloud. Her exact words, not ten minutes before.

The superintendent turned in his chair, but again he did not stand or offer the visitor a chair. "Miss Worthen here asks to know the charges against her."

Mr. Marsden coughed. Lyddie looked up despite herself. At her glance the overseer blinked quickly, then composed himself, his lids hooding his little dark eyes, his rosebud mouth tightening to a slit. "This one is a troublemaker," he said evenly.

She leapt to her feet. She couldn't seem to stop herself. "A troublemaker? Then what be you, Mr. Marsden? What be you, ey?"

The agent's head went up. His body was spread and his eyes bulged like a great toad, poised to spring. "Sit down, Miss Worthen!"

She sank onto the chair.

Her outburst had given the overseer the time he needed. He smiled slightly as though to say, See? No lady, this one.

Satisfied that he had stilled her, the agent shifted his gaze from Lyddie to her accuser. "A troublemaker, Mr. Marsden?" For a quick moment Lyddie hoped—but the man went on. "In what way a troublemaker? Her work record seems satisfactory."

"It is not"—and now Mr. Marsden turned and glared straight at Lyddie, all trace of nervousness gone—"it is not her work as such. Indeed," and here, he gave a sad little laugh, "I at one time thought of her as one of the best on the floor. But"—he turned back to the agent, his voice solemn and quiet—"I am forced, sir, to ask for her dismissal. It is a matter of moral turpitude."

Moral what? What was he saying? What was he accusing her of?

"I see," said the agent, as though all had been explained when nothing, nothing had.

"I cannot," and now the overseer's voice was fairly dripping with the honey of regret, "for the sake of all the innocent young women in my care, I cannot have among my girls someone who sets an example of moral turpitude."

"Certainly not, Mr. Marsden. The corporation cannot countenance moral turpitude."

She turned unbelieving from one man to the other, but they ignored her. She fought for words to counter the drift the interview had taken, but what could she say? She did not know what turpitude was. How could she deny something she did not even know existed? She knew what moral was. But that didn't help. Moral was Amelia's territory of faithful attendance at Sabbath worship and prayer meeting and Bible study, and she couldn't ask for consideration on those counts. She hardly ever went to worship, and Lord knew when she read, it wasn't just the Bible. Still, she was no worse than many, was she? At least she was not a papist, and no one was condemning them.

She opened her mouth. They were both looking at her sadly, but sternly. In the silence, the battle had been lost.

"You may ask the clerk for whatever wages are due you, Miss Worthen," the agent said, turning to his desk.

Mr. Marsden gave his superior's back a nod and tight rosebud smile. Did he click his heels? At any rate, he left quickly without another glance toward Lyddie.

"You may go now," the agent said without turning.

What could she do? She stumbled to her feet and out the door.

They paid her wages full and just, but there was no certificate of honorable discharge from the Concord Corporation, and with no certificate, she would never be hired by any other corporation in Lowell. She walked out of the tall gate benumbed. She had often dreamed of this last day, but in her dream she would be going home in triumph, and now there was no triumph and no home to go to even in disgrace.

22
Farewell

The bear had won. It had stolen her home, her family, her work, her good name. She had thought she was so strong, so tough, and she had just stood there like a day-old lamb and let it gobble her down. She looked around the crowded room that had been her home—the two double beds squeezed in with less than a foot between them for passage. She thought of Betsy sitting cross-legged on the one, bent slightly toward the candle, reading aloud while she, Lyddie, lay motionless, lost in Oliver's world.

And Amelia. Amelia would know what turp—turpitune, turpentine, whatever the wretched word was—Amelia was sure to know what it meant. She could see the older girl's eyebrows arch and her lips purse—"But *why* are you asking?" Indeed. So I can know what they charged against me—why I've lost my job, why I've been dismissed without a certificate. "You?" Betsy would laugh. "Not our Lyddie—Mr. Marsden's best girl." Meanwhile, Prudence would be busy explaining the meaning of the cussed word.

Thank God Rachel was safe. She had a home and food and school. She had a mother. And Charlie. I will not cry. She began to pack her things, stuffing them unfolded into the tiny gunnysack that had been her only luggage when she came. She almost laughed aloud. The sack wouldn't hold her extra clothes, much less her books. Well, she was a rich woman now. She could afford a proper trunk for her belongings even if she had no place to take them.

"They let me go," she explained to Mrs. Bedlow.

The landlady was incredulous. "But why?" she asked. "You were Mr. Marsden's best girl. Everyone said so."

Lyddie gave a laugh more like a horse whinny than any human sound. "Then everyone is wrong."

She could not bring herself to describe to Mrs. Bedlow the two encounters in the weaving room. She must, somehow, have caused the first. She knew so little of the ways of men and women that she must have, without realizing, given him some sign. Mr. Marsden was a deacon in his church. He was not a likable man, but surely . . . And last night. Mercy on her—she'd acted like a crazed beast. Why, even her own mother who died in an asylum had never gone wild like that.

She did not like Mr. Marsden. She had never liked him, but she had tried to please him—tried to win his approval by being the best. And though she needed to know what it was exactly that he was accusing her of, she knew he had not told the agent of those encounters. So, it was something else she had done wrong. She would have asked Mrs. Bedlow, but she was afraid the word would come out "turpentine" and Mrs. Bedlow would laugh. She couldn't bear to be laughed at, not just now.

"I'll be out of my room by tomorrow—the next day at the latest."

"But where will you go?" Don't worry for me. I can't stand it if you are kind, I might break down.

"Back to housekeeping, I reckon." That was it. Triphena would be sure to take her in.

She went to the bank and withdrew all her money—243 dollars and 87 pence. Then she went to the bookstore. She wanted to give Brigid a copy of *Oliver Twist* even if the girl couldn't really read it yet. She'd be able to in time.

"Will there be anything else for you today, Miss Worthen?" They were friends now, the bookseller and she. She hesitated, but what did it matter? She would never be in again. "Do you have a book that—that tells the meanings of words?"

"Ah," he said, "We have an old Alexander dictionary, of course, and then there's Webster's and Worcester's, which are more up-to-date."

"I think I need a up-to-date one," she said. She didn't want to risk buying one that didn't have the one word she needed.

The bookseller got down two fat books, Parts I and II of *An American Dictionary of the English Language* and then a third. "Many people prefer the Worcester," he said, indicating the third book. "It's a bit newer. And all in the one volume." Lyddie paid for the Worcester and forced herself to take it out of the shop before opening it.

As soon as she was out of sight of the bookshop window, she rested her parcels on the sidewalk and opened the dictionary. It took her some time to find the word. The pages were thin and her fingers calloused and clumsy, and she did not know the spelling. But she found it at last.

What? She would have howled in the street had it not been so crowded with passersby. She was not a vile or shameful character! She was not base or depraved. She was only ignorant, and what was the sin in that? He was the evil one to accuse her of such. She had done nothing evil, only foolish.

She rushed back to her room. What could she do? The damage was done. If only she had known what was going on when she was in the agent's office, how that vile man was lying. Oh, the agent was quick to believe him. When I cried out, it was I who was made to seem in the wrong! I was unladylike. That was my crime.

She wrote the letters in a fury, burning herself with sealing wax, her hand was shaking so. She rushed out of the house, her bonnet ribbons loose, her shawl flying. By the time she got to the Acre she was out of breath and could hardly ask the children playing in the streets where Brigid's house might be.

The first child she asked looked up with wide, frightened eyes and ran away without speaking. She stood long enough to tie her bonnet properly and catch her breath before asking another. He pointed dumbly to a shack that turned out not to be Brigid's house at all, but the housewife inside knew Brigid and gave Lyddie proper directions.

Brigid herself answered the door. "Oh Lyddie, what have they done?"

"I'm dismissed," Lyddie said.

"No, it cannot be."

"It can't be helped. It's done. But they must not dismiss you. I've already written a letter to Mr. Marsden. I told him if he dismissed you or bothered you in any way I would tell his wife exactly what happened in the weaving room. Now here is the letter addressed to her. If there is any problem you must mail it at once." Brigid stared at her, mouth open. "At once. You must swear to me you will." The girl nodded. "And now, I'd like to sit down if I could."

"Oh, I'm terrible rude." Brigid stepped aside and let her into the tiny shack. The smell was strong of food and body sweat. It was dark, but Lyddie could see children's eyes large and staring. "Me mother's housecleaning today." Brigid picked up a pile of what looked like rags, but might have been clothing, off a rough stool, and Lyddie sat down gratefully. She was still tired from last night. Tired as she had been after her sickness, her bones aching with it.

"Thank you," she said.

"Where will you be going? Not far from here, I hope."

"They didn't give me a certificate, so I have to go."

"And it's all me fault."

"No, you musn't blame yourself."

There was no place else to sit except the beds, so Brigid stood, watching her. In the darkness of the room, the only noise was the rustle of the children shifting, staring.

She had stopped gasping for breath. It was time to leave. "I'll be going, Brigid. Oh, yes. I nearly forgot." She handed the girl the parcel containing Brigid's old primer and *Oliver Twist*. "So you won't forget me altogether, ey?" she said, and fled so she wouldn't have to listen to Brigid's sobs.

That evening, just at the closing bell, she made her way down the street beyond the boardinghouse row to the trim, frame houses of the overseers of the Concord Corporation. She didn't know which house was his, but it didn't matter. He would have to come this way. She stood in the shadow of the first house and waited.

There was no mistaking his walk. Like a little bantam rooster, he came, all alone. Does he have any friends at all? She shoved the thought aside. She mustn't let anything dilute her anger. "Mr. Marsden?" She stepped out of the shadow and stood in his path.

He stopped, alarmed. They were nearly the same height and she stood close to his face and spoke with deadly quiet, the long brim of her bonnet nearly brushing his cheeks. "Yes, it's me, Lydia Worthen."

"Miss Worthen." He breathed out her name.

"I am mean and I am cheap. Sometimes I am a coward and often times I'm selfish. I ain't a beauty to look at. But I am not vile, shameful, base, or depraved!"

"Wha-at?"

"You accused me of moral turpitude, Mr. Marsden. I am here to say I am not guilty."

He stepped backward with a little puff of a gasp.

"I have here a letter I wrote. I will tell you what it says. It says if you cause Brigid MacBride to lose her position I will see that your wife is informed about what really happens in the weaving room after hours."

"My wife?" he whispered.

"Mrs. Overseer Marsden. I figure she ought to know if there is moral turpitude occurring in her husband's weaving room." She jammed the letter in the overseer's hand and closed his reluctant fist around it. "Good night, Mr. Marsden. I hope you sleep easy—before you die."

She took a stage to Boston. Hardly anyone did these days. The train was so much faster. But she had nowhere to go in such a hurry, and the ride gave her time to compose herself. Boston was a terrible place, older and even dirtier and more crowded than Lowell. The streets were narrow and Lyddie stepped gingerly around the refuse and animal droppings, lifting her skirt with one hand and trying to balance her new trunk under the other arm. She should have found a safe place to leave it, but how did one do that in an unknown city?

At last she found the address. She looked through a glass-windowed door and saw Diana herself, tall and pale, but no longer thin. She was speaking to a customer, her head slightly bent toward the short woman, a polite smile on her face.

Lyddie shifted the heavy trunk under her left arm and pushed open the door. A bell rang and Diana looked up at the sound. At first she nodded politely, her attention still with the chattering customer. Then she recognized Lyddie and her face was transformed.

"Excuse me a moment," she said to the woman, and came over and took the trunk. "Lyddie." Her voice was still quiet and beautifully low-pitched. "How wonderful to see you."

There was no time to talk until the customer's order was complete and the bell rang, signaling her departure. "How are you, Lyddie?" Diana asked.

"They dismissed me," she said. "For 'moral turpitude.' "

"For what?" Diana was almost laughing.

"It means—"

"I know what it means," Diana said gently. "I'm intimately acquainted with the term myself, but you . . . surely—"

"You are not vile, base, or depraved," Lyddie said.

"Thank you." Diana tried not to smile, but the corners of her mouth betrayed her. "And neither are you. What I can't imagine is how—"

"It was Mr. Marsden."

"Ah, yes, dear Mr. Marsden."

When Lyddie told the whole story, nearly crying again in her rage, she realized suddenly that Diana was shaking with laughter.

"It weren't funny, ey!" she protested.

"No, no, of course not. I'm sorry. But I'm imagining his face when you pounced out at him last night. Just when he thought he'd won—when he'd rid himself so neatly of the evidence."

Lyddie saw the rosebud mouth shaped into an O of fright. It *was* satisfying, wasn't it?

"And his wife is a perfect terror, but you know that—"

"I didn't think anyone else would believe me against him."

"Oh, she's a terror, all right. Everyone says so. She's a fright, I promise you." She got up and poured them each a cup of tea. "Let's celebrate, shall we? Oh Lyddie, it's so good of you to come. How can I help you?"

But she had come to help Diana. "I thought—I thought to help you if I could."

"Thank you, but I'm doing all right, as you can see. It was hard at first. No one seemed to want a husbandless woman expecting a child. But the proprietress here was ill and desperate for help. So we needed one another. It's worked out well. She's been so kind. And her daughter will look out for the baby when it comes." She smiled happily. "Like family to me." She reached over and patted Lyddie's knee. "But you understand."

Lyddie spent the night with Diana. Everyone was kind. Diana had her family at last. Then why had something snapped like a broken warp thread inside Lyddie's soul? Wasn't she happy for Diana? Surely, surely she was—happy and greatly relieved. "You must write to Brigid and tell her you are fine, ey?" Lyddie said as they parted the next morning. "She can read now, and she worries."

It rained all the way through New Hampshire, a steady, wearying drizzle. Lyddie rode inside the coach. There was only one other passenger, an old man who took no notice of her. She was grateful because she cried most of the way. She, tough-as-gristle Lyddie, her face in her handkerchief, her head turned toward the shaded window. But the tumult that had raged inside her damped down more and more as though beat into the muddy earth under the horses' hooves. When they finally crossed the bridge into Vermont, the sun came out and turned the leafless trees into silver against the deep green of the evergreen on the mountain slopes. The air was clean and cold, the sky blue, more like a bright day at winter's end than November.

23

Vermont, November 1846

One more night along the way and the sky had turned into the underside of a thick quilt. The coachman pressed the team, eager to get to the next stop before the snow began to fall. It was nearly dusk when the coach took the final dash around the curve in the road that brought it to the door of Cutler's Tavern.

Nothing had changed except herself. At first Triphena pretended not to recognize her at all—"this grand lady come from the city of looms and spindles." But soon the game was over, and the old cook gave her a warm embrace and drew her to a seat by the giant fireplace.

"I would've thought you'd have a cook stove by now," Lyddie said half teasing, as she looked around the familiar kitchen.

"Not while I'm cook here," Triphena said fiercely. "I reckon everyone has those monstrosities in the city, ey?"

"They work fine. We had one at the boardinghouse."

Triphena sniffed. "They'll do, maybe, for those who ain't real cooks." She handed Lyddie a cup of her boiled coffee, thick with cream and maple sugar. "So you're for a visit home, ey?"

Lyddie was brought back with a pang to her present state. "I've left the factory," she said, "for good."

"So it's back to the farm, is it?"

"My uncle sold it."

"But what of your poor mother and the little ones?"

"Mama died," Lyddie said. There was no need to tell Triphena where. "And baby Agnes as well."

"Oh, dear," said Triphena softly.

"So Charlie took Rachel to live with him at the mill. The Phinneys have been good to them both. So—" She took a long drink from her coffee. It scalded her throat but she shook off the pain of it. "So—for the first time, I'm a free woman. Not a care—not a care in the world."

She paused, not knowing how to say, then, that she wished therefore to become once more a housemaid in Mistress Cutler's Tavern. "So—I thought to meself—what fun to work with Triphena again."

The cook threw her head back and laughed. She thinks I'm joking. How to explain? How to say I've nowhere else to go?

And then the girl came in. She was no more than twelve or thirteen, dressed in rough calico with ill-fitting boots. Lyddie's heart sank. That was the housemaid. There was no room for her at Cutler's Tavern anymore.

As it was, she spent the night in one of the guest rooms, paying full price, although Mistress Cutler pretended for a moment that she couldn't possibly take payment from an old and valued employee. Lyddie lay awake, wondering at the silence outside the window, the only light, the cloud-veiled moon. How could you sleep in such a quiet place with no rhythm and clatter from the street? Nothing at all to distract your head from wondering what on earth you could do, where you could go in a world that had no place for you, no need for you at all.

"Then you're off to see the children today?" said Triphena as she fed her breakfast at the great kitchen table. Lyddie was grateful to have plans for at least one day. "The snow is no more'n a dusting. I can get Henry to take you in the wagon." Henry was Willie's successor.

Lyddie chose to walk. The day was cold and clear, but her shawl was warm and her boots stout and well broken in.

She was at the mill by mid-morning. Mrs. Phinney greeted her kindly, but Charlie and Rachel were gone to school in the village, so she just kept walking, her feet taking her up the hill road, past the fields and pastures of Quaker Stevens's farm, and on, up and beyond, until she rounded the last curve and saw it sitting there, squat and homely against the green and silver of the November mountain.

A tracery of snow lay on the fields and in the yard, but it was not true winter yet. In a week or so, everything would be sleeping under a thick comforter, but for now, the cabin stood out in all its sturdy homemade ugliness. Just like me, she thought, and blinked back tears. It was good to be home.

There was no wood piled against the door. Someone had stacked it neatly again in the woodshed. The door itself had been repaired and fit snugly now into its frame. She raised her father's wooden latch and pushed it open.

Even at the brightest midday, it was never really light inside the cabin. On a November afternoon it was truly dark. She found the flint box—no sulfur matches here—and lit the neatly laid tinder and logs. It was as though someone had prepared for her coming. She pulled her mother's rocker close and stared into the flames. Nothing smelled so good or danced so well as a birch fire. It was so full of cheer, so welcoming. Lyddie stretched her toes out toward the warmth of it and sighed, nearly content. She could almost forget everything. She was home where she had longed to be. Perhaps she could just stay the night here. No one would care. How could they deny her just one night before she left forever?

"Lyddie?"

She jumped up. There was the shape of a man, bent over low so as to clear the doorway. He stepped into the cabin and straightened tall. "Lyddie?" he said again, and she knew him for Luke Stevens. She was more angry at the interruption than ashamed to be caught.

"Lyddie?" he said a third time, "is it thee?" He took off his broad Quaker hat and held it over his stomach, squinting a little to see her through the darkness.

"I meant no harm," she said. "I just come to say good-bye." It sounded silly as she said it, coming to say good-bye to a cabin.

"Mother thought she saw thee pass. She sent me to fetch thee for supper and to stay the night if thee will."

She wished she could ask him just to let her stay here— for this one night. But there was no food, and she had no right to use up the Stevenses' kindling. She would not be beholden to them more than she could help. "I'll just be going back—"

"Please," he said, "stay with us. The dark comes so quick this time of year."

Her pride fought with her empty belly. But the truth was it had been hours since Triphena's breakfast, and the walk back would be long and dark and cold. "I've no wish to impose—"

"Thee must not think so," he said quickly. "It would pleasure our mother to have another woman in the house." He smiled shyly. "She often complains that none of us boys can seem to find a woman who will have us." He came to the fireplace and knelt to separate the logs and put out her small fire.

She was glad his back was to her and there was no chance that he could see her face flush red in the shadowy light of the cabin. "About your letter . . ." she began.

He shook his head without turning to her. "It was a foolish hope," he said quietly. "I pray thee forgive me."

They walked side by side down the road, the sun a blazing pumpkin as it fell rapidly behind the western mountains. Luke's long legs purposefully shortened their stride so that she would not have to skip to keep up. For a long time, neither spoke, but as the sun disappeared, and the dusk began to gather about them, he set his gaze far down the road ahead and asked softly, "Then if thee will not stay, where will thee go?"

"I'm off . . ." she said, and knew as she spoke what it was she was off to. To stare down the bear! The bear that she had thought all these years was outside herself, but now, truly, knew was in her own narrow spirit. She would stare down all the bears!

She stopped in the middle of the road, her whole body alight with the thrill of it. "I'm off," she said, "to Ohio. There is a college there that will take a woman just like a man." The plan grew as she spoke. "First I must go tomorrow to say good-bye to Charlie and little Rachel, and then I'll take the coach to Concord, and from there"—she took a deep breath—"the train. I'll go all the rest of the way by train."

He watched her face as though trying to read her thoughts, but gave up the attempt. "Thee is indeed a wonder, Lyddie Worthen," he said.

She looked up into his earnest face as he leaned to speak to her and saw in his bent shoulders the shade of an old man in a funny broad Quaker hat—the gentle old man that he would someday become and that she would love.

Tarnation, Lyddie Worthen! Ain't you learned nothing? Don't you know better than to tie yourself to some other living soul? You'd only be asking for trouble and grief. Might as well just throw open the cabin door full wide and invite that black bear right onto the hearth.

Still—if he was to wait—

He was looking right at her, his head cocked, his brown eyes questioning. His face was so close she could see a trace of soot on it. Like Charlie. The boy could never mess with a fire without getting all dirty. She held her hand tightly to her side to keep from reaching up and wiping his cheek with her fingers.

Will you wait, Luke Stevens? It'll be years before I come back to these mountains again. I won't come back weak and beaten down and because I have nowhere else to go. No, I will not be a slave, even to myself—

"Do I frighten thee?" he asked gently.

"Ey?"

"Thee was staring at me something fierce."

She began to giggle, as she used to when she and Charlie had been young.

His solemn face crinkled into lines of puzzlement and then, still not understanding, he crumpled into laughter, as though glad to be infected by her merriment. He took off his broad hat and ran his big hand through his rusty hair. "I will miss thee," he said.

We can stil hop, Luke Stevens, Lyddie said, but not aloud.

SPECIAL THANKS go to Mary E. Woodruff of the Vermont Women's History Project and Dr. Robert M. Brown of the Museum of American Textile History, who read this book in manuscript and offered suggestions and corrections. Any errors of fact which remain are, of course, my own.

I must also thank the library staff at the museum for their help and patience, Linda Willis at the Mid-State Regional Library of Vermont for locating and ordering materials for me, and Donald George of the Dairy Division of the Vermont State Agriculture Department for answering my questions about cows.

I cannot list all the books and publications to which I am indebted, but I must mention a few without which I could not have written this book:

Thomas Dublin's *Farm to Factory: Women's Letters, 1830–1860* and *Women At Work: The Transformation of Work and Community in Lowell, Massachusetts, 1826–1860*; Hannah Josephson's *The Golden Threads: New England's Mill Girls and Magnates*; David Macaulay's *Mill*; Abby Hemenway's nineteenth century compilation of stories from every section of Vermont, *Vermont Historical Gazetteer*, which includes a story of a hungry black bear that was the seed for the bear story in this book.

And the writings of the Lowell mill girls themselves, including Benita Eisler, editor, *The Lowell Offering: Writings by New England Mill Women (1840–45)*; Factory Tracts published by the Female Labor Reform Association as well as *Voice of Industry* issues from 1845–48; Lucy Larcom's *A New England Girlhood* and *An Idyl of Work*; and Harriet Hanson Robinson's *Loom and Spindle or Life Among the Early Mill Girls*.

What happened to Jip's family?

Why, Jip asked the chickens as he threw them grain, why had no one come back for him? Wouldn't you notice, say, if you began the day with six children and, come night, the count was down to five? Even if you were in a powerful hurry to leave these rocky hills to get West to where the good land lay, wouldn't it cross your mind to wonder what had become of your missing young'un that you once had but suddenly wasn't there any more? Even a goose can count her goslings and know if a fox got one in the night.

Even supposing you were a heartless gypsy who stole other people's children like pies off a cooling sill, wouldn't you care about one of your own?

★"Like Paterson's Newbery-winning *Bridge to Terabithia* and *Jacob Have I Loved*, this historically accurate story is full of revelations and surprise. . . . The taut, extremely readable narrative and its tender depictions of friendship and loyalty provide first-rate entertainment."
—*Publishers Weekly*, starred review

★"Rewards readers with memorable characters and a gripping plot. . . . Resonates with respect for the Vermont landscape and its mid-19th-century residents, with the drama of life during a dark period of our nation's history, and with the human quest for freedom. . . . Readers will be talking and thinking about this book long after they finish the last chapter."
—*School Library Journal*, starred review

PUFFIN NOVELS BY KATHERINE PATERSON

Come Sing, Jimmy Jo
Flip-Flop Girl
Jip: His Story
Lyddie
Park's Quest
Rebels of the Heavenly Kingdom

KATHERINE PATERSON

JIP
His Story

PUFFIN BOOKS

PUFFIN BOOKS
Published by the Penguin Group
Penguin Putnam Inc., 375 Hudson Street, New York, New York 10014, U.S.A.
Penguin Books Ltd, 27 Wrights Lane, London W8 5TZ, England
Penguin Books Australia Ltd, Ringwood, Victoria, Australia
Penguin Books Canada Ltd, 10 Alcorn Avenue, Toronto, Ontario, Canada M4V 3B2
Penguin Books (N.Z.) Ltd, 182-190 Wairau Road, Auckland 10, New Zealand

Penguin Books Ltd, Registered Offices: Harmondsworth, Middlesex, England

First published in the United States of America by Lodestar Books,
an affiliate of Dutton Children's Books, a division of Penguin Books USA Inc., 1996
Published by Puffin Books,
a member of Penguin Putnam Books for Young Readers, 1998

10 9

THE LIBRARY OF CONGRESS HAS CATALOGED THE LODESTAR EDITION AS FOLLOWS:
Paterson, Katherine
Jip: his story / by Katherine Paterson.
    p.   cm.
Summary: While living on a Vermont poor farm during 1855 and 1856,
Jip learns his identity and that of his mother and comes to
understand how he arrived at this place.
ISBN 0-525-67543-4
[1. Identity—Fiction. 2. Fugitive slaves—Fiction.
3. Slavery—Fiction. 4. Afro-Americans—Fiction.] I. Title.
PZ7.P273Ji 1996 [Fic]—dc20 96-2680 CIP AC

Puffin Books ISBN 0-14-038674-2

Printed in the United States of America

for those who
have made this gypsy
feel at home
in Vermont,
especially
Nancy Graff and Grace Greene

Acknowledgments

Particular thanks must go to Nancy Graff for reading this book in manuscript and making several pages' worth of helpful suggestions, though any errors of fact that remain are, of course, my own. Thanks, too, to Larry Gordon, who kindly located the music for the hymn "All Is Well" from his library of early American music, to Lindsay Graff, my moose consultant, and to Alison Hall for sharing her experience with sheep. I am also grateful to the staffs of the Vermont Historical Society and the Vermont State Library, and, especially, to Marjorie Strong of the Aldrich Library in Barre, Vermont.

Although the events of this story are fictional, the character of Put Nelson is based on an actual nineteenth–century Vermonter, Putnam Proctor Wilson, who lived in a cage on the town poor farm in Hartford. According to the town history, when he was rational, Putnam Wilson loved to sing to children and would sing the same song over and over as often as requested. I want to thank Mary Sorum and Dr. Christopher Meyers for their help as I tried to understand in modern medical terms the condition Putnam Wilson's contemporaries regarded as lunacy.

As my pile of books grows ever higher, so does my debt of gratitude to John Paterson and Virginia Buckley. Once again, thank you both.

Contents

My life began the afternoon of June 7, 1847, when I tumbled off the back of a wagon on the West Hill Road and no one came to look for me. I say it began that day, but maybe I'm wrong to say that. Maybe I should say the life I know now began nearly eight years later—when Overseer Flint brought the lunatic to the town poor farm.

1

The Gypsy Boy

Old Berthie was the one that told Jip. "A lunatic, boy," she said leaning so close Jip could count the hairs in her nostrils. "A raving lunatic." She sniffed. 'We're all of us poor and there be some," she rolled her eyes toward Old George and Sheldon Morse, "who is simple. But we're harmless, ain't we, boy? What do they mean bringing a lunatic amongst poor God-fearing folk who done no harm nor had no luck in this cruel world?"

Jip nodded solemnly. He never argued with Berthie. Once he dared question her when she said Ethan Allen had been a fool. After all, Ethan Allen and his Green Mountain Boys were the only genuine Vermont heroes Jip had ever heard tell of.

"Ethan Allen was a hero," he'd said.

She slapped him across the cheek so hard it stung. He wouldn't have credited that old wrinkled hand with such strength. "I said, 'fool,' boy. Don't go contradicting your elders!"

He didn't again. Besides, why *were* they bringing a lunatic to the poor farm?

"Money," Berthie said. "It'd cost the town too dear to send him to the asylum."

The Overseer of the Poor had appeared several days

earlier. Mr. Flint was an imposing man, tall enough to look down his nose at most of the population, with deep, buckshot eyes and sunken cheeks like a skeleton. You could tell from his frock coat and stovepipe hat what an important man he was in these parts. Indeed, he was the wealthiest and most important man that any of the residents knew of. It was he that had put each of them here on the town poor farm and demanded their gratitude on every possible occasion.

Overseer Flint drove his gig down the rutted road that morning in early April, cursing and whipping his mare, urging her through the spring mud. The residents, gathered respectfully in the yard to welcome his arrival, could hear the unchristian language from where they stood, huddled against one another for warmth. They reckoned the overseer above the law—even the biblical injunctions about the Lord's name—that tempered the speech of more ordinary mortals.

Despite the overseer's powerful tongue, the gig's left back wheel stuck, held fast in the greedy clay. "Jip, Sheldon, go help Mr. Flint," Otis Lyman, the farm's manager, yelled. Jip sprang forward, grabbing Sheldon's big, rough hand.

Sheldon looked at him, puzzled.

"We got to get the overseer's wheel loose, Sheldon. You and me together, ey?"

"Awright, Jip." Sheldon was always obliging. He just didn't catch on too fast.

The overseer stopped his red-faced cursing when the two of them got close.

"Good day to you, Mr. Flint, sir. I 'spect you better get down, sir," Jip said.

The overseer peered skeptically at them—the skinny boy and the husky young simpleton. The mare, straining at the reins, was sweating, her eyes wild from pulling. Couldn't the man see his own weight was making the wheel sink deeper and deeper?

"If'n you'd light down—" the boy began.

The man didn't wait for him to finish. His mouth pursed, he climbed down gingerly to the less muddy side, then threw his reins back toward Jip. Jip gathered them in one hand and watched as the tall man tiptoed around the muddiest ruts, picking a cautious way up the road to the crowd watching from the farmhouse yard.

"Wait, Sheldon," Jip said quietly when the man seemed out of earshot. "We got to make friends with this poor critter first. Mr. Flint has aggravated her something fearful with all his whipping and cursing." He moved to the mare's head and began to speak soothingly to the beast. The horse tossed her head once, but when the boy reached a chapped hand to her neck, she let him stroke it—barely stamping her muddy feet.

"Now, Sheldon," Jip said, his voice hardly louder than a spring breeze on a maple branch, "jest put your shoulder on that wheel, and when I say 'gee,' you shove, all right?"

Sheldon grinned, nodding his prematurely balding head. "I'm strong," he said proudly.

"That's right, Sheldon. You ain't got extra sense, but you're lots stronger than most anyone. I can't do without you. All I can do is talk sweet to this here horse. You're the one what's got to save the gig for the overseer."

"He'll say, 'Thank you, Sheldon. You're a good boy.' "

3

"He might, Sheldon. He jest might. Anyhow, we got to do it, thanks or no."

Lacking the overseer's weight and anger, and with Sheldon's strong shoulder against the wheel, the little mare eased the gig from its muddy trap with little effort. Jip patted her neck, kissed it, and praised her.

"You, too, Sheldon, you done every bit as good as the horse. Only she was upset, so I have to pet her special."

"I know, Jip."

They got no thanks from Mr. Flint. By the time horse, boy, and man had walked into the yard, and Jip had tied the reins to the hitching post, Mr. Flint had forgotten all about them. He was deep in a heated discussion with the farm manager, whose bulbous nose gleamed out redder than ever as he tried to argue with his superior. Mrs. Lyman was shooing all the residents into the house and out of hearing. "You, too, Jip, Sheldon. Everyone inside. None of your affair. The overseer has business with Mr. Lyman. Not with you." She was clucking like a mother hen and waving her arms at them. "We mustn't get in the gentlemen's way. Come on now."

They obeyed, if grudgingly. What could they do? They were like chicks here on this farm, pecking about to keep alive. There were seven of them at the time—four because they were old with no one to care for them: Berthie, Joe, Willis, and the silent Throsina. Two were simple—Sheldon in his early thirties and George, who was sickly and old and probably simple as well. Like Throsina, he seldom spoke, so no one could be quite sure.

And then there was Jip. When he arrived, Mr. Lyman had examined his teeth and pronounced that he was two, or maybe three, but no one knew for sure. He had fallen off the back of a wagon on the West Hill Road. Eye-witnesses (at least some who claimed to have been there on the usually deserted road) said the wagon was hell-bent for hades, careening around the sharp curve about a mile out of the village when this odd bit of a boy just tumbled right off the back.

"No one bothered themselves to come back and claim you," Mrs. Lyman had said quite matter-of-factly.

"But didn't I tell you who I was?" Jip had figured early on that the maybe three-year-old child who fell off the wagon was old enough to tell somebody who he was.

"You were speaking nothing but gibberish at the time when you wasn't screaming your head off," she said. "Maybe you was a gypsy babe as some say. Or maybe you knocked your head on a stone when you hit the road." She cocked her head and studied him for a minute. "You ain't overly clever—not simple like Sheldon—but you likely lost something in that fall." She tapped her own head meaningfully.

Still, Jip was smart enough to wonder. There was plenty of time to ponder on things at the farm. He worked hard, as he and Sheldon were the only able-bodied residents, but most of the work left his mind free to ponder.

Why, he asked the chickens as he threw them grain, why had no one come back for him? Wouldn't you notice, say, if you began the day with six children and, come night, the count was down to five? Even if you were in a powerful hurry to leave these rocky hills to get West to where the good land lay, wouldn't it cross your mind to wonder what had become of your missing young'un that you once had but suddenly wasn't there anymore? Even a goose can count her goslings and know if a fox got one in the night.

Even supposing you were a heartless gypsy who stole other people's children like pies off a cooling sill, wouldn't you care about one of your own?

Jip's hair was darkish and on the curly side. His ears stuck out a bit. Did Romany ears protrude? The better to hear with—that was what he told Sheldon, but privately, staring into the wavy kitchen mirror, he thought they gave him the look of a two-handled jug. In the summer his skin burned dark and in the winter it was a perpetual shade of gray. But maybe that was because it didn't often get scrubbed. He was like a barn cat. He didn't mind giving himself a lick or two, but the sight of a tub of steaming water in the kitchen made him race toward the door. When he was tiny, Mrs. Lyman occasionally stripped him and doused him, but now that he was too big to haul about, she gave up on baths.

He might, indeed, be dark like a gypsy babe. On the other hand, perhaps, just perhaps, he was a child the Romanys had snatched from loving parents who were still mourning the loss of their beautiful baby boy.

Deacon Avery of the Congregational Church had come along the West Hill Road in his gig that day. He had gotten down and approached the child and told him to "go home" like he was some stray, but it hadn't worked. So after lengthy hesitation and debate with his wife, the deacon had picked the odd little screaming bundle off the dirt of the road.

His wife had made him take it direct to Reverend

Goodrich. The worthy reverend had thirteen children of his own and a very low salary. With some reluctance, he, in turn, had called upon the authorities—that is to say Mr. Flint, the Overseer of the Poor. It was the overseer's job to clear the town of tramps and transients and sweep the poor and mentally defective out of the village and onto the poor farm, where they would not offend the eyes and nostrils of God-fearing citizens, nor strain their purse strings overmuch.

Mr. Lyman had protested that the poor farm was not an orphan asylum, until Mr. Flint proposed that money could be extracted from the poor farm tax allocation to send the foundling to some distant institution. Or, alternatively, the child could be set up with a worthy Christian household closer by, again with fees from the poor farm budget. Mr. Lyman chose to keep his meager funds intact.

The farm manager prided himself that he had done well by the boy. He tried him in school once. But the other children complained of the smell, and even the little ones could make out the letters Jip could not. With so many citizens fleeing westward, tax revenues plummeted and with them funds to operate the poor farm. In desperation, the manager hired Jip out to a local farmer. To Mrs. Lyman's suggestion that Jip might be a bit too young for a hired man, he'd said the plain truth. "The boy is eating up all the profits, Mrs. Lyman." She couldn't argue. Even the boy, listening to the debate, knew the manager was right. For all his scrawniness, he shoveled in everything that wasn't nailed to the table. "But who will have him?" she'd asked.

Farmer Slaytor would. He would have anything he could beat and bully. His own dog cowered at the sight of him. Jip's most vivid memory of that time was being grabbed by an ear and dragged to see how badly he had swept the kitchen or shoveled out the barn. "See! See!" the man would yell. "A blind idjit could do better." As Jip swept and cried, the dog would find him and rub his body against the boy's legs and whimper its sympathy.

Jip might be there yet—one ear larger than the other from all that yanking—but Farmer Slaytor upped and married a husky widow woman from Chelsea and sent his less than satisfactory hand back to the poor farm.

To Jip it felt like coming home. For the poor farm was the only home he could remember. He loved the rocky pastures. He loved standing in the spring wind, gazing at the distant hills, the green deeply pockmarked with the gray of Deacon Avery's granite quarry and the piles of slag around it. He loved the way the sun glinted off the stone. Perhaps, when he was a man, he would go to work there, driving shivs into the rock face with a great sledge-hammer, filling the holes with black powder, and BOOM! blasting the huge granite blocks from the bedrock.

When he came back to the poor farm after those few months away, he seemed a different boy. Privately, Mr. Lyman wondered why Slaytor had let him go. He wouldn't, of course, have said anything to anyone, for it was the poor who were to be grateful, not their managers. Lyman fancied himself not a fully healthy man, and the beasts and residents of the farm were a constant trial to him. The boy had a way with both, though. He was scarcely more than half the height of summer corn, but the flock of scrawny merino sheep would see him coming across the pasture and lope awkwardly over the hill to meet him. His front teeth were hardly out and in again, yet he was milking old Bonnie twice a day, and somehow, the milk she had been so stingy with—however Mrs. Lyman tugged and yanked—flowed like a fountain under his small hands. And that year, instead of her usual stillbirth, old Bonnie bore a calf alive and healthy enough for Lyman to sell at a nice profit, a bit of which bought him some tobacco and a bottle of medicinal spirits to augment his store of homemade cider fermenting in the cellar.

How much of the manager's secret thoughts Jip knew or sensed it would be hard to say, but he was not dissatisfied with his life. Still, he was a normal boy and curious about a number of things. At the moment, he wished it was his ear against the door and not Mrs. Lyman's. He'd like to know what the overseer was saying about the mysterious lunatic.

"Jip!"

He came out of his daydream with a start. Mrs. Lyman jerked her head to summon him close. He left the cluster of residents at the stove and came around the big table to where she stood. "Mr. Lyman will be wanting you," she said. "But, first, go out to the pump and put a rag to your face. Mercy, boy, the overseer has come calling. We run a clean establishment around here. How will he know that if you go talking to him with a face like a pig snout?"

Jip retraced his steps around the table. He was at the east door and ready to go out when she stopped him.

"Take Sheldon and wash his face, too, you hear?" Jip returned to the stove side, taking Sheldon's big hand in his own. "And get his ears this time," she called out after the two of them.

"Why does Mr. Flint want to see me, Jip? Have I been bad?"

"Bend over, Sheldon. I got to reach your ears."

"Have I, Jip?"

"Naa-h. I don't know but what he's got a job of work for you and me."

"You and me, right, Jip? You and me together?"

Jip nodded. "All right, you can straighten up now, Sheldon. You scrub up pretty as a heifer in a county fair."

Sheldon looked troubled. "Is that a joke, Jip?"

"Ehyuh."

The young man laughed, showing his gaggle of decayed and missing teeth. Jip smiled, rinsing out the rag and then working a little harder than usual on his own face. He took Sheldon's hand and they presented themselves for Mrs. Lyman's inspection. Mrs. Lyman opened the main kitchen door.

As they came into the yard, the two men turned. "A cage," Mr. Lyman said, "a cage, Jip. We need a cage."

Jip didn't ask what for, although he wanted to. The overseer's presence made him shy. "How big?" he asked.

The manager turned to Mr. Flint. "Oh," the tall man said, "about as tall as I am—say, six feet cubed, that should do it without waste. Do you know what a cube is, boy?"

"Yessir."

"But strong. It will need to be very strong." He looked

doubtfully at Jip—up and down as if measuring his height. "Perhaps we should hire it done, Mr. Lyman."

Mr. Lyman was alarmed. "And *pay* to have it done? Above the cost of materials—which will be considerable?"

"Yes, well," the overseer said. "But it must be strong. You'll need to buy iron hinges and a padlock."

"I ain't hardly the budget for such expensive—"

"If we send him to Brattleboro it would take your entire appropriation, Mr. Lyman. Believe me, next town meeting, you'd be out of a job altogether."

Mr. Lyman looked beaten. "The boy and I can do it," he said.

"Sheldon can help, can't I, Jip? Can't I?"

"Sure, Sheldon," Jip said gently, "no one here could get along without you."

"Humph." The overseer untied his horse, and watching his feet in their fancy boots to avoid the mud wherever possible, he walked his mare and wagon back to the main road.

The next afternoon, as soon as Mr. Lyman could fetch the rock maple slats from the lumberyard and the hardware from Peck's store in the village, Jip and Sheldon set about building a cage for the lunatic.

2

The Lunatic

Jip put the straw mattress Mrs. Lyman had made on one side of the cage, sat down, and pulled shut the slat door. He wanted to know how it might feel to live in a cage. There was a chamber pot in the corner. He had made a little trapdoor so it could be taken out and emptied and food could be passed in without having to undo the padlock on the main entry. He looked about, taking in the smell of the new-shaved wood. He and Sheldon had done a good job of it. It felt clean and, well, cozy. It might be nice to have a place of his own like this, away from the snoring of the old men and Sheldon's tossing and restless sleep talk. Well, at least he had a cot of his own now. At first he'd had to sleep with Sheldon and woke up on the floor more mornings than not.

He supposed he'd have slept on the floor the rest of his days, but a lucky thing happened. A year back Old Man Rutherford died, and Jip grabbed the vacant cot before Mrs. Lyman had time even to wash out the raggedy quilt.

He stretched out on the mattress. The straw pricked through the ticking and his thin shirt and britches, but it smelled fresh, unlike his own musty bed. The plank floor of the cage was no harder than the wooden frame of his cot. He sucked in a deep, satisfied breath, gazing up at the strips of wood that he and Sheldon had nailed across the top. Mr. Lyman had grumbled about the waste of nails, which came dear at a penny apiece, but the overseer had demanded that they triple-nail each end of every slat.

It was like looking at the ceiling through an elaborate fence. The sides—the same crisscrossed pattern as the top—felt like a protection. He couldn't ever remember having privacy, even at Slaytor's he had slept in the same room as the farmer. Privacy, or the desire for it, was not an idea that he could put into words. But in the cage he sensed what it might feel like to have a little space all one's own that no other, not even simple, sweet Sheldon or his beloved animals, would intrude upon.

"Jip! Ji—yip!" The boy sighed and left the comfort of the cage to respond to Mrs. Lyman's cry. What he needed was a cage with walls so thick that he wouldn't be able to hear the constant call of his name.

They brought the lunatic that very afternoon. Once more the residents stood shivering in the April chill, watching a horse wagon come up the road. This time, neither Jip nor Sheldon was sent to help. Unlike the gig, this wagon was pulled by a strong team of Morgans, and besides the driver and the overseer on the front seat, four sturdy townsmen sat at the corners of the wagon bed surrounding a strange bent-over figure whose screams could be heard long before any face or recognizable human form came into focus.

"Jeezums Crow!" Old Joe exclaimed, revealing that even a man half deaf could hear the commotion. Sheldon clamped both hands over his ears and squeezed his eyes shut, trying to keep out the terrifying sound.

When at last the wagon pulled into the yard, Jip could

see that the strange form in the center of the wagon bed was a man, with only his head free. A rope wound about his legs and back, bringing his knees to his chest. His arms were around his legs and his huge, gnarled hands were tied together at the wrists. The rough hemp rope had rubbed the flesh raw, and between his shrieks, he would duck his shaggy head to bite at the rope with large, yellow teeth.

The hair was appalling—long as a woman's—but it seemed all of a piece with his beard, both of which were streaked with gray and dotted with spittle.

Sheldon opened his eyes long enough to take in the sight, then grabbed Jip's arm in terror. "It's all right, Sheldon," Jip whispered. "I won't let him hurt you," which was the emptiest promise he'd ever made. The man looked quite determined to burst his bonds and do damage to the whole lot of them.

The four townsmen jumped off the back of the wagon before the driver had halted the team. They were all shouting orders. But the yells of the overseer (in his gardening clothes instead of his frock coat) were louder than even the ravings of the lunatic. "Carry it to the cage!"

Two of the townsmen were up on the wagon trying to shove the lunatic over the side to the other two. It couldn't be done. They called for help, so Jip disentangled himself from Sheldon's anxious grasp and scrambled up to help them lift the trussed creature over the side like a bag of rocks into the arms of the men below. They swayed almost to their knees, cursing at the weight. Then shoving, pushing, and stumbling, they carried him into the house, Mrs. Lyman scurrying ahead to open the doors and the overseer shouting out orders. The lunatic, with all his limbs secured, squirmed and bleated like a hog set for the slaughter.

The men dragged and dumped him in the cage, tripping over the madman's body in their hurry to escape. Mr. Flint slammed the door, clamped the great iron padlock together with a clunk of metal, and turned to present the key to Mr. Lyman. The manager's wide eyes were so fixed on the lunatic that it was several moments and a jab before he saw the key to take it.

"Mind you, take care, Lyman," the overseer said to the manager, who was visibly shaking. "I hold you responsible."

The escorts did not even stay for the cups of hard cider that Mrs. Lyman had poured out earlier. They hurried to the wagon and left the farm as fast as the horses could take them down the muddy track.

"Wal," said Mrs. Lyman, downing a cup of cider, "waste not, want not." She handed a cup to her husband who, without a word, hastily downed two more. Between them they finished off the six cups prepared for the visitors, while the thirsty residents stood by, licking their dry lips.

All but Jip, who, seeing the Lymans occupied, stole the butcher knife and crept back to the room next to the shed where the old lunatic lay. His shrieks had quieted to rhythmic moans.

"Sh-sh-hush, there," Jip said. "Hush, old fellow. We ain't going to hurt you."

For a moment the groaning ceased, and the old man struggled about to fix his bloodshot gaze toward the bars where Jip knelt, crooning. "Can you roll yourself to the side?" the boy asked softly. "Or jest swing close enough for me to cut them ropes for you?" He spoke in the voice he used for Sheldon and George and the poor dumb beasts in his care. Miraculously, the lunatic seemed to understand. With an enormous lunge, he heaved his body against the slats.

The trick was to get the rope cut without giving the lunatic a chance to grab the knife. Sweat stood out on Jip's forehead as he eased the blade through the slats and under the ropes across the man's back. He crooned as he sawed at the ropes. "There, there. It'll be better soon. There. That's the main one. A minute more and I'll have your ankles free."

The lunatic stretched out his cramped limbs, crying a bit with the pain of it.

"Now, can you jest move around to the front?" The man hesitated, trying to unravel the request. "Come close, here to me. Stick those old hands through the slats. Then I can cut loose your wrists, too." He put his own wrists together trying to signal to the man what was needed.

The lunatic shuffled about on his knees, then stretched out his bound hands. He could barely squeeze them through the slats. He flinched slightly as Jip worked the blade between his wrists. "Steady now, quiet. I'd be loath to slice you instead of the rope."

The lunatic obeyed. A little doglike whimper had replaced the moans.

Jip smiled. "See, it's near cut through now. You'll feel lots better without this rope grazing your poor old flesh. There. See?"

The man pulled his hands back into the cage, turning them over as if to study them.

"Maybe I should get you some ointment to put on those rope burns. Want I should do that?"

The man nodded, rubbing first one sore wrist and then the other. His lips parted, showing his great yellow teeth. At first Jip was startled. It took him a moment to understand. The lunatic was smiling. Jip smiled back, shyly at first, but as the lunatic's smile broadened, so did his own.

"There," he said. "Well. I got to fetch the ointment. Don't fuss while I'm gone, old fellow. I won't be long."

"What are you doing with my knife?" Mrs. Lyman was a bit tipsy from her two cups of cider, which she had downed too fast for a woman unaccustomed to fermented drinks.

"I figured Mr. Lyman would want me to cut the lunatic loose. The poor fellow trussed up like a pig ready to be stuck. It weren't human to leave him so."

"He's hardly human, that one," she said.

"I need some ointment—the rope has rubbed his wrists to bleeding."

She fetched the ointment from her cabinet of assorted medications. It was right behind the medicinal spirits.

"You aren't afraid of the creature?" she asked, her back still to the boy.

He shrugged. What was the answer? Maybe he was and maybe he wasn't. He only knew the lunatic needed to have his limbs loosed and his wounds attended to. "I don't figure he'll take unkind to having his wrists soothed."

She turned then and gave him a look before she continued in a sterner tone. "Well, don't forget you've got

17

chores to attend to," she said. "They don't stop just 'cause you've found yourself a new pet."

"I won't," he said and sighed. That was how he had acquired responsibility for all the farm's livestock and the neediest residents. They were "Jip's pets," which out of the goodness of the manager's heart, the boy was allowed to care for.

The cage room was quiet when Jip pushed open the door. He wished he'd scrubbed down the walls after he'd carried all the years of trash out of it yesterday. It seemed so dark in the small room. A high north window let in little light, and the soot on the walls, evidence of the faulty fireplace, made the room even more dingy. The cage filled more than half the space. Beside it there was no furniture. It was a gloomy place to spend one's days. The lunatic was lying stretched out on his mattress. It was too short for him, so his feet hung off the end. The man was staring at the slats, which patterned his view of the cracked ceiling plaster.

"How came I here?" he asked without moving his head.

"What?" Jip would have been less startled to hear Bible verses coming from old Bonnie's bovine muzzle.

"How came I into this cage?" His words were clear, no relation to the ravings of a lunatic.

"You was carried here, sir, on Mr. Flint's wagon."

"The Overseer of the Poor, Mr. Flint?"

"Yessir."

"And does Mr. Flint aim to keep me in a cage like some beast from the jungle?"

The boy hung his head, ashamed to be one of those who had carried the man in here.

"You was raving, sir, somewhat wild and mad. I reckon it was for your safety."

The man sighed deeply and sat up to face him.

"I—I brung you ointment, sir, for your wrists. The rope scraped them something awful."

Again the man raised his hands, turning them over to examine the wounds, as though he'd forgotten.

"If you'll stick them through the slats, I can rub some of this on them—soothe them a bit?" His voice went up into a question as if addressing an elder whose preferences must now be consulted.

The man stuck one large hand through the slats. "You're a kind young feller. What's your name?"

"Jip, sir."

"My friends used to call me Put," the old man said. "I'd like it if you'd call me Put. It's for Putnam, but that's too grand a name for the likes of me, don't you think?"

Jip grinned. "Put's nice," he said.

"Why Jip?"

"Mr. Lyman dubbed me Jip," he said, gently massaging the cold ointment into the raw flesh. "On account of I fell off the back of a wagon and some says it was a gypsy wagon."

"I see." Put pulled the left hand back and thrust out the right. "This is the town farm then?"

"Yessir." He was a little sorry to be the one to give such news. "To save you from being sent to the asylum, it was."

The man didn't remark on that, and Jip decided not to say that the cage was the town's way of saving taxpayer money. The man's plight was harsh enough.

19

"I don't reckon . . ." the man began. "I don't reckon they'd let me take a bath . . . or—" he laughed shortly "—or trim my hair and beard?"

"Likely not." Jip kept his head over his task, avoiding the man's eyes. "They're a bit jumpy, yet. You jest got here less than an hour ago. . . . Maybe when you settle in more . . . There. Does that ease it some?"

The man pulled back his hand. "It does. You're a good lad. Could you make it one more favor? A wet cloth to wipe my face?"

Before the week was out, Jip had cajoled Mr. Lyman into letting him fill a tub in Put's room, so the man could bathe. And although no one, not even Jip, wanted to hand over a straight razor, Jip was allowed scissors to cut Put's wild growth of hair and beard to a more becoming human length.

"Do you like a pleasing tune, my boy?"

"I don't know. I'm not much for music. All I ever heard was hymns in church and most of them is pretty drear."

The man began to sing, then. He had a high voice, clear like sleigh bells across the snow.

As the days passed, Jip came to know that song well, for Put would sing it over and over, never tiring of either the melody or the words. Sometimes Jip would try to sing along, " 'All is well, all is well,' " though his own voice sounded scratchy and tuneless compared to the lunatic's sweet song.

In truth, Jip could scarcely call Put a lunatic. He was not an unhandsome man when bathed, his clothes scrubbed by Jip, his hair and beard neat. His eyes had quite lost their bloodshot wildness.

Put's lunacy had fled or been cast into some distant

swine like in the Bible tale. Every night Jip longed to leave the cage unlocked, for it made his heart sick to clap a padlock against his newfound friend.

"You daren't leave it open, boy," Put said. "If I go raving in the night, I can't think what harm this wretched mind might betray me to."

So, reluctantly, Jip slammed the padlock's shackle into its case and hung the key in the medicine cabinet behind the medicinal spirits.

Then without warning one night, the house awoke to shrieks and terrible banging. Jip threw on his britches and raced down the stairs, his suspenders flying.

"Put, Put," he cried, to make himself heard over the din. But his friend paid no heed to his pleading and hurled his body against the slats until Jip felt sure he would tear all the nails from their holes and splinter the rock maple timbers into kindling.

"Put, Put," he murmured, half crying out his friend's name. "There's no one here would harm you. Rest, rest, hush, don't punish your poor self so—"

In answer Put tore at his face until the blood ran and soiled his shirt.

The Lymans and the residents, all in their nightclothes, stood about in the hallway, terrified to cross the threshold. Only Jip dared approach the cage, but even he stood back lest the lunatic's great hand dart out at him through the slats.

"Come back," Jip crooned. "Don't let the devil possess you. Come back. It's me, your old friend, Jip, what you sings and talks to."

Jip sat on the cold floor, clasped his hands about his knees, and began to sing:

" . . . I soon shall be
From ev'ry pain and sorrow free.
I shall the King of glory see,
All is well, all is well!"

He sang until his throat was hoarse, not loud—he knew that he could not sing above the lunatic's threats and curses—but, rocking his body, he sang on to comfort himself. He had the vain hope that somewhere in that terrible head behind those fearful teeth a bit of the Put he cared for was still alive and could hear that Jip was near and would not desert him.

At some point well past daylight both the madman and the boy fell into exhausted sleep.

Jip was awakened by Mrs. Lyman's call from the hallway. He must get his lazy self to the barn and milk, she said. He stole away from the huge form lying crammed into a corner of the cage, splattered with blood and spittle and worse.

Old Bonnie welcomed him with a gentle low and a barely impatient stomp of her back hoof. "I know, my darling," he said sorrowfully. "I'm late and causing you discomfort. But how could I leave him? And then—" he pulled the stool closer and rested his head against her warm flank "—and then I fell to sleep." He began the rhythmic stroking of her teats, and as the milk *plinked* into the waiting pail, he remembered his sad and desperate singing in the night. He had found a beast he couldn't tame at will. It was like to break his young heart.

3

Newcomers

Put came to himself later that day, but the residents were now more wary of him. Sheldon grabbed Jip's arm and begged him not to go into the cage room. He cried like a child when Jip persisted. Jip never wanted to hurt Sheldon, but Put was—well, he was Put and he belonged to Jip in a way no one else ever had.

There was no way of knowing when one of the spells would come over the man. Whenever Put was out of the cage for even the briefest time, the anxious twittering about of the manager and his wife tainted any small taste of freedom Jip could offer to his friend.

Only Jip remained faithful, daring, when the weather was fair, to take Put out as far as the pasture so that he could feel the sun on his face and welcome the slow approach of Vermont spring.

There were new lambs to count, and, as if to dispel her luckless reputation once and for all, Bonnie dropped yet another healthy calf, a heifer at that.

Put continued in his right mind through the end of April and right on into early May. Perhaps the lengthening of the days cheered his troubled soul, for he sang his songs and played upon a wooden pipe he'd told Jip how to fashion, as he was never allowed anything sharper than his pewter spoon.

He was in his peaceful phase the afternoon the Widow Wilkens appeared, her three unhappy children in tow. Jip's heart danced to see more children come to the farm, having been for all his life there the only one. The oldest was even near to his own size, though a girl. The next was a bit of a boy, just coming into speech, and the youngest a baby girl, still on the breast.

The widow's husband had been, Berthie informed them all, the town's most notorious drunk. Then, during the last big snow, he fell on his way home and froze to death in a snow drift. An empty bottle for illegal spirits was found nearby. No one counted his death much of a loss, though Jip wondered if his wife and children had. They surely might. Still, the taxpayers soon felt the pinch, for the drunkard had left nothing behind save debts, so the responsibility for his family's care fell upon the town.

Jip ran out to meet the newcomers with delight—a delight that was met with cold stares from everyone except for a shy smile from the little boy.

"Show the Wilkenses the empty room next to the gentlemen's quarters," Mrs. Lyman said primly. "Gentlemen" was not a word she was accustomed to use to describe the male residents of the farm.

"Jest follow me, then," Jip called out, running up the stairs. He turned at the top to watch the labored ascent of the new residents.

Lucy, the girl, was carrying a large carpetbag, bumping it from step to step, while her mother juggled the baby on her right hip and dragged the little boy upward with her left hand. "Lift your feet, Toddy, for mercy's sake, jest lift your feet."

Jip went back down, thinking at least to help Lucy with the huge bag, but when he reached for the handles, she snatched it away. "It's ours!" she said, as though he had been intent on stealing it from her.

"I jest thought to give you a hand with it," he said, confused.

"You have a monstrous dirty face."

Jip shook his head and climbed back up to the landing. He didn't tell her that her face wasn't so clean either. Why should he? He knew a hurting animal when he saw one. There was no need to pain her further.

At the supper table, which filled the center of the drab kitchen, the widow and her children sat huddled together at the far side near Mrs. Lyman. The little boy's nose hardly scraped the splintery tabletop. Mr. Lyman served the bowls of mush from the kettle and passed them down. Lucy looked at hers, her face twisting as though she felt nauseous. Her mother poked both her and Toddy and bent to say something sharp and low. Reluctantly, both children picked up their spoons. Jip didn't wait to see how much they ate, he only waited until he had Put's bowl and took it with a spoon down the hall to the cage room.

"Here you are, Put." Jip passed the bowl and spoon through the trapdoor. "Hot at least."

The old man sniffed the steaming mush. "Ah, one of Mrs. Lyman's culinary triumphs." When he smiled like that, his teeth didn't seem so large and menacing.

"We got new residents." Put counted on Jip to bring the news of the world outside the cage room. "A Widow Wilkens and her young 'uns. Berthie says the mister died in the March storm."

"There's unluckier people in this world than you nor me, Jip," the old man said, settling back against the slats with his supper.

"I reckon." It was a new thought to Jip. He never regarded himself as lucky or unlucky. He was just Jip, just here. But he had pitied his friend—a lunatic and a pauper to boot. Was Put right? Was it unluckier still to be the orphan child of a drunken father? Jip returned to the big kitchen table and his own cool mush, determined to be especially kind to the prickly Lucy.

"Make him stop looking at me, Ma," Lucy whispered hoarsely.

In answer Mrs. Wilkens reached past Toddy and gave Lucy's face a slap. "Mind your manners, girl."

Yes, thought Jip. There's some that's unluckier than me.

He felt truly lucky a few days later. He was going into town. A trip into the village for anything besides Sunday services at the Congregational Church was always something of an adventure. Jip liked to study the variety of horses and people on the busy street, to hear the rattle of wagons, the call of greetings. He wished for a cap. If he had a cap to tip, he could have joined in the proper "Howdy-do's" and "Good morning to you's" and made a wise pronouncement on the weather.

Since the day that Lucy had made mention of his face, he had taken more care to splash cold water on it and wipe it carefully on the tail of his shirt. This day he looked down at the raw, red hands sticking out of his skimpy sleeves and washed them as well. There was no mirror over the pump, only the wavy one over the kitchen sink, but he ran his fingers through his tangled curls and patted them to his head. There. At least he felt handsomer.

"Where you off to?" Lucy had come out to the pump.

"Me and Mr. Lyman got to take the heifer in to sell." He lowered his voice. "I got to help. The man's got no way with critters."

"Oh." He tried to figure if she was wanting to go too, but he knew Mr. Lyman wouldn't allow it. He wouldn't even let Sheldon go into town on errands. "I can't be bothered taking care of the idjit," he'd say when Jip begged on Sheldon's behalf, knowing how Sheldon did so love to go places. Though in truth, it would be Jip taking care of both beast and man.

The road was rutted, but the mud was hard, and if Mr. Lyman guided Old Jack around the worst of the ruts, there should be no delay traveling on such a beautiful morning. Jip, sitting in the bed of the wagon, stroked the heifer's neck and half talked, half sang to keep her quiet. In a way, he was sad to see her go, but the sale would help out with the finances of the farm, now seriously strained with the addition of Put and the Wilkens family to the population.

It wasn't hard to tell when money was tight. The meals, meager at best, degenerated into a steady diet of mush, accompanied by a stream of complaints flowing from the head of the table to the foot and back again.

In the good old days, as Mr. Lyman often reminded

them, the able-bodied of the poor would have been let out to the highest bidder and would have brought a good bit of money to the town instead of draining the town purse. But, some do-gooders claimed this practice smacked too close to southern slavery, so they began to put out the poor to the lowest bidder—the householder who proposed to take on the responsibility for the pauper at least expense to the town. This practice, alas, fell into disfavor as the ever vigilant do-gooders sniffed out cases of abuse and claimed near starvation. So out of Christian charity the town had purchased for their benefit—*for their benefit*—this wonderful farm and had hired the Lymans to manage it and the lives of all those unfortunate paupers for whom the town must be responsible.

But, and at this point the manager invariably sighed, the task of keeping the farm from becoming an undue tax burden on those same generous citizens fell entirely to him. Mr. Flint, the Overseer of the Poor, cared for nothing but balanced books and an unruffled citizenry. And how, pray tell, was Mr. Lyman supposed to make the farm pay for itself with only two able-bodied males among the residents—one of them a boy of unknown age who could not or would not succeed when he was hired out and the other a simpleton?

Jip would have felt more guilt or even more sympathy if the manager himself had been more industrious. After all, he seemed perfectly able-bodied, if a bit on the plump side. He was neither young nor simple. But Jip supposed himself only an ignorant boy and not up to understanding the problems of his elders.

The sun warmed Jip's head and shoulders. Winter was

nearly gone at last, and though a May snow was not unknown, it wasn't likely. He hardly minded that by June he would be at work from dawn to dusk. He was not a stranger to work. Sometimes he racked his brains to recall who had done the milking, plowing, seeding, cultivating, picking, and reaping before Mr. Lyman determined that Sheldon had the muscles and Jip had the sense to carry out all these tasks.

Still, he could enjoy a rare holiday from work. He longed to stretch out full length in the wagon and bathe in the sunlight. He was sleepy. He'd hardly had a full night's rest since Put came. Often he slept by the cage, in case the lunatic got to raving in the night. Was it true what Berthie said about the full moon making him crazier? Jip couldn't be sure. Put's bad spells didn't seem as regular as the phases of the moon. And it certainly didn't take a full moon to unhinge him. At least Put was less agitated when the sun was shining, and summer with its long golden days was sure to come.

The wagon hit a bump in the rutted road. Mr. Lyman grunted a curse word and smacked the reins against Jack's patient back. The calf gave a startled little bleat.

"Sh-shhh," Jip whispered. "You ain't going to slaughter. No need to fear. Someone's going to buy you for a nice milk cow. You're a little beauty, I tell you. You'll live to a ripe old cow age, you will."

The little heifer twisted her neck to look up at him with worshipful brown eyes. He did love a calf. When Bonnie delivered a stillborn, it tore him apart, even though, with no calf to nurse, it meant more milk, butter, and cheese for the residents.

They were approaching the edge of the village. As always, he stared at the large houses as they passed. Curtains made the houses look plump and sleepy-eyed as they sat comfortably amongst their luxuriant shade trees. What did people do in the village? They couldn't all work in the mill or the livery stable or at the harness makers. They didn't seem to keep chickens much less a cow, and, aside from the few garden plots, which had not yet been planted, it was hard to see how the rich ate, let alone how they prospered.

Overseer Flint, for example, was called a banker. Jip had even seen the so-called bank, a squat one-story clapboard structure near the village green. But what did people *do* in banks? He knew it was somehow related to money, but what? You didn't grow money. Why would you need a building for it when a mattress or jar or even a drawer would be much more handy?

A visitor to the poor farm years ago had, upon leaving, handed Jip a copper penny. Since it was the only money the boy had ever possessed, he always carried it with him in the pocket of his trousers. The donor had said to Jip: "Now save this, my boy. A penny saved is a penny earned." So Jip had obediently saved it, but it hadn't earned him any more. Jip couldn't figure for the life of him how the man had thought it might. A penny wasn't a hen that could hatch a bunch of copper chicks.

Once, last fall, when he happened to be in the village, he had come close to spending his penny. Peck's store had candies, all different shiny colors, and they were ten for one penny. He was sorely tempted. Those ten candies would give him and Sheldon at least five days of pleasure. But the visitor's warning had stopped him. This particular penny must be destined for greater things than sweets for him and Sheldon to suck.

They were nearly at Peck's now, but the wagon didn't stop. First, they would deliver the heifer on the far side of the village and get the payment for it. Then, perhaps, Mr. Lyman would stop at the store. Jip hoped so. He loved to see the bright candies in their glass jars lined up like a row of rich village girls in their Sunday calicoes. Looking was free and did no harm.

He lifted the calf down from the wagon, nearly falling under the weight of it. Mr. Lyman was in his good suit and couldn't be expected to handle livestock. Jip bent over and gave the calf a secret good-bye kiss and then climbed back up into the wagon.

Mr. Lyman did stop at the store, but to Jip's disappointment, he ordered the boy to stay with the horse while he ran his errand. Jip clambered up to the wagon seat, leaving the reins loose across Jack's broad back and watched as the manager climbed the steps. Just as Mr. Lyman reached the entrance, a man came out, and the two of them dodged each other in the doorway with bows and nods. Jip gazed longingly at the storefront, his mouth all set for the candies he imagined his penny might have fetched.

For a second, the stranger's eyes met his own. The man looked startled, then, shifting his gaze, came down the steps and over to the wagon.

"Waiting for your papa?" he asked. There was something sticky and syrupy about the man's tone that made Jip want to lie, but the sin of lying was too heavy for his conscience, so he shook his head.

"Your . . . uncle?"

Why did the man care who Mr. Lyman was? Besides, he ought to know without asking. Everyone knew Mr. Lyman.

"No kin, eh?"

Jip neither nodded nor shook his head, but turned away to stare at a wagon passing on the road. The stranger was nosy and rude. He had no business asking such questions. Best to ignore him.

"Where you living, sonny?" The man waited, and when Jip failed to answer, added impatiently, "No cause to be unmannerly. I'm just making friendly conversation, you know."

Jip didn't know. That was the point. The man's words didn't seem friendly at all. To his great relief, Mr. Lyman came out of the store soon after, already stuffing his newly purchased tobacco into his pipe. Jip handed him the reins and climbed back to the wagon bed, being careful not to look down at the stranger, who had yet to move away.

"Your pardon, good sir—" Mr. Lyman ignored this greeting, clicked a command to the horse, and with a slap of the reins pulled away, leaving the man standing there red-faced and openmouthed.

"Who was that stranger you was talking to, boy?" the manager asked as they left the village.

"I wasn't talking, sir. He was. He was asking me if I was some relation to you."

The idea clearly displeased the manager. "Don't make up to strangers, boy."

"No, sir. It warn't his business if we was kin or no. Which we are not."

"He's not been in these parts before. What's he doing around here?"

"That I don't know. I didn't tell him nothing, sir."

Mr. Lyman gave a grunt and said no more.

Still, when Jip and Sheldon came in from the hen-house next afternoon, there was the stranger having a cup of tea and biscuits with Mrs. Lyman, right there in the farmhouse kitchen. The stranger must have found out from someone where the wagon had come from. It seemed unlikely to Jip that he had made his way out to the farm by accident. The town farm wasn't what you could call on the road to anywhere else.

The man raised his eyes as the two of them opened the door. Jip caught the man giving him a quick once-over, but he turned right back to Mrs. Lyman, chatting about the prospects for a late frost as though he and the manager's wife were old friends.

Jip washed the eggs and put them carefully into the basket. He wondered if Mr. Lyman knew that the stranger was poking his nose into the very kitchen of the farmhouse. The boy shivered. There was something wrong: The unknown man from the store now chittering away in the kitchen, having himself a cup of the manager's tea as though he was some welcomed and very familiar guest. Not even a parlor visitor—a kitchen one.

"Come on, Sheldon," he said. They left the room as fast as Jip could pull Sheldon out. Jip kept clear of the house until he saw the stranger well on the road toward the village.

He was a tall man, close to Mr. Flint's height, dressed in dark, formal-looking clothes, and walking, not heavy like a farmer, or even proud like a banker, but like a kind of—well, one night Jip had seen a weasel slinking around the chicken house looking for a hole to slide through. It was sort of like that.

The man stopped, looking back up the road toward the farmhouse. Jip jerked out of sight behind the shed.

4

Beware the Stranger

That night Jip waited until the meal was done and everyone had left the table before he took in Put's supper.
Then he settled himself down beside the cage. It wasn't
so much that he wanted to confide in his friend as he
needed Put to help him sort out his own confusion.

"Why you reckon he wanted to know if Mr. Lyman
was my pa or any kin? Everyone knows who Mr.
Lyman is and that he don't have children—nor would
he want a gypsy throwaway mistook for his own flesh
and blood."

"You're a good lad, Jip, gypsy or no."

"Well, you and me is friends, Put, and I thank you for
it, but what I want to know is why sudden like this
stranger pops into town, asks me and Mr. Lyman nosy
questions which we are too smart to answer, and next
thing he's in the kitchen chatting up the missus like they
was old-time acquaintances."

"Strange," Put agreed.

"Powerful strange, I say."

"Did it strike you, Jip—now, mind, I never laid eyes on
the feller—but did it come to mind that he might think
he knows you?"

"Well, he don't."

"I mean from before—that he might know who you belonged to before you fell off that particular wagon?"

"But I was a wee thing, still wobbly on my legs. How would anyone recognize me after all these years? And what if he did? Couldn't he have just said so straight out? Not sniff around like a hound on a trail?"

"Strange," Put repeated.

"If he thought he know'd me," Jip persisted, "how come he don't ask right out, tell me what he had in mind?"

"It would seem the natural, honest thing . . ."

"Well, whatever he is, he ain't honest, Put. I shouldn't be in the way of judging my feller man, but there is something smells very far from fresh about that feller. It gives me the tremblies seeing him in our kitchen. You know something else? Mrs. Lyman never told the mister that he was here."

"No?"

"Not a word passed down the length of that supper table tonight, Put. She says to him like she does every time he goes to the village, 'What is the news in town, Mr. Lyman?' And he says through his slurps, like always, 'Not much, Mrs. Lyman.' And she don't give him any news of the day here a-tall. Visitors is news, Put. You can count on it, visitors of any kind is news, and strangers is enough to call the county press."

"Not a word, eh?"

"Not one little word. Like she was keeping it secret that the stranger come, though he was drinking the tea and eating up the biscuits and Mr. Lyman is sure to notice when he takes to counting stock. He is powerful particular about things that come missing in the count."

"You must be careful, Jip. I don't think this stranger is after Mrs. Lyman's biscuits."

"If he is, he must be near to starvation."

They shared a laugh. Even to those whose memory of tasty vittles was nonexistent or near dead, Mrs. Lyman's cooking was a subject of scorn.

Still, how was Jip to be wary when he didn't know from what direction danger came, if at all? The tremblies persisted for a day or two—once or twice he imagined a figure coming up the road—but there was no one, and life returned to its natural rhythms.

But not quite. For the Widow Wilkens and her children had stirred the still pond of the farm. No one could deny it.

Jip felt responsible for Lucy and Toddy. He could safely leave the cub to her dam, but the other two needed him. Lucy pretended to ignore him, but the little boy took to following him around like a puppy. One day Jip was headed to the far pasture to see if any ewes had dropped lambs during the night and he was startled by the sound of crying. He turned around. Small Toddy was lying on his face in the prickly grass, kicking and screaming. Jip ran back to him, alarmed.

"Too fast!" the child screamed at him. "Too fast!"

"Sorry, little feller. I didn't know you was trotting after." He picked the child up, brushed off the dirt, and swung him to his shoulders. "Here. That better?"

The child shrieked with delight. "Giddap!" he cried, smacking Jip's cheek with his small hand. "Giddap, Jack!"

"Hold tight, now!" As he broke into a canter, he spotted Lucy. She had come running out of the house, after her brother, he supposed, and was standing there watching, a scowl twisting her face.

"C'mon, Lucy!" Toddy yelled.

"Yeah, come on. We're off to see if any lambs were born last night." She shrugged and turned, as if to go in. "Aw, come with us." She didn't move, so he cantered away with Toddy clutching his hair and squealing with anxious joy.

There was a new one—a little black-face love—that bleated so dear and nudged its ma for milk.

Jip swung Toddy gently to the ground. "Shh," he said. "She don't know you yet." The ewe eyed Toddy with suspicion and began to move away, much to the distress of the lamb, who wobbled after her, crying as it went. Toddy made to run after them, but Jip caught him around the waist. "Wait here. See—she's a bit skittish. You're so big. She's feared you might hurt her little one."

"Me?" Toddy was thrilled with being big and scary. "Me?"

"Ehyuh. You got to be still as a rabbit."

"Awright," he whispered, putting his finger to his lips.

"Jest watch. See—that old sheep, she loves her baby jest like—jest like your ma loves hers."

Toddy stuck out his bottom lip.

"Wal, you're right. She does have a new one now. But that's the way with mothers. This ewe will have another next year. And this little one will be big then—like you—running and playing on his own."

There was a grunt behind them. Jip turned to see Lucy standing nearby. She had come after all. Was he supposed to pretend not to notice? Lucy was a contrary creature. He didn't want to start her off by saying the wrong thing.

"All right, Toddy, that's one new lamb. Can you count one?"

The child nodded solemnly, sticking up an index finger.

"Good for you." Jip took his hand. "Now we'll walk quiet so's not to scare them and see if there be any more. This here one's jest fine, ain't he? We can leave him to his ma for now."

There were no more new ones that morning. The rest of the ewes seemed to be taking their own sweet time this year. Jip made a wide circle so as not to bump into Lucy and walked Toddy back to the farmhouse. It was egg-gathering time, and Jip didn't want Sheldon to think he had forgotten. He didn't want Sheldon getting jealous of the attention he was giving to the newcomers. For a long time it had been just Jip and Sheldon, and now it was Jip and Put and Jip and Toddy. Sheldon had already complained about too many Jip and somebody elses.

Jip took Toddy into his ma and began to look for Sheldon, who was nowhere to be seen. He made another circuit around the house and yard to make sure. Then he heard the squawks and protests from the henhouse. Oh, Sheldon, don't go and try to gather them eggs on your own.

He ran to the henhouse, opening the door to find a terrified Sheldon with an angry brown hen crowning his skull. She was flapping her wings and pecking at his sparse hair and pale head. In Sheldon's big hand was a smashed egg, the yellow running down through his fingers and onto his shirtfront.

"Jip! Help me!"

"Oh, Sheldon," Jip said. He reached up and lifted off the angry hen, smoothing her feathers and shushing her furious *arks* until they subsided into annoyed clucks. He placed her gently into her usual nesting box.

"Arabella don't like me," Sheldon said.

"Ah, it ain't that, Sheldon. I think you was jest too quick for her. Scairt her, that's all."

"Scairt me."

"Yeah. Works both ways, I reckon." Jip grinned up at his friend. The poor fellow was close to tears. "How 'bout you put that mess down and we clean you up?"

Sheldon looked unhappily at the smashed eggshell and the yellow goo on his hands and shirt.

"Outside—where the stink won't matter. I guess we better go wash you at the pump. Then we'll gather up the rest of these eggs."

"Will you help me, Jip?"

"Sure. You and me together, Sheldon, I promise."

Lucy was standing just outside the henhouse door. She was pretending to study the empty road as they came out, so he didn't speak to her.

5

An Infinitesimal Chance

The last frost of May had whitened the fields and gone. By five in the morning the sun had topped the eastern hills, turning Deacon Avery's distant woods and sugar bush into a dozen dancing shades of green. Bees hummed in the clover, and the smell of it, mingled in the fresh grass, was more intoxicating to Jip than a drink of strong spirits. In June the world was made new.

The time for planting had come. This year Jip was tall enough and strong enough to grasp the handles of the plow, so it was Sheldon who stood by the horse's head, urging him through the still-damp earth. Jip was full of plans. He would organize all the able-bodied and get the potatoes, corn, beans, squash, and turnips into the fields as early as possible.

In his list of able-bodied he excluded the Lymans. The mister always managed a trip away whenever hard work beckoned and the missus claimed kitchen duties. That usually left just him and Sheldon, but Put hadn't had a bad spell for weeks. He might help, and so might Lucy and Mrs. Wilkens, if he could persuade them. He eased them into it by putting Toddy to work straight off, dropping the sprouted potato eyes into the holes Jip had dug.

Lucy watched. Then she took the hoe from Jip's hands. "I can do that," she said. "It ain't hard."

"Nah," said Jip. "But it's beyond Sheldon, I fear. I'm obliged to you."

He and Sheldon ("Just you and me, Jip?") started on the corn hills. He had to keep reminding Sheldon how many seed kernels to drop into each hill. Sheldon liked the idea of counting. The actual task was a bit daunting.

At length the weather drew nearly the whole household outdoors. It was such a blue heaven of a day. Mrs. Wilkens handed the baby over to Berthie, and she began to plant the beans.

Put took over the squash, and later, when Toddy nearly fell asleep between the rows, Put and Lucy planted more potatoes. Jip and Sheldon sowed the oats. Soon all the crops were put in, and weary but satisfied, the gardeners could welcome the early summer rain when it came.

Only Jip kept working through the rainy days. He fed the chickens, milked the cow, checked the sheep. Late one afternoon, he found the last lamb, the one the oldest ewe had been carrying, lying dead and sodden, its mother bleating plaintively nearby. He got the shovel and buried it, hoping no one would ask after it, especially Toddy.

His heart heavy as his sopping clothes, he replaced the shovel and fetched the bucket for milking.

"Good evening, Jip. I may call you Jip, may I not?" The stranger was leaning against the barn door, holding a huge black umbrella over his head, blocking the entrance with his body.

"I don't know you," Jip said, his lips and throat suddenly dry, though his head and body were dripping wet.

"No, not yet." The stranger flashed a gold tooth. "But perhaps I know you."

"I got to do my chores."

The stranger moved a step sideways, bobbing the umbrella in a sort of nod. "By all means."

Jip passed the man close enough to feel the drips off the edge of the umbrella on his own head. The stranger folded it carefully and followed Jip, closing the door after himself.

In the shadowed gloom of the small barn, Jip took his stool off its peg and sidled under Bonnie's flank. Behind him, the man leaned against the timbered barn wall. Jip could feel the stranger's eyes boring into his back.

For a while—a long anxious while—the only sounds were the *plinking* of milk into the pail and the rattling of rain on the tin roof. Once the stranger cleared his throat. Jip's shoulders tensed, but the man said nothing. The pail was nearly full and the udder dry when Jip broke the silence. He couldn't stand those rabbit-pellet eyes on his shoulder blades.

"Jest what is it you want from me?"

"Want? My dear boy, what a question."

"Then how come you keep hanging 'round, poking your nose here?" He knew how rude he sounded, but he couldn't help it.

The man gave a low chuckle. "My boy, you misjudge me. I only want your good."

Jip didn't answer. He was sure the man wanted his good about as much as a hawk wants the good of a chick.

"But in order to help you—I need a little more information."

"What kind of information?" Hadn't Mrs. Lyman told him all there was to tell?

"I need to know if you might be a certain person I am seeking—have been seeking for quite some time."

Jip waited, hardly breathing. He had a sense that if he waited, the man would tell him more than he meant to. Put had said to be wary. If he was ever to take Put's advice, it was now.

The stranger continued. "A certain gentleman of my acquaintance, I might say, a warm acquaintance, even a friend—" Jip gritted his teeth to keep back his impatience "—this friend of whom I speak had the tragic misfortune to lose his only son—" The man paused. He's trying to flimflam me, Jip decided. That fake voice, like a peddler fixing to sell you something you don't want.

"This gentleman," the stranger went on, "was told that the boy was dead, but though he mourned, indeed, put up a marker, an impressive piece of marble, in the graveyard to commemorate the child—"

Jip had long since given up milking, but he didn't leave the stool. The puzzled Bonnie stamped about a bit and whipped her tail. Jip moved the bucket out of danger and patted the brown flank to tell Bonnie to move on.

The stranger came around to face Jip. He was no more than two arm's lengths away, one hand resting on his folded umbrella, as though it were a gentleman's walking stick.

He smiled down on Jip. "Yes, my boy, an impressive monument it is." Jip looked away. That smile gave him the shivering tremblies for sure. "Then, recently"—he poked at a bit of straw with the metal tip of his umbrella—"a rumor reached my friend's ears that his lost child might not be dead after all." He stopped to let the weight of these words sink in to his listener. Not a peddler, Jip thought, one of those tricksters that sell potions in the traveling medicine show.

"Imagine, if you can, our gentleman's consternation. Could it be that the son he mourned was alive?" The pause this time pulsated with the pounding rain. "How could he be sure? Perhaps fate was playing a cruel joke. Was it only a false hope that would raise his broken spirit, only to dash it into a despair far deeper and darker than even the first had been?"

Despite his resolution, something stirred in Jip's heart. It was a scene he had imagined—that sorrowing parent. He stiffened as the man continued.

"Thus, before he revealed himself to this youth, he must make utterly sure. The chance that his son was alive was so small—infinitesimal indeed—yet if there was any chance however obscure, he must pursue it to the end. And thus—" Here he flourished the umbrella, making Bonnie moo in alarm. He glanced her way, but went determinedly on. "And thus," he said grandly, "am I come."

Jip wished he had not sent Bonnie back to her stall. He longed for the protection of her warm flank between himself and this strange messenger. The thought that he might have a loving parent far away, searching for him, yearning for him—that was a daydream he'd long entertained—but for *that* parent to have sent *this* messenger . . .

Jip studied the figure before him: the narrow head with the pellet eyes, the large-brimmed hat, the tight, thin lips flashing a gold-toothed smile, the long narrow hand with almost pointed nails. It was not the figure, not the hand of an honest working man.

"Well, Jip?"

The boy shook his head. "No use," he mumbled. "I can't help you—nor him what sent you."

"I don't take your meaning."

"Meaning? Meaning I can't remember nothing before I come to this place. It's my home and is likely to remain so for some years to come."

The man lowered his head as if to search Jip's face. "And you are *satisfied* that it remain so? Even when there may be a chance"—he gave a little laugh—"however infinitesimal, that you are meant for something else, something far better"—once more he waved the point of the umbrella about him at the plank boards of the barn—"than *this*?"

Jip got to his feet and picked up the milk pail and stool. He walked deliberately to the peg and hung the stool, then started toward the now unguarded door. "Looks like I'd better be satisfied, don't it?" he said over his shoulder. "Seeings how that's the way things is." He slipped a wooden cover over the open pail, and, willing himself not to look back at the stranger again, he left the barn, carrying the milk through the rain to the safety of the kitchen.

6

All Is Well

The sheep shearers came and went. Summer had truly begun. Jip hardly had time to think about the stranger's visit, and when he did, it was with some relief that he had so easily rid himself of that sinister shadow. And yet, there was a niggling tug at the shirtsleeve of his mind. Suppose there was a chance—and the stranger had emphasized it was infinitesimal (which Jip understood to mean hardly any chance at all)—suppose, given that fleabite of a chance, Jip had been too quick to dismiss the stranger?

Jest because I didn't like the cut of the man. After all *he* ain't the lonely parent longing for his lost boy. And whatever I am or am not, I got to be somebody's lost boy. I wasn't born on the West Hill Road. I jest fell off a wagon there. Whose wagon? And *why* didn't no one come back to look for me? Wouldn't parents worthy of the name come looking? Wouldn't they, like the Good Shepherd in the Gospel, search the earth high and low until they found their lamb what was lost? I would, and my lambs is jest dumb beasts, not a human boy made in the image of God.

He should have asked the stranger straight out why it

47

was that this mysterious gentleman thought even infinitesimally that he, Jip, might be his lost son. Jip remembered that he had been careful not to mention the wagon to the stranger—but Mrs. Lyman was sure to have. She pure loved to tell that tale.

He tried to figure out a way to ask her about that time she'd shared tea with the stranger in the kitchen—the time she never seemed to have mentioned to the mister. Was it somehow connected to the man's popping up at the barn? It had to have been. Well, maybe she told Mr. Lyman about it later, out of Jip's hearing. Maybe she didn't want to mention it in front of the residents. Maybe.

Summer agreed with Put. Like all the plants and animals and residents, the old man was at his best in the long hours of warm sunlight. He was a great help in the farmwork, and Mrs. Wilkens and Lucy took orders from him much better than they did from Jip. Mr. Lyman, true to his nature, was seldom about when there was work to be done. If he knew the overseer was due to call, then he'd put on his old clothes and scurry out to the fields, his sleeves rolled above his elbows, yelling and ordering everyone about, even Berthie and the old ones.

Jip was too soft to make the old ones come to the fields. Besides, they grumbled more than they worked. But Mr. Lyman made a great show of their turning out to Mr. Flint, saying how *all* the residents—men, women, children, simpletons, and lunatics—all were made to bear their fair share of the load.

"Catch him once bending that fat back," Berthie mumbled as she pretended to bend her own. She waited until Mr. Lyman had led the overseer into the parlor for a mug of cider. Then she held up six beans. Jip couldn't help counting—there were exactly six in her gnarled hand when Berthie called out to him, "I'm like to faint in this sun, Jip boy. I jest cannot keep up this slavery at my age."

"All right, Berthie. Take in what you've picked to Mrs. Lyman. You can help her out in the kitchen. Hold the baby or something," though the baby was hardly content to sit on anyone's lap for long these days.

One by one the old ones, except for Put, found some excuse to leave the field. Put, Mrs. Wilkens, Lucy, Sheldon, and, of course, Jip kept on. Even Toddy dodged about pulling a bean now and again, running to Jip for praise each time.

It was shameful to think, much less say, but Jip was nearly glad that Abijah Wilkens had left his family penniless and doomed them to life on the town farm. Toddy was dearer to Jip than any of the animals, and though Mrs. Wilkens was sharpish and Lucy sullen, they hoed and weeded and picked with a will, making life much easier for Jip. The garden was larger and better this year than he and Sheldon had ever managed on their own. The result would be better eating for them all.

And Put. No one worked harder than he. At first Mr. Lyman had resisted the idea that he be let out of the cage to work in the garden and fields.

"I'll be responsible," Jip promised, knowing full well that if Put had one of his spells, four grown men could hardly handle him.

But with the summer, Put seemed so well, so unlike

the raving madman that had arrived down the muddy road three months ago. Jip dared to hope that his friend (he could hardly think of him as the lunatic now) was healed. He ventured to mention the fact.

Put shook his head. "It comes and goes, Jip. I've had my hopes before, and . . ."

"Do you know when it's coming on, Put? Or do it grab you sudden like when you ain't expecting?"

"I don't know, Jip. It seems to grab me without warning. But you might be able to tell."

"How's that?"

"I might start to say something that sounds right sensible to me—but to you is strange like. If you hear words out of my mouth that don't make full sense, you need to lock me up fast. Don't wait, you hear?"

"I won't, Put."

"Now you got to promise me—you won't wait to see if it's a passing thing. Promise, now?"

"I promise you." And on the strength of that solemn promise, he took responsibility for Put's freedom.

Toddy loved Put. He begged Put to carry him and sing and play the pipe for him. Put would sing his own and Toddy's favorite song over and over.

"Again!" Toddy would cry.

And, as though he had not already sung it half a dozen times, Old Put would stroke Toddy's fair hair and sing as sweetly as the hermit thrush of midsummer:

"What's this that steals, that steals upon my frame?
Is it death, is it death?
That soon will quench, will quench this mortal flame,

Is it death? is it death?
If this be death, I soon shall be
From ev'ry pain and sorrow free.
I shall the King of glory see,
All is well, all is well!"

Even though it was a song wholeheartedly dedicated to dying, it was somehow not a sad song. Not the way Put sang it. When he got to the line "If this be death," he'd throw back his hoary head. With his eyes fixed on the sky, he'd sing out like the sight of death was a pleasure—like a colt bolting for the spring pasture.

"More!" said Toddy. And Put always obliged.

"Weep not, my friends, my friends weep not for me,
All is well, all is well!
My sins forgiv'n, forgiv'n and I am free,
All is well, all is well!
There's not a cloud that doth arise,
To hide my Jesus from my eyes.
I soon shall mount the upper skies,
All is well, all is well!"

He sang on through "tune your harps" and "glittering crown," right on to the "blood-washed throng" and their hallelujahs. But on every verse, the words he sang most joyfully were, "All is well, all is well."

Did he really think so? Put with his lunatic mind that lay in wait like a mountain cat, ready to leap down and seize him? Put saw Jip listening and pondering.

"Don't you like Toddy's song?" he asked.

"It's a purty tune."

"Yes," said Put. "I reckon them words seems queer to you at your age. But think on me—how welcome that day—when I'm 'from ev'ry pain and sorrow free,' and 'all, all is peace and joy divine.' "

"Don't you like it down here with us, jest a little bit?"

Put reached out the hand that so often blessed Toddy's head and touched Jip's shoulder. "Of such is the kingdom of heaven," he said softly.

Jip couldn't figure what Put meant by that, but he smiled anyway. He knew it meant somehow that Put thought that he, Jip, had eased the pain and sorrow of this earth, if only a mite.

Was it Jip's fancy, or was it the way life ran, that whenever things were going well, Mr. Lyman would figure out a way to mess them up? At any rate, along about the third week of July he called Jip into the parlor.

"I've got more than enough help on the farm now, boy."

Jip waited. Was Lyman going to send him back to Slaytor's or some other cursed place? He knew the next sentence was leading to no good before it was uttered.

"But we're cash poor, boy. Nothing to show for all my work on this place. The residents will eat up the crops faster than I can grow them or pick them. And the price we got for that paltry show of wool hardly paid for the shearers. We need for someone around here to earn real cash money. Not just eat up all the profits."

Jip held himself still. He had to be that someone. Who else of all the old, weak, young, female, or simple could Lyman mean?

"Sheldon, now . . ."

Sheldon? Sheldon had to have a keeper—someone right beside him to tell him every minute what to do the next minute.

"He's strong as a mule. He can pick up a hundred-pound sheep without breathing hard."

"Yes, but—"

"I've settled it with Avery. He's agreed to take Sheldon on at the quarry. They won't pay him much at first, but when he gets the hang of it . . ."

Sheldon? Sheldon was more like to hang himself in the tangle.

"There's lots of men don't take to quarry work. Say that all that rock blasting makes their brains rattle. But that won't bother Sheldon none. He don't have enough in the upper story to rattle." The manager tapped his head, laughing at his own joke.

A chill went through Jip. He saw the huge granite rocks that must be hauled, heard the blast, and felt in his bones the thundering down of rubble when the blasting went awry. A man needed enough sense to take proper care in a place like that.

"You walk him over in the morning, soon as you're done milking. After that, he can find his own way."

"He can find the way himself anytime," Jip said quietly. "That's not my worry, sir. It's what he won't figure out after that you gotta think to, Mr. Lyman."

"Oh, he got enough sense to haul rock," Lyman said, waving Jip out of the room.

Sheldon was so proud, Jip pushed his own anxiety as far away as he could.

"I have me a lunch pail, Jip," he said. "With bread and cheese. And a apple."

"That's fine, Sheldon."

"And a water jug."

"Good, Sheldon. For when you're thirsty."

"I'm gonna earn cash money for the farm. I ain't never earned cash money before."

"I guess I ain't either. To speak of."

"You ain't?"

"Nah. I'm just a half-growed boy."

"You're a good boy."

"Sheldon . . ." How could he make him understand without scaring him? "Sheldon, you got to listen real careful to what they tell you over to the quarry."

"I will." But Sheldon wasn't paying attention. He was taking his food and the water jug out of the pail and putting them back in again, smiling at each item as he rearranged it.

"I mean it, Sheldon. Listen to me. If they say 'do this' or 'don't do that,' you got to do exactly what they say. That's dangerous work over there."

"Man's work," Sheldon said proudly, glancing down again at the shiny pail.

"Yeah. And a man don't never take his mind off what he's doing. Not at the quarry. You hear me?"

"I hear. I do what they tell me."

"Promise me, Sheldon?"

"I told you I would, Jip."

From the edge of the garden, Jip watched the dying sun turn the trees, fields, and granite trough on Avery's land to burnished gold. Milking and supper were done and still no Sheldon. Lucy and Toddy had been asleep for an hour when Jip finally spied Sheldon's bent figure coming slowly over the pasture hill. He ran to meet him. "How was it, Sheldon?"

"Man's work, Jip."

"Are you terrible tired?"

"I hurt all over, Jip."

"Wal, you been working mighty long and hard, Sheldon, and it's heavy work. If it's too much for you, I can tell Mr. Lyman and—"

"No! I want to go every day. They need me." He straightened up, as though remembering his importance. How he was the only resident able to earn cash money for them all.

So Jip kept silent. Only to Put did he voice his fears. "It worries me silly, Put. I don't think Sheldon's got the sense to be scairt."

"Well, some say it's fearsome work. Me, I like it better than farming."

"I never knew you was a stone man, Put."

"Not for long. One of my spells come upon me. They clapped irons on me and took me away. I was a danger to all, they said."

"Will Sheldon be a danger to all, you think?"

"Not to all. But perhaps to his poor young self."

Jip shivered at the words, but the days went by, and Sheldon came home every night at dusk, tired but unfailingly proud. Jip's mind loosened its grip on worry. Sheldon was doing fine. No need for Jip to cluck around him like an anxious mother hen.

Later, he couldn't remember what he actually heard and what he imagined, but forever afterward the unexpected rattle of a wagon on the road was joined with Put's voice lifted in Toddy's song:

"Hark! hark! my Lord, my Lord and Master's voice,
Calls away, calls away!"

It was noon. A strange time for callers. *Merciful God.* Jip ran toward the wagon. On the bench beside the driver sat Deacon Avery, silent and grim as granite. Jip raced alongside, not tall enough to see over the sides to find what in his heart he knew lay in the wagon bed.

"What is it, Mr. Avery? What're you bringing over here?" he cried.

The driver flicked his whip in annoyance and urged the horses on, leaving the boy standing in the road.

As Jip trudged back up to the house, his whole body so heavy he could scarcely make it move, Mr. Lyman came out the door and the deacon began yelling at him.

"Lyman, come here and look at what you did!"

"What is it, Mr. Avery?"

"Your idjit boy—what's left of him. It's a miracle he killed no more'n his own stupid self."

"You wanted him," Lyman answered hotly. "I wouldn't have sent him else. I could hardly spare him. One of my best hands. And you return nothing to me but a funeral expense, which, heaven help me, I will charge to your account!"

"You dare and I will make it plain to Mr. Flint that it was an idjit you sent when I asked for strong labor."

The argument buzzed around Jip's head like hornets on attack. He flung his arm up as though to ward off the sting of the words. Then while they still yelled, he climbed up into the wagon to look upon what was left of his friend.

Is it death, is it death?

Oh, if he could only believe that poor Sheldon was now from every pain and sorrow free, but it was hard to imagine the saints on high tuning their harps for Sheldon's entrance through the gates of pearl. Or Sheldon wearing a glittering crown singing hallelujahs with the blood-washed throng.

He threw his warm young body across the piece of canvas that covered the already cold one of his friend and sobbed as he never had in all his memory.

7

Jordan's Dark Waters

The Board of Selectmen convened and solemnly determined that Deacon Avery, not the town or the town farm, must pay for Sheldon's funeral. This meant that the residents could see Sheldon out with a proper service—not the quick graveside drop allotted most of the town farm's deceased members.

There was a great discussion as to whether Put should be allowed to attend. In the end, Mr. Lyman decreed that he must stay behind, safely padlocked in the cage, with Mrs. Lyman lurking within earshot from the kitchen.

"But I'll guarantee him," Jip protested. "He ought to be there."

"The townsfolk know him for a lunatic. They'd not credit such a guarantee."

"It's all right, Jip," Put said. "You and Toddy sing loud for me."

"You know I can't sing, Put."

"Yes, you can. There's music inside you, Jip. You just got to let it out."

They didn't sing "All Is Well" at Sheldon's funeral. Jip wished they had. He was trying so hard to cling tight to a picture of Sheldon with all those harps in heaven. Instead, they sang some doleful hymn about when "Jordan's waters encompass me 'round." It gave Jip the chills. He didn't want to think of icy waters closing over Sheldon's sweet, simple face. He wanted to think of Sheldon singing with the angels, "All is well!"

Rather than sitting in the rear of the sanctuary where they were usually relegated, the residents huddled together in a little clump in the first two rows. Jip sat next to Toddy and held his small soft hand. With his other hand, Toddy stroked Jip's arm. It was a comfort to have someone taking care for him even if that someone was a baby no more than four.

Mr. Lyman should have let Put come. There were hardly any citizens there to frighten or offend. Who but Sheldon's fellow paupers would want to mourn the short life of a poor farm simpleton? Never mind. Sheldon would be proud to have a proper funeral with hymns and prayers and even a word from Reverend Goodrich about how Jesus loved Sheldon. "Suffer the little children to come unto me," Jesus had said, and the preacher told how Sheldon in his simple mind was like a little child who had gone to Jesus and no one should grieve overmuch.

Reverend Goodrich, looking the residents right in the eyes as he spoke, gave a pretty sermon, but Jip was glad Sheldon hadn't heard it. He had been monstrous proud to be a workingman at last. That was what had killed him—not the little child part, but the wanting so hard to be a man part.

It was soon over. When Reverend Goodrich pronounced the blessing, they all stood up. Jip was the only resident there strong enough to help carry the coffin but he was too short, so Reverend Goodrich had enlisted six townsmen to hoist Sheldon's remains to their shoulders. Since the residents were all the family Sheldon had, they shuffled down the aisle right after the pallbearers. Toddy still clung to Jip's hand. Neither of them cried. Only Old Berthie cried—almost like the town was paying her to. She hadn't had any time for Sheldon when he was alive, but now she sobbed into her big handkerchief as if she'd lost her only son. Well, it was fitting that someone cry and carry on. Sheldon was due at least that.

Walking home with the able-bodied, which these days meant himself and the Wilkens family, Jip's mind flicked back and forth—from Sheldon gathering eggs and plowing to Sheldon's broken body and the mound of earth in the churchyard.

"Carry me, Jip?"

Jip hoisted the boy to his shoulders.

"Now," he commanded, "sing."

"I can't sing, Toddy. You got to ask Put for music."

"No, you. I want blood-washed frong."

Jip had heard the words so often that he knew them by heart, but they were all about death and dying, and he longed for a little rest from death.

Toddy pounded Jip's head with his fist. "Blood-washed frong!" he cried. "Sing!"

So Jip began:

> "Hail, hail! all, hail, all hail! ye blood-washed throng,
> Saved by grace, saved by grace!

I come to join, to join your rapturous song,
Saved by grace, saved by grace,
All, all is peace and joy divine,
And heaven and glory now are mine,
Loud hallelujahs to the Lamb,
All is well, all is well!"

Toddy chimed in on the "blood-washed frong" and shouted out the "All is well."

"Again!" he cried.

"Do you really think Sheldon is singing hallelujahs with the angels?" Lucy hadn't said a word to him all morning. Now she was looking at him, asking the very question he longed to ask himself.

"I reckon," was all he could say. Secretly he hoped that heaven would have real lambs, too. Not just the Lamb of God. He knew sheep for what they were—stubborn and stupid—but he did love them. Heaven with only the blood-washed throng and no dumb creatures would be a mighty lonesome place.

He reported all the doings of the service to Put, including Lucy's question. "Do you think Sheldon is in heaven, Put? I don't care about the harps and such—jest that he's someplace where somebody will look on him like a man. He wanted to be a full man so bad."

"All is well, Jip. That's all I know."

"I reckon that's enough."

Somehow he was not surprised when he went into the barn that night and found the stranger there waiting.

"Didn't I tell you I was satisfied with how things is?

Why'd you come back to pester me?" He knew he was being rude to his elders, but the man didn't follow any rules Jip knew. "Don't you have more important things than me?"

The stranger smiled, stretching his thin lips back, like a snake fixing to strike. "Oh, I'm always traveling about on important business," he said. "But I was passing through, and I figured you'd had some time to think on what I said to you."

"You was the one who said the chance was in-infinitesimal. Even I know what that means." (He'd checked with Put to make sure.) "It means there ain't hardly no chance a-tall."

"Clever boy, aren't you?" He smiled again. "But don't you want to make sure? Absolutely sure?"

Jip got the stool and clucked at the nervous Bonnie to quiet her so he could begin milking.

"No curiosity even?"

Jip milked steadily, pretending to ignore the question.

"No? Well, a certain other party is curious. A certain very important party."

Despite all his resolution, a little thrill went down Jip's backbone. But he kept a hold on himself. He wasn't about to let the varmint take him for a sleigh ride in summer.

"He just asks I bring you to a place where he can see you for himself. If you aren't the one he's been looking for, he'll never even speak to you—but if you are . . ."

"Why don't he just come and talk to me like the gentleman you say he is? Why's he scairt to meet me face-to-face?"

"It's far more complicated than you could understand, my boy."

"Then it's far too complicated for me to bother with."

The man was quiet for a while, as though listening to the barn sounds—the *coos* from the rafters, the splash of the milk into the pail. From the house, Jip could hear Put's voice lifted up in singing. Toddy must have gone begging to the cage room.

"You got my leave to go—return to your important business."

But the stranger wasn't listening to Jip. He was listening to something else, his tiny eyes intent. "What's that?" he asked in a kind of a whisper.

" 'Is it death? Is it death?' " sang the sweet tenor voice.

"Oh," Jip said as casual as you please. "That's nothing. Jest our lunatic. He sings a lot."

"Your lunatic?"

"Ehyuh. We keeps him in a cage, mostly."

"He's dangerous, then?"

This was getting to be fun. "Nah. Not so long as he's in his cage. It's pretty strong. I don't think he could bust out. Me and our idjit built it. He's never broke out—yit."

The man moistened his thin lips. "I'd think," he began, trying to smile, but not quite managing, "I'd think you'd welcome a chance to leave this place."

"Oh, they counts on me here. I'm the only one what can keep the lunatic calmed down a-tall. I don't know what was to happen if I weren't here. I reckon he'd take it hard if someone was to start picking on me." Jip looked up and made himself smile right at the stranger. "You know how lunatics is," he said deliberately.

The stranger blanched. He does know, Jip realized. He's scairt to death. Not of Put, but of someone else—someone at another time and place. The man opened his mouth, then closed it again. He pulled his hat down firmly before he spoke. "I'll—I'll be back, though it may be some time. Business all over the area, you know. Keeps me—haha—hopping. Meantime, you think on what I've said, my boy."

The man was stumbling over himself to get out of there. He was truly terrified. Had it been anyone else, Jip might have felt sorry for him. But not for the stranger. Jip was too relieved to have some protection against the man. He felt a little ashamed of the way he had talked about his friend, but Put wouldn't mind.

He watched the stranger's hurried retreat, humming along with Put's song. Did he have music in him like Put said? He almost believed it. Some forgotten tune lapped against the landscape of his mind like little waves in a pond disturbed by a pebble.

What a strange day. Jordan's waters washing over Sheldon. Jordan's waters. He shivered. That was the pebble that had disturbed his pond—some song about Jordan he could no longer remember.

With a sigh, he hung up his stool and left the barn. The pail was full. Even with all the distractions, Bonnie had done her best for him. Creatures was so kindly. Wouldn't God want them in heaven? They'd be so much more use to Him than the blood-washed throng strumming around on their harps.

"Who was that man?"

Jip jumped like a cat from the wood box.

"Lucy? What you doing out here?"

"I can come out if I want. It's a poor farm, not a jail."

"You jest gave me a start. That's all."

"Who was that man you was talking to in the barn?"

"I don't know."

"What do you mean, you don't know? You was talking away to him. I heard you."

"I never took you for a sneak." She bristled at that, so he hurried on. "It ain't— The truth is I don't know. He claims he might know something about me. From before."

"Oh? Don't you want to find out?"

"Yeah, sure, I do. But he strikes me 'bout as honest as a fox in a henhouse. He don't want my good—whatever it is he wants. So I told him to leave me be."

She fell in beside him, just as though they were friends, as if they were used to talking together about their problems. Jip liked the feeling. "Put got rid of him for me."

"Put? Put's in his cage, singing to Toddy."

"I know. But when Put commenced to singing, the feller turned white as death."

Lucy giggled. "He was just singing that old song Toddy begs for."

"I know. But it struck me I should kind of decorate it for him—seeing's he was already mighty anxious. I told him how it was jest our lunatic what we keep in a cage— who ain't ever busted out—yit."

She threw back her head and laughed out loud. It was music to Jip. He watched her, then said softly, "That was nice. People don't laugh much here on the farm."

"Ain't much to laugh about," she said, sobering. "I know people say my pa was a worthless drunk, but he could make me laugh."

"You ain't worthless if you can make a person laugh."

She cocked her head. "You ain't, are you?" She opened the kitchen door for him and held it. "He weren't worthless like they say."

"No," said Jip. "Sometimes I wonder at people's ignorance. They said Sheldon was an idjit boy and Put a lunatic. We know better than that and we're only children."

She smiled her thanks to him and later held the cheesecloth tight over the bowl as he poured the milk through to strain it. Lucy was going to be his friend. He felt an easing of the pain that Sheldon's death had pressed upon his heart.

8

To School

Harvest well past, Mrs. Wilkens took it in her head that Lucy should go to school. The closest common school was beyond Avery's—near to a three-mile walk, and Lucy had no interest either in that much exertion or in once again enduring the scorn of her peers. When she'd attended school in the village, she'd been known as the drunkard's daughter. She didn't figure that being a child of the poor farm would raise her status at the district school. But if Jip were to go as well . . .

So Mrs. Wilkens began to work on the manager to send Jip, too. For his own part, Jip had no leisure to waste in the pursuit of education. He'd tried before, but it hadn't been worth the chase. The building was ramshackle, the pupils unruly, and the teacher inept. He had quickly concluded, much to Mr. Lyman's relief, that learning was not for the likes of him.

But last summer between shearing and haying, the farmers in the district had built a new schoolhouse, twenty-two by twenty-eight feet, put in new outhouses, cleaned out the spring and covered it with a small springhouse, and, wonder of wonders, hired a female teacher with a college education. When Mrs. Wilkens got wind of that she was determined for Lucy to come under the influence of the only college-educated woman in the county. And if Lucy wasn't willing to go on her own, then there was nothing for it but that Jip should go, too. Besides, it would be dusk before school let out. She'd feel safer if Lucy didn't have such a long walk alone.

"We tried him at schooling," Mr. Lyman said. "He didn't take to it. Maybe he hit his head when he fell off the gypsy wagon. Leastways he don't have the mind for letters now."

"Oh, he's bright enough," Mrs. Wilkens countered. "He practically runs this place." Her eyes narrowed. "That's the problem, ain't it? Send him to school, the farm collapses."

"I run this farm, if you please, Mrs. Wilkens. It don't depend on no sniveling boy."

"Then he can go to school with my Lucy—like the law says." She was not a great lover of the law, but she didn't mind invoking it when it suited her purpose.

"If the boy ain't mentally fit—"

"Oh, the boy's fit enough. Might be the school weren't fit. I hear tell the big Brackett boys run off that no-count schoolmaster they hired last year. Some teacher what lets himself be run off by his own pupils."

"There's no textbooks to send with him—with either of them."

"So be it," she said. "We can't conjure books out of the air. The new teacher will have to figure something."

On the second Monday of November, a day so warm that the light snow of the previous day had melted by noon, Jip and Lucy set off for the new schoolhouse.

Mrs. Wilkens had been mighty pleased. She had made

Lucy a new dress, cut down from one of her own Sunday outfits. "There," she'd said, smoothing down Lucy's wide white collar. "You look fine. Won't nobody mock my girl at the new school."

Holding tight to the lunch pail he'd inherited from Sheldon, his feet lost inside Sheldon's work boots, Jip waited for Lucy's mother to finish her fussing. She was patting and smoothing Lucy's clothes like a mother cat licking up her scrawny kitten. A pang went though him. Mrs. Wilkens had a sharp tongue and a ready slap, but under it all she cared for her children. Somewhere, sometime he'd had a mother. It stood to reason. Every creature has a dam, a ewe, a cow to lick it to life and nose it fondly. But somehow he had trouble imagining himself with one. It was like he was born the day he fell off the back of that wagon. Even the stranger had failed to mention a mother—only a mysterious maybe of a father. And an infinitesimal chance even of that. He shrugged away the useless thoughts. "If we're going to go, Lucy, best we be going."

Lucy pulled loose from her mother and trailed after him across the rolling fields. "Hey," she said when his long strides took him too far ahead, "wait for me." He turned at the top of a hill to let her catch up, wriggling his toes. Mrs. Wilkens would not hear of his going to school barefoot. "My ma says it will be different at the new school, but I don't believe her."

"What you mean, different?"

"They mocked me in the village school—on account of my pa. She said wouldn't nobody mock me at the new school. But they will. They'll mock me on account of my being from the town farm."

He didn't know how to comfort her. She was probably right. The others would mock them. He could remember learning that much in school. They walked along in silence, crossing the pastures and fields going south. Ahead loomed the expansive scar in the earth that Avery called his stone quarry. It was surrounded by hills of rubble—the waste rock from the hacking and blasting of the stately granite. All this for a stone step or lintel or foundation block. As a little boy, gazing from the pasture, that distant trough of bare rock had seemed beautiful to Jip. He hadn't thought of it as a scar in the green hills. Close as he was now, he could see the gouges of the cutting tools and the blackened rock where the dynamite had blasted out the heart of the stone. It was that terrible black powder that had taken Sheldon from him. He shuddered. "Let's drop down to the road now, Lucy."

"Does it scare you? Knowing Sheldon died up here?"

He didn't answer. Perhaps it did. At any rate they swung down to the road and gave the granite trough and its little mountains of waste a wide berth. There was no one working there this morning. Avery must have his men felling wood up on the mountain. The man always had a half-dozen enterprises going. And there was less blasting lately. The selectmen had warned Avery to take care after Sheldon's death. They didn't want the quarry leaving any widows and orphans to the care of the town. A blessing Sheldon had been an idiot, leaving no dependents, they said.

The schoolhouse was a warm red ocher in the sunshine. Smoke poured from the chimney at the far end.

The yard was empty, the white door was closed. "We're late!" Lucy said. Jip licked his lips and pushed at the door. Lucy was following so close he could feel her warm breath on his neck. Suddenly the door gave way, tumbling them into the room. In the dimmer light inside, it took a minute for Jip's eyes to adjust to the scene. All he knew was that everyone was staring at them. There was a murmur of whispered laughter. He straightened as tall as he could and fixed his eyes on the front. There was a huge potbellied stove in the center. To the right of the stove was the teacher's desk. The teacher was standing behind it. She was tall for a woman and more angular than rounded. Her hair was pulled back as though she meant a stern face, but her eyes were smiling at him.

"I'd say 'come in,' but you seem to have managed that on your own. However, you could help by closing the door."

Jip reddened, much to the delight of the three large Brackett brothers sitting just to his left on the last bench. He turned quickly to obey, his mind working fast. He felt a need to master the laws inside this small kingdom. There were fewer than twenty pupils, boys on the left, girls on the right. The distance from the teacher's desk seemed to be determined by the size of the student— little ones sat on the front benches, biggest ones on the back. But all were under the watchful eye of a single ruler. For she was like a queen—no fancy dress or crown but surely in command. Her voice was low-pitched, but you could hear each word clear across the space of the room.

Jip and Lucy still hesitated in the aisle. Where should they sit? There seemed to be no vacant places on the back two rows, among the students closest to their own size. And the children on the front two rows were hardly larger than Toddy.

"Just put your lunch pails in the cupboard over there beside the chimney and then take a seat down here at the front for now," she said. "I'm still trying to sort out where everyone belongs." Teacher (for no one ever called her by any other name) soon determined that Lucy, who could read aloud a beginning primer with very little difficulty, would sit in the second row with children only a bit smaller than herself. To his immense relief, Teacher never asked Jip to read. "Why don't you sit with the Bracketts," she said quietly. "I think we need a moderating influence in that row." She handed him a book and a slate from the shelf near the cupboard. The shelf must have had several dozen books on it—more books than Jip had ever seen assembled in one spot. "And," she smiled down at him, "when the others go out at noon recess, would you wait and let me talk with you for a few minutes?"

The Brackett brothers were nearly the size of men, but their punches and snorts betrayed a nature that would have made Sheldon seem adult in comparison. They were loath to move their gangly limbs and make room for Jip, but Teacher's stare brooked no disobedience. Jip sat down beside Willie Brackett, the youngest, holding his body stiff so that it wouldn't touch him by accident.

The morning passed slowly. He stole a glance at Lucy.

She had her head bent over the slate Teacher had lent her and seemed to be working on the sums the schoolmistress had set for the older students to add. With the help of his fingers and invisible toes, Jip struggled to do the very simple ones Teacher had quietly written on his slate. Sometimes he just stared at the engravings in the primer Teacher had handed him. He tried to puzzle out the words, but he couldn't get enough of them in a row to unravel a whole sentence.

Finally, Teacher dismissed the pupils to fetch their lunch pails from the cupboard and take them out to the schoolyard. Jip got up and let the Bracketts tumble past him, then sat down again to wait. Already he knew that it was hopeless. Some of the tiny ones in the front row could not only recite their alphabet, they could make out words and whole sentences. Jip would never catch up. He would tell Teacher when the room cleared. He didn't crave the derision of the Bracketts.

"Come up to the front," she said. "And do sit down." He sat on the stool near her desk that in the old school had been reserved for dunces and disobedient pupils. There was a globe on the desk and more books.

"No one has ever told me what your proper name is."

"Jip," he said.

She waited for more.

"Just Jip. On account of some say I fell off a gypsy wagon."

"They never thought to give you a surname? A last name?"

"I'm thinking on the town record it says West—for the West Hill Road where Deacon Avery picked me up."

"I see," she said. But he could tell she thought his was a poor excuse for a name.

"Have you ever thought of giving yourself a name? A new name?"

"No, marm."

"I have a friend who gave himself a new name—Ezekial Freeman . . . Never mind. It's not up to me to tell you what to do." He was beginning to like Teacher a lot. It made him a little sad to think that this would be his last day at school. "Now to business. You haven't had much chance to come to school, have you?"

Jip shook his head. He felt like a shamed pup.

"Listen to me, Jip. You mustn't be embarrassed. It's not your fault."

"They say I ain't got the head for it—"

"Who says?" she asked sharply.

He looked up at her. Her dark eyes were flashing away. "Don't you let anyone say you don't have a head for learning!"

"But—" He needed to tell her that it was true. The sums and words just spun around when he tried to fix his mind on them.

"You're working like a man. Just how old are you, anyhow?"

"I don't know." He hung his head again.

"How could you know? You would hardly land on the West Hill Road with a baptismal certificate sewn to your bib."

Was she teasing him? He peeked a look. But there was no joking in her features. She was madder than Sheldon's hen. But not at him.

"Is there anyone on that farm who could help you if I gave you work to do at home? Someone who could help you catch up?"

"Put. Maybe Put."

"Put?"

"Putnam Nelson, our lunatic."

"The man they have in a cage up there?"

"He's plenty bright, and he don't always rave. He's got lots of good spells. Him and me are regular friends, really."

Some of her primly pulled-back hair was loose from its knot, framing her face. It made her look more gentle like. That and her smile. "How fortunate he is, how fortunate you both are, to have such a friend."

"Yes, marm. And Lucy, too. She knows her letters right smart."

"Yes, Lucy can help you." She looked at him closely. "You wouldn't mind, then, taking lessons from a girl— one younger than you?"

Why should he mind? "I'd like to be able to read and to figure."

"Good. Then you'll do fine. Just don't let anyone talk you out of coming to school now, do you understand? They're sure to try, but it's your right by law—for at least three months out of the year."

"The law says I got to go to school?" Amazing that the law should bother itself about him.

"Yes," she said. "Sometimes even the law is wise. Now"—she stood to let him know he was dismissed— "go out and eat your lunch and enjoy the fresh air. There won't be many more days like this."

75

He grabbed Sheldon's pail from the cupboard and ran outside into the pale November sunshine.

There was some disturbance on the far side of the schoolyard near the springhouse. He would have ignored it in favor of the chunk of bread and slice of cheese he knew to be inside his pail, but he had no sooner sat down on a stump and pried off his tin cover than he heard Lucy's voice. It was coming from the center of the ruckus, shrill and angry—and fearful.

"You leave me be, you dirty bullies. I ain't pestered you none. Leave me be!"

Jip put down his pail and ran across the yard just in time to see Willie Brackett grab Lucy's pail.

"Give it here, Brackett." Jip did his best to imitate Teacher's intimidating stare—the one that stilled the back row whenever it grew restless.

"Who'd want it?" Willie said, trying to sound careless. "Poor farm rubbish." He shoved the pail toward Lucy. With one motion she took the handle and swung it around, bashing the edge into Willie's head. The boy let out a howl like a bobcat. Lucy walked away, the crowd stepping back to make room for her.

"C'mon, Jip," she said. They walked over to the stump. Jip sat down beside his pail, still dazed by the strength of Lucy's anger. "Move over," she said. He obeyed.

Meantime, Willie's shrieks had brought Teacher to the schoolhouse door. She looked around, quickly checking the yard until she spied Willie, fingering the bump that was growing on his skull.

"Come on in, Willie," she said. "Looks as though you might need a cold compress."

Lucy watched warily as Willie stomped past her to follow Teacher into the building.

"Will she cane me, you think?" Lucy whispered.

"Why would she cane you?"

"Ma said you was never to fight on the schoolyard. At my other school—"

"I don't think this is going to be like other schools. But mind who you hit. He might swing back."

She giggled.

Teacher kept Willie on the stool near her desk, a wet rag on his head, for most of the afternoon. Then a half hour or so before dismissal, she sent Willie with his rag to his proper place and told everyone to close their books and put away their slates.

Now it's coming, Jip thought. He glanced down at Lucy. Her head was resting on her hands. He could tell she was scared. But instead of a licking or even a lecture, Teacher pulled a fat book off her desk and commenced to read. She didn't even look about to see if anyone was listening, just sank into the words like someone falling down to rest on a feather bed.

" 'Among other public buildings in a certain town,' " she began, " 'which for many reasons it will be prudent to refrain from mentioning, and to which I will assign no fictitious name, there is one anciently common to most towns, great or small: to wit, a workhouse; and in this workhouse was born; on a day and date which I need not trouble myself to repeat, inasmuch as it can be of no possible consequence to the reader, in this stage of the business at all events; the item of mortality whose name is prefixed to the head of this chapter.'—Oliver Twist."

At first Jip had trouble getting his head around the sentences—like chewing meat that's all gristle—but he let go and listened to the comforting music of Teacher's voice. It was clear how much at home she was with these words, how she loved them.

As they climbed the hill past the quarry, Jip ventured to ask Lucy about the reading.

"It don't seem regular," Lucy said. "I never heard of a teacher reading from a storybook before—a book what don't even teach us how to be good Christians."

"You wouldn't tell on her!"

She spun around as though Jip had accused her of treachery. "Of course I wouldn't. You take me for a fool?"

"That boy in the workhouse—that Oliver—"

"It was just like a poor farm, it was, only worse."

"Him being born there—"

"His poor beautiful young mother dying—"

"He didn't rightly know who he was neither."

Now Lucy snapped out of her dreamy state. "I wager he finds out," she said.

"How come?"

"That's how stories is."

"Truly?"

"I swear it," she said solemnly.

They walked along in silence for a while. Jip kicked a stone for several yards, then gave it up. If he injured Sheldon's boots, he was like to get a licking. "Maybe I could figure out . . ."

"What?"

"Figure out how to—you know, where I come from.

Without no stranger meddling between." He paused.
"You think?"

"Maybe," she said. "We'll have to go every single day
to find out how that Oliver does it."

"Every day," he agreed, squeezing the primer that
Teacher had loaned him.

9

The Celebration

As soon as they got to the pasture that belonged to the town farm, Jip set off on a fast trot. Put. He had nearly forgotten him in all the excitement of the school day. The Lymans would have left him locked in the cage. No one dared let him out except Jip. Poor man, cooped up all day like a rabbit in a hutch. Jip grabbed the key from the cupboard and raced to unlock the padlock. By this time, Lucy had caught up with him, and the two of them led Put out into the backyard. It was past sundown, but the old man must have a chance to stretch his cramped body.

"Dark is dark is dark . . ."

Jip's blood ran cold. "What you say, Put?"

"Dark is dark . . ."

"C'mon, Put," Jip crooned. "Time to go to bed. Like you say, it's mighty dark."

What if it was too late? What if he paid no heed? The dark days of November were upon them, and Put always fared worse in the dark. He took the old man's hand and turned him toward the kitchen door. "C'mon, now, that's it."

"Dark is dark is—"

"Yeah, me, too. I don't care much for the dark, neither. Now come along, ey? You can snuggle up under your quilt, and I'll fetch you something warm for your belly. It'll make you feel better."

Put stood still as a stump. Jip struggled against a rise of panic in his chest. What if the old man refused to go in? What then?

"Here," he said, fighting to expel the anxiety from his voice, "give me your right hand. Lucy will take your left." Good girl, she took the big hand quickly, calm as though she were taking Toddy for a stroll in the fields. "Now, move your feet. That's it. Not far to go. Here, up the stoop, onto the porch. Good."

"Dark is . . ."

"Easy, easy there." Jip pulled the door open with his free hand, and somehow, miraculously, he and Lucy got Put into the kitchen, down the hall, and safely into the cage. Jip was sweating something fierce and his hands shook like palsy as he clapped the shackle into the padlock. At the click, Put's head jerked up, but he didn't cry out.

"Lucy," Jip whispered, his eyes fixed on his friend, "could you get him something warm? Milk, I think, not too hot? I'd best stay here with Put."

She nodded and ran off toward the kitchen. When she brought the steaming mug, Jip took a sip to make sure of the temperature and then handed it through the little trapdoor to Put. "Here," he said. "Lucy's brought you some nice warm milk. Ain't that nice?"

Put turned slowly toward him. Oh mercy. His eyes were like a crazed horse's. Jip backed up despite himself, as the mug was snatched from his grasp and crashed against the slats of the cage, splashing white milk and shards of brown crockery in every direction.

"Put!" Lucy screamed. "Stop that!"

Jip wanted to yell, too, but he knew it wouldn't help. Put was gone from them—at least for a while.

At first, supper forgotten, the frightened residents, with the Lymans among them, huddled in the cold hallway outside the cage room. Then Toddy began to cry, and Mrs. Wilkens took charge, herding the lot of them toward the kitchen table. Jip never went to eat nor did he hear when the others climbed the stairs to bed. The men were all asleep when he stole up to get his quilt from his cot and return to his lonely vigil.

The lunatic raged all night long, cutting himself on fragments of the shattered mug. Jip fetched a rake and stuck it between the slats, trying to clear the pieces out of the cage, but Put grabbed the handle and snapped it in two across his knee. Then he stuck a jagged, splintered end through the slats, wielding it like an ugly weapon.

Oh, Put, Jip sobbed silently, moving out of range of the broken rake handle and Put's fury. Oh, Put, don't leave me now. I need you so bad. How can I do my schooling without you?

Jip slept hardly at all that night, wrapped in his quilt in the far corner of the cage room, listening to the unearthly sounds that filled the darkness like some demon chant. He had no hope of going to school the next morning, as exhausted as he was. Put was finally asleep, but still tossing and crying out. Jip had done no chores, no schoolwork, but Mrs. Wilkens was adamant. "Jest do the milking. That cow won't have none of me.

It seemed unfair to Jip, as though words were unsteady, an undependable commodity. The little ones didn't question the fickleness of the language, but Jip did. You ought to be able to count on it more. It was ornery as some people.

Put, dear old Put, the Put he loved began after a couple of weeks to creep out from under the wild shell of madness that had clamped down on him.

He was full of remorse when he came to himself and saw the state his cage and indeed his own self was in. "The darkness seems to overpower me, Jip," he said. "I wish I could know to fight it. But I lose to it every time."

Jip wanted to say it was all right, that he understood. But it wasn't all right, and how could anyone understand the shadow that hung over his friend, ready to snatch him away with no warning, hardly.

Put—bathed, dressed in clean clothes, his hair, beard, and nails neatly trimmed—oh, this Put was a proper schoolmaster. He insisted, however, that he teach from the cage, as he felt that during the dark days of winter he couldn't be entrusted with even the freedom of the cage room. The one exception was his bath, which soothed him body and mind and gave Jip a chance to neaten up his hair and beard and nails. Jip also took apart the mattress, discarded the stinking straw, and scrubbed the cover. Mrs. Wilkens humphed and complained, but she was finally persuaded to stitch it up.

"I need spectacles, Jip," Put explained, "if I'm to help you with your lessons. They took mine away before I come here."

At first Jip was stumped. How was he to afford

spectacles for Put? He knew Mr. Lyman would refuse. Then Lucy remembered. In the cupboard where Mrs. Lyman stored the clothes left by all the residents who had died, there was a little basket of spectacles as well. Jip had some conscience about stealing anything, but Lucy had no such scruples. She brought the whole basket down, and Put tried on every pair until he found one that suited him.

"How do I look?" he asked.

"It don't matter how you look," Lucy said.

"Can you read now, Put?" Jip asked anxiously.

"Not unless you tell me how handsome they make me."

"Good earth and seas!" Lucy exclaimed. "Did you ever hear tell of such vanity?"

But Jip laughed with delight to see his friend so restored to his true self.

Toddy always wanted to come in, and though Mrs. Wilkens was obviously loath to let the little boy be close to the lunatic and listened warily from the hallway, even she didn't have the heart to keep the child entirely away from the old man he loved so much.

First Lucy, then Jip overheard Mrs. Lyman trying to persuade Mr. Lyman that the time had come to send Put to the asylum. The last episode had unnerved her, and life was always harder at the farm during the cold, bleak months. Mr. Lyman himself was seen scurrying down the cellar steps several times a day to fetch mugs of his ever more comforting cider. But if light was in short supply, money was even shorter, and Mr. Lyman pointed out that Jip liked having a pet, and as long as they kept the lunatic padlocked in his cage, he could do little harm.

"You don't call his shrieking and cursing the name of God harm, then, Mr. Lyman?" she asked.

"Jest shut your ears, Mrs. Lyman. No good Christian woman should allow herself to listen to such speech."

"And jest how is a good Christian woman supposed to shut her ears to such ungodly racket, Mr. Lyman? Will you tell me that?"

But Mr. Lyman continued on his way to his bedroom, cider mug in hand. The matter was closed. At least for the present.

Teacher was planning a celebration for the last day of school before Christmas. All the families were invited to come at two o'clock and bring refreshments to share. "Don't worry, you can be home in time for milking," she said. The students would provide the entertainment. Jip knew full well that Mrs. Lyman would not send poor farm food for rich folks to gobble down and he resigned himself to missing the celebration. Lucy, however, had a sweet voice, and Teacher had asked her to sing a verse of one of the carols alone, so she was determined not only that she and Jip should stay for the party but that her mother and Toddy should come as well. Mrs. Wilkens bullied Mrs. Lyman into letting her have enough flour and maple sugar to make a little cake. For the rest, they would content themselves with bread and cheese, and apples from the cellar.

When the day came, the snow was too deep for Toddy to walk, not being able as yet to manage snowshoes. But Mrs. Wilkens left the two little ones with Berthie and the other old ones and made her way across the fields to the schoolhouse. She had even managed to coax the loan of a lantern for the homeward trek.

The cold weather had put an end to outdoor recess. The students spent the time making decorations for the little schoolhouse. Some kindly farmer gave them a tree and greens, and Teacher had brought candles for each of the four windows. By two o'clock on the afternoon of the celebration the room twinkled and sparkled like a place of enchantment.

The small yard began to fill with sleighs from the surrounding countryside. Teacher sent the older boys out to help with the horses. With noisy cheer, the red-faced farmers and their wives and tiny babes crowded the benches and overflowed into the narrow aisle.

When Jip and the other boys came in they found that Teacher had instructed the children to sit on the floor up front. The Bracketts scowled, but one look from Teacher and they came down the aisle, elbowing one another and mumbling under their breath. She quietly sent Addison, Warner, and Willie to three separate spots on the floor, and when they had folded their long limbs and sat down, the program began.

Deacon Avery's grandson, who was the best reader, read the Christmas story from the Gospel of Luke. Some of the older girls recited poems. The little ones struggled to sing on key the simple songs that Teacher had taught them. Near the end of the hour, it was Lucy's turn. She sang in a firm, clear voice the message of the angel to the shepherds:

> " 'Fear not,' he said, for sudden dread
> Had seized their troubled mind;

'Glad tidings of great joy I bring
To you and all mankind.' "

Jip was only in the chorus, for which he was glad. He
didn't crave the chance to show off in front of strangers,
but he could tell how Lucy loved it. She didn't seem to
care that her dress was cut down from one of Berthie's.
Her chin was up and proud. Her face shone as she sang.

" 'To you, in David's town, this day,
Is born, of David's line,
The Savior, who is Christ the Lord;
And this shall be the sign:
The heavenly Babe you there shall find
To human view displayed,
All meanly wrapped in swaddling-bands,
And in a manger laid.' "

Jip was hardly listening as he joined the others to sing
the final stanza. As poor and meanly wrapped as Jesus
was, he was descended from a king. It was not impossible
that a poor boy . . .

Jip stole a look at Mrs. Wilkens's face. There was a
softening in her usually hard features. Teacher looked
different, too. She had on a light blue dress and above
the lace-trimmed collar, her cheeks were flushed, her
eyes bright. Jip caught her glancing at the back west corner and followed the glance to see what was putting the
extra color in Teacher's face. There was a tall man sitting
quietly there, looking only at Teacher, as though none of
the rest of them had bothered to come into the room.

Willie Brackett poked Jip in the ribs. "Teacher's got a
sweetheart," he whispered under the cover of applause.

Jip's heart gave a little tweak. He shouldn't have been surprised, but still, he'd thought of Teacher as belonging to the school—to them. The idea that someone else might try to lay claim to her attentions created a little pocket of sadness in him. But he couldn't argue with Willie. No matter what happened, who was reciting or singing, the man on the back row was seeing only Teacher.

People were getting up. The children were laughing and seeking out their parents. The program was over. Outside the windows, dusk was gathering. "Please, Ma, we got to stay for the eats," Lucy was begging. She was still riding high on her triumph. People had clapped for her. Even her mother had clapped and smiled, very nearly.

"Not for long. It's dark, most." Mrs. Wilkens reached down to brush Lucy's hair out of her glowing face.

Teacher must have heard, for she came over. "Are you on foot, Mrs. Wilkens?"

Mrs. Wilkens nodded.

"We'll make sure you get a ride," she said. "Enjoy the party."

It was as though on the eighth day God had said, "Let there be food," and there was food: pumpkin and apple and squash and mince pies, plum puddings and jam tarts, gingerbread and little cakes with maple sugar frosting— and behold it was very good.

"What do you call this?" Jip kept asking Lucy as he bit into one new treat after another. She knew the names or invented them. It didn't matter. Jip ate everything. He couldn't decide which he favored most, so he had to go back and have another tart to see if he indeed preferred it to the muffin topped with currant jelly or the iced tea cake or the pumpkin pie.

"You're going to be sick," Mrs. Wilkens warned, but she didn't try to stop them from stuffing themselves.

They were the last to leave. Teacher's gentleman friend put out the fire in the stove—no school tomorrow—while the rest of them took down the decorations and the candles and stored them in a big wooden box for next year. Jip got out the broom and began to sweep pine needles off the floor.

"No, thank you anyhow, Jip," Teacher said. "Enough for tonight. It's late and by the time the holiday is over, I'll have to sweep again. Just take these branches out to the woodpile for me, please, and then Mr. Stevens will give us all a ride home."

She gave the gentleman one of her lovely smiles. Jip rushed outside with the greens. It was dark with only the faint glow of the lamp from inside the building. Willie had said "sweetheart," but Jip had resisted the idea. But that smile . . . He hurried around to the woodshed.

"Hey, boy."

Jip jumped. For a moment he was afraid, but then he recognized the shadow leaning against the building. It was the oldest Brackett.

"Addison? I thought you'd gone home—with the rest."

"I been meaning to tell you something private like, but there's never a private time in school to talk."

"What do you mean, tell me something?"

"There was a feller around town some months ago . . ."

Jip put his armload of greens down. He hoped Addison couldn't see how trembly he was.

"Wal—for some reason he's mighty interested in you. He give me cash money to keep an eye on you."

"Yeah?"

"Just letting you know. I got my eye on you, boy."

"Jip?" Teacher was calling from the doorway.

"I gotta go."

"Wal, you be good now. I don't want to have no trouble doing my job, hear?"

"I ain't going nowhere, if that's what you mean." He hurried off around the building, his stupid heart beating faster than a chick's. It was only Addison Brackett, for mercy's sake.

"Is everything all right?" Teacher asked.

"Fine," he said, "jest fine." But the words came out like panting.

10

The Caller

The three days of holiday seemed to go on forever. Having good things like school and friends and Teacher and stories caused trouble—you came to need them, to expect them as your due, to crave them when they disappeared.

Before there had been such things, Jip had been passing content from one day to the next. His hours had been filled with the animals and with his chores. He'd not much minded the quality of the food and hardly noticed, except when it was scarce. Now it was as though both his mind and his body had had a taste of a rich diet, and they longed for more. They would never again feel satisfied with the tastelessness of the old days. Life was to him now like mush without so much as a dash of salt.

If only Put could be himself—or what Jip thought of as Put's true self—the good, wise Put who sang that all was well and petted Toddy on the head and made Jip feel that he was the cleverest of boys. It was strange, maybe, but when Jip saw himself through Put's eyes, Put's unclouded eyes, he saw a different Jip. He was no longer the waif fallen off the back of a gypsy wagon that nobody even bothered to come back after. He was the

boy that beasts came to without his calling or cajoling—
the boy that ran the farm good as any man—the one
person that Mr. Lyman and the residents could not do
without.

Then, somehow, when Put went away from him into
that fearsome rage or silent curtain of the densest fog, Jip
himself went missing. Oh, he still did the chores, but he
was again the ignorant boy who barely knew his letters—
the boy that was maybe dropped on his head in the fall
from the wagon and left deficient. More kin to the ignorant beasts than to upright humanity.

An ache welled up inside him. This is how it had
always been for Sheldon, a continuous sadness at being
less than others. The hankering to be seen as a man—
that was what had cost Sheldon his life. He was not so
great an idiot as some had thought. He knew the grief of
being cast off as worthless, and then a few days, a tragic
few days of feeling himself grown full into manhood. Oh,
Sheldon, I was never good enough to you. I didn't
understand.

He held tight to the slats of Put's cage. Come back to
me, Put, he begged silently. But today Put lay in a stupor, his back curled away from Jip and the world.

School began, but Jip did not go. Mr. Lyman called
him out of the cage room the night before to tell him he
must stay on the farm.

"I can't have you going off to play whilst Put is in this
state," the manager said. "It frights the women and children too greatly. You've made him your pet and now
you'll jest have to care for him, or I'm forced to send him
down to Brattleboro whether it takes the food from the
rest of your mouths or no. You understand me, boy?"

Jip understood. There was to be no schooling for him. He should never have allowed himself to hope for it. When Lucy heard, she stamped her foot and refused to go alone.

"You got to go, Lucy. I'll never know how Oliver comes out, else. 'Sides, you can come home and teach me what you learn. Then I won't be left so far behind."

"Wal, I tell you, Teacher ain't going to like it a-tall."

"It can't be helped. We can't have Put going off to the asylum, can we? Remember how he come to us tied and ..." But of course she couldn't remember. She hadn't been here then.

"It's the law. Teacher said so. You supposed to have at least three months' schooling a year, and you ain't hardly had one."

"Mr. Lyman'll contend I ain't fit for learning."

She snorted almost loud as a horse. "It'd take ten of Lyman's brains to make the hind part of yours," she said.

He couldn't help but smile at that. "Then you gotta help me, Lucy. Go to school for us both."

"Teacher asked after you," Lucy reported the first afternoon. "So did Addison Brackett, but I told him to mind his own affairs."

He tried not to think of Addison Brackett behind the schoolhouse in the shadow. "Did she read the book?"

"She didn't, almost. She said she hated to go on when some folks would miss out. Only you and the Turner baby was missing, and you know Teacher didn't mean that one. Tarnation! She still sucks her fingers."

He could feel the warmth of Teacher's concern glowing in his cheeks.

"But all the big ones cried out—even the Bracketts—for her to go on. 'I'll tell Jip what happens,' I said, right out loud, and she says quiet like to me, 'Then you got to listen to every word. Jip'll want to know every little thing that happens.' "

"She said that?"

"I wouldn't make it up. You're her pet, for sure." Lucy pushed out her lip in a pretense of a pout.

"No, I ain't. Teacher just knows how much I got to learn fast to catch up even to Baby Turner. It's pity for me, only. Now follow me out to the chicken house and tell me what happened."

"Wal," Lucy began, "you'll remember Oliver got caught when Dodger was stealing?"

"Yeah, yeah." He didn't need a review. How could she think he'd forget anything?

"Wal, they took him before the justice and—" She paused to pet a young rooster, who in return pecked her finger. "Ow!"

"Go on," he begged. He had to finish gathering the eggs before milking time. She told him how the kindly gentleman's heart had gone out to poor Oliver there in the dock, and how he had taken the orphan boy to live with him like an adopted son, near.

"Do you think? Nah . . ."

"Think what?"

"That the kindly gentleman might be—well, suppose he turns out to be Oliver's *real* father."

"Too old," she said. "Besides, he don't have a wife and besides . . ."

"Never mind," he said, although he did mind just a little.

And so it went each afternoon. Lucy kept him caught up as much as she could, but it wasn't the same. Not nearly. He tried as she spoke to hear Teacher's voice reading the words of the book. But it was like a tune you once heard that you could no longer recall—neither the words nor the melody—just snatches of something that made you long for the real thing.

"It ain't the same," he said sadly.

"What ain't?"

"Hearing the things that happen in place of the book words."

"I'm doing the best I can," she said. "I never said I could recite you every word."

"You're fine," he said quickly. "You're doing fine, really." He sneaked a look at her face. If she got put out, she might just stop telling him even the sketchy outline of the tale, and then where would he be?

A week passed and Put had yet to return to himself. Mr. Flint came to call and insisted on seeing the lunatic. Mr. Lyman detained the overseer in the parlor as long as possible while Jip scooted back to the cage room. He stretched an arm through the slats, doing his best to wipe Put's grizzly hair with a damp cloth, crooning to the old man as he did so.

"It's all right, Put, all right, just want to pretty you up for Mr. Flint. He's come to pay you a call, and I'm fearful he will send you off to Brattleboro, and then where would I be? You're my friend, Put, my best friend in all the world. How can I let them put you in irons and carry you off? They'd take you away, Put. They'd lock you up forever. You'd not likely sit in the sunshine ever again."

The body of his friend shuddered, but he did not turn to face Jip.

"You hear me, Put? If you don't care anything for me—and can I blame you for that? You can despise me if you will, but think to yourself, Put. You'd never sing again, locked away with nothing but lunatics to keep you company. No Toddy, Put. No Toddy in Brattleboro. Now stick your hands out and let me wipe them off. You know they need it."

There was no response. Desperation crept into the crooning voice.

"Come on, Put. We ain't got time to spare. The overseer will be stomping down the hall in his shiny leather boots any minute now. You got to least turn over and let me wipe your face and hands. Will you do that for me? For yourself? You don't want Mr. Flint to send you away from us, now do you?"

The door opened. Jip jumped back from the cage, keeping the rag behind his back as though the sight of it would somehow count against Put.

The overseer studied Put's back and then strolled around the three sides of the cage to better study the top of Put's head and the soles of his dirty bare feet. Flint took out his handkerchief and put it delicately to his nose.

"Don't you ever bathe him?"

The question was directed at Mr. Lyman, who looked confused and nodded his head toward Jip.

"You put the boy in charge?"

Mr. Lyman's eyes darted about. He wiped his hands on his trouser legs.

"I asked to do for Mr. Nelson, sir," Jip said. "Me and

Put gets along pretty good, and he's—he's"—he searched his head for the proper phrase—"like a father to me."

"A what?"

Jip's face reddened. "What I mean is, being an orphan, it makes me feel good to care special for someone. Like having family—"

Mr. Flint stiffened, his gaze again on Put's dirty back. He patted his nose. "He seems harmless enough at the moment," the overseer said at last.

Jip dared to breathe. "Yessir," he said, trying to force his lips into a smile.

"Well, carry on, then," the overseer said, giving him a jerk of the head, his large nose still protected by the gleaming linen handkerchief.

The two men slammed the door behind them.

"Rude, ain't they?" Jip said, but the back did not answer.

He tried to tell himself that it was great good luck that Mr. Flint had come when Put was in his deathlike state and not having his howling fit when he threw his body against the slats and screamed the name of the Lord in vain, calling down obscenities and the curses of the devil and all his black angels upon anyone and no one.

But at least when Put was hollering, Jip knew his friend was alive—that there was someone in that filthy shell of a body, raging against the awfulness that had taken possession of him. " 'All is well,' " Jip would sing, trying vainly to pierce the darkness.

A week passed before Teacher came to call. She presented herself at the front parlor door, which upset Mrs. Lyman no end. The door had not been opened for years and it was so warped that no amount of banging and shoving from the inside could force it ajar. The manager's wife sent Jip running around to tell whoever it was out there to come around to the main kitchen door like "any normal Christian soul."

To Jip's surprised delight it was Teacher standing there in the snow, wrapped in a warm shawl with a country woman's bonnet tied under her chin.

"Teacher?" he said.

"Jip. How are you?"

She was so beautiful, even in that homely bonnet—tall and built as strong as a brick house with eyes so lively they made you long to see whatever it was they were looking at.

"You're all right?"

"Fine," he said. He knew his face was red under the dirt. "Uh, Mrs. Lyman? She says to ask you kindly to come to the kitchen door. This here one's stuck fast."

Teacher laughed. "I've been gone from here too long. I should know better than to come to anyone's front door, shouldn't I?" She followed him around to the kitchen, lifting her skirt to keep it from dragging in the snow. "That's my pay for trying to impress people with the importance of my visit." She had a lovely laugh. Though the truth of it was, had he considered it, everything about her seemed to Jip exactly what a woman should be: see the way she stopped at the hitching post to give her horse a pat and a word before she went to the kitchen door.

"We're missing you at school," she said, as she wiped her feet carefully on the gunnysack Mrs. Lyman put out for a mat on the stoop.

"Yes, marm," he said. "I mean, I miss school, too."

"Good," she said. "I needed to be sure we were in agreement."

"I can't come back, though. Leastways not for a while."

"Why not?"

"It's Put, marm. Putnam Nelson? No one else will care for him when he's in a bad way."

"I see."

Did she? "If—if— Oh, marm, I can't let them take him to the asylum. It would kill him."

"So that's it."

"He's my friend."

She looked down at him, her eyes soft and kind. "You're a rare one, Jip," she said.

He opened the door and held it back to hide his burning face. "You best go in. It's cold as hades out here."

"Well, that's a different view of it," she said, laughing again. She gave his shoulder a little pat as she walked past him into the kitchen.

Mrs. Lyman was sitting at the kitchen table. She didn't stand up to welcome the guest, just nodded at a vacant chair. "You'd best be seeing to Mr. Nelson, Jip," she said.

For a minute he didn't move. He was hovering behind Teacher, waiting to take the shawl and bonnet, to pull out the chair, anything to keep close by. She smelled fresh as a barn filled with new-cut hay.

"Jip!"

"Huh?"

Mrs. Lyman gave a great sigh. "We've tried to make him mannerly." She gave a helpless laugh. "Can't teach a sow to sing, I reckon."

Teacher frowned but pressed her lips together.

"Boy!"

He dropped the hands he was holding out for the shawl and bonnet.

"Don't worry about my things, Jip. I'll just lay them here on this chair."

"And close the door behind you!" Mrs. Lyman ordered.

He backed awkwardly out of the kitchen. Mrs. Lyman didn't want him there. She wanted to tell Teacher that he had no head for learning, would probably be a care to the town all his life like Sheldon—being he was thrown off a gypsy wagon and never come back for.

The anger rose up inside him like soap lye bubbling up in a kettle. He could learn. He knew he could. He just had to have the chance for it. Still, how could he leave Put behind? What would they do to him? Send him off to an asylum, locked away from all that made life worth living—the sky, the mountains, the open air, and Jip, his one true friend? Lucy and Toddy, too, of course, and the animals. Put loved them as well. But it's me he counts on. Lucy and Toddy have their mother and the baby, but Put and me only have each other. We're all we got in this world. I already lost Sheldon. I can't lose Put, too.

He was never quite able to ask himself if Put, as he had been for the last two weeks, might be better off in the asylum. With all his heart he believed that only he, Jip, could care for the old man properly.

He opened the door to the cage room and went inside.

"There you are, son. I was wondering if you could heat some water. I need a bath worse than a sheep needs shearing."

"Put! Put!" he cried out. "You come back to me!"

"Have I been gone so long?"

Jip was crying. "Too long, Put, too long." He sniffled and wiped his nose across his sleeve. "I'll put the water on in jest a minute. Mrs. Lyman's got company in the kitchen right now. She won't take kindly to any interruption."

"I forget. Life goes on without me." He sounded so mournful that Jip repented his hesitation at once.

"Never mind about Mrs. Lyman, Put. I'll jest sneak in, put on the kettle, and be right back."

"I'm obliged. And," he added, "a change of clothes?"

"Yes, yes. Whatever you want, Put." The smile was like to crack his chapped face in two. "Oh, I been waiting and watching for you. Thank you for coming back to me."

He raced down the hall, stopping short of the kitchen door. He paused, wiped his palms on his trousers, and knocked gently.

"What is it?" Mrs. Lyman's voice was sharp with impatience.

He cracked the door. "Begging your pardon," he said, smiling at each woman in turn, "if I could just put the kettle on . . ."

"We've no time for tea."

"No, no, it's Put," Jip said. "He wants a wash."

He saw the anger in Mrs. Lyman's face and realized belatedly that he shouldn't have spoken of a gentleman's need for a bath in front of ladies. Teacher must think him rude.

He covered his embarrassment by grabbing the kettle and racing out to the pump with it. Mrs. Lyman was still muttering at him when he returned. He paid her no mind, poked up the fire, and put the kettle on. Put was better. Put wanted a bath. "I'll jest be taking this," he said, hoisting the copper tub over his head and maneuvering it out of the door.

"Jip—" He stopped at the sound of Teacher's voice. "We'll be looking for you next week, then, all right?"

"Yes, marm," he said from under the tub. "Yes, marm."

"That woman came calling today," Mrs. Lyman said down the length of the supper table to her husband.

"What woman?"

"She means Teacher," Lucy said, and got a look from her mother for impertinence.

"What was she doing here?" the manager asked.

"Prying into matters what ain't her concern," his wife said. "She means for the boy to return to school. Won't listen to reason. The woman argues like a politician. Ain't natural."

"Humph," the manager said.

Jip waited anxiously for the conversation to continue, but all that followed were the usual sounds of a tableful of noisy eaters chewing, swallowing, sniffling, coughing. Lucy caught his eye and sent him a knowing grin. Jip's heart gave a little leap. Teacher's won. Whether the Lymans like it or no, I'll be going back to school next week.

11

The Ghost

As the days grew longer, life grew sweeter. It was daylight now when he and Lucy started out for school, and daylight still when they returned. Put hardly had a spell that would count for a real one since January.

Oliver, after many a terrible trial, was reunited with the elderly gentleman who turned out to be not Oliver's father, but his dead father's best friend. To Jip's sorrow, Oliver didn't figure it out for himself.

"He couldn't," said Lucy. "Don't you see? He was born in the plaguey poorhouse with no one to tell him nothing. T'warnt no way for him to figure it."

"I reckon not," Jip said, but he couldn't help his bitter disappointment. He'd looked to Oliver to teach him how it might be done. How an orphan boy might figure out where he come from when no one older or wiser seemed to know nor care—except, except for a menacing stranger who was making business of something that was no business of his.

The all too short school term was nearly at an end. Teacher stood up in town meeting and tried to talk the township into extending another month, but the vote went against it. Partly, it was their resentment of a woman more educated than any of them. But also, times were hard. Money was scarce. School cost money. The local citizenry were loath to spend a penny more than the law demanded. Besides, sugaring was upon them. The farmers needed their children home to fetch the sap and tend the fire and take turns standing by the boiling kettle.

The last day of school Teacher asked Jip to stay afterward. Lucy lingered at her seat, but Teacher sent her out to scrape the ice off the front step. It was just a way of getting rid of her. Lucy knew it, but she only sighed, fetched the shovel, and went out to obey.

"Jip," Teacher said when the door shut behind Lucy, "you've made great progress this term."

He mumbled a thank-you, unaccustomed to praise.

"I've wrapped a few books for you to take home. You must work on your own until school opens again in November."

"Yes, marm. I will."

"And Jip . . ." She was gathering herself up to say something hard, he could tell by the way she hesitated and then moved carefully into the rest of the sentence. "Jip, if for any reason, if anything comes up that—if you find yourself in any trouble—"

"Marm?"

"Do you remember Mr. Stevens, who drove us home after the Christmas event?"

"Yes, marm."

"Well, Mr. Stevens asked me particularly to tell you that you are to call on him—if anything, anyone tries to threaten you or—"

"I can take care of myself. The Bracketts—"

"Not the Bracketts."

"He don't mean Put? He's strange and he do have terrible spells, but he's my best friend in the world."

"I think Mr. Stevens had in mind someone else—a stranger, perhaps."

Jip was sure she saw him start. How did Mr. Stevens know about the stranger?

She was watching him closely. "The Stevens family farm is up Quaker Road on the other side of the village from you. Do you know where that is?"

He shook his head. "But don't you mind. I can take care of myself."

She started to say something more but seemed to change her mind. "Enjoy the books," she said. "I'm counting on seeing you in November now, you hear?"

"Hope so," he said.

"Good-bye then, Jip."

"Good-bye." He gave her one last look to carry him through until November, then started for the door. Lucy would be impatient.

"Jip—"

He turned at the door. Her face was full of concern. It made him want to cloud up like Toddy and cry. But he didn't. He couldn't turn back and be the baby he never was. It was too late for that.

"Jip, if you want help of any kind—and, Jip, it's not a sign of weakness to ask for help—leave a note for me at Peck's store. I pick up my mail there. All right?"

He nodded and hurried out and waited in the cold outside while Lucy replaced the shovel.

* * *

Winter lumbered into spring with the awkward gait of a moose. Sometimes just when the cold grayness of the season seemed immovable, it would disappear. Then just as you started to rejoice in the sunshine, it came thundering back. There was no sugar bush on the poor farm. Except for the few apple trees near the house, the previous owner had cut down all the trees to make way for sheep. Jip was hired out nighttimes to Deacon Avery's sugar operation—the man had more projects going than an anthill has ants. He put aside his feud with Mr. Lyman for the sake of Jip's strong young back and almost boundless energy.

Avery's sugar shack was built to protect his kettle, not the humans who sat by it. Freezing winds found every crack between the timbers. Many was the night Jip got next to no sleep, tending the fire and boiling the sap, his nostrils filled with the sticky sweet odor, the watery sap leaving white stains like strange tracks on his ragged clothes. His friends and comforters in the long, freezing nights were Avery's three dogs, who huddled close to him as though guarding their pup against the elements.

The sugaring season done, Mrs. Wilkens took it in her head (or perhaps Lucy nagged, he was never sure) to make Jip some more respectable garments. She went to the cupboard where Mrs. Lyman stored the clothing left by the residents who now moldered in their graves and found a shirt and a pair of trousers. These she boiled in lye soap within an inch of their lives, and then made Jip a well-faded but indisputably clean and respectable new outfit.

Complaints Mr. Lyman voiced about cutting down good broadcloth for a boy who was growing an inch a week were quickly shushed by Mrs. Wilkens, who pointed out that the clothes had been lying around gathering dust since before she had arrived. "When he outgrows 'em, they can go to Toddy," she said.

Jip, for his part, was mightily pleased with his new shirt and trousers. The shirt cuffs came all the way to his wrists, the trouser cuffs to his ankles, and there was a button to match every single neatly embroidered buttonhole.

"Your mother ought to take in sewing," he said to Lucy when she caught him jumping to admire himself in the wavy reflection of the kitchen mirror. "She's the cleverest person with the needle I ever did see."

"How many you seen?"

It was true, he hadn't seen many, but still, he knew good tailoring from what Berthie or, on rare occasions, Mrs. Lyman had offered him before. If he'd lost a button or suffered a torn sleeve in recent years, it had been up to him to fix it or put up with it as it was. He'd usually chosen the latter course.

He repeated his compliment to Mrs. Wilkens, and regretted it within days. For so encouraged, Mrs. Wilkens walked into town and got herself hired out to the local dressmaker. A room at the back of the shop was nearly empty, and she talked her new employer into letting her have it rent free for herself and the children.

How could he even think of losing Lucy and Toddy—or of losing Mrs. Wilkens and the baby, now crawling about and pulling herself to her feet, providing entertainment for the old folks simply by plopping down again or saying "da da," which all the old men claimed as their own name? The very idea of losing the Wilkenses was as close to losing Sheldon again as he could imagine.

Lucy was no help in his distress. She bounced around with joy. "I won't be a dead drunkard's orphan or a poor farm girl; I'll be a regular somebody, don't you see, Jip?"

Jip saw. Couldn't *she* see that what she was saying was that *he* was a nobody—never had been anybody—never would be?

"Come on, sour face! Be happy for me!"

He tried to say he was. In a corner of his head he was glad for her, but the part of him that reached out to Put and the animals, the part of him so easy to tear that he tried most times to keep it hidden from people, that part of him was ripped. He was afraid to expose it anymore, lest it be torn beyond repair.

His warmth and comfort that spring was Put. With the days growing quickly longer, Put's spirits lightened. So despite the Wilkenses' departure, April and May were not too harsh. These months lacked the deep pleasure of the winter days, which had given him school and the companionship of Toddy and especially Lucy. But Put was like a new man. With the coming of June it was hard for Jip to remember the lunatic of January. They plowed the fields together and planted the crops. The garden would be smaller than last year, but then, there were fewer of them now. It was good to have hard work to do to keep mind and body busy. He tried not to think of what was gone—Sheldon and the Wilkenses—but to be happy with what he had: Put working at his side, animals being born, the apple trees in blossom, the pasture greening up, and crops breaking the soil.

He tried not to let his mind wander, because at the edge of it, something lurked. It was as though he were waiting for someone—for something to happen. It was not the feeling he had when he was waiting to know what would happen to Oliver in Teacher's book. He remembered, with a smile, hugging *that* waiting to himself every night as he dropped off to sleep. Waiting for Oliver had peppered his prayers and invaded his dreams.

This new waiting was quieter—more like a deer who knows without seeing that he's being stalked, but not who the hunter is, what direction he will come from, or exactly when the shot will ring out. None of this can the stag know. But head up, eyes alert, he must be tensed for the shot that will ring out, and be ready to spring into the air, to bound away to the safety of the deep woods.

Meantime that spring and early summer, when the work of the day was done, Jip began to read, or try to read, the books Teacher had lent him. He began with the Bible. There was a huge one on the parlor table, a gift, it said in fancy script, from the Ladies' Missionary Aid Society of the Congregational Church. But it had never occurred to Jip that the parlor Bible was something to be read, like an ordinary book. It seemed more like an ornament.

He took a look at the Bible Teacher had given him. It was smaller and more like a reading book. He tried the first page or so, but it was all in fancy words about the king, far too discouraging for him. Put explained (Put seemed to know everything) that what he was trying to read was just the introduction about how the Bible got to be written down in English and not part of the Bible itself. He should turn over to Genesis and see how God made the world. Jip did so and sure enough, he could decipher the Genesis pages tolerably well.

The second book was about Vermont history. He asked Put to read the part about Ethan Allen and the Green Mountain Boys in that. It seemed that he and Berthie had both been right. The man was part hero, part scoundrel, though Jip could tell the writer was loath to admit the scoundrel part.

The last book, and as it turned out, the one that truly caught Jip's eye, was called *Uncle Tom's Cabin or Life Among the Lowly*.

Uncle Tom was a story, like *Oliver*. Teacher must have suspected that he would work powerful hard to make his way through a story. It wasn't as fetching a story as *Oliver*—more churchy—as though every minute you were paying strict mind to the story part the writer was bound to stick in all the lessons she could while she had your attention. Now Jip was just an ignorant boy and it wasn't his business, he knew, to try to tell a writer how to write a book, but it stood to reason that if you want to catch a reader tight, the trap needs to be plain and strong with no smell of the trapper lingering on it.

But for all her preacher airs, the writer trapped him. Indeed, he was so impatient to know how the lowly of the tale would manage that he did hardly any of the reading himself. He made Put read. He wanted to get the tune of the words in his head. Listening was so much better than pounding out the sounds for himself, for he lost the sense of the story in the struggle to read it. But Put would make him wrestle with the words for a few minutes each night. He said it was for Jip's own good and Jip reckoned he was right about that.

Jip had once heard a guest preacher at the Congregational Church tell about the wicked slave masters down south. Not all the masters in this book were wicked, though. It was just that luck was not on the side of the slaves. They'd get sold down the river to where the masters and their overseers would turn out to be evil as the devil. It was a tragic tale that wrung Jip's heart for all his discomfort about how pretty it was put down on the page.

Put said he'd seen a real live slave once. "He lived on a farm not far from where I worked for some years after I come back from fighting with Old Tippecanoe. That's where my poor head got ruint, you know. Anyhow, the runaway—that's what he was, only we had no way of knowing—he lived right with the folks on the next farm and worked their fields like proper hired help. In those days there warn't a law from Washington that said slavers could come into a free state and track down men and women as though they was strayed cattle. But one day the man up and disappeared. The farmer was hurt like. He had tried to treat the man kind and pay him fair. Then months after, he got a letter from Montreal—that's in Canady, you know. Seems the fellow had gone into town on an errand and seen his old master right there on the street. He never even come back to the farm for his clothes. He just took off running and didn't stop till he crossed over the line."

"Did you ever see a slave catcher?"

"Naw," Put said. "Never saw one of them to my knowledge. Though a man like that ain't going to walk about with a sign hanging 'round his neck, scarcely. But I ain't heard of fugitives in these parts for . . ." He stopped, rubbing his big hand across his mouth, his eyes sad. Jip knew he was realizing that living in a cage at the poor farm he was not likely to hear much of the local gossip.

"Teacher said the law means if you see a slave you're bound to give him up to the slave catcher or pay a whopping fine. Only she says no true Vermonter would send another human being back to slavery."

"Your teacher's a noble woman. Not everyone would agree. But I guess you not going to see any fugitive living in peace on a Vermont farm these days, neither."

"Reckon not," Jip said. But his mind wasn't on fugitives or laws, it was on Put, whose knowledge of the world was limited by the slats of his cage—a cage he and Sheldon had built. It made him feel somehow responsible for Put's pain, though what else could they have done short of sending him to Brattleboro?

Teacher had left a letter inside this book. On the front was her name care of Peck's store. On the back a Montreal address with the name the Rev. Ezekial Freeman. Where had he heard that name before? Oh, yes. Teacher's friend. The one who had changed his name.

Though the warm, long days found Put at his best, Mr. Lyman seemed to suffer continuously from the ague, which responded only to large doses of medicinal spirits, the cider in the cellar having long before been consumed. Truth be known, Mr. Lyman's malingering meant much more freedom for Jip. It was up to him to fetch supplies from the village, and there was no one along to complain of dawdling if he and the old horse, Jack, stopped to admire a pretty view or Jip took time to eye the rows of goods in Peck's store.

On every trip he kept his ears perked for any conversation in the store or on the porch. Somedays an old man in a rocker would read parts of the newspaper aloud to the rest, and Jip would have a bit of news of the country or the world to share with Put when he returned. Put ate it up the way Sheldon would have licked up that penny candy Jip had never been quite generous enough to buy him with his one saved coin.

"Strangers in town." Jip was waiting at the counter to pay for the staples Mrs. Lyman had sent him to buy. The speaker inclined his head slightly, and Jip followed the tilt down the length of the long counter.

He had heard the old men at the farm tell tales of meeting their own ghosts. That was the only way he could explain later what had happened at that moment. As he turned his head to look down the counter, a tall, fair-headed man at the far end met his gaze—gray eyes meeting his own dark ones. He knew that face—it was the one that stared out at him every day from the wavy kitchen mirror.

12

Revelations

Both of them stood paralyzed—the man and the boy—both gaping, transfixed by the other.

"Jip?" The hateful, familiar voice came from someone standing behind the tall yellow-haired man. Jip jumped like a flushed quail at the sound. *The stranger was back.*

He dropped his goods unpaid for on the counter and raced out the open door of the store. His fingers were shaking so, he could hardly untie Jack's reins. By the time he got up on the wagon seat, he knew that the two strangers—one the mirrored reflection, the other like an old nightmare that keeps invading your dreams—that the pair of them were standing in the open doorway, staring after him as he yelled at Jack to get moving.

Poor Jack. Jip had never so much as raised his voice to him before. The old horse threw the boy a disapproving look as though ashamed that Jip had lost his manners, but he sensed the boy's fright and without further reproof picked up his hooves and rattled the wagon down the main street as fast as though he was on the open road.

Jip was sweating under his hair and out of every pore of his body. He didn't ask himself why he was so scared or why his first reaction to the sight of his own face on a strange man's body should compel him to flee, but flee he did, as though for his very life. Something inside not tamed enough to be words or even thoughts forced him on. He was already past the outskirts of the village before he realized that he was headed the wrong way. The farm was on the other side. He hadn't turned the wagon around. But he kept going north until he found himself, hardly without willing it, bouncing up the rough dirt of Quaker Road. He began then to slow, for the road was steep and no horse with a wagon behind, however urged, could take that slope at the clip Jip had been driving it.

With the slowing of the pace, his brain awoke from its stupor and began to buzz gently about as though looking for a spot to set down.

So the stranger had told the truth? Jip couldn't deny the yellow-haired man's uncanny resemblance to himself. His hair and eyes were lighter. Maybe his nose was a trifle longer? Still, all this taken into consideration, what the boy saw was his own face, even his own ears, thirty, forty years hence. He allowed himself a moment of vanity. The man was not ugly. Then he shuddered. It was as though the truth came to him on a chill wind. There was something wrong with the man Jip would someday be, something terribly wrong. He couldn't shape it into words, but the man of forty years to come was not a man Jip even wanted to know, much less become.

"If you want help of any kind . . ." His body had recalled Teacher's words, if not his mind, for he was heading straight for the Stevens farm. Quaker Road was named for him, or for his father, more likely. People talked of them because though they were Quakers, they were rich as any Congregationalist, which seemed hardly proper. Quakers were supposed to be simple, plain folk. Surely only hypocrite Quakers could own that much land and prosper so when their own sons were deserting the hill farms and moving west in waves.

Jip came to a sprawling farmhouse with attached barns, undoubtedly the Quakers' place. He reined Jack in, stopping in the road. How could he turn in at the drive? The whole flight from the village seemed suddenly too foolish for words: racing from the store like one possessed at the sight of a man who at a glance bore him some small resemblance. He should turn around at once. He should go home where he and Put would have a good laugh at his being so easily panicked. Jip had known sheep with more gumption.

"And then you turned tail and run?" Put would say.

"Ehyuh. Like a ruined hound at sight of his first fox."

Something like that. He had all but made up his mind to turn the wagon when someone called to him from near the house. She, for it was a woman, seemed old, at least the hair escaping from her bonnet was white. She wore the plain black dress of a Quaker woman, with a white apron tied under her wide bosom.

"May I help thee?" she asked as she drew close. It was a good plain face, the eyes wrinkled with concern.

"Jip. That is what they call thee, is it not?"

He nodded, though he knew no reason why she should know him. "Is Mr. Stevens about? The young one, I mean."

She smiled broadly. "I've three of those young ones

about, growing older every day. But I think thee means my Luke."

"Teacher's friend?" Jip knew no other way to distinguish Teacher's Mr. Stevens from his brothers.

"The very one. He's hereabouts somewhere. Tie the horse and come in for a cup of milk while thee waits."

Jip obeyed because he had no other plan and because she seemed so kind, and safe. The first stranger knew only that he lived at the poor farm. The two men were not likely to go looking for him elsewhere.

Mrs. Stevens sat him down in her large, warm kitchen filled with smells of meat and vegetables stewing. There was a large loom in one corner with a fat roll of finished homespun on the cloth beam. Mrs. Stevens put a saucepan on the huge iron cookstove, and when it was steaming, she poured him a cup of foaming milk into which she had stirred a teaspoon of maple syrup.

"There," she said. "It's hot, so thee must sip it slowly while I fetch Luke from the pasture. Thee will wait?"

Jip nodded his head. He hoped later that he had remembered to say a proper thanks, but he may not have. All he could recall was her kindness and his own fear—all the more sharp because it made so little sense to him. If you can put a name to fear you have some power over it. He learned that in time, but that day he was too green to have such wisdom.

He had long finished the large mug of hot, sweet milk when Luke Stevens appeared at the kitchen door. He must have run, for his broad hat was in his hand and he was breathing hard.

"Jip," he said. But he did not waste his breath on more

119

welcome than that. "We must get thee away from here at once."

If he had said, "We must hang thee from the nearest elm," Jip would not have been more surprised.

"Away?"

"Yes," he said. Then at the look of utter puzzlement on the boy's face, he stopped, drew up a stool next to Jip's chair, and sat down. "Thee does not know." It was not a question. It was the Quaker's realization that if, at that moment, he had broken into Arabic or Chinese, the boy would better understand what he was about.

"Oh," he said, and Jip could tell he was trying to think out what to say—how to explain. "Oh," he said again.

The impasse was broken by his mother's arrival. She immediately took note of Jip's empty mug and moved to refill it. The kindly woman then cut a slice of bread and a slab of cheese and brought these to the boy as well. She offered her son the same, but he shook his head. He was too busy figuring out what to say to Jip to be distracted with food or drink.

"Jip," he said at last. "What does thee know of thy beginnings?"

Jip swallowed the large mouthful of bread and cheese that he was chewing. The fright had not, it appeared, robbed him of his appetite. "Nothing, sir," he said. "Jest that I fell off a wagon on the West Hill Road." He didn't add that no one had thought to come back for him. He had some little pride.

"Thee does not know any more? Who else was in the wagon?"

"No, sir."

Luke watched the boy take a swallow of milk to wash

down the bread in his mouth before continuing. "Has thee heard of the railroad—the Underground Railroad?"

"Teacher give me the book to read—about Uncle Tom?" Jip watched Luke's face, still near to the fresh face of a boy with its freckles and the sweaty red hair flattened against his skull from the broad black hat. Why was the face so stern, though?

"There is no easy way to tell thee . . ." Luke looked at Jip's hands clutching the mug in one, the bread and cheese in the other, then into his eyes, as though he wanted to take the boy onto his lap.

"Thy mother—thy mother . . ." Luke backed up and began again. "Thy skin is very light . . ." Why was the man talking about his skin? Jip glanced down. His hands were grimy as usual. And in summer his hands were so much in the earth that he never bothered to try digging out the dirt from under his nails.

"Thy mother . . ." Luke began again, then turned to Mrs. Stevens. "Mother, I *would* thank thee for a mug of milk."

Mrs. Stevens brought her son the milk, and then leaned kindly toward Jip. "Any son would be proud to have such a mother," she said, smiling warmly at him before she said quietly, "Thy mother is a slave, Jip, and that makes thee, in the eyes of thy master, a slave as well. Thy skin is light because her blood is a mixture of African and white."

She paused, to let her words find their mark. But Jip did not understand. It was as though he were in a great glass cage and could see the movement of their mouths, but could not hear what was being said.

Luke took up the telling. "You were but a baby when

121

she began her flight, following, as many have, the North Star to freedom. Sometimes, farther south, she received help from the railroad, but by the time she reached Vermont, she no longer asked for help. She had grown confident and was traveling quite openly. Her skin and that of her child were so light, no one took her for an African." He took a long swallow of his milk, as though giving Jip leave to speak, but Jip still sat silent in his glass enclosure.

"Someone offered her a ride somewhere south of here, I don't know just where. She was glad to accept. During her long journey the child had grown larger and heavier to carry. And she could not walk to Canada at a toddler's pace." He put his cup down on the table. "The owner of the wagon—unknown to her, the owner of the wagon meant to turn her over to her pursuers." Luke put his hand on Jip's knee. "Perhaps she fell asleep in the back of the wagon. At any rate, she realized suddenly that the wagon was no longer headed north toward the border. She knew at once that she had been betrayed. When the driver slowed to take the sharp curve on the West Hill Road, she put her child down onto the road . . ."

How could Jip credit such a tale? He couldn't look into that earnest Quaker face and doubt the man's own belief in the outlandish story. But if such a thing had truly happened, why didn't whoever caught her come back at once to search for her child?

"They always told me, sir," he said as politely as he knew how, "they always told me it was a gypsy wagon I fell from. They called me Jip." That last piece of evidence, his name, would surely convince the man, in a kindly way, that this account could have nothing to do with him, Jip.

"In truth, none of us knew where thee came from," Luke said. "The gypsy wagon was someone's fanciful tale. Even we plain Yankees like a good story." He smiled wryly.

Mrs. Stevens was studying Jip's uncomprehending face. "Thee must tell the boy how we know these things, son. Else how is he to believe thee?"

"The Scriptures tell us that we must be 'wise as serpents and gentle as doves.' Those of us of the abolitionist persuasion have taken these words to heart. If our enemies are to have spies and agents to do evil, then we must employ our own covert means to do God's work. Thus when it became known that a stranger had come not once, but three times to our township in the last year, my father sent word of it through what we call our grapevine telegraph—our message route." Jip nodded, pretending to understand. "We knew of no fugitives in our midst. Why had this fellow come? We got no answer until almost Christmas."

The stranger? He must mean the stranger who'd come to the poor farm. But the story still seemed to have nothing to do with him.

Luke stopped to take a sip of his milk, and his mother, seeing his hesitation, took up the story. "Thy mother was caught and returned. But somehow she convinced her master that the babe had died along the journey."

"Why didn't—" Jip cleared his throat. "Why didn't the man with the wagon tell him different?"

"We don't know," Luke said. "Perhaps he feared to

admit he had lost thee along the way. Or perhaps he had some shame to be partner to such evil. We do not know even who he was or what became of him. When we first heard this story in December we could not understand it. There was no African child among us. Then when I met thee at the school program . . . Thee has been here for so long that no one thought . . ."

He stopped, too kind to say that poor farm residents were all but invisible to the rest of the community. He sought Jip's eyes, but the boy ducked his head. "This is a hard tale for thee to credit, I'll warrant." The man could read Jip's disbelief. He continued softly. "Thy mother is a woman brave beyond the telling. Many times, we are told, she sought to break away and come to thee. Each time she was returned."

He waited, the air full of the mother's unsaid pain. Then he went on. "A slave catcher who knew thy master sighted thee by chance in the village. We know this because a friend, one of the house slaves, was present when the slaver appeared, demanding a great reward, but the master was incredulous. For all his cruel questioning, thy mother had sworn that thee was dead. But the slaver insisted—an uncanny likeness, he said . . ." Luke paused to see if Jip had taken his meaning. But Jip was remembering the small eyes of the stranger, his mouth dripping with honeyed words. The man was a slaver, setting a trap there in the barn.

"We heard last night that this master has come with the slave catcher to see for himself . . ." He leaned close to the boy. "Has thee seen either man? Is that why thee has come to us?"

Jip didn't answer. Nor could he question further. He was benumbed, like one struck dead. The bread and cheese he had swallowed so hungrily minutes before now sat like cold stones in the pit of his belly. He put the rest of the food down on the large oak table and stared at it.

"Does thee see, my friend," Luke asked anxiously, "why thee must flee at once?"

"I can't," Jip said at last. "How could I leave Put? Whatever would he do?"

13

The Dilemma

Jip couldn't have said why he replied to Luke Stevens as he did. It wasn't, he knew, because he was such a brave and generous boy that he would place Put's welfare above his own chance for freedom. Perhaps it was because his life had suddenly tumbled over on its head—perhaps he was paralyzed by the news of his birth. He had no tools in head or heart with which to shape these revelations into meaning. He only knew that at that moment Put was all the father or mother he could remember and that to leave him would somehow be the death of them both.

Luke Stevens did not scoff at Jip's answer, nor did he seek to pry him from it. It was Luke's mother who said most gently, "But, my child, if thee stays for capture, will thy friend be better off?"

Jip had no answer for this. He hung his head to think that he was such a simpleton as to imagine the strangers would give up the chase before the fox was seized. They knew where he lived. He had no hope the Lymans would seek to hide or protect him there—the reward for capture and threat of punishment for aiding would prove too much. They would send Put away, or worse, let him die of hunger of body and spirit, locked in his filthy cage—the cage Jip had made so proudly with his own hands.

How long he sat stupefied by what seemed unsolvable questions, he never knew. But at last a whinny from Old Jack, waiting at the hitching post, broke into his thoughts. He hadn't even watered him after that crazy race, much less rubbed him down or tied him where there was grass to graze. What must faithful Jack think? He who had given his whole strength to deliver Jip from harm?

"The horse—" he began.

"Let me tend to it for thee," Luke Stevens said.

"I had him at a gallop most of the way from town, and he don't know to trot, hardly."

Luke touched Jip's arm to assure him. "Finish thy bread and cheese. Then thee can decide what must be done."

Jip tried to obey, opening his mouth and chomping down on the food, but his jaws had forgotten how to chew. It took him ages to break down a single bite and then it caught in his throat when he tried to swallow. At length he lay the food once more on the smooth oak table, mumbling an apology.

Mrs. Stevens took it up and wrapped it in a cloth. "Thee has too many burdens in thy heart, child. Later, when thy hunger returns, thee may need this."

She busied herself about the kitchen as Jip watched. So this is what a mother is, he thought. Mrs. Wilkens was the closest model he'd seen, and he knew her for a scarred and broken one. Mrs. Stevens's mind seemed busy as her hands, and he was prideful enough to wonder if it was turning over the problem of his life, just as her hands were slapping down the dough and kneading it against the table. She had large hands for a woman, but he imagined that rough and red as they were from work, the touch was gentle as her voice. How would it be to have been held in those strong arms against that wide breast?

He sensed a kind of homesickness for arms he could not remember. What would she have looked like—that mother? At least now he knew the reason he appeared on the West Hill Road. She had done it to save his life, for freedom, indeed, is life. She couldn't save herself but she had made sure that her child would not grow up a slave.

Would she sorrow to know that those years of freedom had been spent on a poor farm? Would it sadden her to think that Jip had no family but the town to protect him and no name but the one called forth by the peculiar circumstances that added him to the town's roll of paupers? Some might think a poor farm little better than bondage. But Jip knew better. He had, as Father Adam in the Bible, dominion over the animals in his little Eden. Nor was he lonely as Adam in the garden—he'd had Sheldon and Lucy and Toddy and the rich if painful friendship with Put. Teacher, he knew, cared for him, and now the Stevenses did as well.

If Luke Stevens had ways to get word from the South, then perhaps he could send a message to that grieving mother that she had done right to throw her baby child off the wagon, that her son was rich and free, learning day by day to read and write and figure. She'd be so proud she bore him that she could cast off the shame of how he had been conceived.

Because boy though he was, Jip knew as well as any man what had been done to her. She would not have fled if she had chosen freely to bear her master's child.

It is hard to say if all these thoughts went through Jip's head during the space of time while he waited for Luke Stevens to return or whether they came in pieces later, but when Luke returned, the boy was no nearer to decision than when the man had left.

Perhaps that is why he blurted out so ill conceived a plan that it was bound to miscarry.

"I will flee, as you say," he said. "But I must take Put with me when I go."

The Stevenses, mother and son, passed a look but not a word between them. Luke sat down again on the stool beside Jip and asked with the earnestness of a boy questioning a man: "How will thee accomplish this, Jip?"

Jip had no answer, but he pretended to ponder, thinking out a plan even as he spoke. "We will leave tonight," he said. "If I jest follow the North Star like you said . . ."

"We can help thee," Luke said quietly. "There are friends all along the way northward. We call them stations on our secret railway."

"Then it will be easy," the boy said. "Jest tell me the way."

"I can tell thee one station only," Luke said. "We have found it is safer not to carry too much knowledge."

"Safer?"

"For others," he said. "Sometimes—sometimes, under painful questioning, a person tells what he would not otherwise."

"I'd never betray—" he began and then stopped. Who knew what one might do? To play the man might cost others their lives and hopes. "What's the first station, then?"

"Thee is sitting in it." Mrs. Stevens lifted her floury hands and slapped the dough against the tabletop.

"I'll bring him here tonight," Jip said, "if you will help us on."

Luke stood up, ready to see Jip out. "With God's help, we will see thee both safely on," he said.

Jip untied the horse and climbed into the wagon, not worried so much about the flight as the explanation he must concoct for his long absence from the farm, his winded horse, and his empty shopping basket. His mind elsewhere, he took the food Mrs. Stevens had given him from his pocket and chewed nervously at it, until, to his unhappy surprise, it was gone.

And, as it turned out, he needn't have worried about an explanation. Mr. Lyman's ague was most severe, and he was keeping Mrs. Lyman running back and forth to fetch him relieving medication and between times demanding her attention for his noisy complaints.

Jip led Jack into his stall, rewarding him with a handful of oats as well as a manger of hay, and went directly to milk. When he brought in the pail there was no evidence of supper preparation, so he stoked up the stove, put on a pot of water to boil, and made mush for everyone. After he got the others to the table, he took his own bowl and Put's back to the cage room.

Put was sitting cross-legged in the corner of the cage like a Chinese scholar, his spectacles halfway down his nose, reading Teacher's Bible.

Jip put down the bowls, then, making sure the hallway was clear, closed the door and came close to the cage.

"Hallo, Jip," Put said. He seemed in the brightest of spirits, for which Jip gave fervent, if silent, thanks to the Almighty. "You needn't tiptoe about. The manager's been like a wild brute in bedlam all day. But I thank you for closing the door. Now I can read in peace."

"Put." Jip's mouth was at the slats and he was whispering, which caused the old man to put down his book, remove his spectacles, and study the boy's face as if Jip were the odd one.

"Put," he repeated. "It's too long a tale to tell you now, but the stranger is back and this time they mean to kidnap me."

"Kidnap?"

"Shhh. I know it sounds crazy, but it's full truth. So—"

"So?"

"So I got to run."

"Run?" Now the old man had come close to the bars and was whispering as well. "Why? How? Where would you go?"

"We."

"What do you mean?"

"We. You and me. That is, if you're game to make a run for the border."

Put cocked his head. "Canady?" he asked.

Jip nodded. "There's them what will help us—if you be willing. I won't go without your coming, too."

He set the spectacles back on his nose as though Jip were a book in such small print he couldn't read it else. "Why are you so set on Canady?"

"You remember," Jip cleared his throat. "We was talking about it jest days ago. That law from Washington about runaway slaves . . ."

"You didn't run away, boy. You fell off a wagon."

"Seems I was kinda pushed by—my—my mother. She was fleeing them and about to be caught up to, there on the West Hill Road."

Put's mouth dropped open and Jip found himself studying the poor old red gums and missing and decayed teeth. Put closed his mouth, removed his spectacles, and, folding them carefully, set them on his knee. "I won't be going with you," he said. "I'd only hold you back. You know that, son. What you need is speed—to move fast and invisible. Take me along and it'll be like trying to run with a millstone hung 'round your neck."

"Then I won't go neither."

They were both quiet, each searching the other's face for a sign of weakness, a hint that one would give in to the other's demand. Put looked away first.

"If you stay here, they'll catch you. No mistake about it."

"I'll take my chance."

"That's no chance, boy. It's certain as death."

"Then so be it."

He sighed so deeply that Jip knew he had won.

"When do we leave?" the old man asked.

"Tonight." He could hardly keep the excitement from creeping into his voice. "Tonight. Soon as they're all asleep."

14

Taking Flight

Jip told Old George that he would be sleeping in Put's room that night. As he often did this to keep the lunatic calm, no one would think it strange. Nor did he worry about provisions. It was only a few miles north to the Stevens farm, and he knew he could count on the Quakers to more than supply them with what they needed for the next stage of the journey. He had a bit of pride about taking from the farm's store of food. He didn't want anyone, after he was gone, to remember him as a thief.

There was enough moon for the travelers to see their way as they crept out of the house and across the yard. Jip spared a pang of conscience for the beasts. Who would milk Bonnie in the morning or take Jack out to pasture? And no one would pay those poor stupid sheep any mind at all. But he knew in his heart that there was no help for what he was doing. He was getting away and Put was coming with him. Thank the Lord. He hadn't much fancied sitting around like a prize pumpkin waiting to be plucked.

Where were the strangers sleeping this night? Indeed if they slept at all. How did such men go about the business of tracking and trapping other human beings?

Except for what he had read in Mrs. Stowe's book, he knew so little of it all. He had not realized until yesterday that there were folks close by who were set to disrupt this murderous pursuit. Perhaps Teacher had given him that book on purpose, as a warning, so he would know that he mustn't let himself be caught.

He had to be careful of his pace. They were both barefoot, but Put's feet, too long indoors, were tender and he stepped almost daintily on the rough ground. *If he sees he's holding me back, he'll refuse to go on. I got to watch it. I can't waste precious time arguing whether to move forward or back.*

They would be most exposed during the early part of the trip. Jip wasn't expecting the slavers to be out, but how could he be sure? For the first hour or so they followed the road. The early August moon lit their path. Put stopped to point out the Big Dipper and the North Star the fugitives were said to follow. Jip tried not to be impatient. Perhaps they should have cut across the fields, but that would have meant climbing stone walls and rail fences, moving up and down across the rocky ground. Nor would they be better hidden. Someone's dog was like to set up a bark, causing them to be shot as marauding foxes or thieves. And there was no cover to hide behind in those pastures. Most had been cut for potash years before and kept clear by grazing sheep.

They did go east through pastureland to bypass the village, and then it occurred to Jip that at the rate they were walking it would be daylight long before they reached the Stevenses. Put, so out of practice walking, had to stop and catch his breath at every little hill. Jip decided it would be better not to follow the road any longer but to cut up through the woods and hit Quaker Road at an angle, not far from the Stevenses' farm. He didn't discuss his plan with Put. The old man was tired and looked to be feeling every stone and twig underfoot.

The boy had a fair notion of direction in the daytime. Like anyone who works outdoors, he knew where the sun lay at various times of the year and at different hours of the day. He could not recollect ever being lost in daylight. But he had not reckoned for the night. He did not know his way, as sailors do, by the stars, though knowing how the Dipper pointed helped. Once in the woods, however, with no stars in view and hardly any light of the moon shining through, they might as well have been blindfolded. He could only crash forward. Put was probably trying as hard not to ask if Jip knew the way as Jip was trying not to say how very lost they were.

The way—which was what Jip had to call it even though it was just the direction his feet were taking him—went uphill so steeply that he could hear Put behind him panting. The old man was grabbing branches to pull himself forward, letting each one go with a crash as he reached out to grasp the next. A pair of bucks fighting for a doe would have been quieter. But how could Jip scold Put for trying to keep up on a journey he'd forced him to take? As soon as they reached a level spot, Jip stopped. When Put was beside him, the boy dropped all pretense. "I ain't got the smallest notion of where we are, Put. We might as well find a spot and settle down till morning."

The old man mumbled something Jip took to be

assent. It seemed clear he was too tired to speak. They huddled together for warmth against the broad trunk of a tree. "Best try to sleep," Jip said.

Put may have slept a little. His panting ceased and his breath came more regularly. Jip could have sworn that he never closed his own eyes, but he must have, because suddenly the bright sun of a summer morning penetrated the leafy ceiling of the woods. Jip looked at Put. His eyes were open, though bloodshot and very weary.

His own limbs were stiff, but the boy struggled to his feet, stretched, then reached down to help the old man up. Put tried to make a joke of it. How after all that time sleeping in the luxury of his cage had spoiled his bones. They had plumb forgot how to rough it in the open. Why, when he'd been in the army back in '12, '14, many's the night . . .

At last Jip had him on his feet. "Lead on!" Put said. The tone of fake cheer in his voice made Jip want to cry. If he could get a good glimpse of the sun and take his bearings, he was sure he could lead them to Quaker Road. He hoped he was right—that Quaker Road wound up the far side of the hill on which they stood. "Well, Put," he said at last. "Let's try it this away."

They walked. Jip forced himself to take the pace at nearly a crawl. Finally he figured they must be near the road, if not yet parallel to the Stevenses' farm. They came upon a stream that must be forded. The water was lively and swift, but this late in the summer less than a foot in depth.

"Here, let me give you a hand," Jip said, stepping into the cool water. "These rocks are a mite slippery."

The old man waved him off. "You go on ahead," he said. "Scout it out. Like we used to do in the war. Find us the best route. I'll jest wait here. Get a bit of a rest."

Jip didn't want to go on without him, but he doubted that he could sling the old man over his back and carry him. So he left him there. At least there was water in the stream, even though Put'd have to bend down and lap it like a dog. In all his pride Jip had not even provisioned the two of them with a tin cup for their great journey. For the hundredth time he repented his mindless eating of Mrs. Stevens's bread and cheese.

"I'll be back afore you know it," he promised.

Without Put to slow him down, Jip could move fast as a hare through the brush, and in what seemed to him no time at all, he spied through the trees the winding ribbon of packed earth that must be Quaker Road. He hadn't altogether gotten them lost, or indeed led them far astray of their goal. He allowed himself a moment of pride over that. Then, keeping well under the cover of the trees, he followed the road as it wound farther uphill until, at last, he spied the great red barn and sprawl of white frame buildings that made up Quaker Stevens's homeplace.

Smoke was pouring from the chimney. The boy fancied he caught the smell of corn mush and griddle cakes cooking on the black iron stove. He could have sung out with joy. He would present himself at the door and ask for help bringing Put in from the woods.

He had left the trees and started across the road when a sound came to his ears—the rattle of a carriage and the pounding of hooves on the hard-packed dirt of the road.

He wasn't frightened, but caution sent him back into the trees to let the traffic pass. He knew he shouldn't let himself be seen.

He recognized the horse at once. He knew most horses in the county by sight. It was one from the village livery stable, and it struck him as strange that someone would be out in a hired carriage at this hour of the morning. The lack of sleep must have made him dull. He didn't recognize the driver or the passenger in their top hats and well-cut suits. He was surprised when the carriage failed to continue up the road but turned into the Stevenses' drive and stopped. The driver tied the horse to the same post where Jip had hitched Jack only yesterday. Then the passenger stepped down and the two of them went to the door.

The one who was the driver pounded on the door. Rude, thought Jip. I'd of thought such gentlemen had more manners. An older man, Quaker Stevens himself most likely, answered the door. Jip could not hear his gentle greeting, but his own heart jumped into his mouth as the driver began to wave something in the Quaker's face and a hatefully familiar voice cried out, "Give him up at once! We have a warrant!"

Quaker Stevens did not move, but the driver pushed him roughly aside and the two strangers strode past him into the farmhouse.

15

Hunted

Jip's heart was pounding like summer thunder against his chest. What could they do? He, perhaps, could make his way to the border some whichaway. It couldn't be more than a two-week walk, but what of Put? He had counted on the Quakers to find transport for them. He hadn't thought that Put would need to walk it. What had he done bringing Put along? Would a cell in an asylum be worse than death from hunger or exhaustion in the wild? He must go back at once to where Put waited, confess his selfishness and stupidity, and take his friend back to the poor farm.

For what? Death from despair and neglect? He shivered, then sat down on the floor of the woods, unable to go forward or back. I'll watch the house, he reasoned. When they find I'm not there, they'll leave and go hunt for me elsewhere. They're not so clever. Else they'd have come to the farm last night. He began to sweat. Suppose they had? He'd taken a dreadful risk going back there. Why had they not gone there last night? Why, instead, come here so early in the day? They had wind of the Stevenses, that was it; they suspected them of aiding fugitives.

The slavers must surely have searched every inch of

the house, the outbuildings, and the barn. Or it seemed they had. He sat so long and so still there on the leaves and litter of the forest floor that a little vanguard of ants hurried over the mountain of his bare foot and came back sometime later, lugging a beetle many times their size. Jip watched the little creatures, tugging and pulling and pushing their feast. He almost reached down and lifted the beetle across his foot for them, but he stopped himself. There was something comforting about that kind of grit. It was like a message. The ants were telling him that he mustn't lose heart so easily.

The slavers were out of Jip's sight for near eternity, until at last his straining eyes saw them come out of the barn door, accompanied by a small troop of male Stevenses.

They were too far away for Jip to hear what was being said, but from the gestures of the driver, it was clear that he was furious not to have found his quarry. The other— Jip could not call him master, much less . . . The other stood stiffly by. As far as Jip could tell, the pale man said nothing. At length they left the Stevenses and returned to their hired carriage.

As they turned out of the drive and into the road, Jip could catch bits of their conversation, for the angry driver spoke louder than a gentleman ought. The pale man had apparently proposed that the driver stay behind to watch the house, while he himself returned for his breakfast at the tavern.

The driver, the person that Jip had long thought of as the stranger, but whom he now knew to be a slave catcher, was vocal in his displeasure at the idea. Was he then to be left on a country road with no horse and no provisions, not even a stool upon which to sit? He also made some half-joking remark about the large-sized, unfriendly Friends, betraying a certain nervousness about the Stevenses' household.

The pale man was not sympathetic. His voice was much lower, and Jip caught only the words "yonder woods" as the man tossed his head in Jip's direction. The boy didn't wait to hear more, but slipped away through the trees at once. At least they had no hounds. In the book Teacher had given him, the slavers ran a pack of bloodhounds.

He found Put near the spot where he had left him, though during his long wait, the old man had moved to get himself a drink of water. He had heard the boy coming and was looking up with so much expectation in his old tired face that Jip could hardly bear to tell him the news.

"So," Put said when he heard, "that cursed feller is keeping a watch on the house."

"Yes." How could he soften it? "You figure he's got to eat or sleep sometime," knowing as he said it what cold comfort the words offered.

"Appears to me," Put said, his mouth twisted into an attempt at a smile. "Appears to me, you and me is in a pickle barrel without a fork."

Jip gave a weak laugh. "If only I had brought us food."

"And quilts."

"And a jug of cider."

"And a pouch of tabaccy."

"You don't smoke, Put."

"I was thinking of taking it up, with so much time on my hands."

Who could have guessed that Old Put could get him

laughing—and them in such dire straits? For the first time in hours, Jip felt something like happiness that he had brought his friend along. Though he sobered quickly. He knew their laughter couldn't be heard as far as the road, but they must get into the habit of caution. It didn't come naturally to either of them.

"We got to put our brains to it, Put. I think they're like to give us up in a day or two, but meantime, we got to get off this damp ground and get something into our hollow bellies."

"There's huckleberries over in that clearing near the stream," he said. "I spied them when I was getting a drink."

"Huckleberries is fine," Jip said. "I always fancy them this time of year, don't you?" But the few he found were dried and not too tasty. They both made a show of enjoying the scarce handful. Then Jip took a long drink from the stream to give himself time to think out what they must do next.

Put had been thinking as well. "You're right, you know. The feller can't stay there forever, and I've got a good notion that the other pretty gentleman"—said in a voice to make Jip understand that he could not truly consider a slave owner a gentleman—"will feel himself too proud to take a turn at sentry duty."

"So?"

"So they can't capture you, not legal like, without the sheriff or some such officer of the law . . ."

"Ey?" He hadn't known that. Maybe Put did have an idea that might help.

"You go back there"—he raised his hand to keep Jip from interrupting—"*alone*. Two is two to make noise in the bush. You go there and watch the watcher. When he leaves, for he's going to have to leave sometime, you hightail it to the house. They'll have a place to hide you, won't they?"

"But—"

"You can send someone back for me. Even if they was to stumble acrost me here, they're not likely to trouble themselves to arrest a lunatic. And if they do, they'll just throw me into a cage. And a cage, my boy, is home sweet home to me."

He didn't like Put's plan. It meant leaving his friend alone again, but Jip didn't have another plan to offer. He took off his outer shirt and folded it as a kind of pillow for Put to sit on. Though Put gave a show of protest, he settled his old bones on it, leaning against the sugar maple tree that the two of them had begun to think of as their own—as close as they had to a refuge in the woods.

When Jip started once more for Quaker Road he was conscious of every twig cracking under the soles of his feet, the cry of every startled bird, or scurry of chipmunk, the slightest rustle of the branches he brushed past. He must get close enough to keep the slave catcher in sight without arousing the slightest suspicion in the man that he was being watched.

Perhaps he should climb a tree and hide himself among the branches. Then he could look down upon the whole scene, keeping the sentry in sight as well as the farmhouse and whatever traffic might be coming up the road. The trick was to climb making no more noise than a squirrel. The slave catcher was an edgy sort of fellow. Anything was likely to fright him. See—he had pulled his watch out of his pocket once again. Now he was peering down the road. He was on his feet. Jip froze. But, as he suspected, the man's jerky behavior was just nervousness. Look-a-there. The man couldn't seem to sit still. Down under all that bluster, the man was shaky as an aspen in a windstorm. The slaver tried pacing a bit, as much as one could confined by the trees and hidden from the road. He looked this way and that. Once Jip thought the man might have looked straight at him, but if he had, he'd seen nothing, for he took a step or two in the opposite direction before coming back to sit down again on his fallen log.

Jip crept a few feet deeper into the woods, looking for a tree tall and full enough to suit his need. He spotted a tall beech. He had hardly shinnied up its smooth, gray trunk to a low fork in the branches than he heard the sound of the horse and carriage on the road. A squirrel scolded and birds flew up squawking as he climbed, but he could only hope that the noise of the traffic would cover his scramble. Thirty, maybe forty feet up, he sat himself on a strong limb, holding tightly to the trunk. He had chosen well. His perch lifted him above the canopy of the woods. A good stretch of the road was in sight.

The pale stranger's carriage was followed by someone on horseback. Who was it? Yes, the sheriff had come this time. When they got to the spot where the slave catcher had hidden himself, he stepped out into the road. The carriage and horseman stopped. There was a consultation. Sheriff Glover seemed annoyed. At length, and after extended discussion, the slave catcher climbed up into the carriage. The pale man backed and turned the horse.

Soon they would be returning to the village. Jip waited for them all to move on, but they went no farther. What were they waiting for? All three of them were looking down the road. There was annoyance in the way they held their bodies; even the horses stomped and flicked their tails impatiently.

At long last a single clumsy horse came plodding up the hill, two men on its broad back. Jip recognized the horse before he recognized the riders. It was the Bracketts' much abused plowhorse with Addison and Warner astride.

Judging by the gestures, the slave catcher and the brothers were having a heated exchange. Addison was the talker. Warner just sat there, wiping his face on his sleeve. At length they dismounted. They seemed to be tying the horse, though Jip couldn't be sure. After a few more words, the pale man flicked the reins and the carriage started down the road followed by the sheriff. Jip could no longer see the Bracketts, only the rear end of their horse, his tail sweeping his broad rump. Maybe the brothers had sat themselves down on the slaver's fallen log. But it was clear: They were here to watch that no one entered the farmhouse.

What was he to do? The Bracketts had no love for him. They probably thought stalking a fugitive great sport—and one that put money in the pocket besides.

If he had been less tired, if his belly had been less hollow, he would have seen what to do much earlier. There must be a door to the farmhouse on the pasture side. If he made his way up beyond the next bend of the road, he could cross over, steal down the fields and pasture, and come in from the west side of the house. The land was cleared, but it was hilly. There was a good chance he could make it without the Bracketts seeing him. He didn't give the boys much credit for common sense—or vigilance either, for that matter.

He slid down the beech tree, taking care to land softly on the leaf-strewn ground, grateful the Bracketts hadn't thought to bring their dogs along. His heart was pounding so loud that it was a wonder the boys couldn't hear it. He crept several hundred feet north, well beyond the next curve of Quaker Road.

He raced across the fields, not even daring to check that no one was watching. His goal was a huge wooden watering trough, the only hiding place he could spot in the pasture. The cows coming to and from the trough eyed him with considerable suspicion as he squatted there. He held still for several minutes, both to catch his breath and to let the cows become accustomed to his presence. Then he got to his knees and slowly raised his head, his eyes just above the level of the trough.

The farmhouse complex blocked any view of the Bracketts or their horse. Jip spoke gently to the cows. He couldn't risk upsetting them. It would send an alarm even to the thick heads across the road if they saw a bunch of cattle suddenly dancing out from behind the barn. I can make it easy if I move slow and quiet and don't scare the cows, he thought. He had hardly taken his first cautious step when suddenly, sending his stomach bolting into his gullet, a big hand reached across his shoulder and clamped down on his open mouth.

16

The Cabin

"Jip. I did not mean to frighten thee, but thee must not go to the house. They are watching it."

"Just the Brackett boys," Jip whispered. He knew, if Luke Stevens didn't, that those fellows had less gumption than a lovesick moose.

Luke put up a finger to shush conversation, turned Jip about, and headed him right back the way he'd come. "Stay low," he muttered under his breath. He paused a minute to pump some water into the trough and then began a casual saunter among the cattle, motioning to Jip to stay behind the bodies of the beasts while he stooped now and again to inspect an udder or look at a backside. In this way the two of them made their way northward across the pasture to the curve of the road and into the woods on the other side. In the safety of the trees, he explained.

"We know there are others just down the way. There may be more elsewhere. They hope to trap thee into coming into the house. There's a cabin farther up—at the end of the road. I think thee will be safe there until nightfall. Then, if all goes well, we can convey thee to the next station."

"Put—I left Put . . ."

"Where has thee left him? Tell me and I'll fetch him here. It is not safe for thee to be abroad."

Jip described the place as best he could. Luke knew the spot. The woods were on their land, he said, and he had hunted in them the better part of his life. Jip was not to worry. They were walking as they spoke, keeping to the protection of the trees until, finally, the cabin came into sight—a rough log one-room structure—the kind built in the olden days or even more lately by those too poor to raise a proper clapboard house. Still, weatherworn as the logs were, the roof was newly shingled and the small windows sported glass panes.

Without knocking, Luke lifted the latch and pushed open the door for Jip to enter. There was no fire on the hearth and no sign about of the cabin's residents.

"I think thee should stay in the loft," Luke said. "If by chance someone should peer in the window—though no one has come looking here as yet. I'll bring thee food as soon as I am able. Meantime"—he reached into a crock and took out a handful of hard biscuits—"this is the best I can offer." He grinned. "My mother would be mortified to treat a guest so. Now climb up and I will serve thee thy breakfast."

All Jip could think of was Put. He'd make himself sick trying to eat those berries. Oh, why hadn't he saved the bread and cheese for him? "When you go to find Put, he'll be powerful hungry."

"Don't be anxious. I'll see him to better than this, I promise."

Jip climbed up the ladder, then reached down for the

biscuits and a cup of water Luke had dipped out from a bucket near the sink. The Quaker bade a quick good-bye then and closed the door after him. He was outside for a while, stacking something—was it firewood?—against the door. Not to keep him in, Jip guessed, but to try to keep his enemies out.

He ate the hardtack biscuits hungrily, washing them down with water, and fell back on the mattress to sleep like one dead. He awoke once to hear the sound of rain on the roof, but Put was safe, Luke had promised, so he turned over and slept again. The next sound he was conscious of was a noise at the back of the cabin—that of a window being raised. He peered through the darkness without daring to breathe. A dark round form clanked against the plank floor. Then one long leg followed another across the sill, until the whole of Luke Stevens's body slipped into the cabin.

"Jip," he called softly. Even when there was no immediate danger the man had the habit of quiet.

Jip leaned over the edge of the loft. "Where's Put?"

"He's with my mother. He needs more care right now than either thee or I can give him."

"He's not—"

"No, he has not left his senses, but he is cold and hungry. Providence is testing us with a bitter rain tonight, and thy friend got the worst of it. Even the sentries seem to have left off watching."

"Can I come down, then?"

"Yes and I'll make a fire as well. Unless . . ." He hesitated. "Jip, thy friend will not be traveling tonight. He said for thee to go on ahead. That he would follow."

149

"I can't do that," Jip said.

Luke sighed. "I said as much to him." He had the fire going quickly and hung above it the kettle he had brought. On top of the kettle lid he laid slabs of bread to warm. The smell of bubbling meat and vegetables and the steaming bread was as close to heaven as any boy of a poor farm is likely to get this side of the grave. Luke watched him eat, refusing to join him. "If I take rations my mother has sent for thee, she'll take her broad hand to my hide, woman of peace though she claims to be," he said.

With the last hunk of bread Jip was sopping up every drop of the rich gravy that clung to the sides and bottom of the kettle when Luke began to speak. "We do not know what the slavers intend—beyond their certain intention to recapture thee alive. They will not want to hurt thee, for that lessens thy value to them. But they have many tricks and they have been diligent in this hateful business for so long that we on the other side must be, as I said, wise as serpents when we try to match wits with theirs."

Jip waited, though not with complete patience, to hear what the Quaker would say. The man had been matching wits with the devil for some time and, for all his gentleness, was winning, Jip suspected, as often as not.

"My choice," Luke said, "would be to convey thee northward tonight. The rain is on our side. But," he smiled ruefully in the firelight, "it is not mine to choose. If thee and Friend Nelson are to travel together, we must wait until he is more able to make the journey." He stirred the fire and watched it blaze up before continuing. "The enemy will send word to their spies to watch the suspicious houses in this area. I cannot risk conveyance to a station too near at hand. When they companion can make the journey, I aim to convey you to the railroad at Northfield. There is an agent there who is not loath to conceal our passengers in amongst the freight and deliver them safely across the border."

"A real railway?" Jip asked. He'd never seen a train, but the old men at the farm told tales of them—huge black monsters, puffing fire and brimstone as they screamed down their tracks faster than a prize team of Morgans. How would it be to climb into the belly of such a beast and ride? A thrill went down him all the way to his toes. "An *iron* railway?" he asked again to be sure.

"Yes. Not our poor wagon-and-foot underground route. Thee may ride to Canada in style—if we can get there on the day our friend is on duty." Jip determined not to be afraid. A real railway meant Put could *ride* to Canada. Inside where it was warm and dry. They had only to get down the mountain to Northfield.

He bade good night to Luke and mounted the ladder, still shivering at the thought of the great iron beast that would bear him and Put away to Canada and freedom.

He was already awake and hungry again when the first light of early morning penetrated the dark of the cabin. A fellow could get used to good food with hardly any practice. But his breakfast did not appear. By midmorning, tired of lying on the straw mattress listening to the growls from his belly, he climbed down the ladder and stole over to the biscuit crock. He stuffed his pockets. Keeping one eye on the front window, he poured himself a cup of water and carried it and the hardtack back to the loft.

What followed was the longest day of his life. Even at high noon, the cabin let in very little light, so he sat cross-legged on the mattress, tensed for any sound of Luke at the back window. He could hear the birds outside chittering away. He could hear the rustle of leaves, the clatter of squirrels across the wooden shingles over his head. He even thought he heard the squeaking of mice below him. But there was no sound of footsteps on the path or the raising of a window. Luke had promised to come. Something had happened to make him break that vow. What?

His restless brain skittered back and forth across all the possibilities and from there to all the craziness of the last two days, until finally it lit at last on what had been revealed to him: He was an African slave. Not the child of gypsies much less a victim of such. He was the child of a slave—a colored woman had given birth to him. He looked at his hand. In the gloom of the cabin it shone white—far nearer the wool of a merino than the feather of a raven. But then, what did a black African really look like? He had never seen one. There had been a poster hung in Peck's store advertising an abolitionist meeting. The African on the poster did not seem inordinately dark-skinned, though it was hard to tell. At any rate Jip didn't look like that man. And he certainly didn't look like the outlandish caricatures of Negroes in Mr. Lyman's newspaper. But posters and cartoons didn't really tell him what an African slave looked like in the flesh.

Was he shocked to find that he himself was called one? Somewhat, if he were honest. He'd never entertained the possibility before. Of course he was surprised. But the shock that sent quakelike tremors through him was not that he was African, but that he was not entirely Negro. The greater, far more violent assault on his sense of himself was to see his features mirrored in the face of the pale stranger. The very thought made him want to retch. There could be no doubt that his pursuer, the man set to hunt him down like a varmint, was the one who had sired him.

Hour after hour, his poor mind, already pulled about between his anxiety for Put and worry about Luke's not coming, was flooded with revulsion about this new certainty. At first, when Luke had broken the news of his ancestry, he had been numbed. But there in the loft the terribleness of the truth had pierced through that protective wall, leaving him naked to the pain and shame of the fact of his birth.

All those years when he had wondered why no one had bothered to come back for him . . . God must like bitter jokes. Because someone did come. His question was answered. There was no more mystery to be solved. Someone had come back—not to claim his child but to recover his property. He began to shiver though the loft was warm and airless.

Dark came, and still no one appeared to tell him the state of things at the house down the road. A dozen times, he started for the ladder, thinking how he could creep down there himself and scout out how things stood, but he was able to stop himself from such a fool action. If it were possible, Luke Stevens would have come. He had not come. It could only mean that he must wait.

He waited wakeful as an owl. He nibbled up his supply of hardtack, too tense even to lie down for more than a minute or so at a stretch. Then, sometime past midnight, as he judged it, he saw the lights—bobbing high as though borne by men on horseback.

He did not wait for them to arrive. He shoved the cup into his pocket, scrambled down the ladder, and let himself out through the back window as fast as he could. Once he had dropped to the ground, he stood still, listening. Three, no, four horses, coming at a walk up the road. They could only be his pursuers. Luke Stevens would not have come in company and not likely on horseback, even alone.

He crept from the back of the cabin to the edge of the woods. He could hear them dismount, pause, speak quietly at the blocked doorway, and start around the cabin. He did not stop any longer. It was dark in the woods, but he went ahead. If he could get to the stream, he would be able to find their maple tree. Luke might look for him there. And if he did not? What was he to do then? Try to find the way north on his own with no money, no notion of the way, leaving Put behind? Or try to wait his pursuers out? Surely they would tire of hunting him—one half-grown boy, never taught how to be a slave, who'd turn into more of a troublemaker than an asset.

He'd be like the slave George in Teacher's book, he thought. Yes, if caught, he fancied that he'd be quite as belligerent as George toward captivity. Nor would they break him. But slaves like George just got sold down the river to the cotton fields, where they were forced into submission or, like noble Uncle Tom, beaten to an early death.

By the time he stumbled upon the stream the bravado had drained out from the soles of his feet. He did not want to be captured. He did not want his will tested. Oh yes, he could think brave things about freedom being life, but he did not want to have to choose between them. He wanted both.

Must I then jest forget about Put? Leave him with the Stevenses? Who on earth will treat him more kindly than they? Anyone with half a mind would envy such a fate. But if I leave him and go on to Canady by myself, I will be full alone. I need him worse than what he needs me. If only I knew where Teacher was. She'd help me. She'd get me and Put both out of here, clever as she is. . . .

How he found the camping place, he wasn't sure. But there in the pale moonlight through the trees he recognized their tree and flung himself on the wet leaves at its trunk. Did he sleep? He would have said not, but in the first pale gray of morning, something, some noise, startled him wide awake. A crack and crashing through the bush. It was some distance away, but his ear told him whatever it was, man or beast, it was headed in his direction. Should he climb a tree, or wait quietly where he was? It was not likely his pursuers. They would have gone about the chase with more stealth and cunning. No, he reckoned it to be a wild thing of some sort, a bear maybe? He'd heard tales of bears though he had yet to see one.

17

Cries for Help

Through the crash of leaves and litter he heard a voice, a voice weak with exhaustion and desperation: "Jip? Jip, boy, can you hear me?"

Put! He forgot all caution and cried the name aloud. "Put! I'm here. At our old camp. Stay where you are, I'll fetch you." Then he remembered that even trees have ears and he lowered his voice. "Jest keep calling out my name quiet like so's I won't miss you." If the trackers had followed Put into the woods, why, they were both done for, but nothing would keep him from going to Put. When he found him, standing there, his old back bent, his eyes full weary, Jip threw his arms about Put's shoulders and cried like he was Toddy's age—tears of anger and pain, but mostly tears of joy to see his friend again.

Jip led him back across the creek. As he did so, he could feel the man's body shivering. He tried to tell himself it was like his own tears, that Put was just trembling from the pleasure of their being together, but by the time they reached the maple tree he could no longer fool himself. Put's forehead was as hot as a cookstove and his body vibrating like a frightened old ewe at shearing.

Jip started to take off his undershirt—his shirt was

now somewhere in the Stevenses' farmhouse—but Put wouldn't hear of it. "'Twouldn't be decent, you setting around half naked. Good earth and seas, boy, preserve a little delicacy afore an old man."

Jip tried to laugh as he eased Put to the damp ground. They sat in silence, listening to the sounds of the creek. He hardly dared ask the questions that needed to be asked.

"I thought to bring food for us," Put began, "but they who was keeping me prisoner set up all night through in the kitchen, so I daren't."

"Keeping you prisoner?" Had the slavers taken over the farmhouse, then?

"They told me I must stay in bed and not make a sound," he said. "They pushed something afore the door to make sure I didn't escape. But," he smiled proudly, "I'm not such an old fool as I can't manage a little drop from a ground-floor window."

"But where were the Stevenses?" Jip asked. "How could the slavers take over the house?"

"The slavers?" he seemed confused. "It was the plagued Quakers what shut me in."

"Oh, Put. They're our friends. They were trying to keep you safe!"

"They wouldn't let me come to you. I told them to tell you to go on, but they didn't do that neither. They wouldn't listen to me. They just told me I must stay in bed and keep still."

"Because you're sick, Put. They were afraid for you. You're burning with fever."

"They wouldn't let me come to you," he said stubbornly. "Even when I told them you needed me. They wouldn't let me come. I said you'd be caught if we didn't move on, and they wouldn't pay me no mind."

There was nothing more to say. The sun rose high. Even in the shadowy woods, the air felt a bit less chill than it had in the night. Still Put shivered, what teeth he had rattling in his mouth.

Jip took his tin cup and carried cupful after cupful for the old man to drink and some to splash upon his hot forehead. As the day wore on, he knew that another night in the woods might likely be the death of the old man. The cold ground must be painful for him even when the sun was shining.

"How's your feet, Put? Think they could carry us back to the village?"

Put looked up, his eyes bright with fever, but he nodded and began to struggle to stand. Jip pulled him upright. "No hurry a-tall. We'll just meander over that way. We can't go into the village until well past dark, but Mrs. Wilkens is there with Lucy and Toddy and the baby. They're sure to take us in." Put tried to smile.

Any tracker with half a mind could have followed their awkward trail, but the way was mostly downhill, and in the daylight Jip felt confident of the direction. At last they stopped. They were at the edge of the woods in someone's sugar bush, for the maples were scarred from years of tapping. A few minutes more and they could see open pasture through the trees and a farmhouse on the hill beyond.

He tried to figure whose homeplace it was. Was it likely to be friend or foe? Once he got his bearings, he realized it was Baby Tucker's family. He had no idea whether they'd consider harboring a fugitive a crime or a good deed. Best not take a chance. And there was a dog, barking unhappily as though tied against its will. No, best not risk asking for help here.

"Let's back up a bit into the woods," Jip whispered. "I'll find us something to set on—this wet ground's like ice." He found a short piece of trunk from a broken birch and rolled it over against a maple. "There," he said. "There's a parlor chair for you."

Put sat down and leaned against the maple's furrowed trunk, sighing deeply. Jip had thought to bring the cup, though there was no stream handy now. Why hadn't he at least taken the time to fill his pockets with hardtack? He could hardly bear to look at Put, who was hugging his arms to his body, trying to hide the shaking.

Jip left as soon as it was night—sooner gone, sooner returned, he figured. The village was not in total darkness. The moon was nearly full and there were lights shining from a few windows. He kept in the shadows behind the buildings and made his way to the seamstress's shop. There were no lamps lit in front or back. He waited, listening for any sound of activity inside, but could hear none. Good. They were all asleep. Jip crept to a window at the back and stretched his nose over the sill to squint through the glass. He studied every hump until he felt sure that next to the window from where he hunched was a bed and that the bump on it at his right was Lucy's head and the smaller one at the other end was Toddy's head.

He reached up and gently rapped the pane with his knuckles. Lucy stirred and turned over. He rapped again.

Slowly she sat up, then leaned toward the window to peer out into the darkness.

"Lucy?"

She gave a little start.

"It's me, Jip."

She pressed her face on the pane until they were nearly nose to nose against the glass. "Jip? What're you doing here?" she mouthed.

"I need help. Put and me both."

She put her fingers to her lips, looked behind her into the room, and then indicated that he should go to the front of the shop.

He hesitated, not wishing to reveal himself on the street side, but she nodded vigorously and slipped out of bed. Jip sidled around to the front, waited in the shadows until the front door eased open a crack, then crept up on the porch and through the slit.

Lucy didn't bother with a greeting. "You're in terrible trouble," she whispered hoarsely. "There's slavers after you."

"I know. That's why I come—"

"Oh, Jip. Ma heard the slavers offer a hundred dollars' reward and she's licking her chops. If she sees you she'll give you up faster than a cow flicks a fly."

"Your ma?" Mrs. Wilkens had been, if not his friend, surely on his side at the farm. "Why would she do that to me?"

"Ma's mad, Jip. She says you tricked us—making out like you was white as us, when all the time—"

"I didn't know," he said. "Truly. How was I to know?" How could Mrs. Wilkens accuse him of deception?

"I know it don't make sense. But there it is. I'm forbid to speak to you ever again, and if I see you I'm to tell her. But I won't," she added quickly. "I'd never tell. Not even my own ma."

Despair hit him like a blow in the gut. There was to be no help for them—not for Put nor him. What was he to do?

"Teacher'll help you," Lucy whispered. "She's boarding up at Deacon Avery's place the summer. Keeping the books and helping out."

If his heart could have sunk further it would have. Avery'd had no love for him when he was a poor farm brat. He was not likely to jump to his aid now he was a fugitive.

"Lucy?" a sleepy voice called out from the rear room. "Lucy?"

"I better go," she said.

Jip reached into his pocket and pulled out his long-saved penny. "Take this to Peck's and buy some penny candy for you and Toddy, hear? Something to remember your old schoolmate by?"

Her hand closed over the money. "I'll never forget you, Jip. You're my only true friend. You be careful."

He slipped out without another word. The door closed quickly behind him.

What was he to tell Put? That those they had believed to be friends could no longer be counted on? How was he different from the boy Mrs. Wilkens had trusted her Lucy to all last winter? She hadn't despised him when he was a waif fallen off a wagon. Now she's set to betray me—like I done her or her children bodily harm, he thought. He wished he could think that Lucy was lying—rather than believe her ma had said such awful things. But he knew the truth of it. In Mrs. Wilkens's sight, he was no longer just Jip but a thing to be despised. His heart was no different, his mind no better or worse. Nothing about who he was or how he looked had altered in the least, but, suddenly, in other people's heads he was a whole different creature.

Put seemed to be dozing. Jip wanted to leave him there to rest, but he couldn't do that. Suppose he woke up tomorrow and I was gone and he had no notion of where I was or what I was up to? He'd think I'd run off. It might be enough to make him go off into one of his spells, and then where would we be? I'll take him far as Avery's sugar shack. At least there he'll be off the damp ground and out of the chill.

"Put," he whispered. "We got to get moving again."

"You talked to the Wilkenses?"

"I talked to Lucy. It ain't—well, it won't do to stay there. Too dangerous."

For a minute he didn't say anything. Jip waited, loath to tell the whole story. Then he heard something like a sob. He leaned close.

"Don't cry, Put. It's going to be all right. I'm going now to see Teacher. She'll think of a way. It's all right."

Put wiped his nose on his hand. "I knew I should never have come. You'll be caught and . . . What an old fool I was to let you . . ."

"Shush. You think I'll let them weasels snatch us, Put? Come on, now. You and me. We're Green Mountain Boys, ain't we, ain't we, ey?"

Jip grasped Put's arm and pulled him to his feet. He decided not to share his fears about Avery. They hadn't been caught yet. Luck was on their side. Good earth and seas, God himself was on their side. He wouldn't let those devils win. Surely he wouldn't.

"You know something funny? We got to go straight acrost the poor farm to get to Avery's. Did I tell you? Teacher's staying there now, keeping his books. Probably running his whole plaguey business. She's smarter'n any man in this county. You know she went to college?" He kept talking to Put, who stumbled along, his arms clutching his chest, not answering. They crossed Tucker's land, giving the house a wide berth. There were three more small farms between Tucker's and the poor farm. He avoided Tucker's house and barn, but walked across the pasture. Put was just too tired and sick for lengthy detours. When they came to the fields belonging to the poor farm, he ached to steal into the house and find them some food, but he couldn't risk it. A ewe opened a sleepy eye as they passed, and then, recognizing him, pushed to her feet and came over to meet him. He stopped long enough to stroke her nose and murmur.

"She knows me even in the dark, Put." It was warm comfort.

Once beyond poor farm land they headed toward Avery's stand of sugar bush. The wretched man had padlocked his sugar shack. Nobody else in the county had a lock on his house, much less his sugar shack. Once again Jip found a fallen log for Put to sit on. "I'll get Teacher and we'll come for you," he promised and prayed God not to make a liar of him.

He was no sooner out of the protection of the trees than he saw the lights—the high bobbing lights, then the sound of horses beating the hard earth of the road. He fell on his face in the meadow grass. The sheep had nibbled it too close to serve as cover, but he lay paralyzed, listening as the dreadful beat of the hooves grew louder and louder.

He lay there helpless, the wiry grass scratching his cheek. Finally, he turned his head to watch the approach of the horsemen. Where had these demons got their unnatural sense? How could they know where he was headed before he knew it himself? He nearly cried aloud in frustration. There was no use struggling to escape. He was only a stupid boy put off a wagon and raised on a poor farm. How was he supposed to outsmart the devil's own?

18

Capture

What a fool he was! There he lay, his light undershirt shining against the dark grass like a blazing signpost for his enemies. Soon it would be morning. He slithered across the grass on his belly. Beyond him the gray stone of the quarried trough gleamed in the moonlight. On the far side there were piles of slag behind which he could take cover. Surely they would search the house and barns first. He might have a chance, then, to make a run for the woods. He scrambled over the low wall of granite waste. Avery had piled it along the edge of the pasture to keep his cattle from wandering over into the quarry area, where they would soil the surface of the granite or, worse, break a leg on the guttered rock.

The sounds of the horses were ever nearer. Avery's dogs set up the alarm. The horsemen had left the main road and were climbing the hill to Avery's farmhouse. Jip knew he could not make it across the rough stone to the slag piles before the horsemen reached the crest of the hill. He ran toward a wagon loaded with large foundation-sized stones that stood at the near edge of the quarry trough. There were more stones on the quarry itself yet to be loaded. He crouched down behind these and waited for his chance.

The horses had stopped a short distance from the house. He could hear the stamping feet and low whinnies of reined-in mounts and strained to hear what was happening. It was nearly dawn. He needed to run back to the woods while he still had some cover of darkness. Though perhaps he should head the other way—south over the mounds of slag piled on the far side of the trough, which spilled down over the hillside. It would be rough climbing the rubble, but his feet were as leathery as old boots after years of barefoot life. If he could get across the open rock of the quarry trough without being spied—

Avery's dogs began to bark more frantically. He had no fear of Avery's dogs. They were his friends from sugaring time. But their frenzied barks must mean that the riders were at the house now. He crept around the edge of the stones. He had to see where they were.

He could make out the shadowed bulk of them grouped near the door of the farmhouse. Perhaps some of them had gone in. Now was his chance. He must get over the slag and down the hill. The first light of morning was already turning the dome of the sky to gray.

Jip left the shelter of the foundation stones and made his way up and down the gutters of the quarry, willing himself invisible. Then he heard the dogs bay. Someone had set them loose. Soon they would find him and betray him.

If he could make it to the slag in time—but it was too late. The three dogs spotted him and set up a hunting chorus, leaping nimbly across the pocked surface of the quarry in his direction.

A cry went up. "There he is!"

He tried to scramble up the slag pile, but the stones

were not fixed. They came tumbling down toward him, hitting his ankles and legs until he stood buried, nearly to the knees. Each time he tried to lift his bruised legs out and climb, the stones shifted and held him fast. By now the dogs had recognized their friend. They jumped about to miss the stones his climbing had dislodged. They were barking with joy to see him, wagging their tails in delight.

"Turn around and come down."

Over his shoulder he could see the slave catcher making his way cautiously across the granite face. His hand was out and at the end of it Jip could make out the shape of a large derringer pistol.

Luke had said that they would not want to injure him, but how could he be sure? It hardly mattered. He could not escape.

"Come down off those rocks. I don't want to have to hurt you," the slaver called out.

Others were coming from the house, the pale man at their lead. "Call off your dogs, Mr. Avery," the pale man ordered as he picked his way across the granite.

"They won't bother him none," Avery said.

"Call off your dogs, sir," the man repeated tightly.

Avery whistled. The dogs gave Jip a sad look and reluctantly returned to their master's side.

"Tie them up."

Avery cocked his head and opened his mouth, but seemed to reconsider. "C'mon, boys," he said and started for his house, his unhappy dogs at his heels.

"You can come down now," the pale man said. "The dogs won't hurt you."

Slowly, taking care not to set the stones tumbling

again, Jip freed first one bruised foot and then the other and then half ran half fell back down the slag to face his captors. They backed up hastily as Jip sent more stones tumbling down the pile.

"Tie his hands behind him," the pale man said, throwing a length of rope to Addison Brackett.

"I was right, wasn't I?" Addison said. "Didn't I say he'd run to Teacher?"

"Just tie him up," the man said again.

"Don't you dare, Addison Brackett." It was Teacher herself, calling out as she came as fast as she could make it across the uneven rock. Her dark hair was bound in one long untidy pigtail, her feet bare. Addison, always terrified by what the pupils called Teacher's look, stepped back.

She turned to the sheriff. "What is the meaning of this, Mr. Glover?" she asked.

Sheriff Glover looked embarrassed. "Wal, miss, the gent does got a warrant."

"From God Almighty?" Her eyes flashed.

The pale man stepped between Teacher and the sheriff. "This is not your affair, madam," he said. "It is a matter of law, nothing to concern a lady."

She opened her mouth and would have said more except that the slave catcher, his pistol still trained on Jip, suddenly interrupted. "What's that?"

In the morning stillness Jip heard it, sweet as a birdcall: a high, clear tenor voice singing Toddy's hymn:

"Is it death, is it death?
That soon will quench, will quench this mortal flame?"

At first Jip thought it must be Put's ghost, letting him know that all was well, that his friend was past all worry

168

now, but he could tell that all the others had heard it, too. And then they saw him coming across the grass, a tall ragged form, his head thrown back as he sang to the sky.

"It's our lunatic," Jip said.

The slaver's hand began to shake. He waved the pistol. "You got to call to him," he said. "Settle him down."

"It ain't no use," Jip said. "When he's raving, can't no one calm him, even me." God forgive my lying tongue.

"But he's coming this way."

"He's kinda like my dog. Even when he's craziest, he don't like it if someone messes with me."

> "There's not a cloud that doth arise,
> To hide my Jesus from my eyes.
> I soon shall mount the upper skies . . ."

Still singing, the old man threw one leg over the slag wall and then the other. He kept coming, past the wagon, past the pile of stone, right toward the crowd of them gathered there on the quarry floor. Friend and enemy alike watched as though in a trance as the lunatic started across the bedrock, not bothering to watch his footing, just keeping his eyes on the slave catcher.

"I don't like it," the slave catcher said. He was trembling all over. "I don't like lunatics."

"Quiet, fool," the pale man said.

"You ain't scairt, are you, mister?" Jip asked.

As if to answer, the slave catcher turned the pistol away from Jip and pointed it toward the old man. "Stop! Stop right there!" Put kept walking.

Oh, dear God. He thinks he can save me. "Don't, Put!" Jip yelled out. "Go back!"

" 'Tune, tune your harps, your harps ye saints on high . . .' " He was singing at the top of his voice: " 'I too will strike my harp . . .' " He was nearly upon the slave catcher now.

A shot rang out. Put stopped, a look of utter surprise on his face, then with a shout, " 'All is well!' " he threw his body forward. As though propelled by some supernatural strength, he hurled himself upon the slaver as the man tried desperately to reload. With his clawlike hands, Put grabbed the slaver's arms and drove him back furiously against the piled foundation stones.

His top hat fell off. Then the man's skull struck a jagged edge of granite with a crack like that of a pumpkin bursting. The pistol flew high into the air, bounced once against the quarry floor and lay still. Like partners in some horrible dance, Put and the slaver crumpled, sliding slowly to the bedrock, still locked in their cursed embrace.

Oh, Put, no. Jip started toward his friend, but a hand grabbed his arm.

"Lemme go!" he cried out. "I got to see to him!"

"He's dead." The voice was as tight as the grip on his arm.

"No, no, not my Put." He turned to look at his captor. "Kill me," he sobbed. "Kill me, but don't kill my Put. He ain't done nothing to you. Please, please don't hurt him."

The gray eyes stared into his. There was a flicker of something near kin to shame in them. A shudder went through the man's body as he turned away. "You, boy," he called out to Addison. "I said, tie him up." Without looking at Jip again, he let go of his arm and went over to where Sheriff Glover and Teacher bent over the fallen men.

Jip knew Put was dead. Of course he knew, but, until Teacher came back to where the Bracketts guarded him, and he could see the deep sorrow in her eyes, he had tried to hope.

Avery was coming back across the quarry from his house. The pale man picked up the derringer and, calling out, ordered him to see to the bodies.

"What were you planning to do with the boy?" Teacher asked.

The pale man took a watch out of his pocket as though to check the time. "I'm taking the fugitive back to where he belongs," he said.

"Not until after the hearing, you won't."

"Now listen here, young woman . . ."

"Tell him, Mr. Glover."

Sheriff Glover shifted his gaze uneasily from one to the other. It was plain that he didn't know what Teacher meant.

"Habeas corpus, Mr. Glover. Explain that the boy is entitled to a hearing in a court of law."

"Ridiculous. This is my property."

Sheriff Glover took one last look at Teacher before clearing his throat to reply. "Wal, now, come to think of it, mister, I think the lady's got a point. You may know the boy belongs to you. And for all I know the boy knows that. It's jest that the law don't know that—" He spat on the granite. "Yit."

"You know you are bound by the Fugitive Slave Act to give me every assistance—"

171

"Yah, wal, up here in Vermont folks think you got to prove this here boy's your legal property afore you can haul him acrost the line into Massachusetts, where I hear tell there's some what ain't quite so particular."

The pale man grew whiter still. He looked about. But he stood alone. Even the Bracketts hesitated to cross both Teacher and the law.

"No need to fret, mister," the sheriff continued. "He's jest a ignorant boy raised on our town poor farm. He can hardly best you—a gentleman of your stripe. Meantime, I'll jest hold him in the jail for you."

The Brackett brothers boosted Jip up on the deputy's horse, never daring to look the boy in the eye. And Jip, hands bound, head sagging in despair against his chest, rode into the village behind the deputy, leaving Put stretched out on the bedrock of the quarry, his eyes still wide open in surprise.

19

End and Beginning

What the sheriff had rather grandly referred to as "the jail" was only a small room in the basement of the town hall where the village put public drunks or the occasional vagrant for safekeeping. There were no bars on the one small high window, as no one had ever tried to escape. The cell door was a simple wooden one with a bolt on the outside to keep an unruly inmate from roaming the building during the night.

The pale man spotted the careless security measures at once and paid the deputy from his own pocket to spend the nights in the corridor outside the room until the hearing.

He needn't worry, Jip thought, I ain't going nowhere. He sat on the edge of the wooden cot. The room smelled of the tramps and drunkards who'd been there before him and was none too clean, but he hardly noticed.

Luke Stevens tried to warn me. He tried to tell me not to take Put with me, but I was too proud, too ornery to heed him. Pigheaded fool. Caring more for myself than for Put. I was wrong. The slavers didn't kill him. I did.

The only punishment that nearly fit his monstrous crime was bondage. To go meekly with that pale devil and live out the rest of his miserable life in whatever hell that one chose to confine him to.

The hearing was set for two days hence. Sheriff Glover had explained to the pale man that the prisoner must have a day to make ready his defense, and since the day following was a Sabbath, the judge would not be available until Monday. Jip did not plan any defense, and it was irksome to him to have his sentence so delayed.

He had been in jail for several hours when the door opened and the sheriff told him he had visitors. Teacher had come, Luke Stevens with her. They brought him his overshirt, now washed and mended, and a basket of food.

"I was to bring you food yesterday," Luke said apologetically, handing him the neatly packed basket, "but the slavers seemed to have eyes everywhere. How thy friend escaped their notice, God help me, I'll never know—"

"I ain't hungry," Jip said. "Begging your pardon."

"No," said Teacher, sitting down on the cot beside him, "probably not. But try to take something. You need your strength."

"What—what of Put?" he asked.

"We fetched him back," Luke's voice faltered, "back up to our house, my brothers and I."

"He ought to have—I want him to have a proper funeral."

Teacher put her hand gently on Jip's. "I promise you. In the church."

"With hymns?"

She nodded. "With hymns."

"There's one he's partial to." Jip couldn't quite bring himself to say it was the one Put died singing. "Lucy will know the one."

He began to cry then. He had thought he was past all feeling, but when he thought of the hymn, the picture of Put coming across the pasture, his head thrown back . . . "Do you think—I mean, is it—all well with him now?"

"Yes," she said. "I'm sure."

He wiped his eyes on the back of his hand. Teacher handed him a handkerchief. Her own eyes were bright with tears. "We have to think of you now, Jip."

He shook his head.

"What does thee mean?" Luke Stevens bent his head close to Jip's and whispered hoarsely. "Surely thee is not resigned to slavery?"

Jip couldn't meet the Quaker's gaze, for that was exactly what he had determined.

"Then," Teacher's eyes flashed as though he were an insolent student, "then you mean to throw poor Put's life away?"

"No." He looked at her horrified. How could she imagine—

"He died for you, Jip. And you mean to make that of no account?" She was whispering so no one outside in the corridor could hear, but the whisper only served to make her fury more apparent. She stood up and began to pace the small room.

Now Luke came close to the cot. "I mean to spirit thee away," he said in Jip's ear. "We have a friend in Montreal—Ezekial Freeman. We will get thee there. Very early Monday morning the train will stop in Northfield. Tomorrow night . . ."

"No," Jip said between his teeth. "They'd punish you sure—for aiding a runaway."

"I've been at this game for many a year now . . ."

"Wait." Teacher had stopped her pacing. "No one needs to spirit anyone away. We just need to put on a defense—one that will convince the justice." She smiled. "The man has no love for slavers. He'll not be hard to convince."

"There ain't no defense," Jip said dully. "You know the devil speaks the truth."

"Ah, Jip, boy, he's only a man. A poor sinner like me or thee."

Teacher spun around. "The devil never speaks the truth!"

Jip couldn't tell which of them she was rebuking. She didn't explain, only went on in the same manner in which she'd give out the solution to a problem in arithmetic: "You have never known it, Jip, but you are my son."

"Marm?"

She blew out a sigh and sat down beside him on the cot. "I was indiscreet those years ago when I was a factory girl in Lowell. It happened among us mill girls more often than—"

Teacher was lying! He'd never imagined such a thing. A woman so noble lying like some scoundrel. "It ain't true. You know it ain't true. Why do you say such a monstrous thing about yourself?"

She looked him in the eye. "I'm ready to swear to it before the justice," she said. "I want to acknowledge that you are my child."

Jip turned to Luke. "You won't let her do such a thing, will you? Lying and breaking the law? Bringing disgrace on herself?"

Luke smiled wryly. "The woman has her own mind. If

she's made it up, it's not likely she'll suddenly start listening to me."

"I thought you cared about her!" He said it right out loud.

Now Luke was looking Teacher full in the face. "She knows I do. Surely she does." He walked over to Teacher, took her hands, and pulled her gently to her feet. "If thee is determined on such a headstrong and desperate course, I cannot stop thee. But I will say on Monday that I am the father of the boy. Before the justice I will plead for forgiveness and beg thee to be my wife."

"They'll dismiss you from the Meeting," she said to him, leaving her hands in his.

"They'll dismiss me for marrying anyone who is outside the Meeting," he said, with a little laugh, "even when the Meeting is without young women to marry."

"Then you are determined to do this foolish thing?"

"Since the day thee walked down the hill to sell thy heifer to my father," he said.

"For a Quaker, you are an uncommonly stubborn man."

"And thee, Lyddie Worthen, are the world's most stubborn woman. Are we not a proper pair?"

They said more, but Jip had given up listening. His ears would not let him be party to such a wicked conspiracy. Luke's being cast out of the Quaker Meeting was nothing compared to what folks would say of her.

He waited well past dark, until he could hear the deputy's snoring through the door. The man had been awake all the previous night tracking Jip down, so Jip had reason to hope that his sleep would be deep.

He put the buns and slabs of cheese that his visitors had brought into his shirtfront and tied his shirttails tightly together to keep the food safe. Then he inched the cot over to the window and, covering the food basket with the quilt from the cot, swung it against the glass. There was hardly any sound, but he waited, hardly breathing, to make sure he hadn't waked the deputy.

The snoring seemed as regular as before. By standing on the cot, Jip could just touch the window with his fingertips. He brushed the glass off the frame with the end of the quilt and then pulled himself up to the broad sill. It was easy then, to slide across it onto the ground outside.

He came out into a clear August night. Follow the North Star. Put had showed him the way. Jip looked up at the heavens to get his bearing from the Big Dipper and then began to run.

I found the Reverend Ezekial Freeman in Montreal with very little trouble. Teacher and Luke's friend was the only African minister called by that name in the city. The Freemans have given me the family and the name I was long denied. They have brought me up to be a Freeman among free peoples. I am very grateful. I doubt that I could have learned the art of living as a man both black and free without their compassionate instruction.

But my heart still yearns for the land I left behind. My old country is at war. A Negro regiment is forming in New York, and I have decided to go south and join the struggle. My foster mother weeps to see me go, but my foster father understands even though he is a clergyman and a man of gentle spirit.

It is the opposite with my friends at home. Luke Stevens does not countenance war and begs me to remain here, while his wife, my dear Teacher, sends me her blessing. (It seems that the excuse of my defense was not needed to push the two of them into marriage after all.) Teacher declares that were she not a woman and a mother, she would be at my side, rifle in hand.

But who can say which of us is right in this wretched business? Surely the Almighty, who would not have us enslave one another, does not rejoice to see us kill each other in His name.

Yet, I will return now to do what it seems I must. As I

go, I try to cling to the faith that Put used to sing—to believe that all is well, whether I live a free man or die to secure that freedom for others. Nonetheless, had I a choice, I would choose a little plot of rocky land in the Green Mountains with a flock of sheep and a peaceful old age.

ALL IS WELL

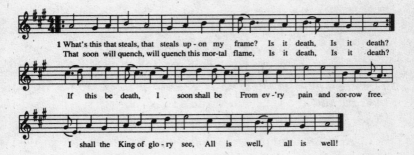

1 What's this that steals, that steals up-on my frame? Is it death, Is it death?
That soon will quench, will quench this mor-tal flame, Is it death, Is it death?

If this be death, I soon shall be From ev-'ry pain and sor-row free.

I shall the King of glo-ry see, All is well, all is well!

2 Weep not, my friends, my friends weep not for me, All is well, all is well!
   My sins forgiv'n, forgiv'n and I am free, All is well, all is well!
   There's not a cloud that doth arise, To hide my Jesus from my eyes.
   I soon shall mount the upper skies, All is well, all is well!

3 Tune, tune your harps ye saints on high, All is well, all is well!
   I too will strike my harp with equal joy, All is well, all is well!
   Bright angels are from glory come, They're round my bed, they're in my room,
   They wait to waft my spirit home, All is well, all is well!

4 Hark! hark! my Lord, my Lord and Master's voice, Calls away, calls away!
   I soon shall see—enjoy my happy choice, Why delay, why delay?
   Farewell, my friends, adieu, adieu, I can no longer stay with you,
   My glittering crown appears in view, All is well, all is well!

5 Hail, hail! all hail, all hail! ye blood-washed throng, Saved by grace, saved by grace!
   I come to join, to join your rapturous song, Saved by grace, saved by grace,
   All, all is peace and joy divine, And heaven and glory now are mine,
   Loud hallelujahs to the Lamb, All is well, all is well!

Words and music Anonymous

Katherine Paterson's books have received wide acclaim and been published in twenty languages. Among her many literary honors are two Newbery Medals, for *Bridge to Terabithia* and *Jacob Have I Loved*, two National Book Awards, and most recently the Hans Christian Andersen Award. Her latest book is *Parzival*.

The author lives in Barre, Vermont, an area she describes in her earlier novel *Lyddie*, and which she researched for the background of this story. The Patersons have four grown children and two grandchildren.

More information about Katherine Paterson is available at her website, Terabithia (**http://www.terabithia.com**).

SCHOLASTIC

Parent

to

Hassle-free

HOMEWORK

Judith Stein, Ph.D.
Lynn Meltzer, Ph.D.
Kalyani Krishnan, M.A.
Laura Sales Pollica, M.A.
Irene Papadopoulos, M.A.
Bethany Roditi, Ph.D.

RESEARCH
INSTITUTE FOR
LEARNING AND
DEVELOPMENT

New York • Toronto • London • Auckland • Sydney
Mexico City • New Delhi • Hong Kong • Buenos Aires

Teaching
Resources

Acknowledgments

We would like to thank Steve Beckhardt, ResearchILD board member, for his dedication and commitment to funding the initial stages of this project. Through his support, we hope that this book will enrich the lives of families and improve the homework experiences of so many struggling learners.

Our colleagues at the Institutes for Learning and Development (ResearchILD and ILD) deserve many thanks for their ongoing support, energy, passion, and numerous creative ideas, which have shaped and contributed to our programs and our writing.

We would like to express our gratitude to the very conscientious, supportive, and creative staff at Scholastic: to Terry Cooper, Vice President, Scholastic Teaching Resources, for her enthusiasm, insights, flexibility, and unwavering support; to Maria Chang, for her ongoing wisdom, encouragement, and patience; and to the design team for creating such a clear and colorful layout that was so faithful to our vision.

Our thanks to all the students, parents, and teachers who have provided inspiration for our work and have contributed in so many ways to the strategies we discuss in this book.

Lastly, we are indebted to our families whose never-ending love, understanding, and patience have nourished this project from start to finish.

Editor: Maria L. Chang
Cover design by Jay Namerow
Interior design by Holly Grundon

ISBN-13: 978-0-439-82131-5
ISBN-10: 0-439-82131-2
Copyright © 2007 by Judith Stein, Lynn Meltzer, Kalyani Krishnan, Laura Sales Pollica, Irene Papadopoulos, Bethany Roditi.

All rights reserved. Published by Scholastic Inc.
Printed in the U.S.A.

1 2 3 4 5 6 7 8 9 10   23   14 13 12 11 10 09 08 07

Table of Contents

No one knows the trials and tribulations of homework better than parents do. Whether you like it or not, you are often drawn into your children's triumphs and struggles over homework. Although working with your children on homework provides a wonderful opportunity to be involved in their education, it often does not feel so wonderful during the process. Given the differences between parents' and children's expectations, learning styles, knowledge, and understanding, conflict is inevitable. On one hand, parents want their children to be the best and brightest students that they can be. They want to do all that they can to ensure their children's success. Children, on the other hand, while wanting to please their parents, may have priorities and capabilities that are quite different from those of their parents. No wonder helping with homework can feel more like a battle than a fun or gratifying experience!

Meet Jessica, a 9-year-old, who often gets upset when she has math homework to do. For hours after school, Jessica will be busy doing anything but homework. No matter how many times her mother suggests that she get started, Jessica finds another activity to distract her or thinks of a reason to delay doing her homework. It is often late into the evening before Jessica finally gets started on her homework. If she has a math assignment, she immediately begs for help. "Mom, I can't do this! This is a stupid assignment, and I don't understand what to do."

> "Mom, I can't do this! This is a stupid assignment, and I don't understand what to do."

When her mother starts to help, the battle begins. No matter how her mother tries to explain the assignment or show her how to do a problem, Jessica resists vehemently. "Mom, that's not the way to do it! My teacher did it differently. I know you're doing it wrong. I don't understand anything that you're saying!" Soon Jessica and her mother are yelling at each other and getting more frustrated by the minute. By the time the shouting match ends, Jessica is in tears, her mother is feeling angry and guilty, and the homework is ripped to shreds on the floor.

Josh, a 13-year-old middle school student, is not nearly as achievement-oriented as his parents. When Josh receives an important homework assignment, the seeds of conflict are already planted as he and his mother begin to talk about the work. Josh thinks, "Oh, just another paper to write. I bet I can write this paper in no time. As long as I write three pages, I should get a B on it. That'll be just fine." Meanwhile, his mother is thinking, "This assignment will be a great opportunity for Josh to work on his writing. Here's a chance for him to write several drafts and hand in an excellent paper. He'd feel so proud if he earned an A." Already their goals, attitudes, and levels of involvement are on a collision course. Josh is satisfied with being a good-enough student and would much rather perfect his guitar-playing techniques or socialize with friends. His mother, on the other hand, knows that he is very capable and is frustrated that academics are not his top priority. She wants to help, not hinder, but her frustration and disappointment become more obvious as she gets involved in the homework process.

> "I bet I can write this paper in no time. As long as I write three pages, I should get a B on it. That'll be just fine."

Then there's Katie, a high school sophomore, who is a hard worker and a high achiever. Getting excellent grades is very important to her. As a result, she spends hours and hours completing her homework and worries that it is not "perfect enough." Sometimes she gets so stressed out about her assignments that she takes out her frustration on everyone else. Her father tries to calm her down and jokes with her so that she will take things less seriously. Although this approach helps sometimes, Katie's parents still worry about how much pressure she puts on herself and how unhappy she seems when she is doing her schoolwork. So often, when they try to help, Katie gets more upset and shuts down completely. By the time she calms down and is ready to work again, it is very late in the evening and she has to either stay up past midnight or hand in her homework a day late.

If these scenarios sound familiar or are ones that you hope to avoid, then this homework book is for you. We wrote this book to help parents manage homework issues that affect all children, especially those with learning and attentional problems. All children sometimes have difficulty getting started on their homework, working to the best of their ability, organizing their assignments, or understanding the tasks at hand. But children with nontraditional learning styles, learning difficulties, or attention problems struggle to complete homework on a daily basis.

Through our work as parents, educators, and therapists at the Institute for Learning and Development, we have worked with a broad spectrum of children who have struggled to succeed in school because of their learning, attentional, motivational, or emotional issues.

Our philosophy is grounded in the belief that all children can thrive if they are given the appropriate environment, tools, and strategies. Your child has a unique learning style and personality—together, these factors interact to shape your child as a learner. By helping your child lead with her strengths, she can often overcome or compensate for her difficulties.

Your job as a parent is to be well informed about your child's learning style and his teacher's expectations, and to provide the necessary structure, support, and encouragement to ensure that he can succeed. As parents and professionals, we know that your job is a lot harder than it sounds! That's why we decided to write this book—to give you the knowledge and understanding that you'll need to negotiate your way through the homework maze with minimum stress.

What makes this book unique is that we have provided you with tools to help you better understand your child's learning style as well as specific strategies to help your child tackle homework assignments with greater ease. We have included research-based strategies to help your child with organization, reading, math, writing, and test taking. Some children will use these strategies easily once they are introduced. Most children, however, will need to be taught these strategies in a stepwise fashion—first modeled by you or his teacher, and then guided in using the strategy to complete a homework assignment. It is important to have your child try several strategies and decide which one(s) work for him or her. If you do not feel comfortable teaching a particular strategy suggested in this book, then you could work collaboratively with your child's teacher, who could introduce the strategy in the classroom. Then you could reinforce your child's use of the strategy at home.

We hope that the information included in this book will ease your worries, reduce homework conflicts, and provide you with new strategies to help your child tackle homework more easily. In the first chapter, you will find background information that will help you to understand the purpose and impact of homework, the amount of time your child should spend on homework, and the various roles that parents can assume in the homework process. Chapter 2 will assist you in identifying your child's particular learning style and in choosing the best ways to support your child while doing homework. In Chapter 3, you will learn how to establish an effective homework routine and solve common homework problems (e.g., procrastination, frustration, outbursts). Chapters 4 through 7 will give you the tools that you will need to help your child with reading, writing, math, and studying for tests. If you are worried about your child's motivation regarding schoolwork, then Chapter 8 will provide you with the knowledge and strategies for inspiring your child to do his best. Finally, in Chapter 9, you will learn how best to communicate with teachers and to advocate for your child.

Chapter 1

Homework:
Why? How? What?

Emma couldn't wait to get home to tell her mother the good news! She had just been chosen to be the lead in the school play, *Oklahoma*. She had worked hard and earned the part. She was so proud of herself. Life couldn't be better . . . if only she didn't have homework to contend with. . . . As she started to think about the evening's worth of reading and math that she had to finish, her enthusiasm and self-confidence spiraled downward. By the time she arrived home, Emma was dreading the workload that lay ahead of her. Luckily, Emma's parents knew how to handle her angst about homework. They celebrated her success in music and drama and provided her with the support and encouragement she needed to succeed in school. Emma's parents had learned to help her increase her efficiency by using their knowledge of Emma's learning style, staying informed about class work and assignments, and teaching her effective strategies.

Why Do Homework?

"Homework is an opportunity for students to learn and for parents to be involved in their children's education" (Paulu, 1995). Parents can help children succeed by teaching them important lessons about learning. Becoming a lifelong learner is a joyful and rewarding experience that requires discipline, commitment, effort, and determination. Most educators agree that homework can enrich children's learning by enabling them to:

◆ review and practice what they've learned in the classroom

◆ apply newly acquired skills/information in new contexts

◆ extend their knowledge through independent research

- integrate knowledge by reflecting, problem-solving, or writing

- further explore content areas by using their creativity

- develop a disciplined approach to learning

- work independently, and in doing so, develop a greater sense of responsibility for, and ownership of, their learning

Yet despite these benefits, experts continue to debate about the positive and negative effects of homework on long-term academic success, family life, and individual growth and development.

In the early part of the 20th century, a national anti-homework movement led some school systems to eliminate homework for students in kindergarten through eighth grade. Support for increased homework resurfaced in the 1950s when the American government became concerned about competing successfully with the Russians in the development of space travel and military technology. While homework was given less emphasis in the '60s and '70s (perhaps because our country was more focused on the Vietnam War and civil rights), in the '80s, educators demanded more homework because they were concerned about the Japanese outperforming Americans. Recent educational reforms, such as the No Child Left Behind Act (H.R. 936/ S. 448, February 2003) and the standards-based education initiatives across the country, have sparked new discussions about the important role of homework in raising academic standards.

Over the past five years, discussions about homework have been a focus of many major newspapers, magazines, and television news programs. Some educators and writers, such as Etta Kralovec and John Buell (2001), argue that homework should be eliminated because it overburdens already stressed children, disrupts families, increases conflict between parents and children, and interferes with learning by contributing to negative attitudes toward school and education. At the same time, many teachers, parents, and principals insist that homework helps develop the discipline, independence, and persistence that are necessary ingredients for academic and lifelong success. The limited research aimed at evaluating the benefits of homework concludes that homework is an essential component of the learning experience, especially in the higher grades when students need time to review, reflect on, and integrate complex material for mastery. Studies have shown that junior high and high school students who complete more homework generally perform better on standardized tests and earn a higher grade-point average than youngsters who spend less time on homework (Cooper, 2001).

Although experts still do not fully agree on the purpose and value of homework at different grade levels, the U.S. Department of Education has proposed general guidelines for the quality and quantity of homework. In *Helping Your Child With Homework* (Paulu, 1995), the author recommended that homework assignments "should have a specific purpose, come with clear instructions, be well matched to a student's abilities, and designed to help develop a student's knowledge and skills." Recommended guidelines for the type of homework have included:

♦ drill and practice (e.g., learning math facts, writing spelling words several times)

♦ working at an independent level (e.g., creating sentences using spelling words, independent reading)

♦ application of well-learned skills (e.g., writing a book report)

♦ previewing the next day's lessons (e.g., reading articles or next chapter in text, brainstorming ideas for a story, pretest in math)

Regarding the right amount of homework, the author suggested the following:

● 10 to 20 minutes for kindergarten through second grade

● 30 to 60 minutes for third through sixth grade

● 60+ minutes for seventh grade and beyond

In general, homework should be well within a child's capabilities both conceptually and in terms of the skills required. The work should be familiar and should relate to concepts that have been introduced or reviewed within the few days preceding the assignment. Ideally, children should be able to complete the homework fairly independently. However, each child develops at a different pace. Therefore, all children may not be equally ready for the same assignment at the same time. Some children may need additional exposure to the material and a few more examples before they can tackle an assignment. Others may need some assistance with finishing their work, such as help with editing or proofreading. Many of these issues will be addressed in the following chapters.

How Can Parents Help?

As mentioned earlier, homework provides a vehicle for parents and children to work together on assignments and to discuss what children are learning. Parents have the opportunity to spark enthusiasm, to encourage learning, to teach study skills, and to enrich their children's knowledge through everyday experiences at home. Becoming and remaining engaged with a child's academic work is also an opportunity to teach a different set of skills and attitudes that include pride in one's work, a strong work ethic, accountability, and independence.

You can become involved in your child's homework in many ways and at many levels. As reported by Kathleen Hoover-Dempsey and her colleagues (2001), parents can participate in their children's academic work by assuming any one or several of the following roles:

1. **Communicator:** interacting with teachers about the children's homework, progress, problems, and instructional needs, as well as the teachers' expectations and concerns

2. **Organizer:** helping children structure time, space, and materials for homework and enforcing expectations for homework completion

3. **Overseer:** supervising the homework process

4. **Encourager:** rewarding children's efforts, encouraging problem-solving and independent work

5. **Reviewer:** reviewing, correcting, editing homework

6. **Assistant:** helping children drill, practice, memorize, and study for tests

7. **Teacher:** directly teaching children concepts, procedures, vocabulary, and problem-solving techniques

8. **Strategy Coach:** teaching children metacognitive strategies for planning, organizing, prioritizing, self-monitoring, and checking their work

All these roles can be effective ways of helping children become enthusiastic learners and successful students. You can choose which of these roles will be best suited to your personality, family relationships, time commitments, and skill set. Becoming involved in your child's homework is valuable no matter which role or roles you choose. Keep in mind that most parents can't do it all, nor should they. You will have to find a suitable role that matches your child's age, skill level, independence, motivation, and openness to help. Throughout this book, you will find invaluable information to help you carry out any of these responsibilities using a positive and rewarding approach. If you are most interested in the Communicator role, read Chapter 9. Chapters 3 and 8 will be most helpful for the Organizer, Overseer, and Encourager roles. Chapters 4, 5, 6, and 7 provide many helpful strategies for reviewing, assisting, teaching, and tutoring your child during the homework process.

What Are Realistic Expectations for My Child?

Children differ in their attitudes toward homework, their motivation, their attention span, their perseverance, and their readiness to learn the material. As a parent, you will need to align your expectations with what you know about your child. A child who is eager to learn but has a short attention span may be able to complete all of his homework, but may need to break up his work time into small chunks, such as 15-minute work periods separated by 20- to 30-minute breaks. A child who is exhausted from a day of school and struggles with homework may need an added incentive to do her work (e.g., concrete rewards or special privileges) or may even need a reduced homework load. A child with learning difficulties may not have the confidence and/or the skills to complete his homework. He may need extra help, extra time, or a modified assignment in order to do his work successfully.

Jonah was a bright, energetic student, who had difficulties
with attention and memory, which in turn affected his ability to
read, write, and do math. While he loved to learn about history

and science, Jonah dreaded his math and spelling homework and avoided reading lengthy texts as much as possible. For many years, homework was a nightmare for Jonah and an ongoing battle for his parents.

Over time, however, his parents learned to set more realistic expectations, advocated for appropriate homework modifications, and learned new strategies and technological tools to support Jonah's learning. Homework became less of a burden and more of an opportunity for learning.

Like Jonah's parents, you may need to tailor your expectations to match your child's goals and priorities, his time commitments to extracurricular activities, and his skills and abilities.

Mr. and Mrs. Kaplan expected their ninth-grade son, Tim, to be a highly motivated, hardworking student like his older brother. Much to his parents' dismay, Tim valued drama and music much more than his homework. He also resented his parents' criticism of his work habits and their constant nagging about homework. Although he was very bright and creative, Tim had difficulty paying attention and concentrating for long periods of time and was an extremely slow reader. As you can imagine, homework was not much fun for him. In fact, most of the time, homework was a time-consuming, tedious, frustrating, and unrewarding task.

In this case, Mr. and Mrs. Kaplan had to let go of some of their expectations regarding Tim's academic work until he was ready to take charge of his own learning. Instead, they advocated for him to receive academic help at school, offered tutoring support as needed, and collaborated with Tim to help him plan and organize his homework more effectively. With less-frequent nagging from his parents, Tim gradually accepted the responsibility of doing his homework and actively sought help when he needed it. As his grades improved, Tim gained more confidence and was more motivated to work harder. Tim was proud of his accomplishments, as were his parents.

To set realistic homework expectations for your child, ask yourself the following questions:

- How long can your child sit still and pay attention?

- Does your child have the skills to handle the current curriculum?

- How important is school success to your child?

- What motivates your child to work hard?

- How does your child handle frustration? Does he give up, ask for help, avoid tasks, or keep working until the problem is solved?

- How willing is your child to accept help from you or others?

Keep in mind that the purpose of homework is to enable children to acquire and consolidate new information and academic skills and to foster their development as independent learners. Within our current educational system and national standards, homework is an important component of every child's education. Moreover, the quality and consistency of homework completion is often a significant factor in determining a student's grade. Nevertheless, homework is not often tailored to the individual student and therefore is not always appropriate or manageable. A child may not be ready to learn the material, may not have the necessary skills to complete the assignment, or may not have the attention or motivation to succeed.

To further complicate the issue, parents often impose their own expectations regarding homework, and sometimes these expectations may be unrealistic or burdensome for the child. For many children, the usual homework routine is not the best way to learn or the best measure of what they know and what they have learned. Whether a child does her homework consistently or not may affect her current performance, but keep in mind that it is unlikely to predict her long-term success in life.

Chapter 2

Understanding Your Child's Learning Style

Much of the time, Seth, a seventh grader, couldn't absorb what his social studies teacher was saying even though he tried to listen as best as he could. The only time he felt that he understood what was going on in class was when the teacher showed pictures, maps, or movies to illustrate the content.

· ·

Wendy loved listening to the stories her social studies teacher told. It was easy for her to remember historical events and cultural characteristics by recalling the anecdotes she heard from her teacher. She had a much harder time learning the locations of cities and societies and struggled to memorize maps.

Understanding how your child learns most efficiently is an important tool you can use to help your child succeed in school. The opportunities to observe and assess your child's learning style are countless. Watching your child play, cook, draw, build, or tackle any new task provides a wonderful way of learning more about your child's natural talents and approach to learning. Moreover, observing your child in the classroom offers a rich opportunity to understand his strengths and preferences for learning.

Imagine a fourth-grade classroom in which students with many different learning styles are tackling their morning assignment. Each student is asked to create a small poster representing a book that he or she has read recently. Lily immediately picks up several markers and begins drawing a picture. Jessica turns toward a friend and begins asking her questions: "Do you think I should tell the story or just describe the characters? Do you think we can print out pictures from the Internet, or do we have to draw them?" In one corner of the room, Jonathan quietly leans on his arm and looks pensively at the paper. Nearby, David shoots his pencil across the chalk tray and seems oblivious to the drawing activities going on around him. Across the table, Nicholas struggles to copy the author's name on his poster. Clara hums a song and sounds out the words as she writes a summary of the book.

By the end of the allotted time, each student has produced a poster. The process has been very different for each child. Some had worked quickly and were on to the next activity before the teacher collected their work. Others had rushed at the end to finish the last details. A few had barely begun before they were asked to stop. While some children were quiet and thoughtful before they started the assignment, others jumped into the project without a second thought. Some relied on visual cues around the room to help them tackle the spelling and drawing, while others sang and asked questions to help them recall and organize the information that they wanted to convey. Their varied approaches reflect differences in these students' attention, processing speeds, levels of organization, orientations (auditory, visual, kinesthetic), and temperaments.

Understanding how your child learns most efficiently is an important tool you can use to help your child succeed in school.

Not surprisingly, the students' diverse approaches and processes produced very different products. Some students created highly detailed, colorful works of art, while others drew simple sketches. Some posters were very organized with words and pictures artfully arranged on the page. Others contained words and figures randomly scattered across the paper. Some children planned or imagined the whole poster before filling in the details (a **top-down approach**), whereas others begun with a flurry of ideas and later organized them into the final product (a **bottom-up approach**).

Top-Down or Bottom-Up

One way of understanding your child's learning style is to think about whether he learns information by focusing first on the "big picture" or main ideas and then the details, or by noticing all of the interesting facts or details before grasping the overall theme or story line. This dichotomy of learning styles can easily be observed by asking your child to describe a

Bottom-Up vs. Top-Down			
	Always (Top-Down)	**Sometimes** (Mixed)	**Never** (Bottom-Up)
If you have a collection of objects, could your child easily categorize them by size, color, and function?			
If your child has a homework sheet, will she read all of the directions and look at the whole sheet before starting to work?			
When your child describes a toy, does he tell you about what kind of toy it is before describing all of the details?			
After your child reads a story, can she easily tell you the moral, lesson, or author's purpose in writing the story?			
When your child describes a movie, do you know what the movie is about before you are flooded with all of the details?			
When your child tells a story, do you understand what it's about?			

movie he's seen, a baseball game he's watched, or a book he's read. Consider two youngsters: David can tell you about a movie from beginning to end and can describe each scene in minute detail, but he can't tell you what the main point of the movie was or why the director ended the movie the way he did. In contrast, Brian can tell you about a basketball game he's watched and focus on the team's strategies for winning and the team's major mistakes. But he'll forget all the specific statistics (e.g., who scored the most baskets, who made the most fouls, who blocked the most balls). These contrasting learning styles will likely define how David and Brian approach a variety of learning tasks, such as reading a book, making a poster, or writing an essay. While David may immediately absorb and present the details, Brian will likely reflect on the overall theme of the material and will focus on the "big picture" in his presentation.

One of the best ways of observing the top-down, bottom-up dimension is to notice how your child approaches a writing assignment. Does she develop an overall theme and write related topic sentences with little difficulty? Or does she readily describe the details and have difficulty stating the general topic or thesis of her writing?

To help you determine your child's preferred approach to learning, consider the set of questions on page 17. You may discover that your child uses both approaches, prefers one over the other in certain contexts, or easily shifts from one approach to the other as needed.

Understanding when and how your child approaches information with respect to the "big picture" and the details will help you support and guide her when she is involved in learning any new skill or accomplishing a complex task.

Auditory, Visual, or Kinesthetic Learner

As a parent, you have observed your child accomplish many kinds of tasks over the years. Think about how your child learned to play a game or build with construction toys. Did he *listen* to your directions, *read* the instructions, or dive right into playing the game or building the model without listening or reading at all? Or think about how your child first learned to read. Did she learn to read by listening to you read her stories and then remembering the words that she heard? Or did she look at the pictures for clues when she didn't know how to read a certain word? Or was it most helpful for her to keep her finger on each word while she tried to sound it out?

If your child prefers to listen intently rather than see or read what to do, then he may be an **auditory learner**. That is, he may take in information best when he can hear the information rather than see or feel it. Conversely, if your child loves to dive right into a project without listening to or reading directions, she may learn best by using her hands rather than seeing or hearing new information. She may be a **kinesthetic learner**. If your child tends to focus on what he sees rather than what he hears or touches, then he is likely a **visual learner**.

Reflecting on the kinds of activities your child prefers also gives you insight into his learning style. Most children naturally choose leisure-time activities that draw on their strengths and preferred approach to learning. Children who tend to be good listeners, enjoy hearing stories, remember dialogue and conversations well, and like to talk are most likely auditory learners. Children who enjoy looking at pictures, tend to be keen observers, remember movies and scenery well, and are artistic are most likely visual learners. Children who prefer to be active, enjoy sports, and like to engage in hands-on activities, such as crafts and construction toys, may be kinesthetic learners.

Another way to learn more about your child's learning style is simply to ask her. In what ways does she like to learn? Does she prefer to listen, to watch, or to use her hands? Is she better at expressing her ideas by using words or pictures? How does she approach learning new spelling words, remembering her math facts, or starting a writing assignment? Does she talk through tasks as she does them, does she visualize what she needs to do or the information she needs to remember, or does she use her body to help her learn or recall new material?

As you observe your child and understand how he learns best, you will be a much more effective partner in his education. Whether you choose to be his guide, coach, teacher, or advocate, you will need to know how your child takes in information, processes it, and expresses himself most efficiently. Here is one model to guide your observations and thoughts regarding your child's learning process. You can simply focus on three aspects of acquiring and integrating new knowledge: receiving, processing, and expressing information.

Receiving Information

We receive information by paying attention to sensory stimuli (sights, sounds, textures, tastes, and smells) and interpreting and assigning meaning to them. For the information to be understood, children need to change the stimuli into meaningful language or a meaningful image. Some children are better able to pay attention to certain stimuli, such as sounds or pictures, and to perceive them more quickly and accurately. For example, when John listens to his teacher's instructions he can understand the assignment more easily than when he silently reads the directions on a worksheet. John's auditory attention and perception are much stronger than his visual attention and perception. John's parents, who understand this aspect of his learning style, help him with his homework by suggesting that he read his assignments and directions aloud before he begins to work.

Processing Information

For learning to take place, information must be organized and then stored accurately so that it can be accessed and available when needed. Before the material can be put into long-term storage, it must first be understood and organized into a chunk or package that can easily be found at a later stage by linking it to other information. Just as you organize computer files into folders and assign them to a specific location on the hard drive, your brain breaks down information into manageable chunks, categorizes them, and stores them in a location that is linked to related pieces of information. The more often new information is linked (cross-referenced) to already known material, the more easily it will be remembered.

Most children remember certain kinds of information better than other kinds. Some children will remember something they've heard more easily than something they've read or seen, and vice versa. Some children can remember isolated chunks of information such as dates or names better than a complex concept, story, or section of text. Others remember stories and pictures more successfully than isolated details.

Children also differ in terms of their ability to hold onto information for a period of time. Some children remember what they're learning only in the moment and have difficulty storing it for later access. Others need to have information repeated many times before they can understand it, but once they store it, they can remember it for a very long time. Some children take longer to absorb and organize information but they can remember it well once they've had more time to process the material.

A child who has difficulty remembering information can improve her memory by learning more effective ways to break down the information, organize it, categorize it, and link it to more meaningful information that she has already mastered. Sometimes changing the form of the information (e.g., from text to a picture, or from pictures into words) will help a child remember it.

By knowing your child's learning preferences, interests, and knowledge base, you can help him process, organize, and store new information in such a way that he will remember it more easily for a long time. Using mnemonics (rhymes, cartoons, silly sentences) is a fun way to improve memory. Read more about this and other strategies in Chapter 7.

Expressing Information

Knowledge is reinforced and integrated and becomes more useful when it is communicated to others. For a child to show what she knows, she can communicate by verbalizing, writing, or expressing her thoughts in an artistic form. Children usually have at least one way in which they can express their ideas and feelings most easily. Some are better at communicating what they know by talking, acting, drawing, building, making music, or writing.

When helping your child with homework, keep in mind which aspects of the communication process come easily and which might be more challenging. For example, if your child is having trouble learning his math facts but is a great singer, you can use familiar songs to "sing" the multiplication facts. Or if your child is struggling to write about a series of historical events but loves to act, you might suggest that he act out the historical events before writing.

Gather information about your child's learning style through your own observations, discussions with teachers, and possibly testing by a psychologist to gain a better understanding of his strengths and weaknesses. Summarize what you've discovered about your child using the checklist on page 22.

Multiple Intelligences

One of the many ways of understanding your child's learning style and her strengths and abilities is to think about the various kinds of intelligences. According to Howard Gardner, author of *Frames of Mind: The Theory of Multiple Intelligences* (1983), there are at least eight different intelligences. Rather than viewing intelligence as a global, measurable trait that can be defined by an I.Q. score, Gardner sees "intelligence" as the ability to solve problems or to create new products that are valued in at least one cultural setting. In his view, each of us has many different intelligences that

Your Child's Learning Style	Strong	Average	Weak
Receiving Information			
How well does your child learn by listening?			
How well does your child pay attention to visual details?			
How much does your child like to learn by touching, building, moving around?			
Processing Information			
How well can your child break down information?			
How easily can your child categorize information?			
How well can your child organize incoming information?			
How well can your child remember information? * short-term vs. long-term? * concrete vs. abstract? * visual vs. verbal/auditory? * rote vs. meaningful?			
Expressing Information			
How well can your child organize ideas when talking?			
How well can your child organize ideas when writing?			
How well can your child express ideas in picture or chart form?			
How well can your child illustrate knowledge by using her hands or body—acting, dancing, building?			

are expressed in a variety of ways. These intelligences can be grouped into the following eight categories:

Linguistic Intelligence

This intelligence is defined by the ability to use language effectively, either orally (as a storyteller, orator, conversationalist) or in writing (as a poet, reporter, playwright). Children who are strong linguistically probably enjoy reading, acting, writing, and talking. Generally they learn well by listening, discussing, and verbalizing information.

Logical–Mathematical Intelligence

This is the ability to use numbers effectively (mathematician, accountant) and to use logical reasoning (scientist, computer programmer). Students who are strong in this area enjoy math and science and learn well using a step-by-step approach to tasks.

Spatial Intelligence

Someone who has strong spatial intelligence has an appreciation and mastery of the visual-spatial world including a sensitivity to color, shape, and space. It includes the capacity to visualize, orient oneself in space, and change perspective easily. Artists, architects, designers, and inventors have high spatial intelligence. Children with these strengths enjoy drawing, building, designing, and imagining.

Bodily–Kinesthetic Intelligence

Intelligence of this kind involves using the body to express ideas (actor, athlete) and being adept at using one's hands to create (sculptor, mechanic, builder). Children who are adept with their bodies generally like to play sports, participate in drama or dance, or build, tinker, or work on arts-and-crafts activities.

Musical Intelligence

This type of intelligence includes the capacity to perceive and appreciate music and to express oneself musically (music lover, performer, composer). Children who have developed skills in this area may love to sing, play an instrument, write songs, or listen to music critically.

Intrapersonal Intelligence

Knowing oneself well and being able to recognize and understand one's moods, motivations, interests, talents, and challenges defines intrapersonal intelligence. Children who are strong intrapersonally are sensitive and insightful to their own moods, can self-soothe, and can express what they want and need. Children with a well-developed self-understanding may enjoy spending time alone and pursuing interests independently.

Interpersonal Intelligence

The capacity to understand the feelings of others, perceive social cues, and respond effectively to those cues characterizes interpersonal intelligence. Children who have well-developed social skills and can respond empathically to others have a high level of interpersonal intelligence. Generally, these children enjoy socializing with friends, helping others, and taking on leadership roles.

Naturalistic Intelligence

A keen interest and appreciation for the natural world and an ability to observe behavioral patterns and natural cycles among plants and animals defines this kind of intelligence. Children with this ability often love hiking, collecting natural objects, spending time outdoors, gardening, and taking care of pets.

Individuals may be strong in a given area even if they do not display all of the abilities listed in that category. Some students with significant reading problems, for example, may still be gifted in the linguistic area and may be talented creative writers or charismatic speakers.

Gardner's theory helps us view ourselves and our children differently. While the traditional classroom supports and applauds those students with strengths in linguistic and mathematical intelligences, it is important that we embrace all students and provide them with opportunities to learn and demonstrate their abilities in multiple ways. We are all unique—and it is essential that we nurture all of the varied human intelligences.

Jesse enjoys being outdoors, hiking in the woods, searching for frogs, and collecting rocks. He is very articulate, loves to tell people all that he's seen on his hikes and all that he's learned. He is easy to get along with and is in tune with others' feelings. Jesse makes friends easily and is well liked by his classmates. He likes to read, especially about animals and nature. Jesse's greatest difficulty is math. He struggles to remember his multiplication facts and doesn't understand fractions and decimals. He also has a poor sense of time, gets lost easily, and often loses his possessions. His backpack is messy and his room is a disaster area.

In other words, Jesse has strong naturalistic, linguistic, and interpersonal intelligences, is average in the areas of intrapersonal and kinesthetic intelligence, and is weaker in the areas of musical, mathematical, and spatial abilities.

Annie is very artistic and loves to draw and work on craft projects. She has a wonderful sense of color and style and is a keen observer of her environment. She doesn't always listen well to what people are saying and often gets distracted when listening to long stories or lectures in class. She is strong in math and science but struggles to express herself in class discussions and in writing. She learns best when she sees pictures, movies, or graphs. She has a few good friends but tends to avoid large groups and is a bit shy in new social situations. Annie knows herself well and is able to identify her strengths and difficulties accurately. She is a good advocate for herself and often asks for help when learning becomes difficult.

From a multiple-intelligence perspective, Annie is strongest in the areas of spatial, kinesthetic, and mathematical intelligence, a little less strong in her intrapersonal and interpersonal abilities, and relatively weaker in the areas of linguistic and naturalistic intelligences.

When parents and children are able to identify and understand their learning styles and use this information effectively, homework can be less stressful and can be accomplished more efficiently.

Chapter 3

Establishing a Positive Emotional Climate and an Effective Homework Routine

Ten-year-old Ben comes home from school, eats a snack, and reluctantly starts his homework by 4 P.M. He pulls out his notebook and homework materials and tries to figure out what he is supposed to do. Within the first 15 minutes, Ben is up and down at least half a dozen times searching for a sharper pencil, getting a drink, checking the baseball scores in the newspaper, looking for his favorite CD, finding batteries for his CD player, and so on. His mother tries to be encouraging: "Ben, let me help you get started. Now, what is it that you have to do? Show me where you need to begin. I know you can do this." As Ben continues to get distracted and stall, Ben's mother becomes increasingly frustrated and angry. Silently, she complains, "I am so sick and tired of this nonsense! When is he ever going to learn? Why can't he just focus and do his work? Why does it take him hours to do 45 minutes worth of homework?" Exasperated, annoyed, and concerned, Ben's mother begins to

> Three hours later, the homework is finished, Mom is exhausted and discouraged, and Ben is either agitated and unruly or sullen and withdrawn. Although Mom knows that something is very wrong with their homework routine, she doesn't know quite how to change it.

nag . . . and direct . . . and yell . . . and threaten. Three hours later, the homework is finished, Mom is exhausted and discouraged, and Ben is either agitated and unruly or sullen and withdrawn. Although Mom knows that something is very wrong with their homework routine, she doesn't know quite how to change it. She only knows that this vicious cycle will certainly begin again tomorrow.

Does this scenario remind you of your household? Do you ever find yourself wondering if there is a better way to manage your child's homework? Do you feel worried, frustrated, disappointed, discouraged, or helpless?

In our experience, most parents struggle with their children and themselves regarding homework issues. Parents and students often are not well-informed about the homework process. The media, school systems, and teachers communicate conflicting attitudes and information about homework. Popular opinion and expert advice can be quite different when discussions arise about the value and purpose of homework, the appropriate quality and quantity of assignments, and the role of parents in helping children complete their schoolwork successfully. It's no wonder everyone is somewhat bewildered about homework!

The homework scene can be quite challenging for parents and students alike under normal circumstances, but it can be an Olympic feat for families with children who have difficulties with attention, organization, and learning. Although the process of writing down one's assignments, gathering the necessary materials and information, and completing them may seem relatively uncomplicated to most adults, children and adolescents may find the homework routine immensely overwhelming. Just look at the multiple demands that successful homework completion entails:

Steps to Homework Success

♦ Write down assignments correctly.

♦ Bring home necessary papers, books, and so on.

- Understand instructions for assignment.

- Decide on a time to do the assignment.

- Gather needed materials, find space, and so on.

- Prioritize assignments in order of importance or ease.

- Get started.

- Work independently or ask for help as needed.

- Persist even when bored, frustrated, or distracted.

- Finish task.

- Transport homework to teacher and hand it in.

Looking at this list, you can understand how any step in the homework process can go awry when a student has problems with attention, memory, language, visual-motor coordination, organization, time management, and/ or frustration tolerance. Imagine what the homework process is like for students who find it difficult to pay attention, to plan ahead, to ward off distractions, and to persevere when tasks are uninteresting and mundane. It can be incredibly challenging for a student to search for his notebook in his backpack (filled with countless pieces of paper), copy the assignment from the blackboard while other students are buzzing with conversation, and write down all the details slowly and carefully so that he can read his handwriting hours later. And that's just the first step!

While doing homework, it is not uncommon for children to become so frustrated that they can no longer cope with either the assignment or your help. In response to feeling anxious, inadequate, or helpless, children often regress and become overly dependent, angry, oppositional, or withdrawn. Even though it is often disappointing, frustrating, and sometimes enraging to see your child flail, explode, or shut down when faced with adversity, you can be helpful only if you remain calm, provide encouragement and direction, and if all else fails, withdraw from the situation.

Establishing the Best Homework Routine for Your Child

While teachers and schools can go only so far in shaping the daily schedule and routine to fit students' natural body rhythms and learning styles, parents have more leeway in creating a learning environment and homework routine that optimizes their child's energy, attention, and mood.

Talk to your child about what kind of homework routine will work best for him. Consider his natural biorhythm, energy level, and learning style. Will he work best right after school when he is still in the thinking mode? Will he be more productive after he has had a chance to relax or to exercise? Is she more of a morning person or a night owl? Would doing homework in the evening or even first thing in the morning optimize her learning? To find out the answers to these questions and others, complete the survey on page 31 with your child, and then design her study routine and space accordingly.

Once you have determined the general characteristics of an effective study time and place, make a daily and weekly plan for homework completion. Review your child's weekly activities (scheduled or otherwise) with him and make sure that his homework preferences fit with his other interests and commitments. In this decade of high-achieving, overscheduled children and families, you may need to set a firm limit on the number of activities, amount of leisure time for friends, hours of TV and game time allowed, and other competing distractions. The older your child, the more negotiating and compromising you may have to do to establish a realistic homework plan that your child can endorse for himself. Fill out the schedule on page 32 with your child, post it in an eye-catching place, and enforce it!

How Much Should You Be Involved in Homework?

Once a plan is in place, parents often wonder how much they should be involved in implementing the homework routine. How much time and energy should you spend monitoring, nagging, helping, and reinforcing your child's completion of homework? Most educators agree that homework is the child's responsibility, and the earlier the child can take on that responsibility independently the better. Many teachers, in fact, discourage parents from getting involved in the homework process other than monitoring the child's progress and helping if absolutely necessary. In one elementary school, for example, the fourth-grade teachers clearly communicated a "hands-off" homework policy for parents. Instructions to their students were as follows:

> "Your homework should be completed by you, without the help of your parents or friends. If you need some help understanding directions, it is okay to ask your parents, but we expect you to do your work on your own, unless we instruct you otherwise. If you are really stuck on an assignment and have tried your best, please write a note to us explaining your problem. Then we can help you here at school."

For many students, this "hands-off" approach to homework works well. After all, if homework is an important part of the learning process, then it is important that each child takes responsibility and ownership for completing the work. Generally, by the third or fourth grade, students are expected to manage their homework fairly independently with parents available only to supply needed materials, explain instructions, monitor accuracy, and edit

Homework Preferences

When is the best time to do homework?	☐ In the morning	☐ Right after school	☐ In the evening	☐ Other
Where is the best place to work?	☐ In an isolated and quiet room	☐ Near some activity	☐ Near a parent	☐ Other
What level of noise will maximize concentration?	☐ Totally quiet	☐ Soft music	☐ White noise	☐ Loud music
What kind of lighting, colors, brightness is preferred?	☐ Very colorful and bright	☐ Soft or neutral colors	☐ Doesn't matter	☐ Other
What kind of space is needed?	☐ Large work surface	☐ Cozy corner	☐ Room to move around	☐ Other
What's the best way to start?	☐ Warm-up with easy tasks	☐ Jump right into the challenging tasks	☐ Preview all of the tasks first, then decide	☐ Other
How long can you study without losing attention?	☐ 15–20 minutes	☐ 20–45 minutes	☐ 45–90 minutes	☐ Other
What kind of breaks work best?	☐ 10–15 minutes after every half hour	☐ Half hour breaks after a larger chunk of work	☐ No breaks until homework is complete	☐ Other
What's the best thing to do when help is needed?	☐ Ask a parent	☐ Call a friend	☐ Have Mom or Dad check work	☐ Yell, whine, or quit

Homework Schedule

	Monday	Tuesday	Wednesday	Thursday	Friday	Saturday	Sunday
2:00							
3:00							
4:00							
5:00							
6:00							
7:00							
8:00							
9:00							
10:00							

writing assignments. By middle school, not only do teachers recommend that parents stay out of the homework routine, but the youngsters themselves demand that parents stay clear of their schoolwork. For emerging teens, this attitude is a healthy one and enables them to establish greater independence from their parents and to take ownership of their own learning.

For students with learning differences and attentional problems, however, a hands-off approach can be a springboard for disaster. In our experience, children of all ages with learning and attentional issues require more structure, direct intervention, support, and encouragement than typical learners.

If your child has a learning disability or an organizational or attentional problem, then knowing what your child's homework is, monitoring his completion of the work, and providing help when needed are essential to your child's academic success. If you are able to stay involved even minimally, it will be easier to intervene if and when your child begins to have difficulty managing the volume or complexity of his assignments. If you allow your child to exclude you totally from his schoolwork, then it will be difficult to reinsert yourself if a crisis occurs. While some parents may decide it is not worth the battle to nag or push their way into their adolescent's homework routine, others will determine that it is in their child's best interest and their responsibility as a parent to stay on top of his homework assignments. To help you decide which way to go, start by asking yourself how well your child manages homework and attains his achievement goals:

♦ How consistently is your child able to complete homework on time?

♦ Does your child work as hard as she is capable of?

♦ Does he keep working even when the work gets difficult?

♦ Does she make a plan of how she is going to accomplish the work and stick to it?

♦ Does he begin working on projects or studying for tests well before the deadline?

♦ Does she schedule in needed breaks?

♦ Can he estimate how long an assignment will take to complete?

♦ Does she check her work before handing it in?

- How much panic/stress does he experience before tests or project due dates?

- How much nagging is required on your part to ensure homework is completed on time?

Your answers to these questions will help you decide how involved you should be in the homework process and what your role should be. Some of the most common homework problems and possible solutions are presented below:

Homework Problems	Possible Solutions
Difficulty getting started	• Have a routine starting time. • Review assignments with child. • Make a plan for completion. • Have child visualize completion. • Select first task and ensure understanding. • Model first step and observe while child completes next step. • Use an incentive: *If you start now and finish this assignment in the next half hour, then you can . . .*
Difficulty scheduling enough time to complete work	• Together, estimate how much time each assignment will take and make a plan on a daily basis. • Use a timer to measure actual working time. • Record how much time each assignment actually takes. • Build in breaks every half hour or less. • Base new estimates on past performance. • Talk to teachers about getting advance notice on assignments.

Homework Problems	Possible Solutions
Isolates self and doesn't accomplish much	• Change workspace so that some monitoring is possible. • Agree on frequent check-ins. • Offer incentives for each assignment completed. • Remove distractions if needed (e.g., TV, computer games, loud music). • Establish frequent communication with teachers to ensure work is completed and quality is adequate.
Rushes through work	• Give incentives for slowing down and producing accurate work. • Review expectations for quality. • Ask teacher for specific rubrics (detailed grading sheets) for major assignments. • Check work for accuracy and insist on corrections. • Use timer to encourage spending more time.

Doesn't turn in assignments even when completed	• Discuss reasons for behavior:
	  ➜ Is it because he forgets?
	  ➜ Is she worried the work isn't good enough?
	  ➜ Is he convincing himself that he's finished before turning it in?
	• Plan to check in with teacher or counselor to ensure assignments are turned in on time.
	• Provide incentives for homework turned in on time.
	• Ask for weekly reports from teachers.

Homework Problems	*Possible Solutions*
Distractibility	• Test usefulness of background noises (e.g., soft music, fan). • Remove real distractions—TV, video games, siblings, computer.
Whining	• Set limits: *I'll listen only if you change your tone.*
Tantrums	• Remove child from homework. • Distract him. • Let him blow off steam in safe ways. • Guide him to calm down by counting to 10, taking a deep breath, drawing who or what he's angry about.
Refusing your help: *Yes, but* . . . or *No, that's not how you do it!*	• Back off—leave the problem for your child to solve or give her a choice: *Calm down and be open to suggestions, or do it yourself.*
Giving up	• Encourage your child to try again using a different strategy: *I know you want to figure this out—let's see if we can approach it differently,* or *Put it aside and try it again later.*

How Do You Decide What Approach to Take?

For Elementary School Children

If your child is in elementary school, you can help by:

♦ ensuring that your child routinely writes down his assignments

♦ assisting your child with organization

♦ providing the necessary materials

♦ reviewing homework instructions

♦ breaking down the assignments into smaller steps

♦ brainstorming ideas

♦ checking work on an as-needed basis

♦ creating a system for storing completed homework so that it is handed in the next day

♦ reviewing content material and quizzing your child before tests

You can also play a role in structuring your child's homework time so that the homework is more engaging and more easily accomplished. For example, if your child has difficulty reading, you can help by becoming an active partner in the reading process. You can read to your child, share the reading by alternating pages, or reinforce her skills by reading a page and then having your child reread the same page. You can also make sure that your child understands what she has read by asking questions such as:

♦ What was the most important event in this chapter?

♦ Did you notice any changes in the characters?

♦ What would be a good title for this chapter?

♦ Why do you think the character felt the way he did?

♦ What do you think will happen next in the story?

To make reading more fun, try to engage your child in his favorite imaginary world or real-life activity:

♦ Would he like to play detective with you and figure out what's going to happen next in the book?

♦ Would he like to play a favorite TV game show by seeing who can answer questions about the plot, characters, and/or title?

♦ Can he become a Master Wizard by drawing what's going to happen in the next chapter?

For more ways to help your child with reading, see Chapter 4.

For Middle and High School Students

When your child is in middle or high school, staying informed and involved in homework will present a greater challenge. You can always encourage your child to do his best while making sure he knows that you are willing to help. Be clear with yourself and your child as to what kind of support and assistance you are willing to give. For instance, in the case of an older child, would you be willing to:

♦ go out the night before a project is due to buy supplies?

♦ type his paper?

♦ help with the research for her paper?

♦ drive him to the library at his convenience so he can do his own research?

♦ discuss her ideas before she begins to write a paper?

♦ help him draw up a reasonable schedule to finish a project?

♦ provide an incentive for her to finish a long-term project on time?

♦ help him edit a paper or put the finishing touches on a poster?

Decide upfront where you want to draw the line. Often, parents feel compelled to expend far more effort and time on their children's work than is necessary or appropriate. Some parents may feel that their child's grade on his homework will reflect on everyone in the family or that so much depends on this assignment that it is imperative to drop everything to make it happen. In reality, a single assignment is rarely that important to your child's overall success. In most cases, teachers are well aware of your child's capabilities and can easily discern when parents contribute significantly to a paper or project. In instances when assignments are not well-matched to your child's skills, it is more important for teachers to realize what your child does and does not understand than it is for you to mask his difficulties.

How Do You Begin to Help?

Think of your role as a problem solver. Keep in mind that nobody else knows your child as well, and as intimately, as you do.

- How can you help your child align his specific skills and strengths to complete the task at hand?

- What "secret" knowledge do you have about your child that you can bring to bear when solving this problem?

Helping your child with homework is no different than the time you helped her learn how to set the table, or tie her shoes, or greet visitors, or do any of the numerous tasks she now accomplishes in the course of the day. You were, after all, her very first teacher.

Of course, academics are a little more specialized, but the same principles apply in this context as well. For instance, research on parent-child interactions in a variety of cultures has shown that parents use many of the same techniques that accomplished and trained teachers do when teaching their children new skills. One such technique is called **scaffolding**. Here, a novice learner is given every support he needs to accomplish a task. With each repetition of the task, his skill increases, and the teacher withdraws the supports one by one until the learner is functioning independently. If the learner makes errors during subsequent attempts at the same task, the expert offers the least possible support to reestablish the learner's competence with the least intervention. Since you would expect that your child has attained a sufficient level of competence in the classroom, difficulty during homework would require only those minimal prompts. If you approach homework assistance from this point of view, you can probably rely on your intuition regarding your child's strengths and weaknesses and be successful.

For example, if your child is having difficulty learning how to take notes from a textbook, follow these steps to provide the necessary support to enable your child to be successful. First, explain and model a technique for taking notes. Teachers at the middle and high school level often recommend the two-column or three-column approach shown on pages 41–42. (See Chapter 7 for a more detailed explanation and examples.)

Partner with your child and have him write the main ideas while you record the details, explaining why you wrote down specific items and providing positive feedback on your child's contributions. After your child demonstrates the ability to write the main ideas, you can then switch roles and have your child write the details while you write the main ideas. Once your child has mastered the details, encourage him to fill in both columns while you supervise, always providing positive feedback and encouragement. If your child is able to fill in both columns successfully, you can then withdraw your support and allow your child to take notes independently.

Note-Taking Strategies

Two-Column Notes

The two-column method involves writing the main ideas in the first column (e.g., major headings, major events, broad concepts) and the supporting details in the second column (e.g., important people, dates, consequences).

Main Ideas	Details
Revolutionary War	1775–1783
Causes	1764 New Taxes
	1765 Stamp Tax Passed
	1765 Sons of Liberty Organized
	1767 Townshend Acts Imposed
	1767 Colonists Impose Boycott
	1768 British Troops Land
	1770 Boston Massacre
	1770 Townshend Acts Repealed
	1773 Boston Tea Party
	1774 Coercive Acts Imposed
	1774 First Continental Congress
Battles	Lexington and Concord
	Bunker Hill
	Attack on Canada
	Germantown
	Valley Forge

Three-Column Notes

The three-column method includes the main ideas in the first column, the details in the second column, and a memory strategy in the third column (a picture, acronym, key word, or diagram).

Main Ideas	Details	Memory Strategy
Revolutionary War	1775–1783	Grandma and Grandpa's ages (75 and 83)
Causes	**S**tamp Tax Passed **S**ons of Liberty Organized **T**ownshend Acts Imposed Colonists Impose **B**oycott British **T**roops Land Boston **M**assacre **T**ownshend Acts Repealed Boston **T**ea Party **C**oercive Acts Imposed First **C**ontinental Congress	**S**trong **S**am **T**ried **B**elching **T**wo **M**ore **T**imes **T**han **C**ramer **C**ould
Battles	Lexington and Concord Bunker Hill Attack on Canada Germantown Valley Forge	Sing battle names to tune of "Twinkle, Twinkle Little Star"

Ways to Encourage Your Child

The messages that you communicate about learning and the language that you use to express your ideas are critical in shaping and sustaining your child's attitude, motivation, and persistence in pursuit of educational success. When you talk with your child about school and homework, your messages must clearly convey empathy, acceptance, encouragement, and optimism.

1. **Empathy:** To be an effective partner in your child's education, you will have to show him that you understand the triumphs, strengths, challenges, and feelings that influence his attitude toward and success with learning. To fully support your child's efforts and to appreciate his learning experiences, you will need to view the situation from his perspective before he will be ready to listen.

2. **Acceptance:** One of the most difficult challenges that parents face is learning to accept their own weaknesses, imperfections, and failures, and their children's flaws as well. Let your child know that you accept her, and help her realize that everyone has flaws and failures. Reading books that focus on this theme is one way to approach this issue in a child-friendly way. (See "Resources for Families," page 158.)

3. **Encouragement:** Encouraging your child means communicating that you have confidence in his ability, that you know he really wants to do well, that his effort is what counts the most, and that you appreciate all the ways in which he makes the world a better place. While emphasizing the positive, encouragement differs from praise in that it is descriptive, specific, child-focused, and confidence building (reflecting your child's unique abilities and efforts). With encouragement, your child will develop more confidence in his ability to learn successfully and the "stick-to-it" attitude to persist even when the work is difficult.

4. **Optimism:** Your child depends on your never-ending trust and belief in her ability to succeed regardless of her difficulties, challenges, or lack of self-confidence.

Praise	vs.	Encouragement
Global: *That's terrific!*		Specific: *The introduction is very clearly written.*
Evaluative: *I love it!*		Descriptive: *Now, that's what I call colorful!*
Parent-focused: *I'm so proud of you!*		Child-focused: *You worked really hard on that project. You should be so proud of yourself!*
Unrealistic: *That's perfect!*		Realistic: *Your work shows that you really understood the book that you read.*
Universal: *What a good job!*		Unique: *Only you could have written that story and made me laugh so hard!*
Controlling: *I love those A's—now you can buy that new computer game you wanted!*		Liberating (communicates your confidence in his/her abilities and intentions): *I know you want to do your best—with a little hard work, I know you will!*

By establishing a positive and supportive communication style, you will be in a better position to structure and reinforce an effective homework routine for your child. Again, take into consideration your child's personal preferences, temperament, and work style when establishing a homework routine that is most likely to lead to success. It is also important to decide how much you want to be involved in your child's homework and in what ways you can be most supportive. Each family will be different with respect to the amount of parental involvement needed and preferred. There is no one correct routine for all.

Now let's return to Ben and his mother from the chapter opening. How could this homework struggle have been avoided or resolved in a more positive way? First of all, Ben's mother could sit down and have a serious talk with Ben about his homework routine. Their conversation might go like this:

Mom: Ben, have you noticed how long it takes you to get your homework done and how often we fight about your homework?

Ben: No kidding, Mom! I hate doing homework! And I wish you would leave me alone!

Mom: I know you don't like homework, Ben. Most kids don't. But homework is important because you have a chance to review what you've learned in school today, learn something new, apply what you've learned to solve a new problem, or create something of your own.

Ben: Who cares? I still don't like doing it!

Mom: Well, maybe when you're older you'll understand why homework does help. But in the meantime, even if you don't like it, it's something you have to do. So, how can we work together so that you get your work done more quickly and have more time for fun?

Ben: I don't know. I always think my homework's going to take so long so I try to avoid it as long as I can.

Mom: Well, how about we make a deal? I know that your teacher expects you to work on homework for less than an hour each day. Let's think about what we need to do to make sure that you get most or all of your work done in that amount of time. Do you have any ideas?

Ben: Not really.

Mom: Well, I have a few suggestions. Have you ever noticed that you spend a lot of time just trying to find a pencil and other materials that you need before doing your homework?

Ben: Yes, I can never find a pencil or extra paper.

Mom: Why don't we set up a homework area that has all the materials that you need. Then let's set a timer for one hour and see how much you get done in that amount of time. When an hour is up, you should stop. If you haven't finished, I'll write a note to your teacher and will let her know that you worked hard and did as much as you could in an hour. I know you can do it, especially if you're not worried about how long homework will take you.

Ben: You mean, I won't have to work longer than an hour? And then I could play a game or watch TV?

Mom: That's right. And if you follow the plan and really work hard for an hour, you could also earn points and cash them in for special treats. Let's say you could earn up to five points a day for doing your homework and following our plan. We'll make a list of prizes and privileges you can earn with your points. What do you think?

Ben: That sounds pretty good to me!

With their agreement in place, Ben's mother can focus her energies on helping Ben implement the plan and can reward his efforts, rather than fight with him. By providing a plan, making sure that he has the materials he needs, adding some structure (i.e., the timer and a time limit), and encouraging him to do his best, Ben's mother will be much more effective and happier with the results. In turn, Ben will probably be able to complete his homework more efficiently without the usual distress and conflict.

Remember, all parents sometimes struggle with their children over homework. So don't take it to heart if you and your child fight about when, how, or why to do homework. However, you can minimize the conflict and begin to encourage your child to approach homework with a more positive attitude and to complete it more efficiently. By using the ideas in this chapter, you will be able to develop a realistic homework routine with your child, encourage her efforts, and decide on a supportive role that works for you and is acceptable to your child.

Chapter 4

Helping Your Child With Reading Homework

Ron is a poised and friendly fourth grader who struggles with reading. As a young child, he had frequent and severe ear infections and had shown some early delays in language development. However, as a result of early intervention speech and language support, Ron entered kindergarten on schedule. By the time Ron finished second grade, his parents and teachers realized that he was having a great deal of difficulty with reading and writing. His teacher spent extra time with him after school, coaching him in reading. Now in the fourth grade, Ron continues to struggle with his homework and does not enjoy reading independently. Any homework that requires reading or writing is a struggle, and Ron is beginning to feel terrible about school. His parents and teachers are extremely concerned about his slow rate of progress and his diminished self-esteem.

Fifth-grader Alex has always lagged behind his peers in reading. Although he is bright and inquisitive, he has never been interested in books. When his parents read with him, they find that he reads very slowly and often repeats words or phrases. These struggles mean that Alex is rarely able to finish the books assigned for homework and has trouble understanding what he reads. In fact, he avoids reading directions even when he is given math or science homework. As a result,

> Fifth-grader Alex has always lagged behind his peers in reading. Although he is bright and inquisitive, he has never been interested in books.

Alex has grown increasingly discouraged. Daily homework has become a struggle for him and his family. He now seems to prefer learning from videotapes and TV programs.

· ·

Julia is a seventh grader who does not enjoy reading. Although she can read accurately and fluently, her comprehension is weak when she reads independently. She tends to lose track of the major themes and confuses characters with one another. Julia reads slowly and is often resistant to doing any homework that involves reading. She struggles particularly with homework assignments that require her to research topics from a variety of sources.

Studies show that parents who read for leisure and who make books available at home are likely to inspire their children to love reading. Weekly trips to the local public library, doing the Sunday crosswords, clipping recipes or cartoons from magazines and newspapers, discussing favorite books, and reading together are all ways of showing children that reading is an enriching and tremendously useful skill. Reading is a source of great pleasure for many people, and parents often wait with happy anticipation for their children to discover this same pleasure.

In most cases, children will begin to read by the latter half of kindergarten if they show normally developing language skills, are exposed to the written word from an early age, and are given routine early educational experiences. Once they "break the code" and understand how printed text relates to speech, these children proceed in leaps and bounds.

However, there are also many children for whom reading is a struggle. These children sometimes have early difficulties with various aspects of literacy. They may have difficulty learning the alphabet, have trouble playing rhyming games, or avoid all reading-related activities in preschool and kindergarten. Small words such as *the, who, what, no,* and *and* may be very troublesome for some children, who don't seem to recognize these words no matter how many times they see them. Some children may reverse words, reading *no* for *on* or *saw* for *was.* Others may sound out words laboriously and may struggle to blend the sounds into words. Reading is not fun or enjoyable for any of these children. Rather, it is a chore, and a difficult one at that.

This chapter examines the process of reading, delineates landmarks on the young child's path to becoming a reader, and offers parents tips for encouraging and supporting their children with reading homework.

The Reading Process

Reading is a multilayered process that includes several subprocesses. A child learning to read moves through these processes until, finally, all the processes are integrated to create a fluent and successful reader.

- -

Processes in Reading

- ◆ Phonological awareness

- ◆ Knowing about print

- ◆ Learning consistent sound-symbol relationships

- ◆ Reading fluently

- ◆ Reading for meaning

- -

Linking Oral Language and Reading

Reading is a language-based skill that is superimposed on oral language skills. Therefore, early language acquisition is closely linked to the later acquisition of reading in literate societies. When children begin to realize that spoken language can be broken up into words, syllables, and sounds, they are ready to learn that each sound is mapped onto a written symbol. This is the basis for reading in an alphabetic system such as English. As children grow and develop, the relationship between their "reading life" and their oral language becomes reciprocal. Thus, as their skill with reading and their sophistication with language use increases, they can read more challenging material. In turn, their choice of reading material helps swell their vocabularies and broaden their horizons with respect to grammar and style.

The Link Between Oral Language and Early Reading Skills: Phonological Awareness

Phonological awareness is the understanding that the stream of speech can be divided into words, syllables, and sounds. This may seem like a no-brainer to those of us who are expert readers. However, this is where the journey to expert reading begins. A child with strong phonological awareness can usually identify word boundaries. A young child who is told to behave, and who responds, "I'm being haive," is in the process of making this journey. He has heard "be good," "be quiet," and now he is experimenting with "behave." Children with strong phonological awareness and phonological processing typically learn to read and spell easily. The phonological-awareness skills necessary for reading and spelling are usually well developed by the age of 7.

The Link Between Oral Language and Later Reading Skills

Since reading is superimposed upon oral language development, a child's early vocabulary and grammar skills provide a basis for understanding picture books and other childhood literature. As your child grows, she will encounter more complex vocabulary and language in reading material, which will challenge and stretch her oral language development. During the middle school years and beyond, a student's oral language sophistication is dependent on her reading habits. Research has shown that in these later years, the bulk of a student's understanding of vocabulary and language comes from the text she reads. Routine and casual oral conversations no longer expand the student's language skills in the same way.

As the reader matures, the relationship between reading and oral language becomes more reciprocal. In other words, while oral language skills may predict early reading success, in older children strong reading abilities are reflected in their oral language, particularly with respect to their understanding and use of novel vocabulary, sophisticated sentence structure, and figurative language. The opposite is also true. A child who has delays in oral language can be expected to have difficulty with aspects of reading, and an older child who does not read because it is not enjoyable for him may show signs of impoverished oral language.

Usually, weaknesses in articulation, phonological processing, and vocabulary can have an impact on a child's ability to decode text.

The Stages of Reading

Note: Please keep in mind that the age ranges below are rough estimates, and there is overlap between the reading stages. Within each stage, some children may be advanced, while others lag behind. These broad age ranges are based on educational research.

Stage 0. Pre-reading (birth to age 6) — Children gain control over language and begin to understand that words are made up of individual sounds. They also begin to learn about print and can often distinguish written language from random scribbling.

Stage 1. Decoding Stage: Grades 1 to 2 (ages 6 to 7) — Children learn the letters of the alphabet and associate these with spoken sounds. Children begin to internalize the awareness of their own errors and gain a greater sensitivity to the differences between words such as *tap* and *ton*. By the end of this phase, they have gained insight into the nature of the spelling system of the particular language they are learning to read.

Stage 2. Ungluing from Print: Grades 2 to 3 (ages 7 to 8) — Children consolidate what they have learned in Stage 1 and begin to read known stories with greater fluency. According to Jeanne Chall, they "gain courage and skill in using context and thus gain fluency and speed." Although additional and more complex elements may be learned during this stage and later, the critical aspect of Stage 2 is that children learn to use their decoding knowledge and the redundancies in language to read more efficiently.

Stage 3. Reading for Learning the New: Grade 3 through middle school (ages 8 to 14) — Children begin to use reading as a tool to acquire new knowledge, information, thoughts, and experiences.

Stage 4. Multiple View Points: High School (ages 14 to 18) — Students are able to read and understand texts that deal with more than one point of view, where material is treated with greater depth.

Stage 5. Construction and Reconstruction—A World View: College (ages 18 and above) — This is the most mature stage and is the adult level of reading. Students can construct knowledge at a higher level and create their own "truth" from others' "truths."

Adapted from Jeanne S. Chall (1983). *Stages of Reading Development*. Harcourt Brace College Publishers

Levels of Language Processing

Articulation: The process of producing speech sounds by moving the "articulators" or mouthparts such as the lips, tongue, and soft palate (velum).

Phonological Processing: Using speech sounds in a meaningful way; for instance, knowing the difference between the first sound in the words *pat* and *bat*, and knowing that this difference also changes the meaning. On the other hand, the difference in the last sound in the words *bugs* and *rats* does not change the meaning of the plural suffix *-s*.

Vocabulary: All the words for which the child knows at least one meaning and which the child can use to express his ideas.

Morphology: The process of changing the meanings of words by adding affixes (i.e., prefixes and suffixes). For example, we can change the word *read* to *reading* by adding *-ing*, and thus modify its meaning so that it belongs to a different grammatical category.

Syntax: Rules of grammar that govern the construction of sentences, phrases, and clauses. For example, in English the rules of syntax state that an adjective must come before the noun. So, we say, "blue ball" rather than "ball blue."

Semantics: The relationship between language and meaning. For example, the child who says, "I want to put socks on so my feet feel cold and cozy," is not fully competent with the semantic rules that govern this statement.

Pragmatics: Rules that govern social conversation. These include taking turns, making eye contact with one's listener, using language that is appropriate to the formality of the situation, using etiquette (e.g., saying "please" and "thank you"), and speaking at an appropriate volume. Pragmatics also includes the skills involved in monitoring what one says so confusion on the part of the listener is noticed and appropriate steps are taken to "repair" communication.

Weaknesses in vocabulary, syntax, semantics, and pragmatics can have an impact on a student's reading comprehension skills.

Common Areas of Difficulty

Phonological Awareness

A child who has weak phonological awareness and who struggles with phonological processing may show the following signs:

♦ A lack of appreciation or enjoyment of early rhyming games or songs

♦ Difficulty using "pig Latin," or appreciating such games

♦ Difficulties identifying or classifying words that start with the same sound or have the same sound as part of the words

♦ Difficulty playing with language by interchanging syllables (e.g., *boat nook* instead of *notebook*).

Sound–Symbol Correspondence

In order to read, a child needs to learn that the sounds she speaks can be mapped onto written symbols. Understanding and learning this relationship is a key step to becoming a fluent reader. A child who struggles with sound-symbol correspondence may show the following signs:

♦ Difficulty remembering letter names and sounds

♦ Difficulty learning the rules of phonics

♦ Difficulty recognizing a letter or group of letters that she's seen before

Automaticity and Fluency

The goal of reading is to extract meaning easily from text. Expert readers can skim a page of text and effortlessly get to the essence of the content. Many are even unaware of having read individual words in the text. Thus, an expert reader spends almost no cognitive energy on decoding and saves all his resources for interpreting the message in the text. This is because they are fluent readers for whom the decoding process has "gone underground." For these experts, not only is the association between the written symbols and the spoken word extremely well integrated, but the information can be retrieved with no overt effort. As students progress through elementary school, the expectation is that they will increase their fluency so that they begin to "read to learn." A student who struggles with fluency may show the following signs:

♦ Reading in a very labored manner

♦ Sounding out each individual word and pausing frequently

♦ Little or no expression when reading

♦ Very slow progress

♦ Little or no comprehension after reading

♦ Lack of enjoyment of reading and fatigue

Comprehension

By third grade, reading instruction shifts to focus on content. Thus, the main focus in upper elementary through middle school is to use reading as a tool to acquire new knowledge, information, thoughts, and experiences. As students mature, they encounter longer and more complex texts. The texts feature complex language including metaphors, advanced vocabulary or even foreign words, and mature themes that stretch students' critical-thinking abilities. However, students often have to go beyond the text in order to understand the content fully. They have to draw on their background knowledge and life experience, rely on their ability to empathize with characters, and work actively to integrate information. In order to comprehend text effectively, students have to sort and prioritize details, link new information with old, and integrate information. Students who struggle with comprehension may show the following signs:

♦ Poor memory for what they have read

♦ Inability to retell what they have read

- Difficulty drawing inferences

- Difficulty gleaning the meaning of novel words through context

- Difficulty keeping the thread of a narrative

- Incomplete or inaccurate answers to questions

- Difficulty summarizing the text

- Slow or poor development of vocabulary and grammar skills

- Gaps in background knowledge that they should have learned from reading assignments

- Lack of enjoyment of reading

- Fatigue and avoidance of reading tasks

How Parents Can Help

Try these suggestions for encouraging and helping a beginning reader:

- Find some quiet time to read each day. A regularly scheduled reading time is a good idea.

- Find a comfortable place to sit, with good lighting.

- Spend a few minutes looking at the cover of the book and talking about the title. Discuss what the title might mean and what the book may be about. Encourage your child to make guesses about the story.

- Leaf through the book, looking only at the pictures and using them to create a first narration of the story so that your child becomes familiar with the themes.

- As your child begins to read, provide assistance as needed. You may need to help your child track the lines correctly. You may also need to help him read some words. Each time you provide help with a word, ask your child to read the word himself.

- When you are reading to your child, allow her to look in the book with you as you read.

◆ As your child becomes more comfortable and independent with reading, encourage him to spend a few minutes leafing through and reading a book of his choice. The book should present an appropriate challenge to him. Remain within earshot so you can listen and provide help when necessary.

Phonological Awareness and Sound–Symbol Correspondence

Parents cannot teach phonological-awareness skills as this requires specialized training and knowledge. Students who have difficulties with these areas into third grade and beyond require specialized reading instruction. Parents who have ongoing concerns about their children's ability to remember the sounds of letters and decode words should bring their concerns to the attention of their children's teachers. Often, teachers are just as concerned about these students. Usually, students who are struggling with decoding skills qualify for specialized reading instruction through the special-education process.

Accuracy and Fluency

As students progress through elementary school, they are usually required to read regularly, often for about half an hour each night. Teachers usually assign books of appropriate complexity based on each student's reading ability and the expectations for that grade level. Assignments vary at each grade but include some combination of vocabulary building, critical thinking, and responsive writing. In grades 4 and 5, teachers may assign art projects to showcase student's responses to the reading text. In grades 5 and 6, written responses may be the norm. Students are expected to read fluently at this level. If your child's reading lacks fluency and accuracy, here are some things you can try:

◆ If your child stumbles on a word, remind him to point to each letter as he reads. If necessary, help with compound words and longer words by covering the second half of the word while he decodes the first half.

◆ If your child misreads a word, prompt her to stop and listen to herself and to ask herself, "Did that make sense?" You could then guide her to use information from the shape of the word (i.e., the sequence of letters in it) and the meaning of the sentence to come up with a better alternative that makes sense.

- If you notice your child reading in a monotone, you can help her read with more expression using the following suggestions:

  - Try an easier text and see if your child's reading fluency improves. To help you select an appropriate text, choose a few hard words from the text and check to see if these are within your child's repertoire.

  - Regular practice with sight words is often the key to improved fluency. Your child's teacher will be able to give you a list of words that he is expected to recognize on sight. You can put these on index cards and help your child practice them a few at a time until she can recognize them easily without errors.

  - Highlight the voice tones and expression that you use when you read.

  - Explain to your child that punctuation marks are a way of writing down the "tune" of our speech.

  - Assign her short paragraphs to practice (read and reread) until she is thoroughly familiar with them. The paragraphs must be well within her capabilities, and she should read them one at a time.

  - Choral reading is an effective way of modeling the appropriate pace and expression for reading. You and your child can read a section together first before she reads it independently.

  - Ask her to pretend she is on a radio or TV program while reading aloud.

- If your child's reading is hesitant because he is not gleaning meaning from the text, use the practice reading trials of short paragraphs to discuss what the story means. You may also "set up" the story before he begins reading by spending time looking at the cover and illustrations and discussing the title.

- If difficulties with fluent reading persist, it is important to discuss this with your child's teacher. She may benefit from accommodations such as taped books or from more intensive instruction at school.

As your child progresses, he will gain more confidence and become more independent with reading. It is, however, a good idea to keep track of his performance by periodically having him read aloud to you, preferably from a text that he is using at school. You can continue to use the strategies and suggestions discussed above as needed.

Comprehension

Reading comprehension requires the coordination of multiple cognitive processes. It is also a process that changes depending on what we are reading. For example, we use different strategies and processes when we are reading a novel or directions for installing a new printer. Our ability to comprehend is influenced by our grasp of the language, our background knowledge, and our ability to monitor our performance as we read. We also need ways to sort and organize information in the text, draw inferences, and understand information flexibly.

As texts become longer and more complex in late elementary school, it is a good idea to check on your child's understanding periodically. You can do this in the following ways:

♦ Encourage her to summarize (e.g., *Tell me what the story was about.*).

♦ Encourage him to predict upcoming events in the text.

♦ Discuss alternate possibilities and encourage her to predict two possible options for the next chapter.

These tips will give your child early practice with the skills involved in stating and supporting a thesis.

In middle school (starting from grade 6 or 7, depending on the school system), students are assigned homework that requires them to read textbooks and longer, more involved novels. They are also expected to read independently, analytically, and quickly and to write book reports and research papers. As students progress into high school, the complexity of texts increases along with the level of analysis expected of them. It is sometimes difficult to intervene with an older child's homework even when you suspect that she needs your help. These issues are discussed at length in Chapter 7. However, you can encourage your adolescent to use some of the following strategies to read textbooks more efficiently:

- Encourage your child to skim chapter headings, section headings, and diagrams. He could write a one- or two-sentence summary of what he expects to learn from this chapter based on this information.

- Encourage your child to jot down, very briefly, any knowledge he may already have about this topic.

- For each section, he could read the subheadings carefully and reformulate them into questions. He could then write these questions in the margin of the textbook. This helps your child think carefully about what he will be reading and to become an "active reader."

- Encourage your child to use a T-chart (Figure 1) to record his questions and answers as he reads the chapter.

Figure 1: T-Chart

Questions	Answers

ResearchILD/Fablevision, 2002

- Your child can use a Triple Note Tote (Figure 2) if he wants to use a third column to note down a strategy for remembering information.

- Next, your child can read the section, paying attention to new vocabulary. He can use the glossary if necessary.

- When he is done reading, your child can answer the questions that he wrote in the margin earlier.

Figure 2: Triple Note Tote

Organize	Plan	Remember
Name the New England colonies.	Maine New Hampshire Vermont Massachusetts Connecticut Rhode Island	Many New Happy Voices Make the Chorus RIng

ResearchILD/Fablevision, 2002

- Encourage your child to write the answer on a sticky note and stick it in the margin. This is a quick section summary.

- At the end of the chapter, he should go back to the initial summary. He could compare what he now knows with what he knew before reading this chapter.

Figure 3: Star Strategy

Meltzer et al., 2005

- Your child can collect all of his sticky-note summaries and combine them to form a chapter summary. This is an extremely useful tool when studying for tests.

- The STAR strategy (Figure 3), which is discussed in Chapter 5, is also very helpful when reading about people and important events in social studies. Your child can use it to quickly answer the key questions: Who? What? Where? When? Why? and How?

- The Venn diagram (Figure 4) provides an effective way to compare and contrast information when reading.

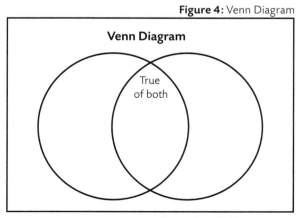

Figure 4: Venn Diagram

ResearchILD/Fablevision, 2002

Novels pose a different type of challenge. Sometimes the length of the assigned novel may overwhelm your child. Other times, he may lack the background knowledge or experience necessary to understand the narrated events. Some novels, such as the writings of Mark Twain or Charles Dickens, are written in dialect, which makes them difficult to read. Finally, your child may have difficulty with the analytical thinking required to complete the reading assignment. Here are some helpful strategies:

Figure 5: Story Grammar Marker

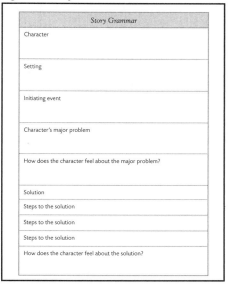

♦ Help your child break down the task if the book is very long. Using a calendar and the table of contents from the book, your child can plan out a schedule for reading her book in the time allotted by her teacher.

Figure 6: Story Plan

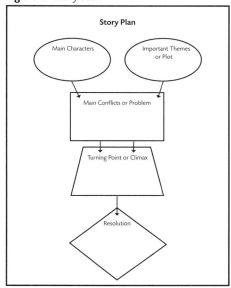

♦ Encourage your child to pause as she reads and check in with herself: "Do I understand what I am reading?" If she does not understand, encourage her to formulate questions and go back and reread text.

♦ Encourage your child to use graphic organizers to help her organize the important information in the story. Different types of organizers will work for different students. Try the samples shown here to see which one your child may prefer (Figures 5, 6, 7).

◆ A Venn diagram (Figure 4) is also very helpful in comparing different characters and their actions, feelings, or motivations.

◆ When your child needs to focus on the attributes of a particular character, she could use organizers that are specifically designed for this purpose (Figure 8).

◆ Sometimes it is helpful if you read the book yourself and discuss the story with your child as she progresses through the book. By doing this, you can prompt your child's memory for important information that she may have missed or help her connect important points in the story.

Figure 7: Chapter Summary Organizer

Chapter Summary Organizer

Title: _____
Chapter: _____
Setting: _____
Characters: _____

Main Character's name: _____

Three facts about the main character
1. _____
2. _____
3. _____

Have you learned anything new about the main character's problem? Write it down.

Summary: (Write down the most important thing that occurred in this chapter.)

New vocabulary from this chapter:

Figure 8: Bubble Map

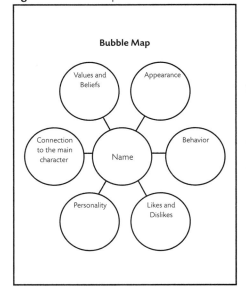

- Many children enjoy having books read aloud to them. If your child's assigned book includes dialogue or is written in a particular dialect, you can take turns reading aloud to make the text come alive.

- Finally, if the book your child is reading has been made into a film that is well reviewed and follows the book closely, it is always a good idea to watch the film. This should be done *in addition* to reading the book. Many children benefit from the multisensory experience of watching a film, and they actually learn and remember more from this than from reading a book.

Reading for Thinking: High School and Beyond

The eventual purpose of reading is that students are able to understand texts that deal with more than one point of view and in which topics are discussed in greater depth. This is the most mature stage and is considered the "adult" level of reading. Here, a student can construct abstract knowledge and create his own "truth" from others' "truths." At this level, reading is merely another avenue for gathering information, similar to listening. In addition, the process of reading may be more like a dialogue with the author, with the reader contributing his or her own understanding. Thus, it becomes a highly individual and flexible tool for personal growth. Your child's success as a reader is no longer dependent only on decoding the text or understanding the structure of the text, but on being able to extract the essence of the text, integrate it with previous knowledge, judge the truth or dependability of the information, appreciate multiple perspectives, and reach a new and deeper understanding of the subject. This is a lifelong process and is shaped by, among other things, the range of writing styles and content that your child chooses, the frequency of reading, and any activity that may follow from the reading (e.g., discussion at a book club or in an educational setting, responsive writing or art, or changes in lifestyle).

Top-Down and Bottom-Up Approaches to Reading: How Parents Can Help

In Chapter 2, you read about the distinction between top-down and bottom-up styles. If your child tends to be a **top-down thinker**, he may focus primarily on the "big picture." Sometimes homework assignments require students to remember important details. If your child is spending hours on his language arts homework but is still getting low grades on assignments and tests that measure his understanding of details, try the following strategies:

- Encourage your child to visualize what he is reading (or listening to) using all the rich detail offered by the text. You may ask him to "make a movie" in his mind as he reads or listens. Stop periodically and ask him to describe the mental picture he has created in as much detail as possible. When your child is recalling the story, encourage him to reflect on these mental images to flesh out his oral narratives.

- Note the types of details your child misses and share this with his teacher.

  - Does he usually forget the characters' names?

  - Does he tend to mix up the sequence of events?

  - Does he have trouble drawing inferences?

  - Is his summary disorganized?

  - Does he tend to remember the beginning of the story and not the end?

- After your child summarizes the story, ask him questions about specific details.

- If his summary is incomplete, ask him if he wants to add anything, as a gentle reminder that he may have forgotten something. If this doesn't jog his memory, ask him a more direct question about a specific detail.

If your child is more of a **bottom-up thinker**, she is drawn to the details. Begin by encouraging your child to summarize a movie she has seen or the text she is reading for homework. Your child may tell you at length about all the interesting details she remembers. Your task, in this case, would be to make sure that your child can tie all the loose ends together and construct an overall thematic understanding of what she has read. Here are some suggestions:

♦ Ask your child to tell you the one most important thing about the movie or story—in other words, what the story is all about.

♦ After she reads a story or paragraph, have her brainstorm an appropriate title. If she struggles, give her a few possible choices to select from so that at least one is too broad in scope and one is too narrow. Make sure you discuss the differences between these choices and help your child justify her choice for a title. For example, *Zuckerman's Farm* would be too broad a title for *Charlotte's Web*, while *Wilbur's Problem* might be a bit too narrow.

♦ Collect some pictures from a magazine, old calendar, or picture post-cards and talk about what each picture might be about. Guide your child to notice that some things are positioned more toward the center of the picture and that some things may be larger or more brightly colored than others. Help her recognize that the more salient items, the "main-idea items," stand out in some way. It may be helpful to place the picture within an old picture frame or even a frame cut out of construction paper.

♦ Play categorizing games with your child. You might take a random assortment of objects or pictures and begin grouping them based on some unnamed principle. When you have placed three items in each group, ask your child to guess the principle you were using. Then let your child take a turn making the groups, while you guess. Take turns in this manner, playing with a variety of objects/pictures. As your child improves in her ability to conceptualize themes and to think in a flexible manner, you can limit your selection to one category with subcategories (e.g., produce to be grouped into fruit or vegetables, salad vegetables, vegetables that need cooking, leafy vegetables, root vegetables, herbs, citrus fruits, melons). When an object can fit into more than one category, discuss the options and let your child decide where the object fits, but always ask her to justify her decision. Card games such as solitaire also provide practice with sorting and organizing details.

- When reading to your child, discuss how the title of the book and the cover illustration give us clues about the main idea of the book.

- Pause periodically while reading together to summarize or paraphrase what you have just finished reading. *Summarizing* refers to the quick restatement of the main points covered. *Paraphrasing* is the restatement of what was covered in one's own words to ensure that it was understood correctly.

- While reading together, point out how the name of the main character or words describing the most important event in the story recur more frequently than words about lesser characters or events.

- Many children benefit from learning to predict alternate outcomes to a story. You can usually achieve this by asking, "What if . . . " Many chapter books provide an excellent opportunity to predict upcoming events at the end of each chapter. Encourage your child to come up with many alternatives and to predict which one would most likely occur. As she reads on, she can see how her predictions pan out. By discussing which ideas worked, which ones did not, and why some predictions were more accurate than others, children can learn a great deal about main ideas, thematic development, and prioritization of details.

- Riddles and jokes also encourage flexibility. It is often an excellent experience for children to read the daily comics in the newspaper. Older students may gain a great deal from reading editorial cartoons. As with any other media, it is always important for you to preview these resources on a daily basis before offering them to your children.

Communicating With Teachers

Teamwork between parents and teachers is critical to the success of children in school. One reason teachers give for assigning homework is that this is a way to keep parents involved in their children's school experience. Communication with your child's teacher is crucial when trying to solve problems with reading. More specific guidelines for effective parent-teacher communication are included in Chapter 9. Here are a few to try:

- Make sure that you and your child are clear about the teacher's expectations regarding daily reading. If your child is struggling with reading or is resistant in some way, you could ask the teacher these questions:

  - Can you read to your child as part of the daily independent reading?
  - Can you choose a different book?
  - Can you be flexible about the amount of time your child spends reading?

- It is important that your child's teacher is aware of any problems that arise during homework. If you feel that the assigned book is too complex or that the open-response questions are not clear to your child, his teacher should hear from you. Rubrics are often helpful in clarifying the particulars of an assignment. Ask your child's teacher if she can provide a rubric for the task at hand.

- If you feel that any assignment your child brings home is more complicated than it should be, discuss this with your child's teacher. Homework is supposed to be an opportunity to review and practice content or skills that have already been taught at school. If your child is struggling with homework, she may need additional explanations or to be taught in a different way. This is important information that should be made available to your child's teacher.

- Teacher feedback is an important component of a child's learning. Ask your child's teacher to provide specific feedback to your child about work that is done well in addition to things that need to improve. This will help you and your child target your efforts at home.

Specialized Instruction and Accommodations

As we have seen in this chapter, parents can help their children learn a variety of strategies to improve reading. Nevertheless, some children need more structured and targeted support, which can often be provided in school. If your child struggles with reading despite his best efforts and yours, he may need classroom accommodations and specialized instructions.

Children whose difficulties are at the phonological level and who are struggling with decoding often respond extremely well to structured, systematic phonics instruction. There are several programs that have produced excellent results with children across the age range. These programs share these particular attributes:

- **Multisensory:** The methods and materials engage the child through the use of multiple modalities including:

  - vision (e.g., color coding, enlarged fonts, sound and word cards)

  - hearing (e.g., listening, repeating, rhyming, rhythm, key words)

  - touch (e.g., tracing, sand writing)

  - movement (e.g., sky writing, manipulating sound cards)

- **Systematic:** The scope and sequence of the program proceeds in a systematic way based on strong theoretical principles. For example, a program may begin by introducing consonants since these sounds are acoustically more distinct than vowel sounds and therefore easier to discriminate. Another program may use a mirror to help a child see how her mouth moves to make specific sounds, providing effective feedback to the student.

- **Structured:** The best programs for teaching decoding skills are highly structured so that they support the student and provide highly specific scaffolds to the learning process. Each lesson proceeds in a predictable manner, using scripted dialogues that help provide the student with a strong basis for understanding and applying rules in a systematic manner.

- **Phonics-based:** The most effective reading programs for students who struggle with decoding teach the rules of phonics in an explicit manner. Research has shown that children who struggle with the foundational skills in reading lack knowledge of phonics. Research has also shown that these students are unable to use implicit information and often need to be taught rules and skills directly. Thus, phonics-based programs that make the rules evident and

Parent Guide to Hassle-Free Homework

accessible to students are highly successful. Examples of programs that meet these criteria include:

- Orton Gillingham Method (www.orton-gillingham.com)
- Project Read (www.projectread.com)
- Wilson Reading System (www.wilsonlanguage.com)
- Telian-Cas Learning Concepts, Inc. (www.readingwithtlc.com)

Students who don't read fluently also benefit from structured programs that include a systematic method for tracking progress in addition to strategies for increasing fluency. Often students who read hesitatingly need practice with decoding rules in addition to direct instruction in vocabulary and grammar. Effective programs include:

- Great Leaps Reading (www.greatleaps.com)
- Read Naturally (www.readnaturally.com)

Difficulties with reading comprehension are often remediated using strategy instruction, sometimes in conjunction with language therapy. This instruction may include specific strategies for identifying main ideas and details, drawing inferences, monitoring comprehension, prioritizing details, and integrating information.

Conclusion

Reading is an important skill, learned early and practiced all one's life. It lends richness and texture to one's life and enhances one's prospects in the workforce. As a result, schools place an enormous amount of importance on the development of reading skills. This is the only area in which homework is assigned from the earliest grades. Nowadays pediatricians are even sending infants home from their well-baby checkups with books! Thus, it is truly a lifelong journey to become a competent and refined reader. As with all other essential endeavors, the family plays a very important role in fostering a child's love of reading and supporting the development of the skills required therein.

Let us return to the children we met at the beginning of this chapter. How did they use these strategies to find success?

Ron was evaluated by his school system. The evaluation showed marked difficulties in phonological awareness, and Ron began to receive specialized reading instruction. His parents remained in close communication with his tutor and helped Ron practice his reading strategies at home. They read to him every day and listened to him read the books assigned to him by his reading teacher. As Ron became more confident, his mother practiced strategies for fluency every day with him. She modeled passages, which Ron read independently. Ron and his mother also practiced choral reading where they read aloud together. Bit by bit, as Ron's skills developed, his confidence returned. He is more engaged with school and with reading and is making excellent progress.

Alex began working with his mother on the sight-word list his teacher gave them. He decided to learn ten words a week. Soon they realized this was too big a goal. Alex decided to try six words per week. This worked better. Soon he had a slew of words that he could recognize on sight. He worked with his parents to practice strategies for fluent reading. Alex's teacher taught him how to use phrasing to improve his reading rate and expression. While doing this, Alex realized that he really liked to read dialogue. His mother helped him become involved in a local children's theater. Alex is enjoying reading plays. He is the star of the show, and his confidence has improved tremendously. His gains have begun to spill over at school as well.

> Alex decided to learn ten words a week. Soon they realized this was too big a goal. Alex decided to try six words per week. This worked better.

Julia and her parents sat down with her teacher to find ways to help her. Julia was quite articulate in describing how she struggled with the long, complex novels she had to read. Her teacher listened patiently and came up with a plan. She developed an organizer that Julia could use to outline each chapter as she read. Julia's mother got a copy of each book that was assigned and read it also. In the beginning, Julia and her mother worked together to complete the outline organizer. Soon Julia was able to outline chapters herself. With hard work and her outlining strategy, Julia earned her first "A" for a book report that year! She has also been pausing to ask herself questions as she reads. As Julia becomes an active reader, she enjoys reading more.

Chapter 5

Helping Your Child With Writing Homework

Sarah comes home with a writing assignment. She tries to think of ideas, but nothing comes. She moves to the computer, hoping that it will get her creative juices flowing. But still nothing.

Sarah, a 12-year-old seventh grader, comes home from school with a writing assignment. She sits at her desk, paper and pen at her disposal. She tries and tries to think of ideas, but nothing comes. She moves to the computer, hoping that staring at a screen will get her creative juices flowing. But still nothing.

Ten-year-old Charlie, a fifth grader, is writing a book report. He has many ideas about interesting characters and suspenseful plots but doesn't know how to organize them. He writes down everything he can think of but doesn't know what to do next.

Anna is ecstatic because she has finished writing her social studies essay and can finally go out with her friends. As she completes the last sentence, she puts down her pencil, hands the essay to her dad, and runs out the door. Anna's father scans over her essay and finds numerous spelling and grammatical mistakes, as well as problems with paragraph organization. He shakes his head in frustration as he thinks about Anna's parting comment that the essay is "ready to hand in."

Many children struggle with written language, whether they have trouble generating ideas or editing the final product. Learning to write effectively is a complex process that takes considerable practice. In the same way you have helped your child develop other skills, there are many activities that you can do with your child to help him become a better writer.

Linking Oral and Written Language

Since oral expression is closely connected to written expression, how your child organizes his thoughts and oral language is often reflected in his writing. You can help your child during formal and informal language activities that occur on a daily basis.

◆ When you pick up your younger child from a birthday party, ask him to tell you about the different activities he participated in or the gifts his friend received. Encourage him to provide the appropriate background information and to sequence events correctly.

◆ When your older child comes home from school, ask her to explain what she did in history class that day, encouraging her to sequence events logically and to provide details.

◆ Categorization, an important skill in organizing written expression, can also be practiced. When writing a grocery list, have your younger child separate the items into categories, such as produce, meats, breads, and dairy, to encourage the linking of smaller items with hierarchical categories. You can also encourage older children to make connections among more abstract ideas in the world around them.

◆ Have children of any age describe the books they are reading, asking them questions to help them focus on both major themes and smaller details.

Most of these informal language activities can be accomplished in the car, at the dinner table, or at bedtime. They are all wonderful ways to give your child the opportunity to practice organizing and expressing ideas.

The Writing Process

When students are given writing assignments, they are often told to follow a series of steps that begins with generating thoughts and ideas and ends with polishing the final product:

1. Planning and organizing

♦ Setting goals

♦ Generating ideas/brainstorming

♦ Organizing and elaborating ideas

2. Writing a draft

♦ Developing a thesis statement/topic sentence

♦ Transferring ideas into sentences and paragraphs

3. Revising and editing

♦ Revising for organization, creativity, and thematic continuity

♦ Editing for sentence structure, spelling, and mechanics

Common Writing Assignments

There are several common types of writing assignments often used in the classroom and given as homework (see page 75). It is important to recognize the purpose of each writing assignment to help your child complete it effectively.

Common Areas of Difficulty

Getting Started

Does your child sit at the table with a pen and paper for hours without writing anything? Getting those initial ideas on paper is one of the most difficult stages in the writing process. Prewriting strategies, such as brainstorming and list making, can "turn on the faucet," helping your child generate thoughts and ideas.

Common Writing Assignments

Informational

Informational writing provides clear information about a topic. Examples include:

- analytic or critical essays
- business letters
- book reports
- character descriptions
- lab reports
- process (how-to) instructions
- object descriptions
- research reports
- summaries

Expressive

Expressive writing creates an impression that causes the reader to have the same perception as the writer. This type of writing includes:

- personal narratives
- anecdotes
- autobiographies
- diary or journal entries
- memoirs
- poems
- descriptions of people or places

Persuasive

The persuasive essay requires students to share their opinion as they analyze or explain why something is the way it is and to persuade or influence the reader in some way. Assignments of this type include:

- advertisements
- complaint letters
- editorials
- speeches
- reviews of books, movies, music, etc.

Literary

Literary writing is intended to tell a story and includes:

- fictional narratives
- dialogues or scripts
- poems

(Adapted from *Language Arts Curriculum* developed by Kathy Boyle Caron and Wendy Stacey, ResearchILD, 2001.)

Organizing Ideas

Does your child have many ideas for the assignment but struggles to integrate them coherently? Students are often able to come up with numerous topics or ideas but have difficulty categorizing and prioritizing them. Encouraging organized oral language and using writing tools, such as outlines and graphic organizers, can help your child organize and present ideas in a systematic fashion.

Elaborating Ideas

Is your child able to develop a topic and some supporting details but struggles to expand ideas? Often, students get stuck when trying to elaborate their initial thoughts and ideas. Strategies such as using guiding questions and simple graphic organizers can help your child develop these ideas further.

Revising and Editing

Is your child ready to hand in her written work after writing one draft? Students often have difficulty editing for broader aspects of writing such as organization and thematic continuity, as well as mechanical errors in spelling, grammar, and punctuation. You can help your child to self-monitor using various editing strategies.

How Parents Can Help

Now that we have identified problems commonly experienced by students when working on writing assignments, we will focus on how you can help your child overcome writing difficulties. In order to help your child perform at her best and to prevent confusion and frustration, it is important to understand the type of writing assignment as well as the teacher's expectations:

- Did your child's teacher provide a chart (rubric) with clear expectations of assignment requirements and grading?

- Did the teacher give examples or models in class for your child to refer to?

- Was your child taught a system for completing writing assignments?

- What writing skills is the teacher emphasizing in the assignment?

♦ What are the teacher's expectations regarding length, format, and due dates?

Helping Your Child Get Started

Getting started can be the most difficult part of the writing process. Find out from your child's teacher the kinds of structures and strategies presented in the classroom to help students generate and organize their ideas before writing. In many classrooms, students are taught to think about the goal or purpose of the writing assignment as a first step. Then, they are often encouraged to brainstorm ideas and organize them into an outline or graphic organizer (chart/diagram). It is important for you to understand the writing process that your child has been taught to use at school so that you can better reinforce this at home.

Goal Setting

For younger children, setting goals for writing is much like getting ready for "show and tell." Just as your child would prepare a discussion of her favorite item to share at school, she can make a plan for structuring her writing. She might ask the same types of question: *What do I want to tell my audience? What is the best way to tell them? Do I have the right information?*

Older children can ask themselves similar questions at a higher level: *How do I best express the information to my audience? What format should I use? Do I have sufficient facts to support my thesis?*

At home, you can help your child by reminding him to think about the following questions before beginning to write:

♦ What is the general purpose of the writing assignment?
- to inform
- to entertain
- to persuade
- to compare/contrast
- to retell
- to present possibilities
- to answer

♦ What is the general structure of the essay?
- story format/genre
- main ideas/details
- comparison/contrast

- Where can you find sources of information?
  - personal experience
  - background knowledge
  - interviews
  - class lectures/discussions
  - textbooks
  - additional research

Brainstorming

The brainstorming process gives your child the opportunity to generate thoughts and ideas freely without having to integrate them into a coherent whole. Brainstorming can be adapted to accommodate your child's individual learning style.

- If your child is a top-down thinker, he may first identify major themes and main ideas and then develop relevant supporting details for each theme.

- If your child is a bottom-up thinker, he could first brainstorm details and later organize and prioritize them.

Making Lists

Making a simple list of ideas is often a great way to get started. Ideas can be written on paper or on a chalkboard or white board. For children who have motor difficulties, listing ideas may be a difficult task. You can make it easier by acting as a scribe, writing the ideas as your child dictates. This will eliminate the physical aspect of writing for him and let his ideas flow freely. If your child has difficulty retrieving his ideas, he may need prompts to facilitate the flow of ideas. Depending on the type of writing assignment, you can ask him specific questions:

For a fictional story:

- *What do you want to be the main idea of your story?*

- *What types of characters do you want in your story?*

- *What happened first/next/last?*

- *Who? What? When? Where? Why?*

For a research paper:

♦ *What are you most interested in learning about?*

♦ *What do you want to learn about your topic?*

♦ *Will you be able to find enough information?*

For a personal narrative:

♦ *Was there ever a time when you…?*

♦ *Remember when you…?*

♦ *Would you like to write about…?*

If your child is having difficulty finding a topic or coming up with ideas, it may be helpful to make specific suggestions and have him choose:

♦ *Was there ever a time when you felt proud of yourself? Maybe at your last piano recital or soccer game?*

♦ *I know that you enjoy horseback riding and that you are also interested in race cars. Is there anything more you would like to learn about either of those topics?*

Taking away the common difficulty or anxiety of getting started with a writing assignment can make a world of difference. Once your child's ideas are out, the remaining steps in the process seem much easier!

Helping Your Child Organize and Elaborate Ideas

Once your child has completed the prewriting step and has generated numerous ideas, it is time to organize the ideas in a way that will help him write a paragraph or essay. Again, before suggesting a particular method to your child, ask his teacher to share any specific strategies or methods that she has presented in class. Some of the most commonly taught organizational strategies are discussed in the next few pages. Depending on your child's learning style and particular strengths and weaknesses, he may prefer one strategy over another. Support his choice wholeheartedly unless you (or the teacher) do not think it is effective. In that case, the teacher or a tutor may need to work with your child to discover which strategy might work better for him.

Semantic Mapping

If your child has strong visual-spatial skills, semantic mapping may help him visually organize ideas (Figure 9). He can use the brainstorming list to group concepts together on a map and elaborate them by categorizing each item further.

Figure 9: Map created by a third grader using Inspiration software

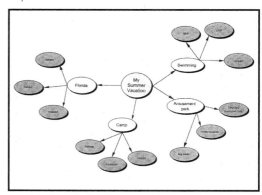

Outlining

If your child is stronger verbally, she may benefit from using an outline to group her ideas from the brainstorming list in a linear fashion (Figure 10).

Guiding Questions

If your child is having difficulty elaborating main ideas, he might benefit from your asking questions to guide him along the way. For example, if your child is writing a book review, you might ask:

- *Why did the main character do what he did?*

- *Where did this occur?*

- *What happened next?*

- *Who else was involved in the plot?*

- *When did this happen?*

- *How was the problem resolved?*

Figure 10: Outline

My Summer Vacation

I. Florida
  A. swam
  B. fished
  C. boated

II. Camp
  A. fishing
  B. baseball
  C. nature

III. Swimming
  A. ocean
  B. pool
  C. lake

IV. Amusement park
  A. big slide
  B. roller coaster
  C. haunted mansion ride

Simple Graphic Organizers

Graphic organizers can help your child organize ideas in a way that is fun and interesting.

Figure 11: Star Strategy

Meltzer et al., 2005

♦ The *Star Strategy* is a prewriting organizer in which your child can elaborate on main ideas by asking *who, what, when, where, why,* and *how* questions. She can then number each aspect in the order they are to be presented in a paragraph.

♦ The *Sandwich Strategy* aids your child in organizing ideas into paragraph form. The bread slices of the sandwich represent the topic sentence and the conclusion, while the meat and fixings hold the supporting details.

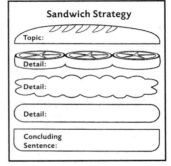

Figure 12: Sandwich Strategy

Houghton-Mifflin, 2001

Paragraph Structure

One helpful acronym for remembering the key components of writing an essay or paragraph is BOTEC (ResearchILD and FableVision, 2005):

B = Brainstorming

O = Organizing

T = Topic sentence

E = Evidence

C = Conclusion

Think 3!

"3" is the magic number when it comes to organizing and elaborating ideas:

- Each essay should contain **three** components:

  1. Topic sentence/thesis statement
  2. Main ideas with relevant supporting details
  3. Conclusion statement

- Each main idea should be supported by at least **three** relevant details.

Helping Your Child Revise and Edit

After your child has used organization and elaboration strategies to integrate his ideas into a paragraph format, it is time to revise and edit. Often, students have spent so much time and energy planning, organizing, and writing that they are reluctant to revise or look over their work once a draft is complete.

This is also the stage that parents find most difficult. Often, parents are drawn into the fray when their child's writing does not seem to match their expectations or their notion of the teacher's expectations.

The following strategies may help your child remember what to look for while revising and editing:

Read Aloud and Tell Back

- When your child has completed a draft, have her read it out loud to you, whether it is a short paragraph or a research paper. Oral reading may help her identify mistakes she may have missed while writing.

- After your child has read to you, summarize the content and tell it back to her. This strategy determines if the reader's interpretation matches the writer's intended message.

- Another version of this strategy is for you to read your child's draft out loud while she follows along with her own copy. If she notices anything that needs to be added or changed, she can mark her copy as you read. Many times, hearing adult intonation and phrasing helps children notice if something "sounds funny," identify run-on sentences or fragments, or become aware of where they have left out punctuation.

Editing Checklists

Editing checklists can be used at all levels. Again, check with your child's teacher to find out if any editing strategies have been taught in the classroom.

Parent Guide to Hassle-Free Homework

If so, your job is to remind your child to use the strategies that have been taught. If not, then you may want to suggest that your child try one of our favorite checklists below:

- In the primary grades, STOPS (Meltzer, et al., 2006) can be used to focus young writers:

  S = Sentence structure (*Check for fragments and run-ons.*)

  T = Tenses (*Make sure that tenses are consistent throughout.*)

  O = Order (*Make sure sentences follow each other logically.*)

  P = Periods (*Check that all sentences end with punctuation.*)

  S = Spelling (*Check for correct spelling.*)

- The above checklist can be modified to SPORTS for the middle grades (Meltzer, et al., 2006):

  S = Sentence structure (*Check for fragments and run-ons. Combine sentences or ask question words to make them longer and more interesting.*)

  P = Punctuation (*Check that all sentences end with punctuation and that quotations are used appropriately.*)

  O = Organization/order (*Make sure sentences and paragraphs follow each other logically.*)

  R = Repeated words (*Check for overused vocabulary and vary word choice.*)

  T = Tenses (*Make sure that tenses are consistent throughout.*)

  S = Spelling (*Check for correct spelling, especially homophones that the computer spell checker does not catch.*)

- Personal checklists are valuable tools that make the editing process meaningful. If your child consistently makes the same types of errors, type out a list.

Self-Monitoring

When helping your child revise and edit her writing, it is important that she becomes aware of common errors that frequently occur. These strategies will teach your child to monitor her writing and develop an awareness of common writing errors.

> **Sam's Hit List**
> 1. Capitalization (proper nouns)
> 2. Repeated words
> 3. Run-on sentences
> 4. Spelling of homophones (there/their/they're, to/too/two)

♦ Have your child go over her work with a colored pencil and circle words she thinks may be misspelled, as well as possible punctuation errors and other suspected mistakes.

♦ When you look over your child's writing, instead of making corrections, count up the number of errors and write the number at the top of the page. Then, have your child find and correct the errors.

♦ If your child frequently makes one type of error when writing (e.g., capitalization), make your child aware of this and have her look for these errors first.

Persistence and Motivation

For many students, the writing process can be very difficult. They may get stuck or give up easily, making it a challenge to complete a writing assignment. The PAUSE Strategy (ResearchILD, 2002) may help your child keep going:

P = Put down your pencil/pen (*take a deep breath and look away for a moment*)

A = Ask yourself questions (*purpose of assignment, who, what, when, where, why, how*)

U = Use strategies (*brainstorming, listing, etc.*)

S = Seek help (*from teacher, friends, parents*)

E = Explore all possibilities and ideas (*write down everything you can think of*)

No matter how much your child struggles, keep in mind that your role as a parent is not to do his writing. Your job is to guide, support, and encourage your child as much as possible. You may or may not be satisfied with the result. If you are frequently concerned about your child's writing, then you will need to communicate with his teacher.

Communicating With Teachers

As a parent, it is important for you to provide consistency between home and school. In order to help your child with written language, communication with teachers is crucial, whether it is through e-mail, written notes, or phone calls. (See Chapter 9 for more details about effective parent-teacher communication.)

- You and your child need to know the purpose of the assignment, the structure of the essay, the sources of information required, the types of writing skills emphasized, and the timeline for the assignment. If any of these expectations are unclear, communicate with your child's teacher to resolve these issues.

- Make sure your child's teacher is aware of problems that arise during homework writing assignments, as well as how much time your child spends on the assignments. If your child is having difficulty or spending too much time, the teacher may be able to modify selected writing assignments for him.

- Ask your child's teacher to provide feedback regarding your child's strengths and weaknesses in written language as observed in the classroom. You can help your child with her areas of weakness by providing strategies and practice.

- If your child is unsure of the teacher's expectations, ask for a rubric (see Figure 14, page 86) or set of criteria that is used to assess writing. This will clarify which aspects of writing are important for your child to include in each writing assignment.

	5	4	3	2	1
Structure	Five paragraphs. Each body paragraph has a clear topic sentence that relates to the thesis.	Five paragraphs. Each body paragraph has a clear topic sentence but one does not relate to thesis.	Five paragraphs. One topic sentence missing or extremely unclear.	Has too many paragraphs. More than one topic sentence missing or unidentifiable.	Has too few paragraphs. No evidence of topic sentences.
Thesis	Thesis is last sentence of first paragraph and has subject, details, and purpose. Is restated in first sentence of conclusion.	Thesis is last sentence of first paragraph and has subject and details. Is restated in first sentence of conclusion.	Thesis has subject and details but is incorrectly placed in first or last paragraph.	Thesis is unclear and/or confusing, but is in both first and last paragraphs.	Unidentifiable thesis in first or last paragraph.
Mechanics	100% accurate. Clearly proofread and edited. Essay has good flow.	1–2 minor errors that do not disrupt the flow.	Several errors that prevent flow. Careless spelling and typos.	Many errors that distract the reader. Grammar/spelling need attention.	Major errors prevent the reader from understanding the topic.
Content	Essay is thorough, detailed, and 100% accurate. Four facts support each topic sentence.	Essay is fairly thorough, detailed, and generally accurate. Four facts support topic sentence.	Essay is generally accurate but has fewer than four facts to support some topic sentences.	Essay has several historical inaccuracies and/or fewer than three facts.	Essay has major historical inaccuracies. Facts are incorrect or missing, or fewer than two.
Writing Process	Final draft is accompanied by all process pieces. Student used class time exceptionally well.	One process piece missing. Student used class time very well.	Two process pieces missing. Student used class time fairly well.	Three process pieces missing. Student used class time poorly.	More than three process pieces missing. Student wasted class time and/or distracted others.
Format	Essay is correctly formatted.	One aspect of formatting is incorrect.	Two aspects of formatting are incorrect.	Three aspects of formatting are incorrect.	More than three pieces of formatting are incorrect.

Figure 14: Sample Rubric

Parent Guide to Hassle-Free Homework

Specialized Instruction and Accommodations

Even with strategy instruction and practice, some students still have difficulty with sentence structure, paragraph organization, elaboration of ideas, and other aspects of writing. If your child is struggling with the writing process, she may need specialized instruction or classroom accommodations.

Many children need explicit instruction regarding the structure of written language before they can become writers themselves. Specialized instruction in writing often provides students with a system for composing sentences, developing ideas, and organizing paragraphs. This type of instruction may occur at various levels and include the following:

At the sentence level:

♦ Explicit rules regarding sentence types and how parts of speech are used to compose sentences

♦ Concrete ways to expand and elaborate on sentences to make them more complex and expressive

♦ Ways to compose topic sentences and provide evidence to support them

♦ How to write conclusion sentences that sum up what was written

At the paragraph level:

♦ Ways to integrate ideas into a paragraph following a logical sequence

♦ How to use specific transition words and phrases to make ideas flow smoothly

At the overall organization level:

♦ Strategies for self-monitoring to ensure that all ideas follow a central theme without repetition

♦ Editing checklists for grammar, sentence structure, tenses, spelling, punctuation, thematic development, and other common errors

Your child may need specialized instruction if she:

♦ does not understand the different parts of speech and their functions.

♦ does not understand rules and requirements for composing sentences.

♦ is unable to put ideas into written form.

♦ has trouble providing evidence to support main ideas.

♦ is unable to elaborate on ideas or form complex sentences.

♦ has difficulty sequencing ideas in a logical format.

♦ is unable to identify errors in grammar, sentence structure, spelling, punctuation, and organization.

In all of these areas, explicit instruction in grammatical rules and writing strategies may help your child obtain the skills and understanding that are needed to improve writing.

If your child has difficulties with visual-motor integration or fine-motor execution, he may need accommodations to bypass the physical aspects of the writing process:

♦ Using a word processor (desktop computer, laptop, or Alphasmart®)— both at home and in school—for brainstorming, outlining, and writing paragraphs and essays often helps students express their ideas without becoming fatigued by the physical demands of writing.

♦ Your child can practice typing at home by using typing software designed for children or by writing e-mail to friends or relatives. Creative or journal writing using a word processor may also enhance typing skills.

Helping Your Child Become a Better Writer

♦ Since you know your child best, it is important to use parent intuition to help your child. Informal language activities that encourage your child to expand and organize language can play an important role in supporting written language.

Parent Guide to Hassle-Free Homework

- Encourage your child to use prewriting, organization, and editing strategies every time he works on a writing assignment. As he uses these strategies more and more, they will become internalized and used spontaneously, decreasing the need for your help and monitoring.

- If your child has learning difficulties, she will need much review, practice, and repetition to be able to use strategies independently and effectively. By recognizing your child's strengths and weaknesses and providing her with positive feedback, you can help her develop confidence as a writer.

Now, let's return to the children we introduced at the beginning of the chapter. How would these strategies help them?

> Sarah begins to ask herself questions to get started: *What is the purpose of this assignment? What do I want to tell my reader?* She makes a list, jotting down any ideas she can think of on a sheet of paper. She asks herself *who, what, when, where,* and *why* questions to further expand on her ideas. Now that she has a starting point, she is ready to write.

> Charlie looks at his jumbled list of ideas and highlights the ideas he thinks would fit best in his book review. He then numbers the ideas in the order they should be presented. He remembers a graphic organizer that his teacher had given him during class and transfers his brainstormed ideas to the graphic organizer. This helps him visualize the structure of his report. He is now able to transfer his ideas into paragraph form.

> When Anna comes home from her friend's house, her father informs her that she still has some work to do on her essay. He counts up her errors and puts a number in the corner of the page. "Okay," he says, "find your mistakes." Anna goes through her essay, finding many errors in spelling, grammar, and punctuation. Anna and her father begin to keep track of the types of errors she tends to make. Anna starts editing her writing and is eventually able to identify many of her mistakes independently.

Chapter 6

Helping Your Child With Math Homework

Fourth-grader Robert comes home from school and sits down to do his math homework. He explains to his mom what he learned in school that day and quickly completes his homework problems. When he is finished, however, his mother finds multiple errors.

. . . .

> Jenna opens her math textbook to begin her assignment. She looks at the page, dumbfounded, unable to recognize a single thing.

Jenna, a sixth-grade student, opens her math textbook to begin her assignment. She looks at the page, dumbfounded, unable to recognize a single thing. She looks over at her dad and says, "We didn't learn this yet."

. . . .

Carrie, a third grader, is working on word problems. She reads a problem out loud to her mother and says, "Okay, I need to add . . . no, subtract . . . no, multiply, yeah multiply . . . no divide . . . What does *product* mean? Why do they use all these confusing words?"

Mathematics is a challenge for many students, as they are required to understand language and concepts that are abstract and often do not relate directly to real life. Math concepts can present an even larger problem for students with learning and attentional difficulties. Students who struggle to understand and organize language, who have difficulty paying attention to details, or who lack number sense often have trouble understanding math and completing their homework assignments. You can support your child by rewarding his use of strategies to help him become a more effective math learner. Math is everywhere, and it is important to show your child concrete examples in everyday life. In addition to formal strategies for schoolwork, there are many activities you can do with your child to enhance the development of math skills and knowledge of math concepts.

Common Areas of Difficulty

Automaticity
Does your child struggle to retrieve simple addition, subtraction, multiplication, and division facts, causing him to take much longer than expected on math homework assignments? Strategies for remembering and practicing these math facts can help your child's computation skills become more automatic, making it easier and less time-consuming to complete math assignments.

Calculation
Does your child make errors in simple calculations even though she understands the math concept and knows how to solve the problem? Strategies for organization can help your child develop a structured method of completing math calculations that will reduce errors. Checking strategies can also reduce the number of inaccuracies due to careless errors.

Understanding Math Language
Does your child get stuck on the language of mathematics even before he can consider a method for problem solving? Your child would benefit from strategies that emphasize math vocabulary and key words to help him solve math problems more effectively.

Concepts
Does your child have trouble understanding quantitative concepts but "gets by" because of a good memory? Your child would benefit from systematic, multisensory instruction that teaches math concepts in a multimodal fashion.

How Parents Can Help

Now that we have identified common problems experienced by students when working on math assignments, how can you help your child overcome her difficulties?

Understanding New Math Programs and Expectations

As a parent, you are not expected to teach your child math concepts. But it may be helpful to understand both how your child's math curriculum is structured and the expectations of your child's teacher.

♦ Many new math curricula and standardized math tests are language-based, requiring students to provide written explanations for math problems in addition to computation. Become familiar with your child's textbooks and other materials used in school so that you understand school expectations when your child asks for assistance.

♦ Have your child explain to you how he was taught to solve a particular problem in school so that you can provide assistance that is consistent with his teacher and curriculum framework. If your child is confused or does not understand how to solve a problem, you may want to communicate his difficulty to the teacher to ensure mutual understanding.

♦ Make sure your child's teacher provides direct, explicit instruction as well as opportunities for "discovery." Your child may need spiral teaching that provides repetition and review of concepts and procedures.

Using Everyday Activities to Enhance Math Skills

It is important and helpful for your child to become aware of the math that surrounds him in everyday life. Discovering math in informal situations may help enforce math concepts learned at school and also help your child make connections between real life and schoolwork.

♦ For younger children, building with blocks or Legos® may introduce them to various types of shapes, angles, and other concepts of geometry that will be learned later in school. Encourage your child to measure his creations and talk about math (e.g., size and shape) while building to further enhance awareness of math concepts.

♦ Putting together puzzles is an excellent way for children to develop awareness of part-whole relationships and visual-spatial reasoning.

- Sorting and organizing are important skills in mathematics, and these can be enhanced by having your child sort anything from laundry (by type or color) to candy to toys! Have your child come up with categories to label each group (e.g., black socks, hard candy, blue cars).

- For older children, money concepts can be reinforced through the distribution of allowance. Have your child figure out how much she will earn in four weeks, five months, or even two years!

- There are plenty of opportunities for math in supermarkets, department stores, or even catalogs. Have your child estimate the total bill from looking at price tags, or ask him to determine how much you have saved with coupons or sales. Shopping can reinforce concepts of money, fractions, and percents, as well as automaticity of mental math.

- Cooking presents a great way to develop and reinforce skills in fractions. Using measuring cups and spoons as well as doubling or halving recipes will help your child understand fractions in concrete terms. Recipes provide good practice for following multiple steps in a math problem. Continue to use fractions when slicing a cake, pie, or pizza!

- Reinforce math skills such as estimation, time, and visual-spatial awareness while traveling. Have your child look at a map to determine the number of miles to the next destination. Ask her to figure out how much time it will take to get there depending on how fast the car is traveling.

- Link math to sports, music, economics, and anything else that is meaningful to your child!

Depending on your child's interests, math concepts can be used in a variety of everyday situations. Help your child discover daily opportunities for using math. The more math your child encounters in the real world, the better she will be able to apply math skills in school.

Helping Your Child Practice Math Facts

Although rote math facts should be taught and reinforced in school, some children need extra time and practice to develop the automaticity needed to solve higher-level math problems in an efficient manner.

General Strategies

♦ Help your child come up with meaningful raps or rhymes, like the one below, to help him remember math facts with which he is having difficulty.

> 4 x 6
> I'm hatching baby chicks,
> If I keep them off the floor,
> I'll have eggs-actly 24.
>
> (Adapted from Schroeder & Washington, 1989)

Practice these rhymes on a daily basis at a certain time of the day (e.g., before bed or after dinner) so that it becomes part of your child's daily routine. The more your child practices, the quicker the math facts will become automatic. Math rap CDs can also be purchased at record stores.

♦ Help your child make flash cards of the particular math facts that are most difficult for her to remember. Have your child come up with a drawing or a mnemonic strategy that will help her remember.

Specific Strategies

♦ For younger children, the **Terrific 10s Strategy** can be used to help them recognize patterns in addition math facts:

1	2	3	4	5	6	7	8	9
+ 9	+ 8	+ 7	+ 6	+ 5	+ 4	+ 3	+ 2	+ 1
10	10	10	10	10	10	10	10	10

By studying the Terrific 10s, your child will realize that as the numbers on top increase, the numbers below decrease. They can then visualize the number pairs. The Terrific 10s strategy can also be enforced using playing cards. Children have to learn only the first five numbers because the last five are the same, except the order of the numbers is reversed.

- The **9s Fingers Strategy** can be used to help your child remember the 9 times table, up to 9 x 10. Have your child put his hands flat on a table. If the problem is 9 x 6, have your child start counting from the left-hand pinky finger and fold down his sixth finger. The remaining fingers on either side of the missing finger (five fingers on the left hand and four on the right) show the answer—54! Count by 10s on the fingers to the left of the folded finger, and count by 1s on the fingers to the right of the folded finger.

   Example: 9s Finger Strategy

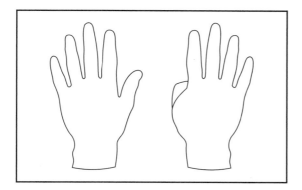

- **Card or dice games** can make the memorization and reinforcement of math facts more fun. Have your child pick two cards from the deck and either add or multiply them as quickly as he can. Add a timer and see how many math facts your child can solve in one minute. Keep track of this number, and each time you and your child play the game he can try to beat the number from the last time. The card game "War" can also be adapted for a math drill. When each player flips over a card, have your child add or multiply the two numbers. Similar games can be played using dice. Use four dice for more advanced students and have your child first add together sets of two and then multiply the sums!

- **Computer software** is a fun, interactive medium for reinforcing math facts and concepts, especially for children who enjoy video or computer games. Check out *Number Maze Challenge* (Great Wave Software) and *Carmen Sandiego Math Detective* (Broderbund Software).

Strategies for Problem Solving

It is important for you to know the types of strategies taught to your child in school so that you can help reinforce them during homework. In many classrooms, children are taught a list of steps to help them solve complex, multistep problems. Also, children are often taught visual strategies that aid in organizing information. If your child is not taught explicit or effective strategies at school, the following may be helpful during homework times:

♦ Keep a list of **problem-solving strategies** handy when your child is working on math assignments. This way, if your child gets stuck, she can refer to the list to jog her memory for effective strategies to use along the way. The following list shows the current strategies presented in many elementary and middle school math curricula:

- Look for a pattern.
- Work backwards.
- Use logical reasoning.
- Make it simpler.
- Brainstorm.

- Act out or use objects.
- Make a picture or diagram.
- Use or make a table.
- Make an organized list.
- Guess and check.

(Goodnow, 1989)

♦ **RAPS** is a strategy that may help your child follow the steps of a word problem:

R = Read and rephrase (*Read the problem and put into your own words.*)

A = Art (*Draw a picture.*)

P = Plan and predict (*Make a plan for solving the problem and estimate the answer.*)

S = Solve (*Solve the problem.*)

♦ **Highlighting and color-coding** can also be used to find the main idea in math word problems. After your child reads a problem, have him ask himself, "What is the problem asking for?" Tell your child to highlight

Parent Guide to Hassle-Free Homework

the important parts of the problem, such as the question, the numbers, and any important vocabulary words. Numbering the steps in a problem may also help your child organize and prioritize information.

Example:
Three boxes of pencils cost **$2.50**. Four packages of paper cost **$5.75**. Two boxes of markers cost $4.95. John bought **(1)** 12 boxes of pencils and **(2)** 12 packages of paper. **(3)** How much change would he get back from $50?

These simple strategies may prevent your child from becoming overwhelmed and from focusing on irrelevant information.

◆ The **"Same but Simple" Strategy** helps your child identify the problem and figure out how to solve it. Replace complex or large numbers in a word problem with smaller, less-complicated numbers. Once your child figures out how to solve the problem, the original numbers can be replaced.

Example:
Steven has 10 $\frac{1}{2}$ pounds of candy that he needs to separate into $\frac{1}{4}$-pound bags. How many bags will he need?

Since fractions are difficult to work with, we can change the numbers to make it easier.

Steven has 30 pounds of candy that he needs to separate into 5-pound bags. How many bags will he need?

Looking at the easier numbers, we know that we have to divide. Going back to the original problem: 10 $\frac{1}{2}$ divided by $\frac{1}{4}$ equals 42 bags.

Some children, especially those with learning or attentional difficulties, need to be taught how to organize information in a word problem. Your child's teacher may have taught her to use specific **graphic organizers** to help organize certain information presented in math problems. If your child still has difficulty, here are some basic strategies to help her organize information visually:

Lists and Tables: Help your child translate information in word problems into organized lists or tables. This may keep your child from getting lost in the complex language of the problem and will help her identify the most important information.

Example:
Three boxes of pencils cost $2.50. Four packages of paper cost $5.75. Two boxes of markers cost $4.95. John bought 12 boxes of pencils and 12 packages of paper. How much change would he get back from $50?

Pencils: $2.50 for 3 boxes
Paper: $5.75 for 4 packages
Markers: $4.95 for 2 boxes

12 boxes of pencils

$$\frac{12}{3} = 4$$

4 x $2.50 = $10.00

$10.00	$50.00
+ 17.25	− 27.25
$27.25	**$22.75**

12 packages of paper

$$\frac{12}{4} = 3$$

3 x $5.75 = $17.25

Personalized Graphic Organizers or Drawings: To make the process more meaningful for your child, you may want to help your child develop her own personal graphic organizer for use with multiple problems.

What do I know?	What do I need to find out?	What operations do I need to use?
Picture/table/calculations:		
Answer:		

- Many children are confused by **math language and vocabulary**, making it difficult for them to understand math problems. It may be helpful to keep a list of important math vocabulary words with their definitions handy for reference during homework. You can help your child spot these words and highlight them before beginning the problem to help him understand what is being asked.

Addition	Subtraction	Multiplication	Division
All together	Difference	Each has	Share
Total	Less than	Each group	Did each one get
In all	Lost	All together	Total is given
Sum	Gave away	What is the area?	Fraction
Got more	Left	Product	Quotient
	How many more . . . than		

Studying for Math Tests

Math tests often cause anxiety among children, especially those with learning difficulties. There are several things you can do to help your child prepare for these tests:

Drill and Practice

- Ask your child math vocabulary and math rules he needs to know for the test.

- Drill math facts, including strategies that have been most effective for your child in remembering them.

- Give your child practice problems or make up a sample test.

- Use your child's textbook or homework problems and change the numbers to give her more practice.

- Ask the teacher to provide a study guide with math problems set up in the same format as the test.

- Refer to Web-based math helping tools, such as www.loisterms.com and the National Library of Virtual Manipulatives (nlvm.usu.edu/en/nav/vlibrary.html).

Organize the Information

As your child's math curriculum becomes more and more complex, it may become difficult for her to organize the material and study effectively.

One common problem with taking math tests is that even when students understand the material in class and are able to solve homework problems on specific subtopics, they may have difficulty differentiating problem types and appropriate procedures on a test where different kinds of problems are presented on the same page in a random order. When your child is studying for a test, you can help him identify the various kinds of problems and learn how to recognize them. For example, if your child is being tested on operations with fractions, take each problem type and write it on an index card with an example of how to recognize it.

Adding and subtracting fractions with the same denominator

Example: $\dfrac{7}{8} - \dfrac{2}{8} = \dfrac{5}{8}$ Add or subtract numerators
Leave denominators the same

How to recognize it: The bottom numbers in both fractions will be the same.

Give your child a practice test with different problem types mixed together. Have her identify what type of problem each one is before solving.

Three-column notes come in handy for organizing math vocabulary, terminology, and rules. Here's an example:

Parent Guide to Hassle-Free Homework

Term	Definition/Rule	Picture
Vertical angles	Are always congruent	

Checking Strategies

As part of the study session, you can help your child become aware of frequent errors and encourage him to check his work when he is finished with a test.

♦ Keep your child's completed math tests together. Look at the tests and praise your child for all of the items she completed accurately. With your child, do an error analysis to determine frequent error types. Then, together, make a list of his "Top 3" errors and discuss how to fix them.

♦ Have your child internalize his "Top 3 Hit List" and recite it to you before a test. When your child is completing a practice test, have him write the "top 3" errors at the top of the page to remind him to check for them when the test is completed. This strategy can then be transferred to the classroom test situation.

♦ Help your child come up with a checklist to follow after he has completed a problem. Your child can personalize the checklist to include particular errors he frequently makes or steps he often skips. The following is an example of a math checklist:

  • Did I write the numbers correctly?

  • Did I line up the numbers correctly?

  • Did I use the correct signs?

  • Did I use the correct operation?

  • Did I label my answer correctly?

- Is my answer close to the estimate?

- Is my answer reasonable? Does it make sense? (This is the most important checklist question. If there is not much time for checking, make sure your child at least asks himself this question.)

Have your child add his most common errors to the checklist to make it his own.

♦ The **POUNCE Strategy** is another example of a math checklist your child could use after completing a math assignment.

P = Pens (*Change pen color for checking.*)

O = Operation (*Did I use the right operation?*)

U = Underline (*Underline the question asked. Did I answer it exactly?*)

N = Numbers and signs (*Did I select the right numbers?*)

C = Calculate (*Did I calculate correctly?*)

E = Estimation (*Does my answer agree with my estimate?*)

The idea is for your child to pretend they see a cat "pouncing" on their homework and finding common errors.

Communicating With Teachers

♦ It is important to keep the lines of communication open between home and school. You should not have to teach your child new math concepts—your job is to help your child organize and reinforce material that was already taught. If you feel that your child has not been taught material he is required to do for homework, discuss this with his teacher to determine the problem.

♦ Make sure that the strategies you use with your child are reinforcing what she has learned in school. Your child may become confused if you teach her an approach to a problem that is not consistent with what she has learned. Your child's teacher may be able to offer suggestions or strategies he uses in the classroom that can also be used at home during homework. If you and your child come up with an effective strategy at home, encourage her to discuss this with the teacher so she can use it in the classroom as well.

♦ If you find your child is spending too much time on homework, then you should discuss this problem with the teacher. Perhaps the teacher could modify your child's assignments, reducing the number of problems if necessary.

Specialized Instruction and Accommodations

No matter how much instruction and practice they get in school and for homework, some students still have difficulty with automaticity, grasping math concepts, or computation. If your child is struggling despite his teacher's or your efforts, he may need specialized instruction or classroom accommodations.

Specialized instruction in math often provides children with a systematic, multisensory approach to understanding math principles and solving problems when they are unable to grasp abstract concepts, memorize math facts, and manipulate information efficiently in their minds. Your child may need specialized instruction if she:

♦ does not seem to have a number sense.

♦ does not understand the concepts of the basic operations of addition, subtraction, multiplication, and division.

♦ cannot identify the main idea or what is being asked in word problems.

♦ has not memorized math facts.

♦ does not link math procedures to math concepts or ideas.

Your child may be eligible for classroom accommodations depending on the type and extent of his difficulties.

♦ If your child struggles with *dysgraphia* (difficulty with the fine-motor aspect of writing), you may advocate for shorter lists of compulsory pencil-and-paper problems for homework to reduce your child's work time and frustration.

- If your child grasps math concepts but has difficulty carrying out calculations due to problems with organization or automatic memory, he may be able to use a calculator to bypass the lower-level skills and move ahead to solve higher-level problems.

- If your child has difficulty remembering what she has learned at school, she may need a homework jumpstart. Your child's teacher can help her begin the homework assignment in school so she understands the requirements. When your child comes home, she will spend less time trying to remember what she needs to do and will be able to complete the assignment more efficiently.

- If your child has difficulty aligning numbers on a page, he may need to use graph paper to help organize math problems visually.

- If your child has problems in the area of language, she may need consistent previewing and reviewing of math vocabulary.

Conclusion

Your most important objective as a parent is to reinforce what your child has learned at school. If you are taking on the job of tutor or strategy coach, discuss your involvement with your child's teacher to ensure that you are teaching your child in a manner that best matches his educational needs and learning style.

Here again are the children we introduced at the beginning of the chapter. Let's see how math strategies worked for them:

> Robert's mother realized that many of his errors occurred because his math facts are not yet automatic. In addition, the problems were written in very tiny print, and Robert often misaligned the columns while solving them. His mother had him redo his calculations on graph paper, where the boxes created a spatial structure for the problems. She began practicing math facts with him on a daily basis, using games and activities to make it more fun for him. Eventually, Robert's calculation abilities improved.

Jenna's parents realized that this is not the first time she has come home without knowing how to do her math assignment. Either her teacher expects Jenna to learn it herself, or Jenna is having trouble remembering what she has learned in class. They decided to call the teacher and set up a parent conference to clarify these issues.

· ·

Carrie remembered that her teacher had given her a chart with key math words on it. She sees that the word *product* is associated with multiplication and knows how to proceed with solving the problem.

Jenna's parents realized that this is not the first time she has come home without knowing how to do her math assignment. They decided to call the teacher and set up a parent conference to clarify these issues.

Chapter 7

Helping Your Child Prepare for Tests

As your child progresses through school, she will be challenged to "show what she knows" on tests. Some children take tests in stride and can demonstrate their knowledge and understanding with ease. However, taking tests is an overwhelming challenge for many students, particularly those with learning, attentional, or emotional difficulties. These students might not know what or how to study, or might have difficulty remembering information even when they've studied well. They may have trouble expressing what they know (especially on an essay test), may make careless errors and not check their work, or may just plain panic! Unfortunately, in some classrooms students are evaluated primarily on their test grades. So those students who have difficulty taking tests can easily spiral downward into a negative cycle where their poor test performance discourages them from putting in effort and learning more effective study strategies.

Assisting an older child with homework or studying may require patience and tact. If your child is already receiving some kind of academic support, he may be open to receiving help. More often than not, however, older students are expected by teachers (and parents) to work independently and to have an adequate grasp of what is going on in class. So if and when they begin to have trouble keeping up with work and studying for tests and succeeding on them, they may find it difficult to let their parents "in" to help them.

Many bright and capable students with subtle weaknesses in organization, planning, time management, and written expression begin to experience such difficulties in middle school with no apparent warning. These students lose confidence in themselves and are not quite sure how to handle these new and unexpected challenges. Some parents have also begun to distance themselves from their children's homework and studying, assuming that they are now older and more capable of working independently. They, too, are taken by surprise and are unsure how to help their children.

To further complicate matters, middle and high schools do not often include instruction on the organizational aspects of independent studying. While they may do an excellent job of teaching content, they may not actually teach students how to take notes, how to plan and complete long-term projects, how to study for different types of tests (e.g., multiple choice, short-answer, or essay), or how to organize and memorize abstract information (e.g., dates in history or valences of elements in chemistry).

How Parents Can Help

This may seem like a very difficult problem to solve, but that does not have to be the case. To help your child with studying, you will need to observe your child and get to know what type of learner he is. Several chapters of this book have addressed various aspects of a learner's "style" and give tips on how this can be done. Here are some general guidelines:

- Share your insights with your child to help her become more aware of her learning style, strengths, and weaknesses. This knowledge is one of the key tools a student needs in order to succeed in school and in life. If your child has been evaluated at some point, share the evaluation's findings with her as much as possible.

- Children often inherit many aspects of their parents' or other family members' learning profiles. Reflect on your learning style with your spouse or partner, siblings, or other family members. In what way does your child resemble you or others in your family? How did you deal with similar challenges yourself? Share your experiences with your child and empathize with him. This will help him cope with the bewilderment and frustration caused by unexpected obstacles in his path.

- Stay involved in your child's school experience. Even if you are not supervising homework anymore, chat with your child about what she is learning at school. Be aware of her likes and dislikes—does she "love" her math teacher but "hate" the history teacher? This could be a red flag—is history a challenge to your seventh grader this year? Why? Could it be the nature of the subject? Or the frequent pop quizzes that challenge a child's ability to access information quickly and her knowledge of the facts? Or, does the teacher have a very loose approach that is leaving your mildly disorganized adolescent at sea?

♦ When your child is doing homework, don't hesitate to check in every now and then, even if you have to use the pretext of bringing a snack. Stay abreast of long-term projects and test schedules. Offer to help edit a draft—this will allow you to read your child's writing and may enlighten you as to how he is coping with the curriculum.

♦ If none of these strategies proves helpful and your child is reluctant to accept your help, consider speaking to a guidance counselor or an academic advisor. You may also want to check in with the teacher to see if her perceptions of your child's performance match yours.

Once you have established the groundwork, you can begin to address specifics. Here are some tips and strategies:

Identify the Problem: What Is Getting in Your Child's Way?

♦ Does your child know **what** to study?

♦ Does your child know **how** to study?

♦ Does your child make a **study plan**?

♦ Does your child **rush** through studying or test taking?

♦ Does your child have trouble with specific **test formats** and **vocabulary**?

What to Study

Often, children may not be aware of the breadth and depth of material to be covered by the test. Here are some things you could check on and, perhaps, bring to your child's attention:

♦ Is there a study guide or practice test she can refer to?

♦ Is there a review session she can attend?

"Active listening" in the classroom during everyday lessons also helps students zero in on key facts or skills that a teacher may include on a test.

Parent Guide to Hassle-Free Homework

Talk to your child about her listening skills, attention, and focus. Encourage your child to listen to teacher "signals" of what is important. For example:

◆ *Write this down.*	◆ *This is important.*
◆ *Let me summarize.*	◆ *I'll write this on the board.*
◆ *Let me say it again.*	◆ *Remember . . .*

Have a conversation with your child and help her understand that her teacher may be sending signals every day on what is important to study for a test. Suggest that your child could use a special color highlighter or sticky note to identify this information in her textbook or notes.

Well-written textbooks also include several clues that identify important information. Encourage your child to review his textbooks carefully and to use all of the tools provided. Remind him to:

◆ look at the sidebars	◆ answer the summary questions at the end of the chapter
◆ review the bold vocabulary words	
◆ read the headings	◆ study the pictures and tables

Look over your child's textbook with her and discuss the use of different size or colored fonts, sidebars, figures, and other features in the chapter. You may also want to share with the teacher what you're doing at home, since focused listening and reading are easily taught and practiced in the classroom.

Helping Your Child Develop More Effective Study Strategies

Does your child know what kinds of study strategies work best for him? As discussed in previous chapters, each of us has our own preferences and unique learning style. Think about what you know about your child. Discuss your child's preference with him based on the following strategies:

◆ **Verbal:** repeating things out loud, reading notes aloud, flash cards, songs, rhymes, acronyms, silly sentences (BrainCogs, 2002)

◆ **Visual:** drawing pictures, charts

♦ **Kinesthetic:** movement, building, using manipulatives, concrete models

Ask yourself, does your child have insights into her own learning style? Is she able to consciously draw upon the appropriate strategy given her learning profile and the task at hand? Observe your child as she works on homework or on projects around the house and try to gauge her level of self-awareness. If you find that your child is inefficient in her approach to tasks and that she seems to be working unnecessarily hard, here are some things you could do:

♦ Talk to your child about what you have observed. For instance, you might say: *You've always been very good at remembering the lyrics to songs. I wonder if there is something about music and rhythm that helps you learn. Or, Whenever you've made something with your hands, you've been able to talk about it really easily. Perhaps building a model for science will help you learn more easily about levers.*

♦ It may also be helpful to your child to think about which subjects are easier for him than others and why this is so. These discussions may help your child gain a deeper understanding of his own learning style. Ask him questions such as: *Do particular teachers do things in class that help or hinder you? Is a subject appealing for a particular reason* (e.g., it involves hands-on projects or class discussions)?

♦ If you share specific attributes with your child, share this information with her and discuss the strategies that have helped you.

♦ If your child is unable to generate appropriate strategies independently, encourage him to work with you to create these.

Here are brief descriptions of some of the verbal strategies named above that may not be as familiar to you:

Rhymes: Rhythmic chants that may also include rhyming words. These help children remember isolated and abstract facts. For example: *In 1775, the Stamp Act was alive.*

Acronyms: These are also useful when your child has to learn a list of information in which the sequence is not important. Take the first letter from the first word of each item on the list and combine these letters to form a unique or meaningful word. Here are some examples:

HOMES helps your child remember the names of the Great Lakes:

Huron
Ontario
Michigan
Erie
Superior

ROY G. BIV is an acronym for remembering the colors of the spectrum:

Red
Orange
Yellow
Green
Blue
Indigo
Violet

Silly Sentences: When the sequence of items in a list is important, it is helpful to create silly sentences instead of acronyms. First, sequence the items in order. Then, take the first letter of the first word of each item in order to form a silly sentence. Make the sentence as vivid, strange, and visually appealing as possible. One seven-year-old was having trouble remembering his first routine of the day at school:

1. Hang up your bag.

2. Hang up your jacket.

3. Sign up for lunch.

4. Get started on your work.

He came up with the sentence *"Baggy jaguars love worms"* to help him remember these steps: bag, jacket, lunch, work. On days when he had to turn in his homework folder, he modified the sentence to say, *"Baggy jaguars love fuzzy worms."* Inserting the word *fuzzy* reminded him of his folders. This sentence worked for several reasons:

◆ The child loved animals, and it was motivating to him to use this sentence.

♦ The image created by the sentence was a really silly one, and he had a lot of fun recalling it each morning.

♦ The words in the sentence sounded like the words he had to remember, making this an easy strategy for him to use.

♦ This was a quick and private strategy—he just needed to remember the words silently or to recall the image to make sure he had remembered all the steps in order.

Helping Your Child Make a Study Plan

Help your child make a study plan and stick to it:

Sample Study Plan for History

Materials: textbook, class notes, old quizzes, homework

Study Activities:

a. Answer questions at end of chapter.

b. Make flash cards for vocabulary terms and important people.

c. Make a timeline of important events in chapter.

d. Review class notes, homework, and quizzes, and highlight important information. Then, look away from notes and recite highlighted information out loud.

e. Make a chart of important events and the causes and consequences of each.

f. Predict possible essay questions—jot down notes for answering each question.

g. Explain the main ideas of the chapter to yourself, a parent, or friend.

h. Have a friend or parent quiz you.

Timetable:

Mon., Wed., and Thurs. — spend one hour each evening

Friday morning — review flash cards, timeline, and chart

Pacing

Does your child rush through her studying or test taking? If so, one of these suggestions might work for her:

♦ Review her study plan and set a timer for a certain study period according to the plan.

♦ Discuss a goal for studying and taking the test: What does he want to master and how well does he want to do on this test?

♦ Offer to quiz her on the material when she's sure that she has learned the information sufficiently.

♦ Analyze the mistakes he made on the last quiz or test and determine how many were due to rushing.

♦ Discuss the value of slowing down and checking her answers before handing in the test.

♦ Make a personal checklist for checking his test before handing it in.

Helping Your Child Understand the Content and Format of Tests

Does your child have difficulty understanding test questions and teacher expectations? Children with learning differences and attentional problems often misread questions or have difficulty understanding the language, determining what's most important, paying attention to all of the details, and differentiating between similar answers. If this description matches your child, here are some suggestions that may help:

♦ Ask the teacher for sample questions and examples of high-quality sample responses and review them with your child.

♦ Many test questions will require your child to be on the alert for key words that can clarify the meaning of the question (for essays and short answers) and help eliminate some of the answer choices (on multiple-choice questions). For example, answer choices that include words such as *always* or *never* are usually not correct. One way of remembering these key words is to use an acronym such as Ann E. Boa (BrainCogs, 2003).

A = Always
N = Never
N = Not
E = Except
B = But
O = Only
A = All

In addition to memorizing the acronym, make sure that your child knows the meanings of each word and can apply this knowledge to succeed on tests.

♦ Encourage your child to read multiple-choice questions, paraphrase them in her mind, and generate her own answers before looking at the possible choices. Remind her that multiple-choice questions often have a correct answer, an answer that is obviously wrong, and then one or two choices that are close to the right answer. She should read each choice carefully and try to eliminate as many answers as possible before choosing one. Encourage your child to stick with her first answer unless she knows that she made a careless error.

♦ On multiple-choice tests, the vocabulary and/or the visual layout of the answer sheet can confuse children. For example, children with visual-spatial or fine-motor difficulties can have a hard time filling in scannable forms accurately or copying answers onto a separate sheet of paper. If your child struggles with the layout of the test or answer sheet, talk to the teacher and advocate for a different format or permission to answer directly on the test.

♦ For matching questions, some students struggle to recognize connected ideas. Again, some children have difficulty with the visual aspect of the task—looking at two lists and keeping track of which answers have already been chosen—while others may have trouble remembering the specific vocabulary or connections between items. When taking matching tests, suggest to your child that he read all of the choices, match the items that he is certain of, and cross off the choices that he has used. Then he can proceed with the remaining items using a process of elimination.

♦ Students often need help planning ahead to compose short and long answers in preparation for tests. You can help your child review study guides, practice tests, textbooks, and class notes with the teacher signals discussed earlier so that she can predict likely essay or short-answer questions. This will enable your child to map out key points and arguments ahead of time. Even if the questions she prepares for are not actually on the test, the work she does will give her practice in thinking through questions and formulating answers.

Helping Your Child With Test-Taking Anxiety or Stress

Sometimes emotional factors may impede a student's performance on tests even when he is well prepared. If your child panics or becomes anxious when studying for or taking tests, suggest these strategies:

♦ Remind your child of the effort expended and strategies used to study.

♦ Encourage your child to focus on his strengths: *Remember, you have a really good memory and can recite all of the important facts.*

♦ Teach your child to take some deep, relaxing breaths before and during the test: *Blink, breathe, and relax.*

♦ Help your child put the test in perspective: *Remember, this is just one test—you've done so well on your papers and projects, it's okay if you make some mistakes.*

♦ Praise your child's strong effort: *You studied really well and can be proud of that. It will really pay off on the test.*

♦ Remind your child not to get stuck on any one item. Teach her to move on to the next question if she doesn't know an answer. The answer will probably pop into her mind later.

If the test requires a few important details, such as mathematical formulas, science equations, brief outlines for possible essays, spelling words, or dates, encourage your child to write them at the top of the answer sheet before even reading the questions so he doesn't have to worry about remembering them later. He can write memory strategies there, too (e.g., silly sentences, acronyms, cartoons) to jog his memory later.

Anxiety can adversely affect your child's memory and attention to details. Encourage your child to check her work for careless mistakes as much as possible. A personalized checklist (like a "Top 3 Hit List") of the most common kinds of errors your child makes (based on previous tests) can help her prioritize which problems or questions to recheck before handing in the test.

Conclusion

Tests and exams are a part of academic life that our children have to be prepared to face. As adults, we know that it is not our performance on specific tests but what we learned along the way that makes us successful in our lives. Nevertheless, it is important to give our children the tools to achieve to the best of their abilities here and now. We hope that the suggestions made throughout this book and this chapter in particular will enable you to support your child and help him reach his full potential.

Chapter 8

Motivation

Jaime worked hard throughout elementary school to do her best. However, when middle school began, she became more interested in socializing with her friends, playing lacrosse, and shopping online. As a result, she spent less time on her homework, and her grades started to decline.

. . . .

Duncan did not take school very seriously until he entered high school. He knew that he wanted to go to a well-respected college and in order to do so, he had to earn top grades. Duncan worked hard to accomplish his goal. Though he had difficulty with math and science classes, he learned that if he studied with friends and met with teachers after school for extra help sessions, he could improve his grades.

The linchpin of any child or adolescent's performance is the motivation to do well. No matter how bright or creative a child may be, if he is not motivated to put in the effort and persistence needed to complete homework, study for tests, and actively participate in his classes, he will not be a successful student.

What Do We Know About Motivation in Relation to Schoolwork?

Research has shown that all children are intrinsically curious and motivated to learn when they:

◆ have some **control** over the learning process

◆ are able to pursue their own **interests**

◆ are sufficiently **challenged**

◆ feel **confident** that they can master the task or body of knowledge

At the University of Rochester, Edward Deci and his colleagues studied motivation during the 1970s and 1980s. They found that for most children and adults, **intrinsic motivation** (an inherent desire to learn) promotes learning and sustains effort far better than **extrinsic motivation** (expectations, rewards, and so on). They discovered that there were several key factors that enhanced motivation, namely:

◆ **autonomy:** the opportunity to choose when and what to learn

◆ **efficacy:** the belief that one is capable of accomplishing the task

◆ **an appropriate level of challenge:** tasks that were too easy or too hard diminished motivation (Deci, 1995)

Several motivational psychologists and educators have identified other factors that contribute to the motivation–learning dynamic as well. For example, Carol Dweck and her colleagues have published a number of research studies that showed a positive relationship between student beliefs about intelligence and their motivation. They found that those students who believed that intelligence was not a fixed trait but something that can be acquired by working hard were far more motivated than students who were convinced that intelligence was something that you either "had" or "didn't have" (Dweck, 1986; Licht & Dweck, 1984). In other words, children who believe that they can be successful by investing time and effort are more likely to have the "drive to thrive" (Meltzer, et al., 2004). They understand that long-term success comes as a result of trying hard, making many mistakes, and persisting even when frustrated (Brooks, 1991). Attributing successes to one's own efforts supports the notion that an individual has some control over her learning and performance and reinforces the belief that she is capable of continued success.

While all children may lack self-confidence when they take on new challenges or learn difficult material, two groups of students are especially vulnerable. Not surprisingly, children who have experienced frequent frustration and failure in school, perhaps because of a learning or attentional problem, are prone to feelings of helplessness and defeat. They have a much more difficult time believing that they are capable of learning and that persisting in their efforts is critical. Until they begin to experience success, it will be difficult to convince them otherwise. Similarly, gifted students (especially girls) have a tendency to underestimate their capabilities. Kids who are used to succeeding without expending much effort are often devastated when they struggle to understand new material or when their grades fall short of their expectations. They may feel incompetent because they (or their parents and teachers) have set unrealistically high standards for themselves, and anything less than perfection may be seen as unacceptable (Stipek & Seal, 2001). Often, these students need help understanding that everyone has strengths and limitations and that real learning involves effort, struggle, and mistakes. For both groups of students, setting realistic expectations and challenging them appropriately are critical for motivating them to succeed.

Relationships also provide an important framework for supporting motivation and learning. For the past several decades, many social-psychological studies have found that when children feel supported and respected by their parents and have strong connections within their community, they are much more likely to embrace learning and to work hard to achieve success (Stipek & Seal, 2001; Hallowell, 1999). Marshall Raskind (1999) reported that an important factor in the lives of many successful adults with learning and/or attentional problems were the emotional connections with parents and teachers. Children have an enormous capacity to overcome personal or familial hardships when there is at least one significant person in their lives who serves as a mentor providing emotional support, encouragement, and guidance.

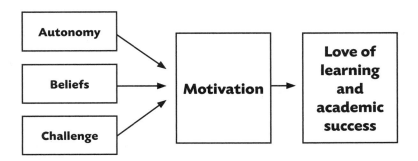

While most children enter kindergarten with an enthusiasm for learning about the world around them, by the time they reach middle school, their love for learning may be diminished (Harter, 1981). For some middle and high school students, schoolwork becomes at best a tolerable chore or at worst, a dreaded nightmare! This phenomenon is understandable given what we know about normal development and motivation. As middle and high school students struggle to understand themselves, to carve out an identity, and to achieve greater independence, they have more difficulty valuing and investing in a curriculum and a set of expectations imposed on them by their parents and teachers. In fact, for many youngsters, their love of learning continues to decline until they are in college, where they are able to identify and pursue a course of study based on their interests and strengths.

Imagine how a learning disability, an attentional or emotional problem, or a major family stressor, such as divorce or unemployment, can further impact an adolescent's motivation. Consider a young woman who has been plagued for years by low self-esteem due to ongoing academic struggles or has suddenly experienced a loss of self-confidence due to a family crisis. In either case, she may have difficulty trusting in her ability to learn, revving up the necessary energy and effort to succeed, and believing that she has some control over the learning process. While some teens are resilient enough to thrive even when faced with devastating circumstances, many will need support and help if they are to succeed.

How Parents Can Help

Even though we know a great deal about motivation in general, it is often difficult to understand why a particular student is not motivated to do her best in school. If your child is struggling to sustain her interest and effort in school, then think about a number of factors that might be affecting her motivation. As a starting point, ask yourself these questions:

♦ How successful has she been in the past?

♦ How hard did he have to work to be successful in the past?

♦ Does she have an opportunity to "shine" sometime during her day?

♦ Does he believe he can succeed?

- Is she a "pleaser" or a "perfectionist"?

- Is he generally oppositional or difficult?

- Could she be depressed or suffering from low self-esteem?

- Is he faced with a curriculum that is either too easy or too difficult?

- Is she reacting to family stresses by trying to get your attention or giving up on herself?

- Is he discouraged because he believes you have given up on him?

- Is she feeling too much pressure to perform at a certain level?

Once you have answered these questions, you might be able to pinpoint where the problem lies. Is your child lacking motivation because he lacks confidence in his own abilities? Does she believe that one is either smart or not? Has he come to grips with the fact that once he gets to middle school and/or high school, he must work hard to succeed? Does she lack motivation because no matter how hard she works, it doesn't seem to make a difference? Is he losing interest in school because he doesn't have many choices about his learning?

One way you can foster your child's motivation is to support his need for autonomy and ownership of the learning process. While you can establish basic rules like, *You must complete your homework every night,* you can give your child a say in when and how his homework is done. Your child will accomplish the most when he knows your general expectations and guidelines, but that he has a choice about how the expectations are met. For example, if he knows that he must complete homework before 9 P.M., but he can choose when, where, and in what order he can do his homework, he may put more energy into doing the work than if he is reminded every 20 minutes, *It's time to do your homework!* or *Haven't you started your homework yet?*

Supporting your child's need for autonomy and choice is often a matter of choosing the right words to show her that she does have some control over her learning. Research has shown that subtle differences in giving people directions or suggestions can influence whether people feel in control or controlled and, consequently, how well they perform. Rather than telling your child what to do, you can empower your child best by asking questions and giving information in a matter-of-fact way. For example, to spur your child to start her homework, you might ask her:

- *Would you like to use the computer for your homework now or after dinner?*

- *Would you like to read your book in the kitchen while I'm washing dishes?*

- *I know you're having a test tomorrow in science. Would you like me to quiz you on the chapter in about an hour?*

- *If you're going to basketball practice tonight, when are you planning to do your homework?*

To give a gentle push toward starting a long-term project, you might ask: *Do you need to go to the library to do some research for your project? If so, I can give you a lift tonight.* Or, *If you are planning to watch the Super Bowl with your friends tomorrow, will you have enough time to write your outline for the history paper?*

Inspiring your child to work hard without nagging is a challenge for all parents. However, if you make suggestions or remind her of past successes, you can help motivate her and preserve her sense of control. A neutral statement can go a long way. For instance, you could say:

- *If you want to do well on that history test on Friday, you might want to start studying tonight.*

- *Remember when you did well on the last paper, you gave yourself plenty of time to write a rough draft and a final copy.*

- *If you want to get a better grade on this paper, you might want to use the thesaurus to improve your writing.*

Challenging Faulty Beliefs

If you think that your child's motivation is inconsistent or on the decline because of a lack of self-confidence, there are many ways you can help. First, try to identify what beliefs might be getting in the way:

- Does she believe that intelligence is fixed and can't be changed?

- Does he believe that only smart kids can do well?

- Does she believe that no matter how hard she tries, she can't do well on a test?

- Does he believe that if he really was smart, he wouldn't have to work hard?

- Is she thinking that success only means getting all A's?

Once you discover what faulty beliefs might be discouraging your child from feeling competent and working hard, then you can help by challenging his beliefs and persuading him to believe otherwise. Following are some of the many ways that you can influence your child's beliefs:

Give Clear, Consistent Messages—A Daily Mantra

As a child, one of my favorite children's books was *The Little Engine That Could* (Grosset & Dunlap, 1978). I can still vividly recall my father reading me the story at bedtime over and over again. Whenever I was frustrated or discouraged, my dad would remind me of the little engine's words, "I think I can, I think I can, I think I can," and tell me that I could do anything if I worked hard enough. His words were a powerful message that motivated me to take on many challenges and to do well in school. Even today, when I am overwhelmed with anxiety and self-doubt, I often rely on the simple mantra, "I think I can," to overcome my fear or frustration.

As a parent, you, too, can find or create a simple phrase that can send a powerful message about the importance of hard work and persistence. When you hear your child make disparaging comments about himself, such as: *I'm so stupid! I can't do these math problems!* try using a consistent "sound bite," such as: *It's not about intelligence, honey, it's all about hard work. I know you can figure it out if you work at it a little longer.*

You can also point out that thinking and saying negative thoughts will make the task even harder. Suggest that, instead, she could give herself a boost by making more encouraging statements, such as:

- *I can do this if I wrap my mind around it.*

- *If I keep working at it, I will be able to figure it out.*

- *Maybe if I try a different approach, I'll be able to solve it.*

Remind Your Child of Past Successes

Sometimes when children feel discouraged and lose confidence in their abilities, all they need is a reminder of how they overcame difficulties in the past. Perhaps your child often gets stuck when he is trying to think of ideas for a writing assignment. Although generating ideas might be an area of difficulty for him, you can remind him of the last time he chose a writing topic and what strategy or approach worked for him.

For example, if your child enjoyed writing about basketball for his last assignment, you might suggest that he choose a similar topic or explore another one of his interests. You can also defuse some of the tension by reassuring him that even if it takes him more time, he will think of ideas because he always has in the past! Finally, you could suggest a strategy to help him, or ask him to think of a strategy he has learned at school, like making a list of ideas or using a graphic organizer. (For specific strategies to use in this situation, read Chapter 5.) Your conversation might go something like this:

John: I've been sitting here for 20 minutes and I can't think of anything to write. I give up!

Mom: What's making it difficult?

John: I don't know. You know I'm not a good writer. I can never think of a good topic.

Mom: Do you remember your last writing assignment? You really enjoyed writing about your basketball game. Once you got started, the ideas really flowed! Could you write about something related to basketball for this assignment?

John: No, it can't be about the same topic. It has to include a character description.

Mom: Well, how about making a list of five of your favorite people and picking someone on your list to describe?

Give Specific Positive Feedback and Constructive Criticism

Children who lack self-confidence often need reassurance that their work is of high quality or, at least, acceptable. When you look over your child's homework, make sure that you always point out something positive, but be specific and sincere.

- *Your introduction is terrific—it really drew me in and made me excited about reading the rest of your paper.*

- *Wow! This paper shows how much your vocabulary has really improved. You are on the road to becoming a great writer.*

You can boost your child's confidence even further by emphasizing her role in achieving success. In other words, it's not just that she's talented or "lucked out," but her effort, persistence, and use of a specific strategy or approach contributed to her achievement. For example:

- *I really liked the way that you worked slowly and carefully on this math assignment. Your effort really paid off! I don't see any mistakes.*

- *Your answers to these questions really show that you understood the story. I bet writing those margin notes helped you identify the important parts.*

Children gain confidence when they understand how their continued efforts and use of strategies will lead to success. They also feel more certain about their abilities when they know that you have confidence in them. Pointing out how your child can improve his work reinforces the notion that you believe that he can do better and are willing to show him how.

Redefine Success

Your child may be discouraged if she feels that no matter how hard she works, her grades don't show it. If you think this is true, then you can help restore her confidence and motivation by helping her redefine success. As renowned special educator and lecturer Rick LaVoie suggests, success should be evaluated in terms of effort, learning, and improvement, not performance or grades. So if your child has worked hard, learned something new, and improved her skills, then she has been successful!

If you keep this definition in mind, imagine how encouraging and empowering your response will be when your child brings home a poor test grade or a disappointing report card. It is important not to get upset or make comments, such as:

> *Oh no, I can't believe you still got 2 C's and a D. What happened? I thought you were doing better!*

You can help him by acknowledging his feelings and then focusing on how hard he worked and how much he learned. For example, you might say something like this:

> *I know how disappointed you must be. It doesn't seem fair that you worked so hard, and your hard work doesn't show as much as you'd like. But you and I know that you did work hard, and it certainly showed when you were telling me about the causes of the Civil War. You learned quite a bit of history this term, and you should feel good about that! Maybe you can talk to your teacher about what else you can do to score better on her tests or find another way that you can show her how much you've learned.*

Another way you can help is by encouraging your child to establish a few realistic learning goals in each subject area and to find ways to keep track of her progress. For example, if your child is in middle or high school, she might decide that she wants to improve her writing and can do so if she gives more examples to elaborate her ideas or to prove her thesis. You could encourage her to make a chart so that each time she writes a paper, she can record how many examples she includes. She could also record the grade she receives on each paper so that she will see that working on her goal can improve her performance. In this way, your child will learn that she can be successful if she focuses on one goal at a time and keeps working toward it!

Praise Effort and Persistence

Effort and persistence are two critical components of academic success. A large body of research supports the idea of a cyclical relationship among motivation, effort, and academic performance (Meltzer, et al., 2004). Moreover, results of several studies of adults who have been successful despite their struggles with learning and attentional problems suggest that the ability to exert the necessary effort to attain one's goals and to persist even when difficulties arise are important qualities that contribute to lifelong success (Raskind, et al., 1999).

As a parent, you have the opportunity to encourage your child to put forth effort and to persist even when her homework is challenging. Even if you are dissatisfied with the amount of effort your child gives on her assignments, don't forget to praise her for whatever level of energy she exerts. You can always make a specific study suggestion (*Do you think making flash cards would help you remember the information better?*) and encourage her to do more (*I'll bet if you spend a little more time reviewing, you'll really master that chapter!*). Every time you use encouragement and praise, you are reinforcing your child's work ethic and motivating her to do even more.

Emphasize the Importance of Making Mistakes and Learning From Them

Your child may be avoiding or forgetting to do homework because he's afraid of making mistakes and feeling humiliated. If this is true for your child, you can help by clearly sending the message that mistakes are not only acceptable and expected, but are essential for learning and succeeding. Your child may understand this concept best if you use concrete examples from your own life. For example, ask yourself the following questions and share specific experiences that you've had:

◆ Have you ever been afraid of making a mistake? Why?

◆ How did you overcome the fear?

◆ Have you ever had a teacher who encouraged you when you made a mistake?

◆ Can you remember a time when you were humiliated for making a mistake?

◆ Have you ever made a mistake or experienced a failure that led you to later success?

Sharing your feelings about making mistakes and the experiences that you've had will help your child feel more comfortable with taking risks and trying her best even if she is likely to make a mistake.

You can also use examples from popular heroes in your child's life. For example:

- George Lucas, famous director of the *Star Wars* movies, was turned down by every major studio after his first film, *THX-1138*, flopped in 1971.

- Steven Spielberg's mediocre grades prevented him from getting into UCLA film school.

- Ray Kroc worked as a jazz musician and a paper-cup salesman before becoming the founder of McDonald's hamburger empire.

- Elvis Presley was told that he couldn't sing by his high school music teacher, who gave him a C. (Green, 2001)

Although having discussions with your child about the issue of making mistakes is often helpful, responding appropriately to your child when his performance is disappointing is most critical. While it is not easy to put your own feelings about his performance aside, it is important that you do so. Try to listen to your child's feelings first and then offer acceptance and encouragement rather than judgment. Can you remember a time when your conversation went something like this?

Jesse: Dad, I did not do so well on my math test. Here it is . . .

Dad: Oh Jesse, you failed another math test? How could you? What happened? I told you not to go out with your friends on Sunday! You should have been studying more!

Jesse: Forget it, Dad. Get off my back! You know I just can't do math. My teacher is so bad, I can't understand anything she says. No matter how hard I study, I never do well!

If you are like most parents, you've probably had dozens of exchanges like that one! Unfortunately, every time a parent reacts with "blame and shame," his child is going to feel more humiliated and discouraged. With these negative feelings, a child is less likely to ask for the help she may need, to learn from her mistakes, and to work harder.

The next time you feel like having a conversation similar to the one above, try an experiment. See what happens if you approach the situation differently. Perhaps, like this:

Jesse: Dad, I really blew my physics test. Here it is . . .

Dad: Ouch, that must hurt! What were you hoping to get on that test?

Jesse: It was a really hard test, and I knew I didn't do very well, but I was hoping for a C at least.

Dad: Well, sorry it didn't turn out the way you were hoping, but maybe this is an opportunity to learn something. Do you think you understood the material before taking the test?

Jesse: I thought I knew most of the material. I even studied longer than I usually do, but obviously I didn't know it well enough.

Dad: What do you think you need to do differently before the next test? Do you think it would help to meet with the teacher for a review or ask her for a practice test?

Jesse: I guess I could speak to her before the next test and try to get some help, and I'll just have to work harder.

With a little guidance and encouragement, you'll usually get a different response. Remember, no matter what messages you try to communicate to your child, how you respond when the "chips are down" will have the greatest impact on her self-esteem and motivation to try again.

Building Connections

Supportive and loving relationships create the "safety net" that nurtures your child's motivation, persistence, and growth. Research shows that children can overcome the worst of adversities when they have at least one close relationship with a caring adult (Higgins, 1994). The power of these relationships in motivating children to push past their difficulties, whether they are learning, economic, or emotional hardships, has been proven over and over again.

Here's the story of one important relationship for Edward Hallowell, M.D., a highly respected and renowned psychiatrist and author, who has succeeded despite, or as a result of, his lifelong struggle with dyslexia, ADHD, and family traumas.

> The connections at my schools saved me. . . . At Fessenden, there was Mr. Cook and Mr. Gibson and Mr. Slocum and Mr. Fitts and many others. They didn't know how much they were helping me by just being there, just by connecting with me in an ordinary, teacher-like way. . . . I'm sure Mr. Maynard, for example, simply thought he was teaching me geography and coaching me in baseball. He didn't know that on the day he stopped me in the corridor and slapped me on the back and told me that I had scored the highest grade on the seventh-grade exam . . . [he was] saving a child from despair. (Hallowell, 1999)

Similarly, Jonathan Mooney, an internationally known speaker and motivator, recalls how his relationship with his family was of crucial importance in his battle to succeed in the face of learning and attentional problems.

> Throughout my childhood, our house was filled with passion and always with the humor and spirit of those that never fit in and fought at all costs to succeed. I grew up there, and although I would leave with my own share of wounds, my family would eventually save my life. (Mooney & Cole, 2000)

Don't ever underestimate the power of your relationship with your child, even when it seems like you're not having much success helping or inspiring her. Developing and maintaining a close relationship with your child, no matter how old she is, requires a few essential ingredients:

◆ unconditional love and acceptance, regardless of his achievement

◆ authentic interest and involvement in her life, no matter how busy you are

◆ respect for his feelings, ideas, and aspirations

As described in many of the examples above, you can nurture a positive relationship with your child by:

◆ celebrating her strengths and talents

◆ showing how much you love him on a daily basis

◆ spending time with her and making it a priority

◆ listening well and reflecting his feelings

◆ supporting her efforts to solve problems her way

◆ asking questions without blame or criticism

◆ describing problems and sharing solutions without preaching

◆ encouraging his pursuit of his interests and passions

◆ accepting who she is, rather than trying to make her into someone you want her to be

As your child grows and transitions into different stages of development, your relationship will surely change. At times, you may feel that special closeness, when communication is easy and spending time together is tension-free. However, even in the best parent-child relationships, there will be stretches of time when conflict and tension seem to dominate your interactions. During these periods, it is critical that you find a way to continue showing your love and support and at the same time, give your child more space and reasonable opportunities for decision-making and autonomy. Letting go is perhaps the most difficult aspect of parenting, but nonetheless, it is crucial. One of the many ways in which you can preserve your relationship and support your child's independence is by encouraging the development of other relationships with nurturing adults. Extended family members, teachers, coaches, tutors, and counselors provide invaluable connections that can enrich your child's supportive network of relationships.

Finding Community Support

If your child has a serious problem with motivation, you probably won't be able to solve it alone. Many forms of help are available, but it will take time and patience to find the right combination of resources. How much and what kinds of help are needed will depend on what issues your child is struggling with and how willing he is to accept help.

◆ Does your child need more structure and support to get started on homework?

◆ Does your child need to learn specific strategies or study skills to succeed?

◆ Does your child need greater self-confidence and encouragement to tackle the challenges of schoolwork?

◆ Is your child seeking more autonomy from you and reacting against your rules, expectations, and involvement?

Start with the people who are already important in your child's life. Is there a coach, guidance counselor, teacher, or neighbor who has a special relationship with your child and could help by being a role model, mentor, or even coach to encourage her to work hard and succeed? Is there a friend or slightly older student whom your child admires and who would be willing to spend some time doing homework with her? If no one comes to mind, contact your child's teacher or guidance counselor to help you find someone. In many high schools, students have the opportunity to help out younger children or peers through Merit Scholarship, Big Brother/Big Sister, and peer tutoring programs. At our institute, for example, we have recently developed the S.M.A.R.T.S. Mentoring Program, in which high school and college students with learning difficulties reach out to younger students with similar challenges to share their personal experiences and strategies for life success. (For more information, contact ResearchILD at www.researchild.org). Some children benefit from making a connection with a similar mentoring program. Sometimes a meaningful connection with someone other than their parents, who will appreciate them just for being themselves, will encourage them to do their best, and will help them if needed (with no strings attached) is enough to help students overcome their motivational block.

> Sometimes a meaningful connection with someone other than their parents, who will appreciate them just for being themselves, will encourage them to do their best, and will help them if needed (with no strings attached) is enough to help students overcome their motivational block.

On the other hand, if your child is discouraged because he can't do the work (or believes that he can't), he may need a specially trained teacher or tutor to teach him specific strategies or study skills to build his competence and confidence. Nothing sparks motivation more than feeling competent. The more children know how to study, the more interested they are in their assignments and the harder they work. Once a student experiences success, the pride and pleasure of learning a difficult concept or mastering a body of knowledge itself stimulates natural motivation and can reverse a longstanding, downward spiral of disinterest and failure.

If your child is stuck in a battle over control or in a never-ending power struggle with you, then a different approach might be in order. First and foremost, you will have to defuse the conflict before any effective solutions can be found. Your first job is to show your child that you are on her side. In other words, you want to fight *with* her, not *against* her, to help her succeed— no matter how she defines success. An open, nonjudgmental discussion of what her goals and hopes are regarding her school life can sometimes shift the battleground and unlock your child's natural drive to forge ahead.

Unfortunately, in most situations, a discussion is not enough. Most children and teens who are used to fighting with their parents will not give up the struggle so easily. Blaming others for our problems is a great way to avoid the difficult task of facing our own downfalls and accepting the responsibility for our problems. As a parent, you will need to work hard at staying calm, making suggestions in a neutral way, and using the "language of autonomy." (Stipek & Seal, 2001)

No matter how hard you try, you can't make your child work hard and succeed in school. However, you can:

♦ establish basic rules

♦ help your child establish a plan or contract regarding schoolwork

♦ encourage your child to ask for help when needed

♦ communicate your respect and confidence that he can succeed

If the battle continues despite your best efforts to join forces with your child, then you will probably need to consult a counselor or therapist to help your family develop effective ways to resolve your conflicts.

Chapter 9

Communicating and Collaborating With Your Child's Teachers

Markella has a math test tomorrow. After coming home from softball practice and eating dinner, she sits down at her desk to start her homework. She takes out her books from her backpack and scatters them across the desk. She picks up her Spanish book, grabs some index cards, and turns to the vocabulary section of Chapter 3 to make her flash cards for Thursday's vocabulary quiz. While working on them, she remembers that she has to write a reflection paper for her English class that is due tomorrow. Markella gets flustered and frazzled with the overwhelming thought of all she has to do tonight, and it's already 7:00 P.M.!

. . . .

While studying for his history test, Raphael gets easily overwhelmed with all the dates, army generals, and war battles associated with each historical event. He constantly confuses the causes for one battle with those of another. The study guide his teacher provided only complicates his studying because it asks him to identify certain causes and generals but not others. Raphael grows frustrated while sifting through the information and feels like he'll never be able to learn the answers in time for the test.

As we discussed in Chapters 1–8, your child may experience difficulty understanding or completing his homework on any given day. In fact, as parents, you are often involved with trying to help your children understand the assignment and encouraging them to finish their homework in an efficient and organized manner. The homework process, however, can become very frustrating when your child is unclear about the homework assignment, procrastinates until the last minute, or is not organized and prepared with his resources and materials.

Consequently, the assignment becomes cumbersome for your child and a burden on the entire family. It is, therefore, critical that you communicate with teachers in order to devise a homework plan that meets the school's expectations yet is manageable and appropriate for your child each night. But how can you effectively communicate with your child's teachers to share your homework concerns while advocating for your child's needs? Let's review some effective strategies for communicating and collaborating with teachers.

Understanding Teacher Expectations Regarding Homework

Every afternoon when your child returns home from school, her workday is not quite over. In fact, after "working" for eight hours, children have a few additional hours (sometimes more, depending on their grade level) of work ahead of them. Homework can have its rewards and drawbacks. It can serve as a vehicle to review previously learned material and as a preview for upcoming attractions. However, some children may perceive homework as tedious, time-consuming, and irrelevant to the learning process. It is, therefore, important for students and parents to have a clear understanding of the homework assignments as well as the teacher's expectations. Ask your child the following questions to help determine if she has a clear understanding of the homework:

♦ Do you understand what you were asked to do? Do you need help in understanding the instructions and expectations of the assignment?

♦ Do you have the necessary materials to complete the assignment?

♦ Have you had any previous practice with the homework material? (Learning the content in class or doing practice problems)

♦ Do your answers make sense?

♦ Are you learning/completing the assignment in such a way that you can refer back to it when you are studying for a test?

If you have laid the groundwork and you observe that your child continues to struggle with homework assignments, then it is important to communicate your concerns and your child's frustrations to his teacher. When working with the teacher, try to understand where your child's difficulties lie with the homework assignments. Ask your child's teacher to explain the goals of the homework assignment as well as how much time is reasonable to spend on the homework. In addition, ask how much or what kinds of parental involvement are encouraged or accepted. By establishing clear requirements as well as understanding the expectations for the assignments, parents, teachers, and students feel confident that what they are doing has a purpose and that it is realistic to accomplish the task.

Advocating for Your Child

As parents, you are the best advocates for your child. You know her in unique, insightful, and profound ways. You are aware of your child's likes and dislikes, talents and shortcomings, strengths and weaknesses. You know how to comfort her when she's sad, encourage her when she feels disheartened, and protect her when she is in trouble. You have learned under what conditions your child thrives or withers, communicates or retreats, participates or withdraws (LDAC, 1998).

Therefore, it is vitally important that you communicate your concerns, questions, and knowledge about your child's learning strengths and weaknesses to the teacher at the beginning of the year by scheduling a school meeting. By opening the lines of communication between home and school, you are informing your child's teacher of his individual needs and, thus, are able to focus on appropriate programmatic accommodations and plans for the school year ahead. When parents let teachers know what works for their child, they increase the chances that their child will experience academic success and will approach learning more strategically, efficiently, and successfully.

When successful parent-teacher communication is established, cultivated, and continued, the benefits are threefold:

1. Children learn more easily.

2. Teachers teach more effectively.

3. Parents parent more successfully by reinforcing appropriate school behaviors and modeling strategies.

Keeping the lines of communication open between home and school involves building and maintaining relationships.

In order to communicate your concerns effectively to your child's teacher, you may want to follow the three C's of successful communication: **converse**, **collaborate**, and **create**.

- ◆ **Converse:** Talk with your child's teacher openly and state your concerns about a specific homework or classroom situation.

- ◆ **Collaborate:** Work with your child's teacher to create a plan of action that will complement your child's learning style.

- ◆ **Create:** While working with your child's teacher, generate clear expectations for homework completion and the amount of parent involvement with homework that is expected.

Establishing Effective Ways to Communicate

Setting up the initial parent-teacher conference is the most important step toward establishing clear communication. Here, you can meet your child's teacher and discuss your child's learning profile. Once initial contact is established, the communication lines are open. It is your job to keep these lines open and to make sure the information and communication continue to flow smoothly throughout the academic year. To help prepare for your first parent-teacher conference, we suggest the following:

Things to Do Before the Conference

Your child spends half of his waking hours in school with his teachers and peers, just as you spend half your day at work with your colleagues and superiors. It is, therefore, important for your child to have a mutually beneficial relationship with his teachers. When both student and teacher have a clear understanding of what's to come, their relationship can begin to grow and flourish. This relationship can be nourished through the role and intervention of parents. If there is a problem in school or a miscommunication between your child and his teacher, you should encourage your child to approach his teacher in an appropriate manner to address the issue. If the

Parent-Teacher Conference Preparation Form

1. My child's learning profile:

Strengths	Weaknesses

2. My child's comments about each subject/class and related teaching style:

Teacher	Subject/Class	Feedback

3. Current home issues or unusual circumstances that teacher(s) should be aware of:

4. Personal information about my child to help teacher(s) understand him/her better (e.g., hobbies, talents, interests, difficulties, etc.):

problem is very delicate and this approach would not be the fitting course of action, then it is your responsibility to bring the issue to the forefront for discussion and resolution.

In order to gain a better understanding of the positive and negative aspects of your child's experiences in school, it is critical to talk to your child. Ask her to explain a typical day in school. What does she look forward to each day? What is her least favorite part of the school day? After discussing with your child her likes and dislikes, interests and areas of difficulty, as well as questions she may have for her teacher, jot down the key points you want to address when you meet with the teacher.

Sometimes it is difficult for parents to get started and to have a clear idea of what it is they want to share with their child's teacher. The "Parent-Teacher Conference Preparation Form" (page 139) will guide you through this preparation process. The form includes a section regarding your child's learning profile that can be completed in two ways: First, if your child has been tested before, you can refer to his previous psycho-educational evaluation reports, which include a breakdown of his strengths and weaknesses. Second, if your child has never been tested, you can include your observations of his learning style and areas of strength and difficulty. The form includes a section for you to note your child's comments concerning his subjects and classes in school. Finally, there is a section for personal information you might like to share with the teacher, such as unusual family circumstances, special interests that your child has, strategies or techniques that have been beneficial in the past and, of course, questions that you may have for the teacher.

There are several questions to consider as you prepare for your parent-teacher conference. Use the sample list of questions on page 141 to guide your thinking, organizing, and planning for this meeting.

Once you have answered these questions, you are prepared to meet with your child's teacher to exchange information and to make a plan for supporting his educational progress and cognitive development in school.

Things to Do During the Conference

Having an effective and successful conference with your child's teacher depends on four key factors: (1) building rapport, (2) obtaining information, (3) providing information, and (4) making a plan for parent-teacher follow-up.

Parent Checklist to Use BEFORE the Conference

✓ Did I review my child's report card or progress report?

✓ Do I understand his/her learning profile?

✓ Did I talk to my child to see if there were any questions he/she wanted to ask?

✓ Do I know how my child feels about each subject and the related teaching style?

✓ Is there personal information to share with the teacher that offers more insight into my child's work habits and learning style?

✓ Have I made a note of any home stressors or unusual family circumstances that may affect my child's academic performance or behavior?

✓ Are there any learning strategies that I am aware of that lend themselves to parent-teacher collaboration?

✓ Did I check in with other professionals (e.g., tutor, educational therapist, psychologist) who are working with my child privately?

Building Rapport

It is critical for your child's academic success in school that you form a cooperative, collaborative, and trusting relationship with your child's teacher. Always try to avoid an adversarial relationship with the teacher and try to find some common ground for discussing your child's struggle with homework. Without a trusting relationship based on understanding and mutual respect, extraneous factors, such as anxiety and defensiveness, may interfere with a successful meeting.

To build rapport with your child's teacher, start the conference with positive comments from your child about his teacher or the subject matter. If you are there to address a problem, take a deep breath and present your concerns in a calm and constructive manner. If you are feeling defensive or if you sense that the teacher is on the defensive, try to relay your concerns in a way that implies that you are interested in working together with the teacher to resolve the problem. Try using "I" statements when talking to the teacher.

For example, you may ask: *What can I do to improve this situation?* or *I think I can use your help in structuring his assignments before he leaves school so that he has a clear understanding of the expectations when he is doing his homework at home.* Positive comments will show that you are taking an active interest in your child's learning.

Obtaining Information

Using your checklist questions as a guide, ask your child's teacher specific questions about his learning, attention, and behavior in the classroom. The following questions may be helpful:

- How is my child doing in all his subjects?

- What do you see as her areas of strength?

- In what subjects is he having difficulty?

- Does my child participate in class discussions?

- Does my child express her ideas clearly?

- How is my child's attention in class?

- Does he appear to be distracted (internally or externally)?

- How can I help my child at home?

- Who are my child's friends?

- Does she have difficulty relating to peers or other adults?

Providing Information

Refer back to your "Parent-Teacher Conference Preparation Form" to help structure your meeting and fill in any gaps. Make a list of your questions and use them as a point from which to elaborate regarding your child's talents and difficulties.

Parent Checklist to Use DURING the Conference

For a "meet-the-teacher" conference:

✓ Begin on a positive note by thanking the teacher for meeting with you and letting her know, for example, how much your child enjoys a certain subject/project.

✓ Ask your questions:

- How is my child doing in each subject?
- What do you see as his/her strengths and weakness?
- Is he/she participating in class discussions and group work?
- How is he/she doing socially with peers?
- Is my child able to pay attention, follow directions, complete tasks on time?
- How can we work together so that my child can improve in this particular area?

✓ End the conference on a positive note.

For an "emergency" conference to deal with a problem:

✓ How is my child doing in the particular problem area?

✓ What do you think is contributing to this problem/behavior?

✓ How often does this problem/behavior occur?

✓ How can we work together to help my child?

Planning for Parent-Teacher Follow-Up

Discuss with your child's teacher particular strategies that have worked for you at home or have been successful with other specialists working with your child. In addition, ask your child's teacher for any strategies or approaches that you can use at home to enhance her learning. Ask the teacher about her perceptions and observations of your child's skills and efficiencies in the areas of attention, language, reading, math, spelling, and writing.

Things to Do After the Conference

It is important to maintain ongoing communication with your child's teacher after the conference and throughout the school year. This collaboration will help you understand your child's progress and challenges. You will also be a valuable resource to the teacher by sharing your child's homework habits, struggles, and successes. Your child will benefit from this collaboration as she will feel supported both in school and at home.

Parent Checklist to Use AFTER the Conference

✓ Discuss the conference with your child. Provide positive highlights first. Then discuss any concerns that were raised along with action steps to be taken.

✓ Immediately begin implementing the action plan decided upon with your child's teacher.

✓ Maintain regular contact with your child's teacher to discuss your child's progress.

Establishing Consistent Communication

Once you have met with your child's teacher, you have the foundation for future conversations and follow-up with regard to your child's progress. If you suspect that your child is still experiencing difficulty with homework assignments, you should contact the teacher immediately. Request a meeting to discuss the problems. Inform the teacher of your child's difficulties, dilemmas, frustrations, and/or boredom with respect to the assignments. Decide on a mode of communication (telephone, e-mail, or written correspondence) with your child's teacher that is manageable for both parties and will encourage the smooth flow of information between home and school. Many parents and teachers find weekly e-mail updates, progress notes, daily homework sheets, or a communication notebook that goes back and forth to be helpful.

Requesting a Team Meeting

If your child's difficulties continue despite your efforts to communicate with the teacher and to make any necessary accommodations for homework, you may want to consider gathering all the school professionals involved with your child's education. A team meeting may be warranted if you observe suspicious behaviors. Below is a list of behaviors that your child may exhibit

Parent Guide to Hassle-Free Homework

that should be considered "red flags" for calling a team meeting attended by you, your child's teacher, the school counselor, school psychologist, and special-education coordinator:

◆ He is spending twice as long to complete the homework.

◆ She usually turns in her assignments late or forgets to turn them in even though complete.

◆ He frequently loses his assignments.

◆ She tends to forget to bring home the right materials (books, note-books, worksheets).

◆ He has trouble carrying out a series of steps in order to achieve a goal (multiple steps toward completing a science project, research paper, studying for a test).

If the above-mentioned "red flag" items are a hallmark of your child's homework behavior, it will be important to consult with the larger school team in order to discuss possible courses of action (e.g., classroom/homework accommodations, academic testing).

Encouraging Your Child to Advocate for Himself

In the school setting, self-advocacy refers to a student's ability to explain her learning strengths and needs. As parents, you are responsible for helping your child be attuned to and understand what elements of the academic environment enhance her learning. If your child has been evaluated, then you can explain to your child the findings from that evaluation, which should include a profile of cognitive and educational strengths and weaknesses along with a diagnosis. It is important for your child to gain a solid understanding of her learning style and learning challenges.

Once you and your child understand his learning profile, you can both begin to advocate in school. Your child can explain to the teacher how he learns best and can share which strategies, techniques, or accommodations will aid his learning and success in the classroom. Specifically, your child will be aware if he requires more time on a test, an extension on a project, graph paper for math problems, directions in written format, or other accommodations. Your child may also be aware of factors that may interfere with his learning. This information can then be discussed with the teacher. Establishing effective and open communication between student and teacher will help your child learn optimally. Below is a list of strategies that will encourage your child to advocate for himself:

Strategies for Student Self-Advocacy in the Classroom

- Set up a parent-teacher conference to discuss self-advocacy skills that might benefit your child and minimize learning problems.
- Inform your child of the results of the meeting. Present a visual reminder (list, chart, pictures) of the desired behaviors.
- Ask the teacher to encourage your child to ask for what she needs in the classroom.
- Encourage your child to practice self-advocacy skills.
- Praise your child for positive outcomes of self-advocacy.

In elementary school, children could ask teachers for extra handouts, repetition of directions or homework assignments, a quiet space to work if distracted, and a scribe or computer if handwriting is a struggle.

In middle school, students could be encouraged to seek extra help from teachers after school when confused about assignments, to call a friend to get the homework assignment, or to ask for instructions to be repeated.

In high school, students should ask for accommodations as needed for extended time for tests and papers, taking tests in a quiet room, or extra-credit assignments if he did poorly on a test or project.

As this chapter comes to a close, let's revisit the two students we encountered at the beginning:

> Markella would benefit from engaging in self-evaluative behavior. She should monitor her schedule to see if she has a tendency to overextend herself and to overcommit to other

activities. If this is the case, time-management and organization strategies are of utmost importance to help her plan her time more efficiently and effectively so that she can complete her homework. If this does not work for her, she should consult with her teacher and advocate for time extensions or modified assignments.

Raphael would benefit from utilizing a structured and strategic study plan for his history test. He should use strategies that help him learn the broad themes of the material as well as the details so that he can recall the information with greater ease. Using selected memory strategies will help him recall the relevant dates, war battles, and generals. Finding ways to network the information and make it both accessible and meaningful will allow him to feel confident about the material he has learned. Before his next test, Raphael could talk with his teacher about what kind of study guide would be most helpful to him. If test-taking continues to be a problem, then his parents could meet with his team of teachers to discuss the need for accommodations, extra review sessions, or specialized instruction to help him improve his test performance.

Glossary

Attention: the ability to focus one's conscious mind on a particular sensation, thought, or emotion

Auditory: information that is heard or internally verbalized

Automaticity: rapid processing of information that requires little effort or attention

Kinesthetic: something touched or felt

Long-term memory: the ability to recall past sensations, emotions, experiences, or events

Memory: the ability to recall information, thoughts, emotions, sensations, or experiences

Organization: the orderly arrangement of materials, space, and/or information

Orton-Gillingham: a systematic, multisensory method of teaching reading. This method focuses on the sound–symbol relationships in the English language, sight words, syllables, and finger-spelling (i.e., marking each sound in a word with one finger).

Phonological awareness: an understanding of the sounds and the structure of spoken language, including rhyming, blending, segmenting, deleting, and substituting words, syllables, and sounds

Phonological memory: the ability to remember individual sounds, combinations of sounds, and/or words

Processing speed: the speed with which one perceives information and performs relatively easy or overlearned cognitive tasks, such as scanning visual information, recognizing simple patterns or symbols, or identifying similarities or differences

Short-term memory: the ability to recall recent sensations, emotions, experiences, or events

Visual: information that is seen

Working memory: the ability to temporarily store and manipulate information in one's conscious mind

Story Grammar

Character
Setting
Initiating event
Character's major problem
How does the character feel about the major problem?
Solution
Steps to the solution
Steps to the solution
Steps to the solution
How does the character feel about the solution?

Strategy Card: An index card with a question and a strategy on one side and the answer on the other

When: Helpful when learning and reviewing vocabulary words or terms in social studies, science, language arts, math, or a foreign language

How:

1. Write the question or term on the front of the card.

> chlorophyll

2. Write the answer or definition on the back of the card.

> Molecule in plants that makes cells appear green; used to trap the energy needed to make food

3. Add a memory strategy or strategy cue on the front to help you.

> chlorophyll

4. Practice!

Strategy Card

Question:

Strategy Clue:

Strategy Card

Answer:

My strategy:

Triple Note Tote Instructions

Triple Note Tote: A 3-column chart that helps you organize information you need to know

When: Helpful when taking notes from a textbook or reviewing terms or information you need to know for a test

How:

1. Write the main idea, question, or term in the first column.

2. Write the details, answer, or definition in the second column.

3. Add a memory strategy in the third column when it is time to study for a test.

4. Practice!

Question/Term	Answer/Definition	Strategy	
What are the steps of photosynthesis?	1. **Water** and nutrients are transported from the roots, up the stem (xylem) to the leaves. 2. **Light** from the sun shines on leaves and light energy is trapped by chlorophyll and stored. 3. Energy trapped by the chlorophyll turns carbon dioxide from air into **sugars** and releases oxygen into air. 4. Sugars are **transported** down the stem (phloem) to be stored in other parts of the plant. Cell uses this food to grow.	**W**e **L**ove **S**ugary **T**reats	1. **W**ater 2. **L**ight 3. **S**ugars 4. **T**ransport

Triple Note Tote

Question/Term	Answer/Definition	Strategy

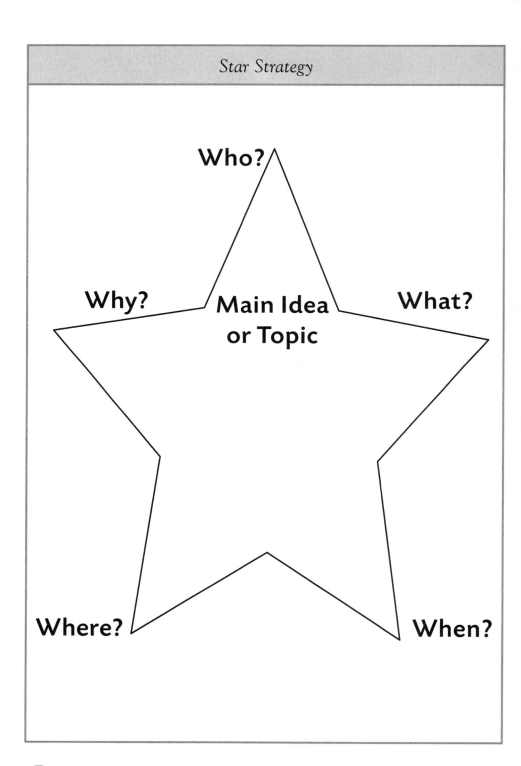

Who?

Why?

Main Idea
or Topic

What?

Where?

When?

Chapter Summary Organizer

Title: _____

Chapter: _____

Setting: _____

Characters: _____

      Main Character's name: _____

      Three facts about the main character

      1. _____

      2. _____

      3. _____

Have you learned anything new about the main character's problem?
Write it down.

Summary: (Write down the most important thing that occurred in this chapter.)

New vocabulary from this chapter:

Your Personal Checklist

My Checklist for Writing:

1. _____

2. _____

3. _____

A strategy to remember my checklist:

First letter of number 1: _____

First letter of number 2: _____

First letter of number 3: _____

Acronym: _____

or

Crazy Phrase: _____

_____

_____

_____

References

Brooks, R. (1991). *The self-esteem teacher: Seeds of self-esteem.* Circle Pines, MN: American Guidance Service Publishing.

Caron, K. B., & Stacey, W. (2001). *Language arts curriculum.* ResearchILD: In-house report.

Chall, J. S. (1996). *Stages of reading development* (pp. 1–296). Fort Worth: Harcourt Brace.

Cooper, H. (2001). Homework for all—in moderation. *Educational Leadership, 58,* 34–38.

Deci, E., & Flaste, R. (1995). *Why we do what we do: Understanding self-motivation.* New York: Penguin.

Dweck, C. (1986). Motivational processes affecting learning. *American Psychologist, 41,* 1040–1048.

Gardner, H. (1983). *Frames of mind: The theory of multiple intelligences.* New York: BasicBooks.

Goodnow, J., in Coburn, et al. (1989). *The problem solver with calculators.* Mountain View, CA: Creative Publications.

Green, J. (2001). *The road to success is paved with failure: How hundreds of famous people triumphed over inauspicious beginnings, crushing rejection, humiliating defeats and other speed bumps along life's highway.* New York: Time Warner.

Grimes, S. (1998). Key points about multiple intelligences and teaching. *The Learning Disabilities Network Exchange,* Spr/Sum.

Hallowell, E. (1999). *Connect* (pp. 26, 303–311). New York: Pantheon Books.

Harter, S. (1981). A model of mastery motivation in children: Individual differences and developmental change. In W. Collins (Ed.), *Minnesota Symposium on Child Psychology* (pp. 14, 215–255). Hillsdale, NH: Erlbaum.

Higgins, G. (1994). *Resilient adults: Overcoming a cruel past* (pp. 1–23). San Francisco: Jossey-Bass.

Hoover-Dempsey, K. V., Battiato, A. C., Walker, J. M., Reed, R. P., DeJong, J. M., & Jones, K. P. (2001). Parental involvement in homework. *Educational Psychologist 36(3),* 195–209.

Institute for Learning and Development/ResearchILD and FableVision. (2001). Brain Cogs: The test-taking survival kit [computer software]. (Available from http://www.fablevision.com/braincogs)

Kralovec, E., & Buell, J. (2001). *The end of homework: How homework disrupts families, overburdens children, and limits learning.* Boston: Beacon Press.

Learning Disabilities Association of Canada. (1998). *Advocating for your child with learning disabilities.* Ottawa, Ontario, Canada and Exceptional Children's Assistance Center NewsLine. Retrieved from http://www.ldac-taac.ca/indepth/advocacy_parents-e.asp.

Licht, B., & Dweck, C. (1984). Determinants of academic achievement. *Developmental Psychology, 20,* 628.

Meltzer, L. J., Roditi, B. N., Steinberg, J. L., Biddle, K. R., Taber, S. E., Caron, K. B., & Kniffin, L. (2006). *Strategies for success: Classroom teaching techniques for students with learning problems, 2nd ed.* Austin, TX: Pro-Ed.

Meltzer, L., Katzir, T., Miller, L., Reddy, R., & Roditi, B. (2004). Academic self-perceptions, effort, and strategy use in students with learning disabilities: Changes over time. *Learning Disabilities Research and Practice, 19(2),* 99–108.

Meltzer, L. J., Roditi, B., Taber, S., Kniffin, L., Stein, J., Steinberg, J., Caron, K., Papadopoulos, I., Pollica, L. (2005). *Essay Express.* Watertown, MA: FableVision. www.fablevision.com

Meltzer, L. J., Roditi, B., Taber, S., Stein, J., Steinberg, J., Caron, K., & Papadopoulos, I. (2001). *Brain Cogs.* Watertown, MA: FableVision. www.braincogs.com

Mooney, J., & Cole, D. (2000). *Learning outside the lines: Two Ivy League students with learning disabilities and ADHD give you the tools for academic success and educational revolution.* New York: Simon and Schuster.

Paulu, N. (1995). *Helping your child with homework.* Retrieved June 15, 2003, from the World Wide Web: http://www.ed.gov/pubs/parents/Homework/title.html

Piper, W., Hauman, G., & Hauman, D. (1976). *The little engine that could: Original classic edition.* New York: Platt & Monk

Raskind, M. H., Goldberg, R. J., Higgins, E. L. and Herman, K. L. (1999). Patterns of change and predictors of success in individuals with learning disabilities: Results from a 20-year study. *Learning Disabilities Research and Practice, 14(1),* 35–49.

ResearchILD and FableVision. (2005). Essay Express. [computer software]. (Available from http://www.fablevision.com)

Roditi, B., in Meltzer et al. (1996). *Strategies for success: Classroom teaching techniques for students with learning problems.* Austin, TX: Pro-Ed.

Schroeder, M.A., & Washington, M. (1989). *Math in bloom.* East Moline, IL: LinguiSystems

Stipek, D., & Seal, K. (2001). *Motivated minds: Raising children to love learning.* New York: Henry Holt.

Walker, J. M. T., Hoover-Dempsey, K. V., Whetsel, D. R., & Green, C. L. (2004). Parental involvement in homework: A review of current research and its implications for teachers, after school program staff, and parent leaders. *Harvard Family Research Project.* Cambridge, MA: Harvard Graduate School of Education

Resources for Families

Resources About Learning Differences

Raising Lifelong Learners: A Parent's Guide by Lucy Calkins (Perseus Books, 1997)

Overcoming Underachieving: An Action Guide to Helping Your Child Succeed in School by Sam Goldstein, Ph.D. and Nancy Mather, Ph.D. (John Wiley & Sons, 1998)

A Mind at a Time by Mel Levine (Simon and Schuster, 2002)

Reaching Minds audiotape series by Mel Levine (Educators Publishing Service) – Available at: www.allkindsofminds.org

Strategies for Success: Classroom Teaching Techniques for Students with Learning Problems by Lynn Meltzer, Bethany Roditi, Donna P. Haynes, Kathleen Rafter Biddle, Michelle Paster, and Susan Taber (Pro-Ed Publishers, 1996)

The Complete IEP Guide: How to Advocate for Your Special Ed Child by Lawrence M. Siegel (Nolo Press, 2001)

Motivated Minds: Raising Children to Love Learning by Deborah Stipek and Kathy Seal (Henry Holt, 2001)

Parent Guide to Hassle-Free Homework

Look What You've Done! Stories of Hope and Resilience for Parents and Teachers by Bob Brooks (PBS Videotape)

The Self-Esteem Teacher: Seeds of Self-Esteem by Bob Brooks (American Guidance Service Publishing, 1991)

Raising Resilient Children: Fostering Strength, Hope, and Optimism in Your Child by Robert B. Brooks and Sam Goldstein (McGraw-Hill/Contemporary, 2001)

The Childhood Roots of Adult Happiness: Five Steps to Help Kids Create and Sustain Lifelong Joy by Edward Hallowell (Ballantine, 2002)

No One to Play With: Social Problems of LD and ADD Children by Betty Osman (Academic Therapy Press, 1996)

Taking Charge of ADHD by Russell Barkley (Guildford, 1995)

Driven to Distraction: Recognizing and Coping with ADD, from Childhood through Adulthood by Edward Hallowell and John Ratey (Pantheon, 1994)

Understanding Girls with AD/HD by Kathleen G. Nadeau, Ellen B. Littman, and Patricia Quinn (Advantage Books, 1999)

The ADD/ADHD Checklist by Sandra F. Rief (Prentice Hall, 1998)

Books for Teens About LD and ADHD

Learning How to Learn: Getting Into and Surviving College When You Have a Learning Disability by Joyanne Cobb (Child Welfare League of America, 2001)

School Survival Guide for Teenagers with LD by Rhoda Cummings and Gary Fisher (Free Spirit, 1993)

Learning Outside the Lines: Two Ivy League Students with Learning Disabilities and ADHD Give You the Tools for Academic Success and Educational Revolution by Jonathan Mooney and David Cole (Simon & Schuster, 2000)

Survival Guide for College Students with ADD or LD by Kathleen G. Nadeau (Imagination Press, 1994)

Help4ADD@HighSchool by Kathleen G. Nadeau (Advantage Books, 1998)

Straight Talk About Learning Disabilities by Kay Marie Porterfield (Facts on File, 1999)

ADD and the College Student by Patricia O. Quinn (Imagination Press, 1994)

Access to Textbooks and Novels on Tape

Library of Congress
1291 Taylor Street, NW
Washington, D.C. 20542
(202) 707–5100

Recording for the Blind & Dyslexic (RFB&D)
20 Roszel Road
Princeton, NJ 08540
(609) 452–0606

General Web Sites

http://www.schwablearning.org
A well-put-together site by a nonprofit organization, dedicated to helping parents of children with LD; very clear and easy to get around (also in Spanish)

http://www.bigchalk.com
Serves students from elementary school through college levels

http://homeworktips.about.com
Provides links to various educational sites in the areas of English, math, history, science, foreign languages, and more

http://www.eduplace.com/kids/
Interactive website of Houghton Mifflin serving students in grades K–8

http://www.bjpinchbeck.com
Contains over 700 homework links for English, math, science, social studies, art, music, and more

http://www.edhelper.com
Contains skill reviews, concept explanations, sample practice sheets, writing prompts, math problem sets, samples quizzes for elementary, middle school, and high school

Web Sites for Specific Content Areas

Math

http://mathforum.org/dr.math/
Students submit questions by filling out a web form, and answers are sent back by e-mail

http://math.rice.edu/~lanius/Lessons
Provides math lessons for students from kindergarten to adult

http://www.coolmath4kids.com
Lessons, games, puzzles, and brain benders for students ages 3–12

http://www.coolmath.com
Provides activities and lessons in algebra, trigonometry, geometry, fractions, calculus, and more for students ages 13 and up

http://www.allmath.com
Contains math tools such as flash cards, metric converter, math glossary, and multiplication tables

http://www.gomath.com
Provides mini-lessons in numerous math topics on all levels

http://www.loisterms.com
Designed primarily for middle school math, this site has great "stories" for helping students remember math principles and operations

English/Language Arts

http://www.wsu.edu/~brians/errors/
Guide to common errors in the English language

http://www.netnaut.com/mnemonics/spelling.html
Fun mnemonics that help students remember difficult spelling and grammar rules

http://www.bartleby.com
Internet publisher of literature, reference, and verse

http://www.indiana.edu/pamphlets/wts/thesis_statement.shtml
Information and examples on how to write a thesis statement

http://onlinebooks.library.upenn.edu/
Provides free online books (over 25,000 titles on many different subjects)